THE
GOLDEN CITY

JOHN TWELVE HAWKS

THE
GOLDEN CITY

Book Three of
The Fourth Realm Trilogy

DOUBLEDAY
New York London Toronto Sydney Auckland

DD
DOUBLEDAY

www.doubleday.com

DOUBLEDAY and the DD colophon are registered trademarks of Random House, Inc.

Published simultaneously in Canada by Doubleday Canada.

Library of Congress Cataloging-in-Publication Data
Twelve Hawks, John.
 The golden city / by John Twelve Hawks. — 1st ed.
  p. cm. — (The fourth realm trilogy ; bk.3) 1. Brothers—Fiction.
2. Supernatural—Fiction. I. Title.
 PS3620.W45G65 2009
 813'6—dc22

2009018975

ISBN 978-0-385-51430-9

PRINTED IN THE UNITED STATES OF AMERICA

10 9 8 7 6 5 4 3 2 1

First Edition

AUTHOR'S NOTE

Seven years ago, I had a vision that evolved into *The Traveler*, the first book of the Fourth Realm Trilogy.

Looking back, I realize that a lifetime of thoughts and experiences were expressed within this fiction. Both the story and its characters couldn't be held within one country or even a particular reality.

The Golden City is the final book of the trilogy, and it seems as if I'm leaving a familiar place. I'm sad to be moving on, but I feel that I have explored every part of the landscape.

Some people have enjoyed reading the books for entertainment, but others have been inspired to start Web sites and groups that are beginning to resist the various manifestations of the Vast Machine. I will continue to support these efforts in any way possible.

This third novel is dedicated to my readers. It's been a privilege to communicate with you. I hope that you and those you love are surrounded by Light.

—John Twelve Hawks

THE
GOLDEN CITY

PRELUDE

Although it was clear that no other car was traveling down Sycamore Lane, Susan Howard switched on her turn signal and glanced in the rearview mirror before pulling into the driveway. Susan lived in a two-bedroom cottage with rosebushes bordering the front walkway. There was a birch tree in the back and a detached garage that resembled a cowshed, covered with ivy.

The garage was filled with storage boxes and old furniture from her mother's house. Whenever Susan arrived home she felt a brief moment of guilt. *I really should clear everything out,* she thought. *Sell Mommy's couch and the dining room chairs or just give them away.* Because of the furniture, she had to keep her car in the driveway. Whenever it snowed, she spent twenty minutes warming up the car and chipping the ice off the windshield.

But now it was spring, and the only thing she noticed when she got out of her car was the sound of cicadas and the smell of wet grass. Susan gazed up at the night sky, looking for the Big Dipper. Usually it pleased her that she lived far enough from New York City to see the constellations, but tonight her eyes focused on the dark, cold spaces between the stars. They were watching her. She could feel it. Someone was watching her.

"Stop it," she said out loud. And the calm tone of her own voice made her feel better.

Susan pulled a handful of bills and catalogues out of the mailbox, then unlocked the front door. She heard a familiar *yip-yip!* and a cocker spaniel raced out of the kitchen, his nails clicking on the linoleum. It was wonderful to be greeted by a friend when you came home, and Charlie really was her little friend. But the dog was mischievous, too—especially if Susan was late. She walked through the cottage and made sure that there hadn't been an accident before she gave Charlie a treat and let him out into the backyard.

Up until a few months ago, she had followed the same routine: she would let the dog out, pour herself a glass of Chablis, and then turn on her computer to answer her e-mail. But she rarely used that computer anymore, and drinking alcohol made her feel sloppy and unaware. They were watching her. She was sure they were watching her. And now she had broken the rules and done something very dangerous.

* * *

SUSAN WAS A computer programmer working for the Evergreen Foundation Research Center in Westchester County. She was involved in creating the software interface for the new quantum computer and had been part of the small group in the observation gallery when Michael Corrigan had left his body for another world. The Crossover Project was top secret, but Susan's team had been told that their work involved national security and the war on terror.

Maybe that was true, but it was still strange to spend part of your workday staring down at a man lying on a table with wires attached to his brain. For several hours, it had been difficult to detect Mr. Corrigan's pulse. Then suddenly he opened his eyes, got off the table, and shuffled out of the room.

A few weeks later every Foundation employee was called into the administration building and told about a new program called Norm-All. The slogan for the program was "A good friend cares about you." The cheerful young woman from Human Resources explained that Norm-All would automatically monitor their physical and mental health. There was a permission form (which everyone signed), and then her research team went back to work.

Susan was the only one who took the program's informational brochure. She studied it during lunch. Norm-All was something called a "personal parameter program." Thousands of people working for the U.S. Defense Department had been monitored for five years, and this had established the benchmarks for acceptable behavior. Each person was given a number—a sort of equation—that gradually changed as the computer gained more data about their particular lifestyle. If the number went beyond a certain parameter of normalcy, then the employee was more likely to have mental and physical problems.

A few days later infrared cameras appeared in all the buildings. The cameras automatically scanned everyone's body and recorded blood pressure, heart rate, and body temperature. There were rumors that phone calls at the Foundation Research Center were evaluated by a computer program that measured the stress level in your voice and the use of various "trigger" words.

Most of the monitoring was unobtrusive. Norm-All could track the movement of your car and evaluate the purchases you made with your bank card. Susan wondered how much weight was given to certain negative actions; your personal equation would certainly be damaged by an arrest for drunken driving, but how much did the number change when you checked out a "negative" book from the public library?

There were rumors that two people were fired because of unacceptable Norm-All equations, and several part-timers were not given full-time jobs. Within a month, her research team stopped talking about anything controversial. The three acceptable topics of conversation were shopping, sports, and TV shows. One Friday they all went to a bar to celebrate a colleague's birthday; when they ordered a third round of drinks, a programmer joked, "Well, this is going to screw up our Norm-All equations!"

Everyone laughed, but there was no discussion about it. They just resumed their conversation about the new models of hybrid cars, and that was it.

Susan had spent her life working with computers and knew how easy it was to trace IP numbers on the Internet. In March, she stopped using her home computer, bought a used laptop at a swap meet, and began to access the wireless connection at a local café. Susan felt like an alcoholic or a drug addict—someone with a shameful problem she couldn't control. When she left work and drove to the café, she felt as if she were entering a bad part of town with broken streetlights and abandoned buildings. In obscure chat rooms, people who called themselves Free Runners made allegations about the Evergreen Foundation. Apparently the Foundation was the public face of a secret organization called the Tabula that wanted to destroy freedom. This plan was opposed by an alliance that called itself the Resistance.

At first, Susan did nothing but read the various discussion threads. But three days earlier, she had taken the first step and begun to chat with a few Free Runners based in Poland.

I work for the Evergreen Foundation, she typed. *We are about to start testing a new version of a quantum computer.*

Where are you? a person asked.

Are you in danger? asked another. *Can we help you?*

Susan switched off her notebook computer and immediately left the café. On the way home, she obeyed the speed limit and waited a few extra seconds when the stoplight turned green.

* * *

SHE PLACED A frozen dinner in the microwave oven and stepped out into the backyard to find Charlie. The dog had disappeared and she could see that the door to the garage was half open. That was unusual. On two occasions, the gardener had forgotten to lock up, but he didn't come on Wednesdays. Cautious, she stood in the doorway, found the switch, and flicked it on. Nothing happened. And then she heard the dog whimpering in the darkness.

"Charlie?"

A man stepped from the shadows and grabbed her arms. She fought back, kicking and screaming. Suddenly a light came on and she saw a second man standing on a kitchen chair. Someone had loosened the lightbulb and now the man was screwing it back into the fixture. Susan stopped fighting and gazed up at the person holding her arms. It was Robert—no, everyone called him Rob—a big man in his thirties who worked as a guard in the administration building.

"What are you doing?" she asked.

"Don't kick me," Rob told her. He looked like a little boy with hurt feelings.

The man standing on the chair had a military haircut and slender body. When he stepped down and approached her, she saw his face. It was Nathan Boone—head of security for the Evergreen Foundation.

"Don't worry, Susan." Boone had a calm, measured voice. "Your dog hasn't been hurt. But we do need to talk to you."

Rob guided her over to the center of the garage and made her sit down on the chair. Charlie had been leashed and tied to a support column. The dog watched as Rob knelt down and placed plastic restraints around Susan's ankles and wrists.

Boone took a biscuit out of his nylon jacket and fed it to Charlie. The dog wagged his tail and waited for more. "Dogs are like humans," Boone said. "They value small rewards and clear lines of authority."

He untied the leash and offered it to Rob. "Take the dog outside while I talk to Susan."

"Yes, sir."

Boone's shadow touched her and then glided away as he paced around the garage. "Do you know who I am?"

"Of course, Mr. Boone."

"And you know why we're here."

"No, I—"

"That was not a question, Susan. We're here because you were disloyal and because you tried to contact our enemies."

"Yes," Susan whispered. It felt like the only true thing she had ever said in her life.

"Good. Thank you. That saves a lot of time." Boone glanced to the right when Rob returned to the garage.

"For the most part, our employees have accepted our system, but a few people have ignored their commitments and chosen to be disloyal. I want to understand this phenomenon, Susan. I really do. I've studied your Norm-All data closely and found nothing unusual in your profile. Your personal equation was well within the parameter of acceptable behavior. So what compelled you to violate the rules and engage in such perversity? You have deliberately turned away from a system that protects what is good and right."

Silence. The plastic restraints were so tight that Susan's ankles were beginning to hurt.

"I'm just—just stubborn. That's all."

"Stubborn?" Boone shook his head as if that wasn't an adequate answer.

"Yes, I've always had a core inside me that's very independent. I want to make my own decisions without people watching me."

"We're watching you for your own good and the good of society."

"People always say things like that when they're about to do something really selfish and bad."

"You violated our rules, Susan. Your own actions have caused the appropriate punishment."

Boone reached up and grabbed a rope that had been tied to the rafters. He dropped a loop around her neck and tightened it.

"A lonely woman gives into her depression," Boone murmured

and motioned to Rob. It felt as if the big man were embracing her like a lover as he picked Susan up and made her stand on the chair.

I can't die now, she thought. *It's not fair*. She had all these thoughts that would never be expressed, all these dreams that would never march off into the world. "There's a movement called the Resistance," she said. "People are waking up and seeing what's going on."

Rob glanced over his shoulder and Boone nodded slightly. Yes. He knew all about the Resistance.

"We're going to fight you and we're not going to back down! Because people want the freedom to choose their own—"

Rob kicked away the chair and Susan swung back and forth. Her feet were a few inches above the floor. Boone stood beside her like a concerned friend, checking the noose and the rope. When he was sure that everything was secure he cut off the restraints with a knife, picked up the bright yellow fragments, and followed Rob out the door.

She was still alive, grabbing at the rope as it cut into her windpipe. And then thoughts flooded through her brain in one final wave of consciousness. Her mother lying in the hospital bed. A Valentine box in grade school. The sunset on a beach in Jamaica. And where was Charlie? Who would take care of Charlie? Was she already dead? Or had she finally been set free?

No one was watching her anymore.

I

Early in the evening, a North Sea storm swept through the German countryside and drenched Berlin. Raindrops rattled on the glass panes of the greenhouse and the orangery in Babelsberg Park. The willow trees around the lake swayed back and forth like underwater plants while a flock of ducks huddled together on their little island. In the streets around Potsdamer Platz, the traffic was slow and halting, the cream-colored taxicabs honking at one another in the clogged intersections while delivery trucks grumbled like large shambling creatures.

Windshields were streaked with water and it was difficult to see the faces of the drivers. The sidewalks in the Mitte district were empty, and it seemed as if much of Berlin's population had disappeared. But the surveillance cameras remained like mute guardians of the city. They tracked a young woman holding a newspaper over her head as she darted from an office doorway to a waiting car. They followed a restaurant deliveryman as he pedaled a bicycle up the street, a life revealed in a series of grainy black-and-white images: a desperate face with wet hair plastered to the forehead, legs moving frantically while a cheap plastic poncho flapped in the wind.

On Friedrichstrasse, a license-plate scanner mounted on a building photographed a black Mercedes stopped at a traffic light. The plate number was recorded and automatically checked against a central database as Michael Corrigan and Mrs. Brewster sat in the backseat and waited for the light to turn green. Mrs. Brewster had taken a tube of lipstick out of her purse and was studying her face in a compact mirror. This was behavior quite out of character for the current head of the Brethren's executive board; unless there was a party or some other kind of special event, Mrs. Brewster paid minimal attention to her personal appearance. She was a tweed-and-practical-shoes sort of woman, whose only gesture to vanity was the artificial color of her chestnut-brown hair.

"God, I look tired," she announced. "It's going to take an effort to get through dinner with Hazelton and his friends."

"If you want, I'll do all the talking."

"That would be wonderful, Michael. But it's not necessary. There's been a change of plans."

With exaggerated decisiveness, Mrs. Brewster snapped the mirror shut and dropped it into her purse, then slipped on a pair of sunglasses. The dark glasses covered her eyes and upper cheekbones like a half mask.

"Terry Dawson just sent me an e-mail from the research center in New York," she said. "They've finished building the new version of the quantum computer, and Dawson has been testing the system. I want you to be there tomorrow afternoon when the computer becomes fully operational."

"Perhaps they could postpone everything for a few days so I could attend the executive board meeting."

"The Crossover Project is a good deal more important than any meeting. The original version of this computer put us in contact with an advanced civilization that began to supply us with technical data. Dr. Dawson wants you to be there if the civilization contacts us again."

The Mercedes turned another corner. Michael stared at Mrs. Brewster for a few seconds, but the sunglasses and the dim light made it difficult to know what she was thinking. Was she telling him the truth, or was this just a strategy to separate him from the rest of the Brethren? Her mouth and neck showed some tension, but there was nothing unusual about that.

"I think it would be easier if we interviewed Dawson with a video conference camera," Michael said.

"I want a full assessment of the project, and you can only do that if you're at the laboratory. Your clothes are packed and waiting at the hotel. A chartered jet is fueling at Schönefeld Airport."

"We've been meeting people for the last three days . . ."

"Yes. I know. Everything is rather frantic. But the quantum computer has always been our top priority. After the first computer was destroyed, we shut down the genetic research program so that we could increase Dawson's funding. Kennard Nash was convinced that this other civilization was eager to send us technological miracles. Before we spend more money, we need to see if this new machine actually works."

Nash's name ended the conversation. Both Michael and Mrs. Brewster had watched Nathan Boone kill the head of the Brethren as he ate lunch on Dark Island. It felt as if Nash were still with them, sitting in the front seat and frowning like a father displeased with his children's activities.

The car stopped in front of the Hotel Adlon, and Mrs. Brewster said something in German to the driver. Moments later,

Michael's luggage was carried from the hotel and loaded into the trunk.

"Thanks so much for doing this, Michael. I can't rely on anyone else."

"Don't worry. I'll handle it. Get some rest."

Mrs. Brewster gave him one of her more gracious smiles. Then she slipped out of the backseat and hurried into the hotel.

As the car pulled away from the curb, Michael used his handheld computer to access the security system at Wellspring Manor—the country estate in southern England controlled by the Evergreen Foundation. Moving the cursor, he clicked through surveillance videos of the front door, the service entrance, and, yes, there it was: a black-and-white image of his father's body lying on a medical table. Matthew Corrigan looked like a dead man, but sensors attached to his body detected a sporadic heartbeat.

The Traveler turned his eyes away from the small screen and gazed out the window. *Still there but not there*, he thought. *An empty shell.*

* * *

THE CHARTERED JET stopped in Maine for refueling and customs inspection, and then continued to the Westchester County Airport, located in the suburbs north of New York City. A town car was parked on the tarmac and a member of the security staff stood beside it like an honor guard. Then it was *Yes, Mr. Corrigan. Hope you had a pleasant flight, Mr. Corrigan*, and the car carried him down a two-lane country road. They glided past stone walls that had once surrounded apple orchards and dairy cows. These days, the land was too expensive for farming, and the area was dotted with corporate headquarters and the renovated farmhouses owned by investment bankers.

The Evergreen Foundation's research center was at the end of a long gravel driveway. Flower beds and pine trees were a pleasant distraction from the high wall that kept out the rest of the world. The compound was dominated by four glass-and-steel buildings that housed the foundation library, genetic laboratory, administrative center, and computer research facility. At the center of this quadrangle was the neurological cybernetics building where Michael had once been attached to the sensors of the quantum computer.

Michael turned on his handheld computer and checked his daily schedule. This was one activity that truly gave him pleasure. Every morning he was sent a schedule that told him what he was going to do in fifteen-minute segments; the activities and the tight schedule confirmed that he was an important member of a powerful organization. When he looked back on his past life in Los Angeles, there were always hours and sometimes days when nothing was going on. The empty time made it difficult not to feel weak and pathetic.

Now that Michael was a Traveler, the schedule helped him stay focused on the reality in front of him. If he thought about it—really thought about it—the other realms made the human world appear false or unreal. But that was a road straight to craziness. His schedule showed that all his actions had order and meaning. Even ordinary activities like "lunch" or "sleep" were on the list. His occasional encounters with prostitutes were placed in the category of "entertainment."

"Now what?" Michael asked the driver. "The schedule doesn't say where I'm supposed to meet Dr. Dawson."

The driver looked confused. "I'm sorry, Mr. Corrigan. But no one gave me any instructions."

Michael got out of the car and walked up a sloping flagstone path to the administration center. He still had a Protective Link chip implanted beneath the skin on the back of his right hand. As he approached the building, it sensed his arrival, verified his identity, and confirmed that he had passed through the main gate. The glass door glided open, and he entered the lobby.

There was no need for a security guard or a receptionist; the lobby scanners tracked his passage across the room. But when Michael reached the elevators—nothing happened. Feeling like an unwelcome guest, he waved his hand at the elevator doors. The lobby seemed very empty and quiet at that moment, and he wondered what to do.

Michael heard a sharp click and turned as Nathan Boone emerged from the side door. The head of security for the Evergreen Foundation wore a black business suit without a necktie. Boone had fastened the top button of his white shirt, and this small detail gave him a severe appearance.

"Good morning, Mr. Corrigan. Welcome back to the research center."

"Why can't I enter the elevator?"

"We had a personnel problem a few days ago, and I restricted access to the offices. I'll reauthorize your chip this afternoon, but right now you need to meet with Dr. Dawson."

They left the lobby together and walked across the compound. "What kind of problem?" Michael asked.

Boone raised his eyebrows. "Excuse me?"

"You mentioned a problem with the staff. As a representative of the executive board I need to know what's going on at this facility."

"An employee named Susan Howard ended her life. She had problems with depression and contacted the so-called Resistance using an Internet chat room. We thought it best to change our security codes."

Did he kill her? Michael wondered. It bothered him that Boone could destroy someone without board authorization, but before he could ask any more questions, they entered the computer building and Terry Dawson hurried out to greet them. The scientist was an older man with white hair and a broad, fleshy face. He seemed nervous about showing the computer to Michael.

"Good morning, Mr. Corrigan. We met several months ago when General Nash gave you a tour of the research center."

"Yes. I remember."

"Nash's sudden death was a real shock to all of us. He was the principal force pushing for the quantum computer."

"The board has decided to rename your building the Kennard

Nash Computer Center," Michael said. "If the General were still alive, he would also want to see some results. There have been too many delays in this project."

"Of course, Mr. Corrigan. I share your concern." A door opened automatically and Dawson led them down a hallway. "I do need to mention something before we enter the laboratory. Our research team is divided into two groups with different security clearances. The technicians and support staff have blue-level access. A much smaller core group, with red-level access, knows about the messages we've received from our friends."

"How do you know they're friends?" Michael asked.

"That was General Nash's view. He believed that the messages came from an advanced civilization in one of the different realms. Anyone who gives us such useful technical data should be considered friendly."

The three men entered a control room filled with computer monitors and equipment panels that glowed with red and green lights. A window looked out on a much larger room where a woman wearing a hijab and two younger men in lab coats were testing the quantum computer. The computer itself was visually unimpressive, a stainless-steel box about the size of an upright piano. Large electrical cables were attached to the base of this box, and smaller cables were attached to the side.

"Is this the quantum computer?" Michael asked. "It looks very different from what I remember."

"It's a whole new approach," Dawson explained. "The old version used electrons floating in super-cooled helium. This new computer uses an oscillating electric field to control the spin-up or spin-down direction of individual electrons. The electrons serve as qubits—the quantum bits—of our machine."

"So the technology is different, but it works the same way?"

"Yes. It's the same principle. An ordinary computer—no matter how powerful it is—stores and processes information with bits that exist in either of two states: one or zero. But a qubit can be a one, a zero, or a superposition of both values at the same time, allowing for an infinite number of states. This means our machine can calculate difficult problems a great deal faster than any computer currently in operation."

Michael stepped closer to the computer, but he kept his hands away from the cables. "And how does this lead to messages from another civilization?"

"Quantum theory tells us that electrons can be multiple places at the same time. This is the reason why the atoms in a molecule don't shatter when they bump into each other. The electrons act as both particle and wave—they form a sort of cloud that binds atoms together. Right now, our qubit electrons exist here, inside this machine, but they also 'go away' for a very brief moment."

"They can't just disappear," Michael said. "They have to go somewhere."

"We have reason to believe that the electrons enter a parallel world and then, when observed, return to our particular reality. It's clear that our distant friends have designed a much more sophisticated quantum computer. They capture the particles, rearrange them into messages, and send them back to us. The electrons shuttle back and forth between worlds so quickly that we only detect the result—not the motion itself."

One of the young men rapped his knuckles on the window. Dawson nodded and switched on an intercom.

"We've done the system check three times," the technician said. "Everything is ready to go."

"Good. We're going to start up now. Dr. Assad, would you please come into the control room."

Dawson switched off the intercom as the young woman with the headscarf entered the control room. She had a round face and very dark eyebrows. "I'd like you to meet Dr. Assad. She was born in Syria, but has spent most of her life here in the States. With Mr. Boone's permission, she's been given a red-level security access."

Dr. Assad smiled shyly and avoided looking into Michael's eyes. "It's an honor to meet you, Mr. Corrigan."

Everyone sat down and Dr. Dawson starting typing commands. Boone was the last person to find a chair, but he never relaxed. He was either watching the people in the room or studying the computer screen.

For the first hour, they followed an established protocol. Michael heard an electrical humming noise that started and paused and started again. Sometimes it was so loud the observation window began to vibrate. As different levels of the computer were tested, Dr. Assad spoke with a calm voice.

"The first ten qubits are operative. Now activating group two."

The computer woke up and became aware of its power. Dawson explained that the machine was able to learn from its mistakes and approach complex problems from different angles. During the second hour, Dr. Assad asked the computer to use Shor's algorithm—a sequence of instructions that broke large numbers into smaller divisors. During the third hour, the machine began to examine the symmetries of something called an E8, a geometric solid that had fifty-seven dimensions. After five hours had passed, Dr. Assad's monitor screen went blank for a few seconds, and then the calculations continued without further pause.

"What just happened?" Michael asked.

The two scientists glanced at each other. "It's what we saw last time," Dawson said. "At a certain point, the computer begins sending substantial amounts of particles off to another realm."

"So it's like radio signals sent off into space?"

"Not exactly," Dawson said. "It takes light-years for radio and television signals to reach another galaxy. Our computer's electrons are going to a place that's not so distant—a parallel level of reality."

Around the sixth hour, one of the technicians was sent out to get dinner. Everyone was munching on chips and sandwiches when the monitor screen flashed several times. Dr. Assad put down her mug of coffee and Dawson scooted his office chair over to her workstation.

"It's coming," he said.

"What are you talking about?" Michael asked.

"The messages from our friends. This is what happened before."

A dark wall of plus symbols flashed onto the screen. Then spaces appeared between them like holes in a wall. A few minutes later, the computer began creating geometric patterns. The first ones were flat like paper snowflakes, but then they gained dimension and symmetry. Balls, cylinders, and cones floated across the screen as if they were being pushed by underwater currents.

"There!" Dawson shouted. "Right there! See it?" And everyone stared at the first number—a three.

More numbers appeared. Groups of them. Michael thought they were random, but Dr. Assad whispered, "This happened before. They're special numbers. All prime."

The monitor screen showed equations using different symbols, and then the equations vanished and shapes returned to the screen. Michael thought the shapes looked like balloons, but then they became living things: fat, globular cells that divided in two, reproducing themselves.

Then—letters. At least, Dawson said they were letters. At first, they were geometric scribbles and scrawls that looked like graffiti scratched on a window. Then these symbols become solid and more familiar.

"That's Hebrew," Dr. Assad whispered. "That's Arabic . . . definitely. Chinese . . . I think. I'm not sure."

Even Boone looked enchanted. "I see an *A* and a *T*," he said. "And that one looks like a *G*."

The letters arranged themselves in lines. Were they in code or just random groups? Then spaces appeared between the letters, forming three-letter, five-letter, and twelve-letter segments. *Was that a word?* Michael asked himself. *Do I see words?* And then words appeared in different languages.

"That's the word *read* in French," Dr. Assad said with a flat voice. "And that's the word *see* in Polish. I spent a month in Warsaw when I was—"

"Keep translating," Michael said.

"*Blue. Soft*. In German. Those new words look Coptic. English now. *Infinity. Confusion* . . ."

The words joined one another, forming phrases that sounded like surrealistic poetry. *Dog take the star road. The random knife with whiskers.*

By the eighth hour, messages were being sent in several languages, but Michael focused on nine words written in English.

come to us

come to us

COME TO US

2

When she had finished her geometry problems, Alice Chen slid off the bench, grabbed a scone from the bread box, and pushed open the cooking hut's heavy door. It was cold and windy on Skellig Columba, but Alice left her quilted jacket open. Her black braids swung back and forth as she hurried up the pathway that connected the three terraces on the northern edge of the island. Two rainwater catch basins and a garden with parsnips and cabbage were on the final terrace, and then the pathway disappeared and she was striding across rocky ground dotted with sorrel and sow thistle.

Alice scrambled up a boulder, kicking off bits of black lichen as if they were ashes from an ancient fire. When she reached the top, she turned slowly around and surveyed the island like a guard who had just climbed up a watchtower. Alice was twelve years old—a small, serious girl who had once practiced the cello and built forts in the desert with her friends. Now she was living on an isolated island with four nuns who thought they were taking care of her—not realizing that the opposite was true. When Alice was alone, she could assume her new identity: the Warrior Princess of Skellig Columba, Guardian of the Poor Claires.

She could smell peat smoke coming from the cooking hut and the rotting odor of the seaweed hauled up from the shore and used to fertilize the garden. The cold wind coming off the water touched the collar of her jacket and made her eyes water. Directly below her were the chapel and the four convent huts, each one re-sembling a stone beehive with slit windows and recessed doors. Looking out at the ocean, she could see the whitecaps on the waves and a dark line on the horizon that marked the circumfer-ence of her world.

The Poor Claires cooked special treats for Alice, mended her torn clothes, and poured pots of hot water into a galvanized wash-tub so that she could enjoy a once-a-week bath. Sister Maura made her read Shakespeare plays and Irish poetry, and Sister Ruth, the eldest nun, guided her through a Victorian-era textbook of Euclidian geometry. Alice slept with the nuns in the dormitory hut. There was always an oil lamp burning in the room; when Al-ice woke up in the middle of the night, she could see the nuns' heads lying in the centers of their goose-down pillows.

She knew that these gentle, devout women cared about her—perhaps they even loved her—but they couldn't protect her from the dangers of the world. A few months earlier, Tabula mercenar-ies had landed on the island in a helicopter. While Alice and the nuns hid in a cave, the men broke down the door of the storage hut and killed Vicki Fraser. Vicki was a very kind person, and it was painful to think about her death.

Alice believed that everything would have been different if Maya had been on the island. The Harlequin would have used her sword and knives and shotgun to destroy all the men on the helicopter. If Maya had been living at New Harmony when the Tabula arrived, she would have protected Alice's mother and the rest of the people living there. Alice knew that everyone at New Harmony was dead, but they were still with her. Sometimes, she was doing something completely ordinary—tying her shoes or mashing her potatoes with a fork—and then she saw her mother getting dressed or heard her friend Brian Bates playing his trumpet.

Alice jumped off the boulder, turned away from the convent, and headed west across the rocky ground. The island had been formed when two mountain peaks pushed their way out of the water, and the bluish-gray limestone was riddled with caves and sinkholes. During her months on Skellig Columba, she had stacked up columns of rocks; some were signposts for her different pathways around the island, while others were false clues that might lead a careless invader off the edge of a cliff.

Her storage spot was a badger-sized hollow hidden inside a patch of weeds. She kept a rusty butcher knife that she had found in the storage hut and a paring knife stolen from the convent kitchen wrapped in a sheet of plastic. Alice thrust the butcher knife beneath her belt, wearing it like a short sword, and strapped the paring knife to her forearm with two large rubber bands. There were no trees on the island, but she had found a walking stick down by the landing dock, and she used it as a tool to probe mysterious places. Now that she was armed, she tried to walk like a Harlequin—calm but alert, never fearful and uncertain.

After hiking for about twenty minutes, she reached the western end of the island. The constant attack of the waves had cut away chunks of limestone, and the cliff looked like five gray fingers reaching into the cold water. Alice walked to the largest of the fingers and stood near the edge. It was a six-foot jump over a crevasse to the next section of cliff. If she slipped and fell, it was a long drop down to the jagged rocks that received the surge of each new wave.

The gap between the two sections of cliff was wide enough to make the jump difficult, but not impossible. She had already imagined what it would feel like if she didn't reach the other side. Her arms would flap wildly like a bird that had just been shot. She would have just enough time to hear the waves and see the rocks before the darkness reached out and claimed her.

A flock of shearwaters circled overhead, calling to one another with wavering cries that made her feel lonely. If she looked toward the center of the island, she could see the cairn that marked Vicki's grave. Hollis Wilson had dug a hole and piled up stones like a madman. He had refused to speak, and the only sound came from the blade of his shovel as he jabbed it into the rocky ground.

Alice turned and stared out at the empty horizon. She could walk away, returning to the warmth of the cooking hut, but then she would never know if she was as brave as Maya. Alice placed her walking stick near a clump of grass and adjusted the two knives so that they wouldn't shift around when she moved quickly. She stood at the far edge of the cliff and realized that she had only about ten feet of running space before she had to leap across the gap.

Do it, she told herself. *You can't hesitate.* Clenching her fists, she took a deep breath, and then dashed forward. As she approached the edge, she stopped suddenly. Her left foot kicked a white pebble into the gap; it bounced off the walls and disappeared into the shadows below.

"Coward," she whispered as she backed away from the edge. "You *are* a coward." Feeling small and weak and twelve years old, she gazed out at the seabirds riding the air currents up to the heavens.

When she took a few steps back to level ground, she saw a black shape come over the ridge. It was Sister Maura, red cheeked and breathing hard. The wind grabbed at her veil and the sleeves of her dress.

"Alice!" the nun shouted. "I'm not pleased with you. Not pleased at all. You didn't finish diagramming your sentences and Sister Ruth said you didn't peel the carrots. Back to the hut. No dawdling. You know the rule—no play until work is done."

Alice took a few more steps back and concentrated on a patch of red lichen on the other side of the gap. There must have been something in the way she held her body that told Sister Maura what was going to happen.

"Stop!" the nun screamed. "You'll kill yourself! You'll—"

But the rest of the words were absorbed by the wind as the Warrior Princess ran toward the edge.

And jumped.

down the sidewalk or sat in an underground train. Even when he wore a business suit and necktie, there was something in the way he carried himself that seemed a bit too confident—almost defiant. The guitar case was the perfect camouflage. When Hollis encountered a police officer near the entrance of the Camden Town Tube station, the young woman glanced at him for only a second and then turned away. He was a musician—that's all—a black man in a shabby overcoat who was going to play on a street corner.

The rifle shifted inside the case as he passed through the turnstile. For Hollis, the London Underground always felt less intense than the New York City subway. The cars were smaller, almost cozy, and the train made a soft whooshing sound when it entered the station.

Hollis took the Northern Line to Embankment and then switched over to the Circle Line. He got off at Temple, walked along the river for a few minutes, then climbed up the stairs to New Bridge Street. It was about eight o'clock in the evening; most of the suburban commuters had already left their jobs and hurried home to the warm light of their televisions. As usual, the drones were still working—sweeping the street, painting women's toenails, delivering take-out food. Their faces showed hunger and exhaustion, a grinding desire to lie down and sleep. A billboard hanging on the side of a building showed a young blond woman looking ecstatic as she spooned a new kind of custard out of a carton. HAPPY TODAY? asked the billboard, and Hollis smiled to himself. *Not happy,* he thought. *But I might get some satisfaction.*

*   *   *

DURING THE LAST few months, his life had been transformed. He had left New York, traveled to western Ireland, and buried Vicki Fraser on Skellig Columba. A week after that, he was in Berlin, scooping up Mother Blessing and carrying her out of the Tabula's underground computer center as alarm bells rang and smoke flowed up the stairwells. Before the police arrived, he had

3

Hollis Wilson carried his new weapon in a guitar case stuffed with wadded-up newspaper. A few weeks ago, he had asked Winston Abosa to supply him with a bolt-action rifle capable of hitting a target at least a hundred yards away. Winston owned a drum shop in Camden Market and he used his contacts there to purchase a stolen Lee-Enfield. The original Lee-Enfield rifle was used in World War I; this No. 4 Mark T with a telescopic sight had been developed in the 1930s. After Hollis had fired the rifle, he planned to leave it on the rooftop and walk away.

London police officers usually noticed Hollis when he strolled just enough time to walk two blocks and hide the body of the dead Harlequin behind a dumpster. Then he stripped off his blood-stained jacket and went to find the car they had left near the dance hall on Auguststrasse.

It took him several hours to get back to the body and dump it into the trunk of the Mercedes-Benz. The Berlin police had blocked off the area around the computer center and he saw the flashing lights of fire engines and ambulances. Eventually, a reporter would show up and receive the official story: MADMAN KILLS SIX—POLICE SEARCH FOR VENGEFUL EMPLOYEE.

Hollis was out of Berlin before sunrise and stopped at a motorway service center near Magdeburg. At a little shop in the area, he bought a road map, a fleece blanket, and a camper's shovel. Sitting in the service center's restaurant, he drank black coffee and ate bread with jam while the waitress kept yawning. He wanted to fall asleep in the back of the car, but he had to get out of Germany. The Tabula search engines were gliding through the Internet, comparing his photograph to the images picked up by the surveillance cameras. He needed to get rid of the car and find someplace that was off the grid.

But the burial was his first objective. Hollis followed the map to a place called Steinhuder Meer, a nature park northwest of Hanover. A descriptive plaque in four languages showed a pathway that led to Dead Moor, a low, boggy area of heather and brown grass. It was a weekday, not quite noon, and there were only a few cars in the area. Hollis drove down a dirt road a few kilometers, wrapped Mother Blessing in the blanket, and carried her across the moor to a cluster of bushes and dwarf willow trees.

When she was alive, Mother Blessing had radiated a constant rage that people sensed the moment they encountered her. Lying on her side in the shallow grave, the Irish Harlequin appeared smaller than he remembered, less powerful. Her face was covered with the blanket, and Hollis didn't want to look at her eyes. When he shoveled in the wet dirt, he could see two small white hands still clenched into fists.

Hollis abandoned the car near the Dutch border, took the ferry to Harwich and then a train to London. When he reached the apartment hidden behind Winston Abosa's drum shop, he found Linden, the French Harlequin, sitting at the kitchen table, reading a stolen bank manual about money transfers.

"The Traveler has returned."

"Gabriel? He's back? What happened?"

"He was captured in the First Realm." Linden pulled the cork from a half-filled bottle of Burgundy and poured some wine into a glass. "Maya rescued him, but she could not return to this world."

"What are you talking about? Is she okay?"

"Maya is not a Traveler. An ordinary person can only cross over through one of the few access points around the world. The Ancients knew where they were. Now most of them are lost."

"So what happened to her?"

"No one knows. Simon Lumbroso is still at the Mary of Zion church in Ethiopia."

Hollis nodded. "That's where she crossed over."

"*C'est correct*. Six days have passed, but Maya has not reappeared in the sanctuary."

"Is there a plan to save her?"

"All we can do is wait." Linden took a sip of wine. "I got your e-mail about what happened in Berlin. Did you leave Mother Blessing's body in the computer center?"

"I drove north and buried her in the countryside. But I didn't put up a headstone or any kind of marker."

"Mother Blessing would not care about that. Did she have a Proud Death?"

Hollis was confused for a moment and then he remembered Maya using the phrase. "She killed six men and then someone shot her. You decide if that was a Proud Death." He opened the metal carrying tube, took out Mother Blessing's sword, and placed it on the kitchen table. "At the last moment, she handed me this."

"Please be precise, Mr. Wilson. Mother Blessing *gave* you her sword or you *took* it from her body?"

"She gave it to me, I guess. So I'm returning it."

"Perhaps she wanted you to accept her obligation."

"That's not going to happen. I didn't grow up in a Harlequin family."

"Nor did I," Linden said. "I was a soldier with the First Marine Infantry Parachute Regiment until I had a disagreement with a senior officer. For two years, I worked as a bodyguard in Moscow and then Thorn hired me as a mercenary. Right away, I knew this was what I was meant to do. We Harlequins don't waste our time defending the rich and the powerful. We protect the prophets and visionaries, those Travelers who push history in a new direction."

"You do what you want, Linden. I've got my own objectives."

Linden waited a few seconds, as if he wanted to confirm what he had just heard, and then seemed to shut down one of the compartments in his mind. He flicked his fingers and that was it. Hollis left the room.

¥   Y   Y

FEELING CONSCIOUS OF the hidden rifle, he turned right onto Ludgate Hill and took the first left onto Limeburner Lane. The Evergreen Foundation occupied a large glass-and-steel building about a hundred yards down the street. Black support beams and black granite panels framed the building's tinted windows. From a distance, it looked as if a massive vertical grid had been dropped into the middle of London.

The building was guarded by an armed security staff. Pretending to be a bicycle messenger, Hollis had entered the building a few days ago and asked for directions. Anyone visiting the Foundation had to pass through a short L-shaped corridor made of green glass that allowed a backscatter X-ray machine to look beneath their clothes.

A Victorian-era office building was on the other side of street. An international architectural firm was the sole tenant and photographs of buildings in Dubai and Saudi Arabia had been placed in the ground-floor window. Hollis had studied the photographs and decided that the architects had simply taken the designs for a prison and added palm trees, fountains, and a pool.

He rang the doorbell at the architectural firm and waited to see if anybody would come to the door. When no one responded, he stood directly in front of the entrance door and unbuttoned his overcoat. A crowbar hung from a cord around his neck. He forced the edge of the bar between the door and the lock and then pushed sideways with all his strength. The screws holding the drop-bolt lock were ripped away and the door popped open.

When Hollis got inside the building, he took a steel wedge out of his pocket and kicked it into the crack beneath the door, jamming it shut. He decided to avoid the elevator and climbed the emergency stairs to the top floor. Inside the men's room, a short wall ladder led to a Plexiglas skylight in the ceiling. Hollis pushed back the latch with one hand and was on the roof seconds later.

The cold night air touched his skin and he could hear the distant sound of a bus moving up the street. Slipping a little on the wet roof slates, Hollis reached the iron railing at the edge of the roof. He sat down and opened the case.

The Lee-Enfield was a long, heavy rifle that had been modified to shoot 7.62 mm cartridges. Hollis pulled the bolt handle straight back and then shoved an ammunition clip into the receiver in front of the trigger guard. When he pushed the bolt forward and down, a cartridge was forced into the firing chamber. Hollis felt as if he had become part of the weapon: locked, loaded, and ready to fire. Peering through the scope, he saw two bisecting lines that met in the center of the door across the street.

His hatred of the Tabula was powerful, sustained emotion— unlike anything he had ever experienced in the past. After he buried Vicki on the island, he had covered her grave with a pile of large gray stones. Sometimes it felt as if one of those stones had been absorbed by his body.

He waited for a target, not knowing what to expect. A few minutes later, a Land Rover pulled up in front of the Foundation building and two people got out. Hollis raised the rifle and peered through the sight at a bald man in his sixties and a young woman wearing a fawn-colored overcoat. As they stood on the sidewalk and gave instructions to the driver, a blond man carrying a brief-case strolled down the street and joined them. The blond man said something and the young woman laughed as the Land Rover left the curb.

Hollis aimed his rifle at the blond man's head. A gust of wind made Hollis shiver and he realized that his face was covered with sweat. *Calm down*, he told himself. *Breathe slowly*. Then he pulled the trigger.

He expected a loud noise and recoil, but nothing happened. Without taking his eye from the scope, Hollis moved the rifle bolt. The unfired cartridge was forced out, and a new round entered the firing chamber. Once again, he pulled the trigger.

Nothing happened. Time itself had vanished, and the only reality was the present moment: the rifle and the blond man's head held within the circle of the scope. *Move the bolt again.* Snap. Click. Nothing.

The third cartridge fell beside his right foot. It bounced off the roof and hit the sidewalk below. No one heard the sound. The three targets had already climbed up the stairs and were entering the building.

Hollis heard footsteps on the roof and twisted around. Linden was ten feet behind him, looking down at the street. The French Harlequin was wearing a black wool overcoat. With his broad shoulders, shaved head, and blunt nose, he looked like a me-chanical creation built to resemble a human being.

"There's nothing wrong with the rifle," Linden said. "I told Winston to give you dead bullets."

"If you didn't want me to use this weapon, then why did you let me come here?"

"You had some sort of plan. I wanted to see what would hap-pen." Linden nodded in the general direction of the Foundation building. "Now I know."

"You've killed a lot of people, Linden. So don't tell me this is wrong."

Linden shoved his hands into the outer pockets of the

overcoat and his right foot slid a few inches forward. Hollis knew it was impossible to stop the Frenchman from drawing and firing a handgun. A minute ago, Hollis had been a human being with a name and a past. Now he was simply a target.

"Harlequins are not terrorists or assassins, Mr. Wilson. Our only obligation is to defend the Travelers."

"Why should you care what I do with my life?"

"Your actions will only bring unwanted attention to the Traveler and I cannot allow that. This means you have two options. You can leave Great Britain or . . ."

The threat was unspoken, but the message was clear. A bullet from Linden's gun would push Hollis over the railing. Within his mind, Hollis saw his body falling, a flurry of arms and legs and then stillness. After the police photographed his body, he would be scooped off the pavement, tagged, and discarded like a piece of trash. The vision didn't frighten him, but it didn't soothe his anger. If he died, then his memory of Vicki would die with him. She would perish a second time.

"And what is your response?" Linden asked.

"I'll— I'll go away."

Linden turned his back and disappeared through the open skylight. And Hollis was alone again, still clutching the useless weapon.

4

The next morning, Hollis woke up in his rented room on Camden High Street. He felt like the last man alive as he started his daily routine: two hundred push-ups and an equal number of sit-ups on the stained rug, followed by a series of martial arts exercises. When his T-shirt was soaked with sweat, he took a shower and cooked a pot of oatmeal on the hot plate near the bathroom sink. After cleaning up and leaving no visible sign of his presence, he went downstairs.

Only a few people were out, mostly shopkeepers receiving morning deliveries and sweeping their little patches of sidewalk. Hollis strolled up the High Street, crossed Regent's Canal, and entered the maze of shops and food stands that occupied the area around Camden Lock. It was Saturday—which meant the market would start to get crowded around ten or eleven o'clock. People would come to the market to get tribal tattoos while their friends bought black leather pants and Tibetan prayer bowls.

The "catacombs" were a system of tunnels built beneath the elevated railway tracks that ran through the market. In the nineteenth century, the tunnels had been used as stables for canal horses, but now this underground area was occupied by stores and artists' studios. Halfway down one of the tunnels, Hollis found Winston Abosa's drum shop. The West African was standing at a back table in the main room, pouring some evaporated milk into a large cup of coffee.

When Winston saw Hollis, he retreated behind a sculpture of a pregnant woman with ivory teeth. "Good morning, Mr. Hollis. I hope all is well."

"I'm leaving the country, Winston. But I wanted to say good-bye to Gabriel."

"Yes, of course. He's in the falafel shop meeting people."

Because the Tabula was searching for him, Gabriel had to spend most of his time in the hidden apartment attached to the drum shop. If members of the Resistance wanted to meet, he would talk to them at a second location. A Lebanese family ran a falafel shop in a market building that overlooked the canal. For a modest payment, they let Gabriel use their upstairs storage room.

In the falafel shop, Hollis stepped around a sullen girl chopping parsley and passed through a doorway concealed behind a beaded curtain. When he climbed the stairs to the storage room, he was surprised to see how many people were waiting. Gabriel was over by the window, talking to a nun wearing the black robes of the Poor Claires. Linden stood guard near the door with his massive arms folded over his chest. The moment he saw Hollis, his hands returned to his overcoat pockets.

"I thought we had an agreement," Linden said.

"We do. But I wanted to say good-bye to my friend."

Linden considered the request and then motioned to one of the chairs. "Wait your turn."

Hollis sat in the back of the room and checked out the rest of the crowd. People were speaking Polish, German, and Spanish. The only people he recognized were a pair of British Free Runners—a pudgy young man named Jugger and his quiet friend, Roland. It was clear that people all over the world had heard about the Traveler.

Back in Los Angeles, Gabriel had had long brown hair and worn a stained leather jacket. He had been quick to smile or show anger, a combination of home-schooled innocence and cowboy swagger. During their time in New York City, Hollis had helped Gabriel cook spaghetti and listened to him sing off-key at a karaoke bar. Now everything had changed. These days, Gabriel looked like a shipwreck survivor. His face was gaunt, and his shirt hung loosely on his body. There was something strange about his eyes—they were clear and very intense.

After each person had spoken to Gabriel, Linden guided them out of the room and pointed to whoever was next. Gabriel would rise to shake hands, then sit down and listen, focusing on the faces of his followers. After everyone had a chance to express their views, he would lean forward and speak quietly—almost a whisper. When the meeting was over, he would touch hands a second time, look directly into their eyes, and say "thank you" in their own language.

The two British Free Runners were the last to meet the Traveler and Hollis could hear every word of conversation. Apparently, someone named Sebastian had traveled to France to organize resistance to the Tabula, and Jugger felt that he wasn't following orders.

"When we started this movement, we came up with a few rules."

"Six, exactly," Roland said.

"That's right. Six rules. And one of them was that each crew would plan their own strategy. My friends in Paris say that Sebastian is talking about organizing a steering committee . . ."

Gabriel kept quiet until Jugger had finished his oration. Once again, the Traveler spoke with such a soft voice that the two Free Runners had to lean forward to hear every word. Gradually, they began to relax, and they both nodded their heads.

"So we all agree?" Gabriel asked.

"I guess so." Jugger glanced at his friend. "You got anything to say, Roland?"

The big man shrugged a shoulder. "No worries."

The Free Runners stood up like chastened schoolboys and shook Gabriel's hand. When they left the room, Linden jerked his head in Hollis's direction. *Your turn.* Then he clomped down the staircase to the falafel shop.

Hollis threaded his way through the tables and sat opposite Gabriel. "I came here to say good-bye."

"Yes. Linden told me what happened."

"You're still my friend, Gabe. I would never do anything to put you in danger."

"I realize that."

"But someone has to be punished for Vicki's death. I can't forget what they did to her. I found her body and dug the grave."

The Traveler got up from the table, walked over to the window, and gazed down at the canal. "When we act like our enemies, we run the risk of becoming just like them."

"I'm not here for a lecture. Understand?"

"I'm talking about the Resistance, Hollis. Did you see those two women from Seattle? They've accessed all the surveillance cameras that are outside the buildings used by the Evergreen Foundation. For the first time, we're using the Vast Machine to *watch* the Vast Machine. It's a well-organized plan that doesn't put anyone in danger, but it still bothers me. It feels like I'm building a house, but I don't know what it's going to look like when it's finished."

"Is that nun also part of the Resistance?"

"Not really. That's a different problem. The Poor Claires on Skellig Columba think that Alice Chen is turning into a wild child—completely out of control. In the next few weeks, they're going to bring her to London, and we have to find a safe place for her to live. I wish Maya was here. She'd know what to do."

"Can Maya ever return to our world?"

Gabriel returned to the table and poured himself a cup of tea. "I could cross over again to the First Realm, but I wouldn't be able to bring her back. Simon Lumbroso is searching through old manuscripts and history books. He needs to find another access point—a place where an ordinary person can cross over and then return. Thousands of years ago, people knew where these sites were. They built temples around them. Now that knowledge is lost."

"And what happens if Simon finds one of these access points?"

"Then I'll go find her."

"Linden won't like it—and your new followers won't be too happy either."

"Why do you think that?"

"Those people you just talked to are taking risks and changing their lives because of you. If you go back to the First Realm, you're basically telling them: 'The Resistance isn't that important. I'm going to put this one person above your problems and maybe I'll never come back.'"

"It's a *particular* person, Hollis."

"Maya wouldn't want you to take the risk. You're a Traveler, Gabe. You have a larger responsibility."

"I need her." Gabriel's voice was filled with emotion. "When you first met me in Los Angeles, I didn't know who I was or what I was supposed to do with my life. Now I've crossed the barriers and visited two realms. Those places are as real as this table and this room. When you've had experiences like that, it changes you. Nowadays it doesn't feel like I have a *connection* to anything. Maya is a cord tied to my heart. Without her, I'd float away."

"You think your brother has the same problem?"

"I doubt if Michael worries about anyone else. All he can think about is power and control."

"There's nothing wrong with power," Hollis said. "Our only problem is that we don't have the power to destroy the Tabula."

"We can't just destroy our enemy. We need to an offer an alternative. Linden said you've been crawling around rooftops with a sniper rifle."

"That's my choice."

"I'm just trying to understand your actions."

"You don't have the right to judge me. You've been protected by the Harlequins for the last year. They'll kill anyone."

"You've studied *The Way of the Sword*. The Harlequins are controlled and disciplined. They only defend themselves and the Travelers. They're not looking for revenge."

"I'm not a Harlequin, so I don't follow their rules. The Tabula killed Vicki, and I'm going to destroy every last one of them."

"You still care about her?"

"Of course!"

"And you remember what kind of person she was?"

"Yeah . . ."

"Do you really think she'd want you to do this?"

Gabriel raised his eyes and Hollis sensed the full power of the Traveler. He felt like a child at that moment. *Embrace me. Comfort me.* But then he remembered the stone inside his body and he covered his chest with his arms.

"There isn't a single thing you can say that will make me change my mind."

"All right. Don't listen to me. But why don't you ask Vicki? What if you could speak to her one last time?"

Hollis felt as if Gabriel had leaned forward and slapped him. *Is this possible? Could a Traveler make this happen? Of course not.* Furious, he slammed his fist on the table. "I don't want to hear any of that spiritual shit. Vicki is dead. I buried her on the island. She's not coming back."

"I didn't say she was coming back. When a person dies, the Light leaves their body forever. But in certain circumstances— a suicide, a violent death—the Light remains for a while in this world. A small group of people have the ability to channel this energy. In the past, they've been called shamans or mediums."

"I know what you're talking about. Ghosts and goblins. Gypsies and crystal balls. It's all fake."

"Most of the time, you're right. But some people really can speak to the dead."

"You?"

Gabriel shook his head. "No. I don't have that gift. But Simon Lumbroso told me about another possibility. When Sparrow was the last Harlequin left in Japan, Maya's father visited Tokyo to see him. Sparrow took Thorn to see a traditional spirit reader who lived on the northern coast of the main island. Thorn said that the woman was very powerful—the real thing."

"It was probably some kind of trick."

"You no longer have a home, Hollis. You can't go back to Los Angeles. If you're leaving London, then why not fly to Tokyo?"

"You're manipulating me . . ."

"I'm offering you a different kind of journey. Any one of us can dedicate our lives to hate. It happens every day. This is your moment to consider an alternative. Go to Japan. Look for this spirit woman. Perhaps you won't find her. Maybe you'll come back and tell me, 'We've got to be like our enemies if we want to defeat them.' If you say that, if you *believe* that, I'll listen to you."

Footsteps on the stairs. Hollis glanced over his shoulder and saw Linden return to the room with a cup of coffee in his massive hand.

"I'll think it over," Hollis said. "But I still don't believe you can talk to the dead."

Maya reached the fourth floor of the abandoned office building and passed slowly down the central hallway, checking for new footprints in the dust. When she was sure that no one had visited the building since her last visit, she scattered broken glass on the hallway floor, then approached a suite of rooms once occupied by an insurance company. Her hand touched the handle of her sword and she got ready to attack.

Moving as quietly as possible, she slipped into the reception area. *Stop. Listen.* No one was there. Maya pushed a desk against the entrance door and opened a hallway air vent so that she could hear anyone approaching. There was no electricity on the island and the only light in the room came from a gas flare out in the street. The flame wavered back and forth, burning with a dirty orange light. Shadows touched the old-fashioned office furniture and the wall of rusty file cabinets. During one of her earlier visits, Maya had searched through the cabinets and found water-stained files filled with insurance contracts and payment stubs.

She entered one of the offices, found an executive chair, and brushed off the dust. Something moved in the next room and she drew her sword. The inhabitants on the island could be divided into two categories: the "cockroaches" were weak, frightened men who tried to survive by hiding in the ruins; the "wolves" were much more aggressive, roaming in groups through the city, looking for prey.

The sound came again. Maya peered through a crack in the door and saw a rat scurry across the floor and disappear into the wall. There were rats all over the island as well as gray animals resembling ferrets that darted through the undergrowth of the abandoned parks. *No danger*, Maya thought. *I can rest here.* She returned the sword to its scabbard and pushed the padded chair into the reception room. After checking the door one last time, she sat down and tried to relax. On the floor near her feet were a steel-tipped club and a shoulder bag that held a bottle of water. No food.

This dark world had many names: the First Realm, Hades, Sheol, or Hell. It had been described in many myths and legends, but one rule was always the same: a visitor like herself should never eat anything while she was here—even an elaborate meal offered on gold plates. Travelers left their real bodies in the Fourth Realm and could escape this danger, but if an ordinary person swallowed a crust of bread, they could be held here for eternity. Maya felt like one of the fires that burned in the rubble, a bright point of flame that was slowly consuming itself. Most of the city's mirrors had been destroyed, but she had seen herself in a sliver of window glass near the city's abandoned museum. Her hair was matted and her eyes were dead.

Her appearance didn't bother her as much as the deterioration of her memory; sometimes it felt as if entire periods of her life were melting away. She guarded the vivid images that still remained. A long time ago, she had spent a winter's day in the New Forest watching a herd of wild horses run across a snow-covered pasture. Within her mind, she saw stocky legs and tangled manes, hooves kicking up the snow as white breath lingered in the air.

She could recall scattered moments with her father and mother, with Linden, Mother Blessing, and the other Harlequins, but Gabriel was the only voice she could still hear, the only face she could still see. So far, her love had protected these memories, but it was becoming more difficult to bring them back. Was Gabriel fading away like a photograph exposed to sunlight, the colors less vivid, the shapes less distinct? If she lost him a second time, then she would become just like the others on the island— dead within, but still alive.

* * *

MAYA HEARD A scraping noise in the hallway and opened her eyes. She had only a few seconds to draw her sword before the door opened an inch or so and hit the desk. She grabbed her shoulder bag, slung the strap over her left shoulder, and stood listening. The intruder knocked on the door.

"Are you there?" asked a soft voice. "It's Pickering. Mr. Pickering. I'm Gabriel's friend."

"There aren't any friends on this island."

"But it's true," Pickering said. "I swear that it's true. I helped Gabriel when he first came here and then the wolves captured us. Open the door. Please. I've been looking for you."

She vaguely recalled a man in rags. He had been chained to a pipe in the abandoned school used as headquarters by the wolves. As Maya wandered alone through the city, she had encountered a few of the human cockroaches that hid themselves within walls or beneath floors. They always seemed frightened and talked rapidly, as if the constant flow of words would prove they were still alive.

o go to the library. I've searched the entire building and fi-
ound the map room. The door to the room is still locked. I
think it's been looted."

he people here don't care about maps. They want food—
eapons."

es. Quite true. That's all they want. But I believe that a map
island is in the library. There have always been rumors
a tunnel beneath the river. A map might show us how to
he tunnel entrance."

aya's fingers tapped nervously on the sword handle. Her
geway back to the Fourth Realm was in the middle of the
On two occasions, she swam out and attempted to find it,
e current was too strong and she barely had enough strength
irn to the shore. She had no idea what existed in the shadow
on the other side of the water, but she couldn't remain on
and. As time passed, her body grew weaker. Eventually, the
s would hunt her down.

o why haven't you taken this map and escaped?" she asked.
need your help." Pickering looked down at his ragged pants
ismatched shoes. "It's not easy to get into the room."

he part of his story was true: there was a library in the city.
had walked past the ruins several times, but had never gone
. As she wandered around the island, she kept finding little
reality in the rubble; if shopping lists and school report cards
irvived, then there might be a map that showed a way out.

his sudden feeling of hope was so powerful, so unexpected,
he was unable to speak or move. It was like finding a red em-
a cold fireplace, a speck of warmth and light that could
nd fill a room.

ll right, Pickering. Let's go to the library."

d be happy to guide you there. And if we find the right kind
o—"

hen we'll leave the island together."

hoped you would say that." The little man grinned. "No one
n this island will keep a promise, except you."

aya shoved the desk back against the wall and followed

The cockroaches were the intellectual
schemes and lengthy explanations.

Maya returned the sword to its lea
to the door, and pulled the desk a few
ing must have heard the desk legs squ
because he immediately turned the
opened wide enough for him to stick
"It's Mr. Pickering, at your service. I
the trouble started. The finest ladies'
breath. "And whom do I have the hon

"Maya."

"Maya . . ." He savored the word.

Pickering had a ferret's ability to s
large as his head. Before Maya could r
crack in the doorway and was sudden
a skinny, trembling man with long ha
green silk wrapped around his neck
noose, but Maya realized that it was
ject—a necktie.

"So, how did you find me?"

"I know all the hiding places on th
and saw a footprint on the stairs."

"Did you tell anyone?"

"I was tempted. Anyone would have
showed his yellow teeth. "The new co
offered one hundred food units to who

"If he really wants me dead, he sho

"Most of the wolves are scared of y
or a demon. You can't be killed, becaus

Maya sat back down on the chair.

"You're alive. I'm quite sure of that.
you came here to rescue him. But now
rest of us."

"And that's why you tracked me o
trapped?"

"I'm here to save you. And save mys

Pickering out of the office. They climbed down the building's circular staircase and stepped onto a street littered with rubble and the blackened shells of torched cars. Pickering's head jerked back and forth. He was like a small animal that had just left its burrow.

"Now what?"

"Stay close and follow me."

A thicket of dead trees and thornbushes was at one end of the island, but it was dominated by a ruined city. Maya had given names to the different locations: there was the insurance building, the school yard, and the theater district. She tried to imagine what the city had looked like before the fighting started. Were there ever leaves on the trees? Did the trolley actually roll down the central boulevard, and did a conductor ever ring its little brass bell?

Pickering had a different vision of Hell. He ignored the few remaining signposts, but appeared to know the location of every gas flare that roared fire and smoke from a broken pipe. His city was comprised of different intensities of darkness and light. For most of their journey, he remained in a shadow land, avoiding the flares as well as the black tunnels where someone might be hiding. "This way . . . This way . . ." he hissed, and Maya had to run to keep up with him.

They entered a looted department store filled with smashed display cases and a pile of dress mannequins. The mannequins were smiling as if pleased by the destruction. When Pickering reached the store entrance, he looked out at the library across the street. The library was designed in the same neoclassical style as the other public buildings in the city. It looked like a Greek temple that had been attacked in a bombing raid. Some of the marble columns had been reduced to rubble, while others leaned against each other like dead trees in an overgrown forest. A large statue had once stood guard at the base of the outer staircase, but all that remained were sandaled feet and the hem of a stone toga.

"We have to cross the street," Pickering explained. "They may see us."

"Keep moving. I'll handle any problems."

Pickering took three quick breaths like a man about to dive

underwater, and then dashed across the street. Maya followed him, walking slowly and deliberately to show that she wasn't afraid.

She found Pickering hiding behind one of the columns, and they entered the library's main lobby. Chunks of plaster and concrete were scattered across the floor, and a brass chandelier had been ripped away from the ceiling. Books were everywhere, littering the floor and staircase. Maya picked up one near her foot and searched through the pages; it was written in a language she had never seen before and featured delicate drawings of plants that looked like ferns and palm trees.

"We're going to the third floor," Pickering said. She followed him up the staircase. Maya tried to avoid the torn and stained books, but sometimes she stepped on the loose pages or kicked them away. It was dark on the staircase; the oppressive gloom seemed to add a weight onto her shoulders. By the time they reached the first landing, her entire body felt heavy and slow.

On the third floor, books had been stacked against the wall as if someone had tried to sort through the collection. Pickering led her down a corridor, made a sudden turn through a doorway, and stopped. "Here we are," he announced. "The reading room . . ."

They stood at one end of the large public space that dominated the top floor of the building. The reading room had a forty-foot-high ceiling and a green-and-white checkered marble floor. It was filled with long wooden tables and chairs. The room's bookshelves were on two levels—a floor-level row of shelves and a second tier that began halfway up the wall. Some of the gas pipes in the library hadn't been destroyed, and a few of the desk lamps were still burning. Their sputtering flames gave off an oily smell.

Pickering's shoulders were tense and his lips were pressed tightly together. Maya wondered if her lack of fear made him nervous. She followed her guide between the rows of tables to a point halfway across the room where the floor suddenly disappeared. Apparently there had been an explosion—and then a fire—and a large portion of the library had collapsed.

What remained was a three-story fragment of the building, a pillar made of brick and stone and concrete, surrounded by twenty feet of empty space. At the top of the pillar was a fragment from the reading room—a single table on a patch of checkered floor and a barred door that looked like the entrance to a prison cell.

"There. Do you see it?" Pickering pointed at the door. "That's the entrance to the map room."

"So how do we get there? Can we climb up from inside?"

"No. I tried. I thought you'd know what to do."

Maya paced back and forth, trying to figure out a way to get across the gap between the pillar and the reading room. A rope was useless unless she could climb to the top of the ceiling. They could build a ladder from pieces of wood and old nails, but that would take too much time, and their activity would be noticed by the patrols. Still silent, she turned away from Pickering and climbed up the staircase to the top level of bookshelves. She grabbed the metal railing and began to push it back and forth. Books fell off the walkway with a flutter of white pages and hit the floor below.

Pickering scurried up the staircase and stood beside her. "What are you doing?"

"Grab the railing," she told him. "Let's see if we can break it off."

Together, they pushed and pulled the railing until a section broke free of the walkway. Maya lay the section flat, and then shoved it forward until the one end rested on the spire like a narrow bridge.

"I knew you'd think of something," Pickering said.

Maya adjusted the scabbard strap and stepped onto the improvised bridge. It shifted, but didn't collapse. She took a first step, then another—trying not to look down. The railing flexed slightly when she reached the center, but she took a few more steps and reached the other side.

Using her club as a pry bar, she ripped the door from its hinges and entered the map room. It was a windowless storage space about the size of a walk-in closet. The walls were lined with shelves that held black cardboard storage boxes. Each box was tied shut with a silk cord and labeled with faded numbers.

Maya grabbed a box from the shelf and placed it on a table. At that moment, escape seemed possible, but she tried to control her emotions. Slowly, she untied the cord, opened the box, and found a faded lithograph of a creature in human form with wings and light emerging from its body. An angel. Beneath that lithograph was another angel, wearing different-colored robes.

Furious, Maya ripped open two more storage boxes, stacking them on top of each other. She found full-color prints of angels carrying swords or gold caskets. Illustrations ripped from books. Watercolors and wood-block prints. But the subject was always the same: Angels on earth and in heaven. Angels floating and flying and sitting on golden thrones. Black angels, white angels, and even one with six arms and green skin. But no trace of a map anywhere.

She heard a banging from outside the room. Holding one of the cardboard boxes, Maya stepped out of the doorway. Her improvised bridge had been kicked away and was lying on the rubble three stories below.

Pickering stood on the edge of the walkway, smiling triumphantly. "Don't go anywhere," he giggled. "I need to find one of the patrols."

"They'll kill you."

"No they won't. They know me. I can find anyone who's lost or missing—even a demon like you."

"What about the maps, Pickering? I just found a map that shows a passageway under the river."

"Show it to me. Let me see it."

"Sure. No problem." Maya waved the box. "Just help me get off this platform."

Pickering considered the idea and then shook his head. "There can't be a map, because there's no way off the island."

"Help me and I'll defend you from the wolves."

"If I stayed with you, we'd both be killed. You still have hope,

Maya. That's your weakness. That's why I could lead you to this place."

As he turned and hurried away, Maya reached into the box and tossed a handful of brightly colored angels into the air. The prints and illustrations fluttered downward into the gloom. *Hope. That's your weakness.*

Now it was gone.

6

Michael woke up and took a shower in a suite decorated with flowers. Two dozen red roses drew his eyes to the bedroom dresser. A spray of white hawthorn blossomed from a crystal vase near the bathroom sink. Little cards had been attached to these offerings—personal messages from Mrs. Brewster and other members of the Brethren. GOOD LUCK, announced one. YOU CARRY OUR HOPES WITH YOU ON YOUR JOURNEY.

Michael had no illusions about the sincerity of these statements. He was still alive because the Brethren believed that he could help them increase their power. When the monitor screen attached to the quantum computer flashed the words *come to us,* he knew that the executive board would demand that he cross over. That was his role—to go off into the darkness and come back with technological miracles.

He pulled on a T-shirt and sweatpants and walked into the living room. An hour ago, the security staff at the research center had placed yet another elaborate flower arrangement on the coffee table, one of a ceramic Japanese village with straw-yellow orchids twined around a pagoda.

Standing at the window, Michael gazed at the Neurological Cybernetics Research Facility, a windowless white box of a building that looked like a sugar cube dropped from the sky. Now that he was a Traveler, he didn't need special drugs or wires inserted into his brain to cross over. But going back into the building was a public act, a demonstration of his unique power. It was clear that he was no longer a prisoner, but becoming a member of the Brethren had only increased his enemies. If he returned with some new form of technology, then his position would be much stronger.

The six realms were parallel worlds, alternative realities. He had already crossed over to the Second Realm of the hungry ghosts. The First Realm was a version of Hell and Michael had no intention of visiting that dangerous place. There was a Third Realm that was filled with animals, but it wasn't the place to find an advanced civilization that used a quantum computer. Michael had decided that the beings who sent the message were either in the Sixth Realm of the gods or the Fifth Realm of the half gods. He had read the diaries of past Travelers, but none of them could describe these worlds in great detail. The half gods were supposed to be clever, but jealous of everyone else. The gods lived in a place that was difficult to find—a golden city.

Although the Brethren assumed they controlled him, Michael had his own agenda. Yes, he needed to gain access to advanced technology, but he was also looking for an explanation for his own actions. It was a waste of time to study philosophy or pray in churches if a superior being could give him a direct answer.

Did the gods possess magical powers? Could they fly through clouds and toss thunderbolts with their hands? Perhaps the human world was simply an enormous anthill, and the gods stopped by to blow up the mounds with firecrackers or flood the passageways with water. And then, every few hundreds of years or so, they would drop morsels of knowledge in the dirt so that humanity would be inspired to keep working.

Someone knocked softly. When he opened the door, he found Nathan Boone and Dr. Dawson waiting for him in the hallway. Boone was as stolid as ever, but the scientist looked anxious.

"How you are feeling, Mr. Corrigan? Did you have a good night's sleep?"

"I guess so."

"The staff is ready," Boone said. "Let's go."

They took the elevator to the lobby and walked outside. The wind was coming from the northeast and the tops of the pine trees beyond the wall swayed as if an army of woodcutters were attacking them with chain saws. When they reached the white building, Boone waved his hand. A steel door slid open and they entered a large room with a glass-enclosed gallery twenty feet above the concrete floor.

As Dawson and Boone climbed the stairs to the gallery, Michael pulled off his shoes and lay down on the examination table in the center of the room. A Taiwanese physician named Lau came over and began to attach sensors to Michael's arms and skull. Michael smelled Lau's twist-of-lemon cologne and heard the sound of an air-conditioning fan. The shadows on the wall changed when the doctor moved to the other side of the table.

"All done," Dr. Lau said quietly. "The microphone is on. They can hear us up in the gallery."

"Okay. I'm ready."

Several minutes passed and nothing happened. Michael's eyes were shut, but he knew everyone was watching him. Maybe something was wrong. If he failed, Nathan Boone would tell Mrs. Brewster, and she would start a whisper campaign against him. Michael remembered what had happened to Dr. Richardson several months ago: the neurologist fled from the research center, but Boone's men found him on a night ferry heading to Newfoundland and tossed him into the ocean.

He opened his eyes and saw Dr. Lau standing beside the table. "Are you comfortable, Mr. Corrigan?"

"You've done your job. Now go away."

A shadow hand emerged from his skin and then was reabsorbed. Michael forgot about the watchers in the gallery and concentrated on his own body. He was aware of the energy inside him—the Light contained within every living thing. Slowly, the energy gained intensity, and it felt as if he were glowing.

He moved his right arm and something forced its way out of his skin. And there it was, an arm composed of little points of light, like a tiny constellation of stars. Within seconds, the rest of the Light followed, and he broke free of the cage that held him, the awkward heaviness of flesh and bone. He drifted upward and then was gone as the Light was pulled into the dark curve of the infinite.

* * *

THE FOUR BARRIERS of air, earth, water, and fire stood between him and the other realms. He passed through them quickly, moving toward each black space that allowed him to continue on. The fire barrier was last, and he paused there for a second, staring at the burning altar before he entered the passageway in the stained-glass window. Something powerful was guiding his light in a particular direction; he felt as if all the atoms in his brain had been split apart and squeezed back together again.

When the moment passed, he was awake and floating in water. Michael panicked, reaching out with his arms and kicking his legs. His feet touched ground and he stood up, blinking and shivering like a shipwreck victim just rescued from the sea.

There was no immediate threat to his life—no sign of any other person or animal. His arms and legs could move. He could think, hear, and see. The air was warm and the clouds above him were billowy and gray. He was standing in the middle of what looked like a massive rice paddy, divided by a grid of narrow levees. Every few yards, a thin stick emerged from the surface.

He examined the area around him and realized that whatever was growing here had nothing to do with rice. Broad leaves with thick stems lay on the surface of the water, and floating among the leaves were flowers that looked like cups molded from orange candle wax. Each flower gave off the wet odor of decay.

Before he could explore the area, he needed to mark the passageway back to his own world. Keeping his eyes on the spot, he gathered three sticks and jammed them into the mud, forming a crude tripod. As he sloshed through the water to get one more stick, his leg brushed against a round, submerged object about the size of a pumpkin.

Michael reached into the water to investigate and something touched his hand. It was an animal—moving quickly and aware of the intruder in its world. The creature slithered through his legs, and then teeth as sharp and pointed as rows of needles pierced his skin. As Michael jerked up his leg, he saw a glistening black creature near the surface of the water. It had the body of a snake and the head of an eel.

Shouting and chopping at the water with his hands, Michael ran through the paddy. His wounded leg burned and he wondered if he had just been poisoned. A few yards from the levee, he stepped into deep mud and he had to force his way forward to the strip of dry land.

Pulling up his pants leg, he examined the wound, a jagged V made of little points of blood. Once the burning sensation faded, he stood up and surveyed this new world. The tripod of sticks that marked the passageway was about two hundred yards in front of him, and the dark green water of the paddies extended to the horizon. Directly above him were three suns grouped in a triangle and half obscured by the gray clouds. When crossing over, he moved toward light—the so-called higher realms. But there was no golden city in the middle of the dirt levees.

"Hello!" he shouted. "Hello!" His voice sounded weak and plaintive.

Michael pivoted on his heel and saw something he hadn't noticed before—a bonfire burning in a distant thicket of brush and trees. Staying on dry land, he followed the levee bordering a watery rectangle. A light wind made waves that splashed against the reddish-brown dirt. The only other sounds he could hear were his own breathing and a squishy noise from his wet socks. After a while, he made a left turn onto a new levee and passed scraggly bushes that reminded him of wild sage and dwarf trees with twisted branches jabbing at the sky.

He heard voices and began crawling through the tangled vegetation. When he reached a thicket of plants with leaves that looked like strips of old leather, he moved cautiously.

Eleven men and women sat around a fire. It was a woeful, ragged-looking group—like the survivors of a flood or a tornado. Both sexes wore wide-brimmed hats woven from straw and long boots with the top part folded down at the knees. The women were dressed in black skirts and blouses with red or green trousers underneath, while the men's clothing displayed bright geometric designs—mostly squares and triangles. Each person also wore something around his or her neck: a red collar about three inches wide with a silver clasp. Their only other possessions were long curved knives that hung from their belts.

The group was arguing about something. When the voices became louder, an old man struggled to his feet. He had bandy legs, stringy hair, and a paunch that sagged over his belt buckle. "He's a thief!" the old man announced. "He's a squat-house thief who cared nothing for the boots working beside him. But the trouble is—he's the thief and *we're* the ones that pay."

A young woman stopped feeding twigs to the fire. "The wet crawlers are on their way here. And now we're one beneath twelve."

Michael could understand most of what they were saying, but the rhythm of their speech, the inflection of their words, seemed to come from an earlier time. Trying not to make any noise, he crawled a few feet to the right and saw a dead man hanging from a noose tied to a tree.

He considered crawling back through the undergrowth to the levee, then rejected the idea. *Come to us* was the message that appeared on the monitor screen. Yes, these people were carrying knives, but the sheaths were stained and smeared with dirt. They're tools, Michael thought. Not weapons. He stood up, pushed his way through the underbrush, and stepped into the clearing. Everyone in the group looked startled and the old man began blinking rapidly, like a cave creature pulled into the light.

"What's the name of this place?" Michael asked.

"The—the waterfields," the old man stammered. "That's the old name. Of course maybe they'll hammer up a new one."

"And what are you doing here?"

"We're faithful servants, sir. All of us. As you can see." The old man touched his collar. "We're here to harvest the spark."

Michael pointed at the hanging man. "And who is that?"

"He's a thief." This announcement prompted grumbling and comments from the rest of the group. "Yes . . . a thief . . . worse than a contempter . . ."

"What did he steal?"

The old man seemed astonished at the question. "He killed himself and stole his life, sir. The gods own that and only the gods can take it from you."

Michael glanced at the suicide and saw that the branch was too low for a quick, neck-snapping death. The man's eyes were open and the toes of his boots touched the ground as if he were an awkward ballet dancer.

A broad-faced man stood up and spoke angrily. "No more teeth and tongue. We're all in the same pot and you're puttin' it on the fire."

"He's not a servant," the old man said, nodding at Michael. "He's not a militant either or we'd be burnin' on the ground. Don't know what he is and what he wants—so what's the harm in talkin' to him?"

"He's a guardian," the young woman said. "Just like the ones on the visionary."

"That's right," Michael said quickly. "I'm a guardian. And I'm here to see the waterfields."

"Well, now you've seen them," a voice said. "So run back to the center."

"Wait! Wait! Let me calculate now," the old man said. "Grant me a short measure." Everyone watched as he paced back and forth in the narrow clearing. Whenever the old man stopped and changed direction, he kicked a divot in the packed dirt. After a minute or so of this ritual, he made a quick about-face and approached Michael. The few teeth left in his mouth were crooked and stained, but he smiled broadly.

"To your ears, sir—I'm Verga sire-Toshan. And what would your tag be?"

"Michael."

The name sounded odd to Verga, but he shrugged and continued. "Now, you say you're a guardian here to see the waterfields. But we've all heard tales of contempters running from the city with militants after them. You're like a finner on dry land—flopping around while the night birds gather. But we can save you if you help us with our error."

"What kind of help are you talking about?"

"*Three must be,*" Verga intoned, as if reciting a passage of scripture. "If we're one short of three, then the church militants will appear. Join us. Be a faithful servant. Help us cut the spark."

A murmur of approval came from the others. Michael realized that if he joined them, the number of workers once again became a multiple of three. He had no idea who the militants were, but it was best to keep a low profile until he learned more about this realm.

"Three must be," Michael said, and everyone smiled. Verga knelt in front of the dead man and began to pull off his boots. Two women left the group by the fire and removed the suicide's hat, clothes, belt, and knife. These possessions were placed at Michael's feet, and the youngest woman smiled shyly.

The dead man's boots and clothes smelled moldy, but they fit. By the time Michael was dressed, the naked thief had been cut down, and Verga had used his knife to snap open the silver clasp and remove the suicide's red collar. As the others rolled the body into a shallow ditch, Verga fit the collar around Michael's neck and forced the clasp back together. The collar was smooth, but fairly heavy; it felt like a thick strip of plastic. Michael wondered if it was an electronic tracking device or just a mark of servitude.

Everyone worked quickly to cover the dead man with branches and brush. When they were done, Michael followed them through the undergrowth to the waterfields. Three of the machines they called "wet crawlers" were a half mile away, grinding toward the levy. The largest of these machines looked like a crazed mechanic's amalgamation of a farm tractor and an old-fashioned locomotive. It had a pair of large wheels in back and a smaller single wheel in front, a long cylindrical body, and a black box like a riverboat wheelhouse on top. A black cloud of smoke puffed from a red smokestack and drifted across the water. Two smaller machines that looked like dump trucks with three wheels were on opposite sides of the main crawler—meek attendants for a roaring dragon.

Michael touched the handle of the dead man's knife. He had been expecting a high-tech world that looked like a cinematic version of the future. Where were the talking robots and massive skyscrapers that glowed like crystal spires? Where were the space vehicles floating down from the heavens and gliding into a vast loading dock?

He realized that the wet crawler would destroy the stick marker he had left in the water. If he lost the passageway, then he would be trapped in this primitive world forever. Trying not to look nervous, he approached Verga.

"Where are we harvesting today?"

"Just follow the tips of your boots." The old man motioned to the area directly in front of them.

Michael pointed in the direction of the passageway. "Are we also going over there?"

"Three suns gone. Three suns come," Verga said, as if this phrase answered the question.

"We guardians don't speak the same way," Michael told him. "We're harvesting here until darkness and then—"

"Three suns gone," Verga repeated.

While they were talking, the other harvesters had fastened the top part of their boots to their belts. Now their legs were protected from anything swimming in the water. When the wet crawlers were about fifty feet away, they began to make slow turns in the water. One servant controlled each machine while boys tossed chunks of fuel into fireboxes and adjusted the valves.

Verga slapped Michael on the shoulder as if he had just joined a football team. "From now on, you're 'Tolmo.' That was the thief's tag."

"What if someone asks about him?"

"They don't care about our faces. That's as clear as the boots I'm standin' in. Only the gods watch our lives."

The harvesters clutched their knives as if they were going to climb onto the crawler and kill everyone onboard. The machinery squealed and chugged and spat little jets of steam. Suddenly, Verga reached into the water and pulled up a green, pumpkin-sized plant still attached to its leafy vines.

"This here's a spark. Don't know what you guardians call it. Now, you want to take your knife and cut right around the base root. Trim the side vines off and toss your harvest into the feeder." He picked up a smaller plant. "Now, this one is still growing. And this one . . ." Verga grabbed Michael's hand and pushed it below the surface so he could feel a large, smooth object. "That's a mother plant. We leave that to birth the next measure."

"I understand."

"Slow and steady wins the day. Don't cut your leg with your blade."

"There are creatures in the water. I got bit."

A few people laughed, and Verga tugged down the brim of Michael's hat. "If a finner starts chewin' on you, just let me know. He'll end up in the pot."

Now that the main crawler had stopped, Michael could see the equipment attached to the back of the machine. A metal frame held a long conveyer belt that was only a few inches above the water. The horizontal belt fed the harvested spark to a vertical wire tube with a screw device revolving inside. Once the spark reached the top of the tube, it could be directed into the hoppers carried by the two auxiliary machines.

"May the gods reward us," Verga prayed. The harvesters drew their knives. Steel poles extending from the conveyer belt established twelve separate work areas. If Michael hadn't substituted for the dead man, it would have been immediately clear that someone was missing. The loud noise from the machinery and the shimmering space of the waterfields were almost overpowering. For a moment, Michael wanted to turn away and slosh his way back to dry land.

A steam whistle blew with a high-pitched shriek and the crawler began to roll forward. Startled by this disturbance, one of the finners broke the surface of the water. The old woman grabbed its tail and flipped it onto the conveyer belt, where a man sliced off its head and another man tossed its body onto the back of the frame. The crawler kept shaking as if it were about to fall apart. Michael stared at the eel head with its needle teeth as it floated past him.

"Tolmo!" Verga shouted. "What's your task now? Where's your blade?"

Michael drew his knife and caught up with the others. Both the men and women worked quickly. They gauged the size of the unseen spark with their feet and legs, then reached into the water, grabbed a stem, and pulled the plant to the surface. One or two quick cuts and the spark was free. Then they had to catch up with the crawler and toss their harvest onto the conveyer belt.

Michael could feel the spark hidden below the surface, but it was difficult cutting them free. Their stems were thick and tangled. Everything was a mess of leaves and mud and his own confusion. *Bend down. Grab. Cut. No, that's not right. Too small. Toss it away.* Finally, he cut a plant of the right size and realized that the crawler was now thirty feet away from him. He had to run through the muddy water, splashing and swearing to himself until he dumped the spark onto the belt.

Verga smiled. "Good. That's an offering for the gods."

"So how long do we have to do this?"

"'Til the midway resting."

"And when is that?"

"The crawler stops and turns when it reaches a boundary mark. You'll have time to fill your lungs . . ."

The crawler blew its whistle and Michael had to run again to catch up with the machine. Back in his own world, he and Gabriel had worked in a cattle feedlot, and one hot summer they had mopped tar onto roofs. But this didn't feel like a job at all. It was a muddy battle with the living world—grabbing the spark, slashing its stem, and flinging it away as if it were the head of a dead enemy.

7

The hazy triangle of suns moved higher in the sky and one of the smaller machines left with its load of spark. Still squeaking and blowing off steam, the main crawler stopped beside a levee, and the harvesters stepped onto dry land. Near this resting point, someone had set up a large cone of hammered copper filled with clean water. Cups were attached to the cone with little chains. While the harvesters took turns with the cups, a young woman opened a sack and passed out small loaves of something that looked like bread. Michael took a loaf and bit off a piece of the end. The midday meal had a brownish-orange color and a coarse texture; it tasted like roasted hazelnuts.

Verga sat near the edge of the levee gobbling down one loaf with two other loaves on his lap. "It's the gunder-spark today. Thought they'd serve us the rasten-spark, but this is better."

"Is that all you eat?"

"I forgot—you guardians eat more of the world. We servants eat finners and shantu and rake, but mostly it's spark, cooked different ways."

"You ever want to eat like the guardians?"

"Here I am and here I should be," Verga said as if this one phrase could refute any argument. "We servants are the hands and arms and legs, standing strong on the ground. And the militants are here . . ." He touched his heart. "And you guardians are here . . ." He touched his head. "All is just when each does his part."

When the harvest resumed a short time later, Michael felt stronger and was able to keep up with the others. What had looked like a haphazard operation turned out to be an efficient system of farming. There was no need to plant seeds or pull weeds as long as the mother plants were left alone. Drainage pipes connected the different fields, and a weak current kept the water from turning stagnant. Even the clanking, hissing wet crawler followed an established pattern: the servant operating the machine steered a straight line by aiming at the sticks embedded in the mud.

Toward the end of the day, the workers put away their knives, rolled down their boot tops, and followed Verga through the grid of levees to the dry land that surrounded the waterfields. After twenty minutes of walking, they reached three railroad tracks set on a gravel bed. The tired workers lay down on a weedy strip beside the tracks until a steam engine arrived, pulling a line of flatcars. The steam engine itself was as simple as a teapot on a three-wheeled wagon: a steam cylinder and a single piston transmitted power to the crankshaft that propelled the train.

If the train carried him to a new area, he might find it difficult to return to the passageway. As the harvesters began to climb onto the flatcars, Michael looked around for landmarks and saw a rusty handcart that resembled an old-fashioned rickshaw. At night, he could follow the railroad tracks back to this point and then retrace his steps to the sticks he left in the water.

His new friends waved their hands and called to him. "Hurry up, Tolmo! We're leaving!"

Michael jumped onto one of the flatcars, and the rickety train started down the tracks. They followed the perimeter of the waterfields, stopping every ten minutes or so to pick up another group of harvesters. Although the flatcars were moving about as fast as a Sunday jogger, there was a lively, excited feeling in the group. Everyone knew one another and people shouted jokes back and forth about the amount of spark each group had harvested that day. The wheels clicked with a quick rhythm as the wind of their passage ruffled the women's hair and the hems of their skirts.

Michael sat at one end of the flatcar with his hat pulled low over his face. He thought again about the summer he and Gabriel worked at the cattle feedlot. They didn't usually have money for gasoline, so, at the end of the workday, an older man named Leon would give them a ride home in the back of his pickup truck. It had been just like this: rolling down a road past the countryside.

Forget all that, Michael told himself. *Focus on the present situation.* Listening to the conversations around him, he figured out the system of two-syllable names used by the servants. Verga was also called Verga sire-Toshan—which meant he was the father of the man named Toshan sitting a few yards away. Mothers added their oldest daughter's name, and so the woman next to him was called Molva san-Pali.

In the distance, huge white shapes seemed to emerge from the ground. As the train drew closer, Michael saw that they were approaching a cluster of triangular buildings with steep roofs. The steam engine blew its whistle loudly, the engineer pulled back a brake lever, and the entire train screeched to a stop. Everyone jumped off the train, and Michael followed Verga across the tracks. A line of railcars had been left on a sidetrack; some of them held wire hoppers filled with harvested spark. A few cars carried stacks of bricks and a work crew was unloading them into wheelbarrows.

A pathway led them to a central courtyard surrounded by the triangular buildings. The courtyard was dominated by white brick structures that were as large as the barns back in South Dakota. Near a machine shop, men were repairing a vehicle that Verga called a "dry crawler." It looked like a nineteenth-century stagecoach with a driver's box and a steam engine in front. But there were also three-wheeled carts pulled by shaggy ponies with blunt noses and handcarts pulled by the older children. An open cooking area was at one end of the courtyard; women scooped out the pale orange pulp of the spark plant and molded it into loaves that they baked in an outdoor oven.

"Stay with my boots," Verga said, and Michael followed the old man through the crowd to one of the barns. He found himself in a cavernous room where sunlight streamed in through high windows. The building was used as a dormitory for all the men in the community. There was a mound of straw at the center, pegs for hanging blankets and clothes, and a trough for waste that was continually flushed out by the water flowing from the bathing area. Imitating the old man, Michael washed his face and hands beneath a stone spout.

"Some say guardians could never cut spark in the waterfields," Verga announced. "But you carried your blade better than that thief ever did."

"What happens now? Do we eat?"

"Eat all you want, Tolmo. And then it's the night for the visionary . . ."

Michael nodded as if he knew what the old man was talking about. They returned to the courtyard and followed the crowd to a trellised area where stew was being served in metal bowls. No spoons or forks were on the tables, so they ripped off chunks of gunder-spark and used them to scoop up their food.

Verga led him over to a long table where their work crew was eating dinner. As they approached the others, Michael was startled by what he saw. About a hundred yards from the dining area was a screen as big as a billboard with a shimmery gold surface. The screen was about six feet above the ground, and benches and stools had been placed in a semicircle in front of it.

The faithful servants gobbled down their food, laughing and gossiping, but Michael stayed quiet and studied a line of black and white circles on the surface of the screen. Every few seconds, the circles changed their configuration, like an odd clock keeping time.

It took him some time to realize that the circles represented a binary number system—the same system used by computers back in the Fourth Realm. Each digit in a line of numbers was either on or off, one or zero. When number eleven (●○●●) was transformed into number ten (●○●○), people tossed their empty bowls into a bin and sauntered over to the viewing area. Parents called to their children and, for a few minutes, Michael felt as if he were back in a small-town movie theater where people arrived a half hour before the show to save seats for their friends.

The three suns were a hand's width above the horizon. The cooks had finished their jobs and found their seats in the little amphitheater. Michael was cautious about asking too many questions, but he wanted to know what was going on. "How long do we have to wait?" he asked Verga.

"Soon enough. When the dark sky comes." The old man jerked his head at the screen. "Just keep watchin' the visionary."

As dusk fell, the sound of a choir singing came from hidden speakers, and then the image of a crystal sphere appeared on the screen. Stars floated on the surface of the sphere, changing positions as it rotated in space. The camera passed through the translucent surface to a second sphere that held the triad of suns and then through a third sphere that held comets and asteroids. At the center of all this was a round disk, colored with patches of blue and green. Like an avenging angel, the camera swooped down from the sky, and Michael saw that they were entering a world with grasslands, forests, and waterfields. A city was at the center of this world, and now the camera was gliding past brick buildings and streets filled with steam-powered crawlers.

A group of nine towers dominated the only hill in the city.

They were tall, bright spires, composed of translucent glass or plastic that concealed what was inside but allowed light to glow from within. Just down the hill from the towers was a white triangular building with an open roof. As the music reached a climax, the camera floated downward to where one man was standing on a stage.

The guardian was a slender blond man in his thirties with a pallid face. He wore a dark green robe that resembled a priest's vestments, but he had the ingratiating manner of a game-show host. "Welcome, everyone!" he shouted. "This could be the night the gods smile on *you!*"

Music boomed from speakers and beams of light shot across the stage. The camera angle changed and Michael saw that the guardian was facing an immense audience in an amphitheater. Men and women were sitting in different sections of the room, and quick close-ups revealed that everyone was young and enthusiastic. Most of the audience were faithful servants, but a smaller segment of the crowd wore silver tunics and black trousers. Michael decided that these people were the church militants that acted as both police force and army.

"This is the moment when two halves become one." The guardian spread his hands and then slowly brought them together. "This is the moment when the gods create a new unity, a new creation."

Again, the lights changed and laser beams moved around the amphitheater as if searching for someone. Onstage, a row of lights on a panel began to blink rapidly.

"And the gods have searched and the gods have chosen . . ."

The row of lights froze—expressing a binary number. There was a brief moment of silence and then a woman in the audience screamed and jumped up, waving a slip of paper that showed her number. Her girlfriends hugged and congratulated her as she hurried to the central aisle and climbed a staircase to the stage.

The young woman had wrapped silk flowers around her red collar, transforming it into a necklace. She seemed awed by the bright lights and the fact that she was now a participant in this event. When one of her friends shouted from the audience, she giggled nervously and waved.

"And what's your name?" the guardian asked.

"Zami."

"Welcome, Zami! Did you think this was going to happen to you tonight?"

"I— I prayed to the gods . . ."

"And now we'll see how they answered!"

The binary lights began blinking rapidly as Zami clasped her hands together. When the flashing stopped and a number appeared, shouts and laughter came from the men's section of the auditorium. A broad-shouldered servant emerged from the crowd and ran toward the stage. The moment he reached Zami, his aggressive energy disappeared. He glanced down at his feet and smiled nervously.

"We—we know each other," Zami said.

"Wonderful! Sometimes that happens." The guardian shook the young man's hand. "And who am I speaking to?"

"Malveto."

"You look like a happy groom."

"Yes, sir. Yes, I am."

As the evening continued, more brides were introduced to their grooms. Some of the couples were strangers, while others had known each other since childhood. At certain intervals, the guardian presented wedding gifts: tools, clothes, and simple furniture. No one seemed to find it surprising that lasers and video screens existed in the same world as wet crawlers and horse carts.

Finally twelve new couples were led offstage. The lights dimmed and the music became slow and solemn. The harvesters sitting around Michael stopped chattering to one another. They looked tense and expectant. Verga leaned toward the screen.

"Each of us is a strand of thread woven tightly into a piece of cloth. The faithful servants are strong. The militants are brave. We guardians are thoughtful. But all of us serve the gods," the guardian said. "Unfortunately there are a few heretics who attempt to destroy the sacred unity that binds us together."

Militants waiting in an offstage area rolled out three men strapped to heavy wooden chairs. The prisoners had shaven heads, and bandages covered their necks. They wore only flimsy white robes that reminded Michael of hospital gowns.

The guardian approached the oldest prisoner. "This enemy of the gods was once a faithful servant."

The prisoner was trembling. His mouth and tongue moved, but only a gurgling sound came out. Now the reason for the bandages came clear—someone had removed the man's vocal cords.

"But he was a servant who committed a vicious crime!"

The visionary screen showed the prisoner chasing a young woman through a warehouse filled with storage bins. As the woman fumbled with a door latch, the man grabbed her from behind, threw her to the ground, and began to rape her. The surveillance cameras photographed the scene from a variety of angles, but no one called for help.

The auditorium reappeared on the screen and a camera moved into a close-up of the man strapped to the second chair. This prisoner was younger than the rapist. His face was slack and his eyes rolled upward as if he had been drugged.

"And now we have a church militant who became a traitor and murderer," the guardian said. "He was taught to be brave and faithful, but he violated his oath and killed a superior."

The screen switched to surveillance footage of the prisoner standing in what appeared to be a military barracks. He was arguing with an older man and suddenly began beating him with a length of pipe. As the attack escalated, the harvesters stood up and shouted at the screen. When the militant finished, he turned and ran between two rows of cots. It seemed as if he were coming toward the harvesters, trying to attack them.

"And now a true sacrilege," the guardian said as he walked over to the third prisoner. "This wretch is a fellow guardian. A man I once called *brother*."

The visionary showed the third prisoner using a hammer to destroy an altar in one of the crystal towers. The harvesters watching the screen began shouting, "Kill him! Kill them all!" Fists were raised and faces were distorted with rage. Michael could hear babies crying, terrified by their mothers' anger.

"There's no doubt of these crimes," the blond guardian said. "No doubt of the punishment."

Militants readjusted the hinged parts of the chairs so that they became wooden racks with the prisoners still fastened to the frames. While the prisoners' gowns were ripped away, another group of militants appeared, pulling large hooks fastened to steel cables. The cables were attached to struts that extended over the stage.

A choir began singing as men with hammers pounded the hooks into the flesh of the prisoners. When the cables were pulled tight, the rapist was pulled up into the air. Naked and bleeding from his wounds, he trembled and fought to break free. Then the murderer was lifted up, followed by the guardian who had defiled the sanctuary. Each man twisted on three pairs of hooks that were buried in his shoulder blades, torso, and legs.

The cables holding up the servant tightened and then strained. First his legs were pulled away, then both arms. The two remaining cables pulled even harder until there was an explosion of blood as his torso was ripped in two. The chunks of flesh and bone still attached to the hooks swung back and forth like bloody pendulums as the other two prisoners were executed in the same manner. When it was over, the cables were released and everything dropped to the floor at the rear of the stage. A spotlight focused on the blond guardian. With a solemn look on his face, he clasped his hands together and murmured the phrase Verga had said earlier that day.

"All is just when each does his part."

The music changed, and after a moment the twelve brides and twelve grooms returned to the stage. All the young women had been dressed in dark red gowns and the men in black uniforms. A blaze of stage light made them look as if they were floating in darkness, but Michael could see the blood-splattered floor behind them. There was a crescendo of music and singing as the walls behind the stage opened like two immense doors. In the distance, the nine towers glowed with such power that they illuminated the city below. A final blast of music came, and then the visionary went dark.

For a few seconds, the crowd of faithful servants sat quiet and motionless. Then children began moving and the parents were pulled from their trance. Oil lamps were lit and the orange flames showed contented faces. They were tired—yes, it had been a long day—but somehow the visionary's presentation of hope and happiness and cruelty transformed them all. Life was good. Time to go to sleep.

Michael felt as if he'd been thrown off a building and somehow survived. He kept staring at the visionary as if a face would suddenly appear to explain everything he had just seen. Opposing ideas pushed through his mind and he was startled when someone touched his shoulder.

It was only Verga, holding an oil lamp. "Follow me, Tolmo. You sleep with us in the Sire House."

Entering the three-sided building, Michael discovered that the mound of straw was being used for bedding. Men would take three or four armfuls of straw, pile it against the wall, and burrow into their little nests. It took him an extra amount of time to make his own nest comfortable. One by one, the lamps were extinguished—leaving a faint buttery scent. Michael felt tired but wary. He removed the knife from its sheath and kept it close to his right hand.

Come to us, he thought. From what he had seen, this could be the advanced civilization that had sent that message. *Come to us* . . . and then what? Would they bring him up on stage and tear him apart for pretending to be a guardian? Michael sat up and tried to figure out what to do. He definitely couldn't stay here. It was too dangerous. When everyone was asleep, he would follow the railroad track back to the handcart, then wait for sunrise. With a little bit of light, he could find the passageway.

Deciding on a plan made him feel detached from what he had seen on the visionary. Mrs. Brewster and the board members of the Evergreen Foundation thought they were tough-minded, but they were children in comparison to the leaders who ran this world. The acts of torture displayed on the visionary were about as subtle as a Mayan priest cutting open a prisoner's rib cage and pulling out a still-beating heart. And then they put the couples together and married them. He puzzled out the connection between these two events, and then it came to him. *We have the power to kill you or bless you*—that was what the guardians were telling their audience.

Grunts and snores came from the darkness. The only light in the cavernous building came from a single oil lamp burning near the concrete trough. Michael's arms and legs felt heavy, and he decided to nap for an hour or so before he ran away.

He snuggled deeper into the straw and went to sleep. At some moment during the night he woke up hearing the hiss and squeak of a steam-driven crawler entering the courtyard. Men spoke to one another in soft voices, and then boots moved across the bricks. Suddenly, Michael's body was hit with a surge of pain that came from the red collar. The pain spread though his body—a sensation so powerful that he stopped breathing.

The collar lock had been broken when Verga took it off the dead harvester and Michael was able to rip it from his neck. Men were screaming and thrashing in the straw as men with handheld lights searched the room.

Clutching his knife, Michael jumped up and ran for the doorway. *Get out*, he thought. *Hide in the darkness. They're going to kill you.*

8

Travelers could break free of their
bodies and cross over to another world. The rest of humanity
needed an access point, one of several portals known in ancient
times. Since Maya hadn't returned, Gabriel would have to find
another way to bring her back. Simon had spent several weeks in
the British Library studying Greek and Latin texts that mentioned sites of prophecy and transformation. Most of these possibilities were in Egypt, so Gabriel asked Linden to arrange a trip
to Cairo.

Jugger and Roland were given the passport Gabriel had used
to enter Great Britain and hair that would match the DNA

samples the Tabula had obtained from his house in Los Angeles. The two Free Runners took the ferry to Calais and then traveled by bus and train across France. Using cybercafes and cell phones, they created the impression that Gabriel was on his way to Eastern Europe.

While the Free Runners were leaving a false trail in various hostels and hotels, Linden prepared cloned passports for Gabriel and Simon. When governments inserted RFID chips into passport covers, forgers quickly learned how to use a machine called a skimmer to read the information. If the skimmer was hidden in a doorway or an elevator it could read the passport carried in someone's pocket or handbag. Linden didn't waste time with skimmers and simply bribed a hotel clerk to scan tourist passports with a legally obtained inspection reader.

Once Linden had the information, he created a cloned passport with a duplicate chip. The information could be altered so that the person carrying the clone matched the embedded photograph and biometric data. In developing countries, the match didn't have to be perfect; ignoring their own instincts, immigration officers tended to wave a passenger through if a machine announced that everything was correct.

"So who I am supposed to be?" Gabriel asked Linden.

"A young man named Brian Nelson who lives in Denver."

"And what about me?" Simon Lumbroso asked.

"You're Dr. Mario Festa—a psychologist from Rome."

Simon grinned and leaned back in his chair. "Good. I'm enjoying this. And, of course, Dr. Festa thinks his government is protecting him."

* * *

A FEW DAYS later, Gabriel, Linden, and Simon flew to the West African country of Senegal. At the Dakar airport, Linden paid a bribe that inserted their new passport numbers into the global monitoring system. They quickly transferred to a different airline and took an overnight flight to Egypt. In the morning, they arrived and took a taxi from the airport into Cairo. Their cab moved through the crowded streets of Cairo like a boat floating in a labyrinth of muddy canals. Drivers kept honking their car horns while the traffic police stood listlessly on the sidewalks. But the Cairo jaywalkers displayed grace and confidence: old people, street sellers, and pregnant women glided through the traffic as if they had given their souls to Allah before stepping off the curb.

Simon told the taxi driver to take them to the City of the Dead on the east side of the Nile. Qarafa cemetery had once been the site of the Roman fortress of Babylon, and the brick-and-stone ruins had been transformed into a burial ground by the Mamluk rulers in the fifteenth century. Over hundreds of years, squatters had built huts among the tombs, and these improvised dwellings evolved into four-story tenements built with a grayish-brown concrete that resembled dried clay.

The cab passed through a square where men were selling canaries and parakeets, the little birds calling to one another as they fluttered back and forth in their cages. Men approached their car offering melons, shoes, and lottery tickets pinned to a cardboard sign. Veiled women walked arm in arm through the crowd while a recorded voice wailed from the speakers mounted on each mosque.

The driver got lost a few times, but eventually they reached the tomb of Imam al-Shafi'i, a Muslim holy man. A mosque with four minarets had been built around the grave site, and an elderly caretaker gave them a tour of the complex—stone walls and a faded green carpet, swallows darting around the interior of the cupola. When they had seen enough of the mosque to provide a reason for their presence in the neighborhood, they walked across the dirt street to a storefront café. Each customer sat at his own little table as the pudgy café owner bustled back and forth with glasses of hot tea that had sprigs of mint floating on the surface.

Simon Lumbroso could speak basic Arabic and had business contacts in Cairo, but as an Orthodox Jew he felt self-conscious about his appearance in a Muslim country. At the hotel, he slipped on a djellaba—a long cotton robe that covered his shabby black suit and the fringe from his *tallit katan*, the ritual Orthodox garment.

Linden and Gabriel were wearing cotton trousers and sports jackets without ties. Gabriel didn't mind looking like a businessman, but he wondered if Linden could truly disguise himself. The big Frenchman moved with an aggressive confidence and constantly surveyed the space around him as if he were preparing for an attack. Beggars and stray dogs sensed the danger and stayed away from him.

Simon lowered his cell phone and wrote a number down in his memo book. "I just talked to the priest's wife. She thinks he's at his uncle's house."

"But he was supposed to meet us here."

"This is typical for Cairo. What is expected never occurs. And what occurs is never expected." Lumbroso started dialing a new number. "Don't worry. We'll find him."

"While we wait for the priest, order some coffee," Linden said. "This tea tastes like dishwater."

Simon spoke to the café owner and then began punching in a new number. Gabriel looked up at the hazy sky above them. The soot and dirt particles in the air softened the light and changed the color of the sun. In the morning, the sun was a yellowish white, but now it looked like an old bronze coin nailed to the ceiling.

Something was about to happen. He felt a change coming; it was a moment when he saw the world clearly and all distinctions melted away. In the past, these incidents had frightened and overwhelmed him. Now, sitting in this street café, he could watch and wait and anticipate what was going to happen. The Light inside him was gaining power like a wave hidden beneath the surface of the sea.

The owner brought out coffee on a tin tray. Gabriel drank quickly and stared at the black grains at the bottom of the glass. A fly landed on his wrist and he flicked it away. More flies circled his boots while others rested on the café tables—tiny silver islands made of hammered steel.

He turned his head slightly, glanced down the street, and then the world opened up before him. During the interval of one heartbeat, his mind pulled back and he saw the city with total detachment. Everything before him—the sky, the flat-roofed tenement buildings, and the scrawny ficus trees—was a complete unity, but he could also perceive each detail. He saw motes of dust rising and falling—smelled garbage and baking bread—heard a woman singing on the radio.

The world enveloped him with its intricate variety, and he watched it all as if it were a photograph projected on a wall screen. He saw the faces around him just as clearly—Simon, Linden, the other customers sitting at the café, a woman carrying a white bird in a silver cage, and a group of boys kicking a bandaged soccer ball. When his mind was detached in this way, he could float above the street like an angel gazing down on fallen souls. The children radiated joy and happiness, but the adults shuffled along with faces that showed weariness, anger, and pain.

"Maybe that car was at the airport," Linden said. "Someone could be following us."

Gabriel's vision melted away and the world was ordinary again—with a feral dog staring at him and a black car parked at the end of the street.

"It is just a Renault sedan," Simon said. "There are thousands of them in this city. Cairo is where old Renaults come to die."

"This one has mud on its left headlight."

"Are you sure you've seen it before?"

"It's possible."

"Possible? Or just Harlequin *follia*?"

"Even crazy people have enemies . . ."

Both of them stopped talking as a battered taxicab came around the corner and stopped in front of the café. A door popped open and a bearded Coptic priest got out. Using his hands to hold up the hem of his robes, he marched over to their tables. The priest's blue jogging shoes had lightning bolts on the sides.

"Mr. Lumbroso?"

"Yes."

"I am Father Youssef from the Church of Saint Bartholomew. My cousin Hossam says you are looking for me."

Simon got up and shook the priest's hand. "It's a pleasure to meet you, Father Youssef. We just arrived in Cairo this morning. These two gentlemen are my friends."

They circled the chairs around one little table and Father Youssef ordered a glass of tea. All the windows on the street were either darkened by curtains or concealed behind shutters. There were no surveillance cameras in the City of the Dead, but Gabriel felt as if someone was watching them. When the black Renault made a U-turn and vanished around the corner, Linden relaxed slightly and leaned back in his chair.

The priest stirred sugar into his tea, and then used a spoon to mash the sprig of mint against the side of the glass. "How do you know Hossam?"

"I've done business with him involving antiquities," Lumbroso said. "Your cousin has a good eye for what is real and what is a fake."

"Hossam says you are a man who keeps promises. That is difficult to find in this city."

"I know that the Coptic Church is being persecuted."

"Our young men are beaten and arrested for nothing. My church has no electricity and the roof leaks when it rains."

Lumbroso touched his breast. A wallet filled with Egyptian pounds was concealed within the inner pocket of his suit coat. "We would reward the person with accurate information. We are looking for—"

"Hossam told me everything. You want a passageway that will take you to another world." Father Youssef drank his tea with a loud slurping sound and put down the glass with a click. "Most people do not care about these passageways. All they want is a new car and a big television."

Simon dropped a lump of sugar into his coffee. "We thought that a passageway might be connected to the pyramids. They've been a special location for thousands of years."

"The pyramids were built for the dead. A passageway is for the living."

Linden leaned forward and touched the priest's arm. "Tell us something of value and your church will get a new roof."

"The Coptic Church is poor and persecuted. They have taken everything from us, including our sacred chapel. It guards the way to another world."

"And who controls this chapel?" Linden asked.

"The Greek Orthodox Church. I talk about the Sacred and Imperial Monastery of the God-Trodden Mount of Sinai."

Lumbroso turned to Gabriel. "Most people know it as Saint Catherine's Monastery. It was built by the Emperor Justinian during the sixth century."

"Our church had a shrine at Mount Sinai before the monastery was built. Do you think Moses got his vision from a plant on fire? The burning bush was just a children's story that someone invented to protect the passageway."

"Can we go there?" Gabriel asked. "Will the priests let us in?"

Father Youssef spat on the dirt. "When pilgrims arrive at the monastery, the Greeks show them a bush growing outside the chapel. The passageway is in a room behind the altar."

"What if we offered them a donation?" Lumbroso asked.

"If the monks think you know about the passageway, they will call the police and have you arrested."

Looking annoyed, Linden shook his head. *"Ce prêtre est inutile,"* he whispered to Simon.

"I want to be helpful," Youssef insisted. "I can draw you a map of the chapel and show you the hidden room. But you should forget about this and go back to Europe. Passageways are dangerous. If you cross over, you can be trapped in a world with demons or ghosts. Only a saint can take such a journey, and there are no more saints."

Simon Lumbroso smiled. "Certain rabbis tell us that a handful of hidden saints keep this world from being destroyed."

"That's a big responsibility," Gabriel said. "I don't know if that's true."

"It is *not* true." Father Youssef tapped on the table with his spoon. "The Age of Saints is over. God no longer speaks directly to men and women. We speak to ourselves and pray to the echo."

9

Simon Lumbroso arranged for a car and driver, and they left that night for St. Catherine's Monastery, Gabriel and Simon in the backseat and Linden in front with the driver. The Renault sedan had a scratched and dusty exterior, but the driver had installed red velvet carpet on the floors and decorated the dashboard with plush dogs. A family of Yorkshire terriers stared at Gabriel with little glass eyes as the car glided past the walled palaces of the Egyptian military and headed east.

The four-lane highway cut a straight line across a flat desert landscape. Occasionally they passed a military installation protected by a high wall or a barbed wire fence, but no one other than soldiers appeared to be living in the area. Their Egyptian driver was a small, quiet man with a pencil-thin mustache. He kept the Renault in the middle of the road—aiming straight at each pair of oncoming headlights, and then swerving to one side at the last possible moment before they smashed into a trailer truck or a lumbering gasoline tanker.

The sun was coming up when they reached the outskirts of Suez. The driver showed his travel permit at three army checkpoints, and then they entered the tunnel lined with white tile that passed beneath the canal. When they reemerged into the sunlight, they had left the African continent and entered the Sinai Peninsula. Linden stretched his legs and arms, then tilted the rearview mirror so he could see out the back window. The driver began to protest, but Linden glared at him. "If you want some extra money, then leave the mirror alone. I like to travel this way, looking at my past."

The sun rose higher and the driver switched on the air conditioner. Every hour or so they passed a city with a smokestack and a power plant, a mosque, and a cluster of pastel-pink apartment buildings—the entire community dumped into a bare landscape of sand and scattered rocks. All the Egyptians had disappeared except for women on the side of the road selling melons that looked like little green cannonballs.

By nine in the morning, they had reached the seaside resorts on the Gulf of Suez. For Egyptians, recreation and luxury were all about palm trees: each resort would announce its presence with date palms in the median strip or a row of weary-looking doum palms by the side of road. Finally, billboards would appear and then a boulevard lined with royal palms that led to a hotel and a strip of beach.

More checkpoints—some run by the police, others by the army. Linden glanced over the seat at Simon Lumbroso. "It feels like half the population of Egypt is checking the passes of the other half."

"There's a lot of unemployment in this country," Simon explained. "This gives them something to do."

After stopping at a gas station, they left the beach resorts and headed inland toward a range of gray mountains. The cliffs and hills around them were eroded by the wind, and sand covered portions of the two-lane road. Simon was dozing now, but Gabriel sensed that something was wrong. Linden adjusted the rearview mirror a second time and then his hand brushed against one of the knives strapped to his lower legs.

"Stop the car," he said.

The driver looked startled. "Is there a problem, sir?"

"Stop the car. Now."

"We are about thirty minutes away from the monastery."

"I want to contemplate *le paysage*."

The driver turned off the road and parked on a sandy patch of ground. Linden grabbed his knapsack with one hand and glanced over the seat at Gabriel and Simon. "All of us want to look at the scenery," he announced. "Let's go."

The two men followed Linden up a hill covered with desert vegetation. It was hot and dry on the ridge and there were no shade trees to protect them from the sun.

"I enjoy looking at a picturesque landscape," Lumbroso said. "But this scrap of desert is not particularly impressive."

"We might have a problem." Linden reached into the knapsack and pulled out a pair of binoculars. "A silver pickup truck has followed us for about ten kilometers. I want to know if they made the same turn."

Simon and Gabriel stood quietly as the Frenchman studied the road.

"See anything?" Simon asked.

"No."

"Good," Gabriel said. "Let's get back in the car."

Linden lowered the binoculars, but he didn't hike back down the hill. He was larger than Gabriel and armed with two ceramic knives. Like most Harlequins, he displayed a certain arrogance about his power.

"I think this expedition is a foolish idea. There is only one road to the monastery, and that will be guarded by several police and army roadblocks. Most people come here in a tour bus. Arriving in a car is going to attract attention."

"There's no way around that," Gabriel said.

Linden didn't bother to hide his disdain. "First we have to find this secret chapel and then we have to get inside. And then what happens?"

"It sounds like you're going to tell us," Gabriel said.

"Then you cross over to the most dangerous realm. And maybe you can find Maya and maybe you cannot because she is already dead."

"She isn't dead," Gabriel said.

"Maya would not want you to risk your life for her. There is only one logical plan. If we find an access point in the chapel, then I will be the one to cross over."

"You've never been to the First Realm," Gabriel said. "I know the city."

Linden turned to Simon Lumbroso. "Explain why this is the correct decision."

Simon raised both hands. "Please. I am not part of this argument."

Gabriel stood on the ridge, trying to figure what to say. He couldn't use the word *love*. That was a meaningless emotion for a man like Linden. "Maya went there to save me. I feel the same obligation."

"Travelers don't have obligations to Harlequins!"

"I'm going to the monastery, Linden. And when I find the access point, I'm crossing over on my own. If you don't want to be part of this, I'll tell the driver to take you back to Cairo."

Gabriel trudged back down the hill to the car and Simon followed. A few minutes later Linden followed and climbed back in the car, slamming the door shut. All three men stayed silent for the rest of the journey. The Egyptian driver seemed to realize that his passengers had argued. He kept glancing at Linden as if the Frenchman were about to explode.

The road followed a dry riverbed up a canyon. They passed through one guard post, and then another. The final checkpoint was run by a bored group of police officers who were sipping tea and smoking from a hookah. Tour buses were parked a hundred yards up the road; they had their engines on and their air conditioners running.

"Most of the tourists come here at two o'clock in the morning to climb Mount Sinai," the driver explained. "If they're too fat to walk, the Bedouin carry them up the trail on camels."

The monastery guesthouse was a complex of white buildings with a terrace shaded with Italian cypress and olive trees. The guesthouse manager checked them in while a teenage boy with a crippled leg carried their luggage to their rooms. The flushed-faced tourists who had just returned from their climb were sitting on the terrace next to the guestroom gift shop and restaurant.

"Go to the chapel and look for the hidden room," Linden told Gabriel and Simon. "I will talk to the abbot and see if I can establish a financial rapport."

As Gabriel and Simon followed a stone walkway up to the monastery, they could see two Bedouins helping an elderly man off a camel while tourists hiked down a switchback trail. "Many years ago, my brother climbed this mountain," Simon said. "There were Bedouin all the way up, selling bottled water and candy bars. The price rises as you get closer to the top."

The monastery had been built like a fort to defend the monks from desert raiders. A rectangular wall made of massive sandstone blocks encircled the Chapel of the Burning Bush and all you could see from the walkway was the top of a bell tower. After paying admission, Gabriel and Simon entered the monastery through a small door cut into the wall. The chapel was at the center of a courtyard surrounded by three levels of monastery offices and dormitories. The gap between these monastery rooms and the chapel itself was quite small—about twenty feet on the western half of the chapel and less than eight feet on the opposite side.

Different groups of tourists squeezed into this gap while their guides shouted at them in various languages. Most of the women wore tank tops and Capri pants, and for modesty's sake they had covered their heads and bare shoulders with gauzy scarves. While

Simon inspected the outside of the chapel, Gabriel followed the crowd to the north end of the court. There was a bush growing there—supposedly the descendant of the original flaming bush—and the tourists pushed and shoved one another to grab souvenir leaves.

Simon touched Gabriel's shoulder and spoke quietly. "No sign of the hidden room. The chapel itself is forty meters wide and one hundred twenty meters long. Let us see what it looks like inside."

They passed through two sets of doors and entered the chapel. Frayed carpets covered the marble floor and muffled their footsteps. The bright desert sky disappeared and the only light came from oil lamps and candleholders hanging from chains attached to the blue-green ceiling. The most striking feature of the chapel was an elaborate gold and silver screen between the public area and the altar. A monk wearing black robes stood in front of the screen and hissed at anyone who tried to take a photograph.

Gabriel and Simon inspected a reliquary for St. Catherine that held a section of her arm; it looked like an old chicken bone found in the backyard. Then Simon paced out the interior dimensions of the chapel while Gabriel sat in one of the wooden pews. A massive brass chandelier hung overhead, and he realized that it was in the shape of a dragon. Icons of saints and martyrs covered the walls. They stared at him with large black eyes and Gabriel felt as if he were being judged by some heavenly tribunal.

A chattering group of Christians from Goa left the chapel, followed by a crowd of Russians and a third group of Poles. At that moment, the chapel became silent, peaceful, extraordinarily holy. Even the monk seemed to relax. He stared at Simon and Gabriel—decided they were harmless—and left through the main entrance.

"Follow me," Simon told Gabriel. "I think I found the hidden room."

Gabriel left the pew and hurried down the aisle. A tapestry hung on the wall at the front of the church. It was a murky image of Moses parting the Red Sea. Touching the dusty cloth lightly, Gabriel felt the outline of a door handle beneath it.

"Is it the right location?"

"Yes. It matches Youssef's map . . ."

Before they could pull back the tapestry, the main door squeaked open and the monk reappeared with a new group of tourists. Gabriel and Simon left the chapel, crossed the courtyard, and passed through the gate in the monastery wall.

"I paced the length of the chapel when we were inside," Simon said. "Factoring in the thickness of the wall, I think there is just enough space for a hidden room."

"Do you think Linden can make a deal with the monks?"

"Who knows? I'm sure he is prepared to offer a bribe."

The two men circled around to the eastern side of the monastery. During the modern era, the monks had decided to install running water and a sewage system. Instead of drilling through the wall, they had bolted a four-inch water pipe to the outside of the sandstone. Gabriel touched the rough surface of the pipe and looked up.

"I could climb this to the roof. Once I was up there, there's a gap between the monk's living quarters and the chapel. I could jump onto the roof of the chapel and get inside through the bell tower."

"That sounds like a good way to break your neck," Simon said. "Let us go back to the guesthouse and see if our friend had any success."

They found Linden sitting on the terrace near the guesthouse restaurant. The French Harlequin looked out of place among the pilgrims. Most of them were women wearing black dresses with white scarves covering their hair and heavy silver crosses hanging from their necks. The few men in the group wore frayed suit coats and white shirts buttoned up at the collar. They chain-smoked cigarettes while chatting with the Greek Orthodox priest who led the group.

Gabriel sat down at the white plastic table. "What happened?"

"I distributed some money to the staff, then went to the monastery and talked to the abbot." Linden tossed a fake business card on the table. "I said I was a film producer who wanted full access to the chapel to take photographs. The abbot said that it would take at least six months to negotiate permission from the Patriarchate of Alexandria. I offered him a small amount of money, then a much larger amount. He looked tempted, but he still said no."

Simon wiped the sweat off his forehead with a handkerchief. "Gabriel thinks he found a way in."

"If I were you, I would go tonight. Visitors stay here for only one or two days. They climb Mount Sinai, see the sunrise, then buy a T-shirt, and get back on the tour bus. If we stay here any longer, someone will get suspicious."

The three men went inside the restaurant for dinner. When they returned to the terrace, the mountains were black silhouettes while the sky held on to the fading light. A figure passed through the shadows and stepped onto the terrace. It was the teenage boy with the crippled leg who had carried their luggage to the rooms. Looking nervous, he approached Linden and whispered something in French. Linden slipped some money into the boy's hand, and then motioned him away.

"We should take our walk *now*. The boy's cousin works at the guard station. He says that men in a silver pickup truck just arrived and they are talking to the captain."

Gabriel and Simon stood up immediately. They followed Linden off the terrace and hiked a few hundred yards into the darkness.

"Are they from the Tabula?" Gabriel asked.

"I doubt it. The boy said that they are military policemen. If they find us, they will ask some questions and make sure we are not Israeli spies."

"Let's make them work hard for their bribe," Simon said to Linden. "I will only speak Italian. You can speak French."

"What if they ask about me?" Gabriel said.

"I will explain that you hiked up Mount Sinai to pray."

"Yes. You are very religious." Simon laughed softly. "We won't tell them that you're breaking into the chapel."

Trying not to trip over stones, the three men headed up the canyon to the monastery. Gabriel could hear camels grumbling in the darkness as the Bedouin got them ready for the pilgrims that would appear a few hours before dawn. The night landscape and the dark shapes of the mountains made him feel tired and lonely. This wasn't heaven or hell—just an odd sort of purgatory.

After ten minutes of walking, they found the drainpipe Gabriel had noticed earlier that day. The monastery wall appeared more formidable in the darkness—a massive stone barrier.

"Stay here," Linden whispered. "I will see if anyone is in the area." He passed through the shadows and vanished around the southeast corner of the wall.

Simon Lumbroso sat down on a boulder and contemplated the moon rising over Mount Sinai. "I am starting to understand why Moses led the Israelis to this awful place. It is about as spare and simple as an empty room. You do not want distractions from the word of the Lord."

Gabriel looked upward at the night sky and found no beauty in the stars. Some of them had perished billions of years ago, but their light still traveled through the universe.

"Linden thinks that Maya is dead."

"No one knows what happened to her. Anything is possible."

"She crossed over into the First Realm and sacrificed herself . . ."

"That was her choice, Gabriel. We talked it over when she came to Rome."

Linden came around the corner of the wall. "The outer doors are locked and no one is in the area. Start climbing. Let us hope that the monks are asleep."

Gabriel grabbed the water pipe and began to climb upward, using both his hands and feet. Even in the dim light, he was aware of the different layers of the wall. The first forty feet consisted of massive sandstone blocks, quarried and dragged to the site by Emperor Justinian's soldiers. The stone blocks in the second layer were much smaller—about a foot square—and held together by mortar. As his arms and shoulders began to ache, he reached the top of the wall: a three-foot layer of irregular stones and pebbles that the monks had picked up on their walks. Gabriel looked down and saw that Linden and Simon were moving away from the monastery. He reached out to the edge of the flat roof and pulled himself up.

The roof was a dumping place for broken bricks and rusty pipes. *Be careful*, he thought. *You're right above someone's bedroom.* Trying not to make any noise, he crossed the roof and looked at the gap between the monks' living quarters and the roof of the chapel. It was too dark to see the courtyard below. It felt as if he were about to throw himself into a bottomless pit. He remembered what one of the Free Runners told him before he ran across the roofs of Smithfield Market. *Watch your feet, but don't look farther down.*

He paced out three steps from a starting point to the edge. One deep breath, and then he was running, jumping, flailing his arms as he fell through the darkness and landed on the chapel's red tile roof. He slipped, started to fall, and then held on to the tiles and lay flat. *Everyone heard me*, he thought. *Everyone knows I'm here.* His brain conjured up scenes of monks jumping out of bed and running downstairs to sound the alarm.

But nothing happened. All he could hear was his own breathing and the faint scratching sound of his fingernails on the tiles. Gabriel crawled across the roof to the bell tower and climbed inside. Once again, he waited a minute or so to see if anyone was coming, and then he climbed down the steps to the foyer. The inner door squeaked faintly as he turned the handle.

Votive candles in red glass holders burned like coals in a dying fire. The faces of the icons were absorbed by the darkness, but the candlelight was reflected by the gold frames and brass chandeliers. When Gabriel walked over to the left aisle of the chapel, he saw one of the monks in front of the altar screen. He was an old man—very short with hunched shoulders—and he held a length of prayer beads with a spindle at one end. As he prayed and paced, he manipulated the chain with his thumb and forefinger. The spindle turned clockwise like a miniature prayer wheel while the monk's sandals scuffled across the stone floor.

Gabriel stood on one side of a pillar and wondered what to do. If he moved forward, the monk would see him immediately; if he tried to leave the chapel, the outer door might be locked. He waited in the shadows for over twenty minutes until the inner door swung open and a second monk entered. The two men spoke to each other in Greek, and Gabriel wondered if someone had heard his footsteps on the roof. The old monk headed toward the side aisle, then changed his mind and followed the younger man out of the chapel.

Were they gone for the rest of the night or just a few minutes? Gabriel grabbed one of the candles and hurried past the altar screen to the tapestry. Pulling back the dust-covered fabric, he found an oak door with a cast-iron door handle and keyhole lock. Quickly, he tied back the tapestry. The lock looked fairly new, but the monks hadn't installed a new door. Standing sideways, Gabriel kicked above the lock. He kept kicking until a section of the wooden frame cracked off and the door popped open.

The room was smaller than he had imagined—about twelve feet long and six feet wide. A white stone altar displayed a gold cross and two candle holders. Directly above the cross was a murky-looking painting of Moses standing beside the burning bush. There was a three-legged stool in one corner next to an embroidered pillow, but no other furniture was in the room.

Gabriel circled the small space again and again until he noticed a marble slab resting on the floor below the altar. It was a rectangular piece of stone that looked like the top of a sarcophagus. A cross and Greek letters were carved into the surface.

Kneeling on the floor, he pushed the slab back a few inches and saw darkness surging and flowing like black oil in a white stone box. The Traveler reached out his hand and moved his fingers. No burning bush. No voice of God. He was in this world, this particular reality, but that was only one thin layer of a far more intricate system. Then he lowered his hand into the darkness and watched it disappear.

10

Hollis met Linden in the store-room above the falafel shop a few days before the Harlequin escorted Gabriel to Egypt. Linden sat by the window dropping shreds of black tobacco into a square of cigarette paper. He rolled the cylinder between his stained fingers and then nodded in Hollis's direction. *Go ahead. Talk.*

"Gabriel said you could help me get to Japan."

The big Frenchman lit the cigarette and flicked the dead match through a crack in the window. The tobacco gave off a faint odor of burnt sugar. "I bought you a plane ticket using one of my Luxembourg corporations." He reached into the inside pocket of his jacket and pulled out an airline ticket and a packet of British pounds. Both gifts were tossed onto the table.

"Thank you."

"*Pas de quoi.* This was not my idea."

"Then thank Gabriel."

"You are not connected to us any longer, Mr. Wilson. But remember this fact: you will be punished if you mention the Traveler to anyone."

A stack of newspapers were on the table and Hollis assumed that a handgun was concealed beneath *Le Monde.* If there was a confrontation, he wondered if he would have enough time to draw his knife and drive it into the center of Linden's chest.

"I respect Gabriel," Hollis said. "And that's never going to change. I keep my promises. You know that."

Linden appeared to be calculating an equation with a half-dozen factors that related to Hollis's death. Apparently, there was some advantage to letting him live. The Harlequin shrugged his shoulders.

"*Au revoir*, Mr. Wilson."

"Not yet. I want to meet this Japanese woman that Gabriel told me about—the one who speaks to the dead. He said you'd know how to find her."

"She is called an *Itako*. You should speak to Sparrow's old friend—a high school teacher named Akihido Kotani. After Sparrow was killed at the Osaka Hotel, Kotani claimed the body and helped get Sparrow's pregnant fiancée out of the country. I was in contact with Kotani for a few years, and then he stopped answering e-mail. But he sent me some books once, and I still have his card."

"That's all? Just his card?"

"This is your problem, Mr. Wilson. You have to solve it on your own." Linden pulled out a dog-eared business card and placed it on the table. A name was given in Japanese and English.

AKIHIDO KOTANI—WHITE CRANE BOOKS—JIMBŌCHŌ—TOKYO

* * *

HOLLIS'S PLANE ARRIVED at Narita Airport early in the afternoon. It took an hour to get through passport control. After a series of polite questions, the immigration officer ordered the foreigner to open his suitcase. The atmosphere was tense and slightly hostile until Hollis held up a karate uniform and two books on Japanese martial arts that he had purchased in London. The immigration officer nodded as if this answered all his questions, and Hollis was allowed to leave the detention area.

He exchanged his money and took a train into Tokyo, passing through suburbs crammed with two- and three-story concrete block buildings. Each residential apartment had a little balcony with a hibachi, a few plastic chairs, and a potted bush that offered a splash of green. Winter had passed, but it was still cold. Little chunks of ice clung to the blue tile roofs beneath a pearl-gray sky.

The conductor was neatly dressed and very efficient. He stared at Hollis when he punched his ticket, then relaxed when the foreigner took out the martial arts book. "You are student?" the conductor asked in English.

"Yes. I've come to Japan to study karate."

"Good. Karate is very good. Always obey your sensei."

At the Ueno train station, Hollis went into a cubicle in the men's toilet. He opened up the back of his notebook computer, took out a ceramic knife blade and handle, then joined them together with epoxy glue. The eight-inch-long ceramic knife was light, durable, and very sharp. Hollis slipped the weapon into a nylon sheath strapped to his arm and then threw away what remained of the computer.

As far as the Japanese were concerned he was a *gaijin*: an "outside person" who would never fit in. Hollis left his bag in the checkroom and stepped out onto the street. Everyone was staring at him; he fumbled through his canvas shoulder bag, found his sunglasses, and put them on to conceal his eyes.

* * *

IT TOOK HIM three hours to reach Jimbōchō—a Tokyo neighborhood comprised of small buildings and shops near Nihon University. Hollis quickly discovered that most of the streets and alleyways in Tokyo were unnamed and that addresses didn't follow the Western system. Usually, a small plate was attached to each building. It showed something called a *banchi* number, which indicated the district and lot. But the numbers weren't always consecutive, and he saw a few Japanese men wandering through the area with an address on a slip of paper.

He searched through his phrase book, learned how to say *sumimasen*—"excuse me" in Japanese—and began to ask directions to White Crane Books. No one in Jimbōchō had ever heard of the place. *"Gomennasai,"* everyone answered—"I'm sorry"—as if their lack of knowledge had caused his confusion. Hollis followed side streets that wandered left and then right like ancient pathways. There were very few children or teenagers on the streets. The city felt like the Kingdom of the Old, a land occupied by short elderly women who wore running shoes and pushed portable shopping carts.

Hollis had grown up in cities and didn't particularly care about nature. But in Tokyo he became aware of the crows, large black birds with jabbing beaks. Everywhere he walked, they were watching him, perched on telephone poles or strutting down the middle of alleyways like little potentates of darkness. A few of them made a screeching sound when he waved his hands or kicked a piece of trash in their direction. It sounded like they had their own crow language they expected him to understand: We see you, *gaijin*. We're watching you.

He stopped at every bookstore he could find and asked if they had ever heard of White Crane Books. After two hours of searching, he saw a bookstore that looked like a hole burrowed into a shabby apartment building. Two bookshelves on wheels were out on the street with plastic tarps attached in case of snow or rain.

Hollis looked inside the shop. It was a dark tunnel lined with books—some of the volumes were arranged on shelves, but most of them were stacked on top of one another or dumped into cardboard boxes. An older Japanese man wearing a tweed jacket sat at the end of the tunnel and read a book stuffed with pieces of paper. A wad of tape held his eyeglass frames together.

"Good afternoon, sir. Can I help you?"

"Just looking . . ." Hollis entered and found a wall of books in various foreign languages. "You got a hell of a lot of books here."

"It is a small shop, sir. I never have enough room."

"Ever heard of a store called White Crane Books? A friend told me to check it out when I came to Tokyo."

The shopkeeper laughed, and then covered his mouth to be polite. "You have reached your destination, sir. This is White Crane Books and I am the owner, Akihido Kotani."

"I'm looking for a special book. It might be difficult to find."

"Is it a foreign book or Japanese?"

"I only know the English title. It's called *The Way of the Sword*."

Looking frightened, Kotani held up both hands. "I am sorry, but do not know this book."

"Of course you do. It was written by a fighter who called himself Sparrow. He was close to a German named Thorn and Frenchman named Linden."

"You must be mistaken. I have never heard of these people. Excuse me. I must close my shop now. *Gomennasai* . . ."

Kotani wheeled one of the bookshelves into the tunnel while Hollis stood on the sidewalk. "You were Sparrow's friend, Mr. Kotani. You got his fiancée out of the country and she had a son named Lawrence Takawa. He was a brave young man, but the Tabula killed him."

"Do not bother me. Please . . ." With frantic energy, the bookseller grabbed the second shelf and pushed it into his shop.

"I need your help, Mr. Kotani. It's important."

Kotani hurried into the bookstore, then pulled the door shut and locked it. Seconds later, he peered out the display window. When he saw that Hollis was still there, he retreated into the darkness.

* * *

HOLLIS WANDERED DOWN the street to a bus stop and sat on a wooden bench. He had concentrated so much on finding the bookshop that he hadn't considered an alternative plan. Should he search for this spirit woman on his own or should he return to London? Although he had never totally believed that he could speak to Vicki again, he had felt a spark of hope. Once again he sensed the stone inside him, that constant anger that never seemed to go away.

"Excuse me, sir. Excuse me." Hollis glanced up and saw that Akihido Kotani was standing beside the bench holding a plastic shopping bag. "I am sorry to bother you. But you left this at my shop."

Confused, Hollis took the shopping bag. Kotani gave him a quick bow before hurrying away. *Why didn't he stay and talk?* Hollis wondered. *Are surveillance cameras watching on this side street?* He returned to the main avenue before he inspected the bookseller's offering. Inside the bag was a copy of *The Way of the Sword* and a cell phone.

11

Michael was locked inside a metal container carried by a steam-powered crawler that was bumping its way down a country road. No one had explained where they were going. He had been dragged out of the men's dormitory, carried across the courtyard, and thrust through a narrow opening like a log being tossed on a fire.

The holding container had a teardrop shape and sloping sides. It reminded Michael of a water boiler built with sheet metal and rivets. The only light came from an air vent near the top of the container, and he spent most of the morning gazing up at a rectangular patch of clouds and sky.

Late in the day, the crunch of steel wheels on gravel changed to a steady grinding noise. Michael scrambled to his feet, grabbed the grate covering the air vent, and pulled himself up. Peering through the bars, he saw that the crawler was passing through a city. The buildings that lined the street had slate roofs, brick walls, and round windows made of yellow glass. The visionary screen had revealed a society with sophisticated technology, but Michael couldn't see any electric lights or power cables. Porters carried baskets filled with chunks of a black substance that looked like coal, and smoke trickled out of crooked pipes that jutted from the roofs.

Michael saw one guardian wearing the distinctive green robe and two church militants patrolling the streets with clubs hanging from their belts. But the city was dominated by the faithful servants. Men and women baked bread, cobbled shoes, and stitched clothing. There were street sweepers with long, feathery brooms.

The crawler made a great deal of noise as it turned to the left and began to climb a low hill. Michael let go of the bars and slid back down to the bottom of the container. He sat quietly and waited as the machinery creaked and shuddered and stopped moving. A few minutes passed, then the door was unlatched and light streamed through the opening.

Michael crawled out and encountered three militants holding thick wooden clubs. Maybe this was a different world, but the militants resembled the police officers he had met in the Fourth Realm. Michael wondered if there was some kind of universal cop attitude toward suspects: *mess with me and I'll put you down.*

He was standing in a courtyard circled by the nine crystal towers he had seen on the visionary screen. At night, the towers had glowed with light; they had looked like magical creations that could detach from their foundations and float into space. In the daylight, Michael could see that the towers were built with steel girders and thick panels of glass or plastic.

"Now what happens?" he asked. "What am I supposed to do?"

"Wait for the guardian," answered the tallest man.

"I haven't done anything wrong," Michael said. "I harvested spark and followed your rules."

The youngest guard repeated what Verga had said when they were out in the waterfields. "All is just when each does his part . . ."

Someone wearing the dark green robes of a guardian emerged from one of the towers and walked across the courtyard to their little group. It was the same blond man who had directed the weddings—and the executions—on the visionary show.

"Did he give you any trouble?" he asked.

"No, sir."

The guardian scrutinized Michael's face. "I think he wants to run away."

Holding his club with two hands, the tall militant approached Michael. He hit his prisoner in the stomach, directly below the rib cage, and Michael went down—gasping for air.

"You can't escape, so don't even consider it," the guardian said calmly. "Now get up and follow me."

Michael struggled to his feet and staggered forward. When they were about twenty yards away from the militants, the blond man stopped and faced him.

"What do you call yourself?"

"Tolmo."

"A deliberate lie is like mud smeared on the altar of our Republic. You're not a servant named Tolmo. Each collar has to match its owner. I'm sure he's floating in the waterfields or rotting in a hole scratched in the ground."

Michael nodded. "He killed himself."

"Ahhh. Now I understand. So the servants were worried about *three must be*, and then you appeared."

"Yes, that's what happened. I'm called Michael."

"You have an unusual name. But that's common for barbarians that find their way here from the outlands."

They reached the base of a tower, and the guardian led him down a sloping causeway. The guardian pushed open a sliding door and they entered an underground area lined with glass panels that gave off a greenish light.

"Electricity," Michael said.

"What?"

"You're not using torches or oil lamps."

"Our temples and the visionary can use the sacred machines."

An elevator door opened at the end of the corridor, and the guardian motioned for Michael to step in. The elevator glided upward with a soft grinding sound. When the door opened, Michael found himself in a large star-shaped room. There was no furniture of any kind—just a bare stone floor. The steep walls of the tower were composed of interlocking triangles reaching upward to an apex lost in the gloom.

The guardian remained in the elevator. He pressed his hands together in a pious gesture. "You have been given a great privilege: a chance to feel the power of the gods. The servants and the militants worship them from afar. We guardians encounter them only once or twice in our lives."

"What do you mean—the gods?" Michael looked around. "No one's here."

"The gods will display themselves if you show obedience and faith." The elevator door closed and then Michael was left alone.

The tower's glass panels were tinged with a smoky gray color that allowed some light in, but made it impossible to look outside. "Hello?" Michael said. "Anyone here?" He whistled and clapped his hands, and the noise echoed off the walls.

He sat on the floor and leaned against one of the panels for a while, then lay on his side with his arms for a pillow. The image of the prisoners being torn apart on the visionary screen kept floating through his mind. There were only three classes in this society—servants, militants, and guardians—and he didn't belong to any particular group. The blond man had called him a "barbarian," but he might also be considered a heretic and a criminal.

When he woke up a few hours later, the room was dark and much colder. Light came from the other eight towers, but he felt as if he were trapped in a cave. Michael stood up and began to pace across the floor. He noticed a breeze touching his face. *How is that possible?* He was inside a building with no windows. Michael touched one of the panels with his hand, feeling the cold, smooth surface. His heart was beating faster and he sensed that someone—or something—had entered the temple.

He spun around quickly and saw that three columns of light had appeared in the center of the room. The light seemed grainy, almost textured, and each column resembled a luminous green cloud with specks of gold dust floating within its gravitational field. Were these the gods that controlled this world?

The light grew more intense until the columns appeared solid—green pillars glowing in the middle of the temple. And then he heard an older man's voice coming from the center column.

"Who are you?" the voice asked.

"Are you a barbarian?" a woman's voice asked. "A stranger from the outlands?"

Trying to figure out what to say, Michael took a few steps toward the light.

"We are waiting for your answer!" the first voice said. "We are the gods of this world and all other worlds . . ."

Michael laughed softly and the sound filled the room. "I'm Michael Corrigan and I've traveled a long way to get here. Who am I? I'm a man who has made money selling things to other people." He sneered at the light wavering in front of him. "And that's how I know what this is—bells and whistles, tricks and mirrors to sell the product. It may be enough to impress the locals, but I'm not buying."

"He's a heretic!" a young man's voice shouted. "Call the guardians and give him his punishment!"

"You can do whatever you want," Michael said. "But then you'd punish the very person the gods asked to come here. I'm a Traveler from another world."

The columns of light gained power and intensity; they were so bright that Michael had to shield his eyes. Wind howled around him, almost pushing him off his feet. Then, just as quickly, the wind stopped. There was a moment of darkness, and then lights attached to the struts of the tower were switched on.

Michael heard the elevator door open and three people—two men and one woman—stepped out and strolled across the stone floor. "Welcome, Michael," the older man said. "We've been waiting for you."

12

The young man on the right had a muscular neck and shoulders, and long black hair that covered his ears. He carried himself in a confident manner and raised his chin slightly as if he expected to be obeyed. In contrast, the older woman on the left looked delighted to meet the Traveler. She leaned forward as if she were going deaf and didn't want to miss a word. The oldest man—clearly the leader—stood in the middle. His hook nose and sunken eyes remind Michael of a marble bust of a Roman emperor.

"We apologize for the severity of our demonstration," the older man said. "But we needed to discover if you were a Traveler or someone from the outlands."

"A barbarian would have fallen to his knees," the woman explained. "They weep and shiver and pray to our light."

"Do you have names?" Michael asked.

"Of course," said the older man. "But they would sound strange to you and you wouldn't understand their meaning."

"We want you to feel like you're talking to *friends*," said the woman.

"So we've picked names from your world," said the older man. "I'm Mr. Westley. This is Miss Holderness and—"

"I'm Dash," said the young man. "Mr. Dash." He looked pleased with the name he'd given himself.

"Are you the people who contacted us using the quantum computer?"

Mr. Westley nodded. "For many years, we've been trying to communicate with your world. Finally, you reached the level of technology that could pick up the messages we sent across the barriers."

"We wanted a Traveler," Miss Holderness explained. "But we didn't know if they still existed in your world."

"And you call yourself gods?"

"We *are* the gods of this reality," Mr. Westley said. "There are more of us, but we three were given the task of meeting you."

"In my world, we have a different image of God. He's a powerful force who knows everything."

"We know about everything that goes on in our Republic," Miss Holderness said. "The computers track every negative thought and sign of rebellion."

Mr. Dash looked annoyed. "And we're just as powerful as gods. If we gave the right order, half the population would kill the other half."

"But God is . . ." Michael hesitated, not knowing how to finish the statement. If he thought about God, he pictured the man with the white beard painted on the ceiling of the Sistine Chapel. "God is immortal."

The three half gods glanced at one another, and Michael sensed that death was a sensitive topic.

"Our power isn't dependent upon an individual being," Mr. Westley said. "If one of us disappears, a new god is chosen from the guardian class. Mr. Dash is our newest recruit."

"The faithful never see us directly," Miss Holderness said. "Sometimes we punish citizens who have prayed every day and followed all our laws. People fear us because they can't predict our actions."

"But you didn't create this world," Michael said. "You're not—"

"Of course we created the world," Miss Holderness said. "Ask anyone who lives here. They'll tell you that we placed the three suns in the sky and made the spark grow in the waterfields."

Mr. Dash was getting angry. "God is whatever is worshipped. Perhaps you are a Traveler, but you seem rather ignorant about religion."

"There's no reason for an argument," Mr. Westley said with a soothing voice. "Michael has never been to our world and he still doesn't understand our system."

"I'm sure he's tired and hungry." Miss Holderness turned to the others. "Aren't we going to feed him?"

"An excellent idea." Mr. Westley pulled a black disk out of his shirt pocket and pressed one corner. There was a humming sound directly behind Michael. When he turned around, he saw sections of the floor open like an elaborate trapdoor. Slowly, a metal platform with furniture on it was raised up from a lower level.

The three half gods guided Michael over to benches surrounding a glass table covered with plates of food. The meal looked fairly simple. Red and green plants had been cut into geometric shapes. Everyone sat down, and Mr. Dash mixed water and a blue liquid in a gold drinking bowl.

"We've had Travelers visit us as long as we have recorded our history," Mr. Westley said. "Some of the Travelers were here only for a brief time. Others, like Plato of Athens, stayed and learned from us."

"We started out with three divisions of society: workers, soldiers, and rulers," Miss Holderness said. "At a certain point, our ancestors introduced a series of myths to justify our system. The first myth is that there is a fundamental reason for our three divisions. The faithful servants are the arms and legs of the Republic. The militants are the heart, and the guardians are the head."

"I heard the same story from a servant in the waterfields," Michael said.

Miss Holderness looked pleased. "Our ancestors also created a wonderful story where everyone is imprisoned in a cave, gazing at shadows on the wall. Only we gods can leave the cave and truly see the light."

"The myth justifies our existence," Mr. Westley said. "The major threat to stability is when people think and act freely. With a hierarchy of consciousness, you can say that anyone's perception is foolish—or blasphemy."

"The men you executed were called heretics."

"The most significant challenge to stability is the perverse impulse toward freedom. You can't control this desire for freedom entirely with threats and punishments; it's more effective if you teach people to doubt the reality of their own perceptions. When the system is working correctly, they censor themselves."

Mr. Dash finished mixing the water and the blue liquid. He drank first and handed the bowl to Mr. Westley. The older man drank, and then handed the bowl to Miss Holderness, who took several swallows and gave the bowl to Michael. All three half gods were silent, watching him. Mr. Dash sat on the edge of his couch as if he expected an unpleasant surprise.

Michael raised the bowl and took a sip of the turquoise-colored liquid. It had a slightly bitter taste, but when he swallowed, he felt warmth spread through his body. He decided that it must be alcohol or something like that. At least they weren't trying to poison him.

"The guardian who brought me here said you can track anyone wearing a red collar."

"There are a variety of other ways to monitor the population,"

Miss Holderness said. "The militants watch the servants. The guardians watch the militants. And we make sure the guardians aren't organizing some kind of rebellion."

"If you have that kind of technology, I don't know why you use horse carts and steam engines."

"Would you give explosives to a child?" Mr. Westley asked. "It would be a disaster if everyone in our society were granted access to the machines—so we've created a two-tier system. Over a long period of time, we have developed computers, the visionary screens, and the monitoring collars. But this technology is restricted to religion and security. We keep food, clothing, and medicine at a simpler level. This allows us to create miracles every day. As far as the people are concerned, we gods see everything, know everything . . ."

"Yes, I came here because of the quantum computer. You were sending us technical data and then it stopped."

"We assumed that any government or organization that could create a quantum computer would also have knowledge of the Travelers," Mr. Westley said.

"This was all about you," Miss Holderness said. "Our goal was to get a Traveler to come to our world."

Although the blue liquid had made Michael feel a little woozy, he sensed that something significant was about to happen. This was the moment in a sales presentation when someone produced a contract and pushed it across the table.

"So now I'm here," Michael said. Trying to hide his own tension, he picked up a piece of food that resembled a slice of watermelon. Michael was surprised that it tasted salty—like Korean kimchi. He swallowed it down and drank from the bowl. "Why did you want to meet me?"

"For some unknown reason, you and the other Travelers have a power that was not given to us," Mr. Westley said. "You can escape your world."

The three half gods stared at him. There was an uncomfortable moment of silence. Michael took another sip of the blue liquid and tried not to smile. They were jealous. Yes, that was it. Jealous of his power.

"We want to cross over to the different worlds," Mr. Westley said.

"We've done everything we can in *this* place," Mr. Dash said. "All of us are bored. We want to go to the Dark Island and the realm of the hungry ghosts. But most of all, we want to travel to the golden city."

"I don't know what you're talking about."

"Travelers have come here in the past and they have insulted us," Mr. Dash said. "They call us 'half gods' and say that the 'real' gods live in this special place."

Miss Holderness tapped her fingers on the table. "Some creatures might appear to have a higher form of consciousness, but we know how to *use* our power. It wouldn't take much effort to make them bow to our true divinity."

"I can't teach you how to be a Traveler," Michael said. "My father had the power and he passed it on to me."

"It's simply a way to focus and send energy," Mr. Westley said. "I think we could duplicate the process with our quantum computers."

Miss Holderness sipped some more of the blue liquid and passed the bowl to Mr. Dash. "Look at Michael," she said. "He's trying to figure out how this is going to increase his own power."

"Help us become Travelers and we'll show you how to take control of your world," Mr. Westley said. "We'll be in charge of the other five realms, but you'll be the god of your own particular reality."

"The Fourth Realm is a big place," Michael told him. "A lot of people live there."

"You're not going to be watching them all," Mr. Dash explained. "Other people can do that job—your church militants and your guardians. However, you'll be in charge of the system. And you'll become a god, just like the three of us."

"Forget about art and philosophy," Mr. Westley said. "There is only one truth, and we see it clearly. The permanent force in the universe is the Light held within each living thing. If you control another person, you control their Light."

"It's a game—only much more elaborate," Miss Holderness said. "We make our citizens march around and fight each other. We make them weep and laugh and pray."

Mr. Dash raised the bowl and grinned. "And after we're done with that, we can always make them die, sometimes in spectacular ways."

Sweat trickled down Michael's neck. He felt as if he had just finished running a race on a warm summer's day. "My world has different governments and armies and religions."

"There's no need to fight against any of these groups," Mr. Westley said. "We'll show you how to guide them in a particular direction. First you create a frightening story, and then you provide a happy ending . . ."

13

For the next few hours, Hollis wandered through the Ginza district waiting for the phone to ring. If the Tabula knew about his passport, their computers might have registered his arrival in Japan. Once his presence was confirmed, the Tabula's local contacts would start looking for him.

As the sun went down, the neon signs of Ginza began to glow red and green. An enormous video screen on the side of a building flashed pictures of young women who smiled and pointed to new products. Hollis wandered through the canyons of skyscrapers and found himself on a street that was devoted to gift giving. Each shop sold a particular kind of luxury: aged sake or expensive luggage, orchids wrapped in white tissue or chocolate candies wrapped in red. Even these gifts made him think about Vicki. Would she have liked a silk scarf or a bottle of perfume? Why didn't he buy gifts for her when they were living in New York City?

When it felt like too many people were staring at him, he wandered north to the modest buildings of the Asakusa district. As the streetlights began to glow with a dark yellow light, he entered an *onsen*—a public bath that used the water from a hot spring. The small entryway had lockers for your shoes, and he found himself hopping on one leg as he untied his laces. A sliding door glided open and a short, burly Japanese man came out to get his shoes. The man's pant legs rose up slightly when he squatted down to open his locker, and Hollis saw that he had tattoos. More tattoos were visible on the patch of chest exposed by his partially unbuttoned shirt. Hollis wondered if the man was *Yakuza*—a Japanese gangster. In a culture that valued conformity, you had to have a good reason to change your appearance.

After leaving his clothes in a locker, he followed a yellow line into a washroom and sat on a plastic stool. The Japanese men stared at the black foreigner as Hollis soaped himself, filled a bucket with hot water from a faucet, and poured it over his head. After repeating the process a half-dozen times, he entered a larger room with four baths—each providing a different temperature. The first bath was so hot his feet and fingers began to tingle. The *onsen* water smelled like sulfur and was the color of weak tea. After a while, the Japanese ignored the foreigner and concentrated on their own soaking. *Am I safe here?* Hollis wondered. *No computers. Paid cash.* Breathing in the steam, he lay back against the wall of the bath.

* * *

HE LEFT THE *onsen* a few hours later and ate dinner at a restaurant where plates of sushi were served on a conveyer belt. After he had consumed the food on six different-colored plates, the book-seller's phone played a few notes from Beethoven's "Ode to Joy."

"Do you know who this is?" Kotani asked. It sounded as if he was still frightened.

"Yes. Thank you for contacting me."

"I am sorry for my cowardly behavior this afternoon. But I was not prepared to meet you."

"I understand."

"Go to a bar called Chill at ten o'clock this evening. It is in the Golden Gai near Kubukichō . . ." The phone went dead as little plates of sushi continued to glide around the room.

* * *

KUBUKICHŌ TURNED OUT to be a red-light district for peep shows, strip clubs, and massage parlors. A plastic sign with a gi-gantic pair of lips hung from one of the buildings. Women's voices whispered from loudspeakers, and the sidewalk was littered with handbills for prostitutes. Hollis was surprised to find Jamaicans working as touts and bouncers for the different establishments. Wearing tropical suits in bright pastel colors, they strutted up and down the sidewalk, speaking Japanese to the businessmen who wandered through the area.

A Jamaican man with a shiny bald head stood outside a bar called Le Passion Club. "Hey, my brother—where you from?"

"The United States."

"Is that so? Why you in Japan?"

"I'm going to study karate at a dojo."

"Best pray to God, brother." The bald man laughed loudly. "Those karate masters gonna kick your black ass."

"I can handle myself."

"You take care. Japan is a tough place for a black man. Just do your business and go on home."

After getting lost a few times, Hollis found the Golden Gai— a grid of narrow streets lined with shabby two-story buildings.

Over twenty bars were crammed into the area. Electric cables were draped across the street as if everything were powered from a single socket. None of the bars had windows; only a few bothered to put up signs. Hollis walked up and down the streets for ten minutes before he noticed the word CHILL written in tiny letters on a green door.

He went inside and found a staircase so steep that it looked like a wooden ladder. Using both hands and feet, he climbed up to the first floor, passed through some red velvet curtains, and found himself in a bar that was about the size of his bedroom back in Los Angeles. Jazz played from hidden speakers while a bartender stood in front of shelves displaying different brands of vodka.

Akihido Kotani sat at a small table against the wall. He was staring at a vodka bottle that had been frozen in a block of ice and then placed inside a brass cylinder. The cylinder was held by a steel frame that could be tipped forward whenever you wanted to pour more alcohol.

The bartender glared at the black foreigner, but Hollis ignored him and sat down at Kotani's table. "Good evening."

"Ahhh, you found this place. Would you like a drink, Mr. Wilson? At this bar, the sake is served warm and the vodka is always cold."

"Sake sounds good."

Kotani ordered some sake from the bartender, and then turned the brass cylinder on its pivot to pour more vodka into his own glass.

"Sparrow came here in the old days when this bar was called Nirvana. Every night from nine until three, they had incense burning and a Zen master meditating over there." Kotani motioned to one side of the room, now occupied by a tropical fish tank. "Sparrow said that the monk created a peaceful atmosphere."

"And you were his friend?"

"I met him before he took his Harlequin name. Even in school, he was the brave one and I was the coward."

THE GOLDEN CITY   115

Kotani stopped talking when the bartender served Hollis a bottle of warmed sake and a ceramic cup. The stereo system started playing a cut from the Miles Davis album *Kind of Blue*.

"Listen, I need to—"

"I know what you want. Sparrow said a Harlequin needs 'a horse, a scroll, a purse, and a sword.' It is not wise to carry a sword in Japan unless you're going to a *kendo* demonstration. But I think I can supply a handgun."

"From the Yakuza?"

Kotani shook his head. "The Yakuza killed Sparrow. They work on contract with the Tabula and other powerful people in this country. They will not help a Harlequin."

"What about the Jamaicans who work for the nightclubs?"

"Those men are *gaijin* with passport problems. Ask for a gun and they sell you to the police. What you need is someone flexible about the law. Japanese born in Peru and Brazil have come home. They look and talk like everyone else, but they see the world in a different way. My landlord, Senzo, is one of these people. He knows a man with a handgun. You can buy it tonight for two hundred thousand yen. Do you have money?"

Hollis nodded. "Will they come to this place?"

"We will meet them at a love hotel over in Shibuya. It is private there. No one will see us." Kotani extended his hand. "I need my phone, please."

Kotani dialed a number on the cell and said a few words in Japanese. "It is okay," he said after he switched off the phone. "They will meet us in an hour."

Hollis sipped the warm sake and Kotani poured himself more vodka from the frozen bottle. "So why are you in Tokyo?" he asked. "There are no more Travelers in Japan. All of them were killed after Sparrow died. Japan isn't waiting for the Vast Machine—it is already here."

"I'm looking for someone who can talk to the dead. When Thorn was in Japan he met a spirit reader, a woman."

"Yes. An Itako. The one Thorn met lives in the north."

"How do I find her?"

Kotani poured some more vodka. His face was flushed and he spoke slowly, trying to pronounce each word. "Sparrow and I went to see this Itako. She said that Sparrow would die because of cowardice and I would die because of bravery."

"And was she right?"

"Not for me. But Sparrow was killed by a coward—a Yakuza who shot him in the back."

"I want to meet her."

The bookseller took a sales slip and a ballpoint pen out of his tweed sports jacket. He wrote Japanese characters on the back of the slip and pushed it across the table. "Her name is Mitsuki. Take the train up to Hachinohe and show this to the people there. You will need a translator. On Sunday afternoon, we will go to Yoyogi-Kōen. That is when the different tribes—the *zoku*—are in the park. One of my old high school students named Hoshi Hirano will be there, dancing to rock-and-roll music. He will help you travel north if your plan sounds exciting." Kotani smiled and raised his glass. "Hoshi is a rebel who needs a cause."

"But you won't come with us?"

"Never." Kotani stood up awkwardly and almost knocked over the chair. "The Itako talks to ghosts. There are too many ghosts in my life."

They left the bar, found a taxi, and asked the driver to take them to the Shibuya district. Kotani closed his eyes and lay back against the seat. The bottle of vodka had helped him overcome his fear.

"So what was Sparrow like?" Hollis asked. "Can you describe him?"

"In the last year of his life, he knew Yakuza were going to kill him. That knowledge made him very calm and gentle—except when he was fighting. I was a high school teacher. Sparrow used to sit in my apartment and help me correct my tests. Then we would go to the Nirvana bar and watch the Zen master try to break free of his body."

"When did you start selling books?"

"When Sparrow was killed, I went to the hospital to claim his body. Someone took my photograph and it was in the newspapers. Underneath my picture were the words 'The Madman's Friend.' One of my enemies cut out the photograph and pinned it up in the teacher's room. I was humiliated. The students laughed at me. So I started selling books. I was no longer respectable, so I could not get married." Kotani made a fist and struck his chest. "I should have died with Sparrow that night, but I was a coward."

The taxi stopped outside the Shibuya subway station, and the bookseller led Hollis up a low hill to a neighborhood filled with hundreds of love hotels. A few of the hotels had bland white façades, but most of them were brightly lit and painted with garish colors. They walked past a miniature French chateau, a Swiss cottage, and a fake Greek temple with plaster nudes in wall alcoves. When cars arrived at the hotels, they disappeared down ramps into underground parking garages.

Halfway up the hill, Kotani stopped in front of a hotel designed to look like a Gothic castle. There was a moat and a drawbridge and a stucco façade that had been painted to resemble blocks of stone. Pink banners flapped wearily from flagpoles at the top of a steep roof.

"This is where we meet Senzo and his friend," Kotani explained. "He did not want you to go to the apartment building."

They crossed the fake drawbridge and pushed open a heavy wooden door. The hotel lobby lacked furniture, but it had a row of brightly lit vending machines that sold condoms, beer, and energy drinks. The framed photographs of twelve different rooms were hanging on the wall. One room was designed to look like a medieval dungeon, another was a cabana.

Kotani picked a room with an African theme. He pushed a red button and the light over the photograph immediately went out. A half curtain covered part of an alcove opening so that the clerk and the hotel customers would never see one another's faces. When Kotani placed a wad of cash on the counter, a woman's hands took the money and offered a plastic key card. A few seconds later, a speaker played the sound of wind chimes, and an elevator door glided open.

Kotani dialed a number on his cell phone and said a few words. They stepped into the elevator, and it moved slowly upward. "Why can't we operate the elevator?" Hollis asked.

"You can only go to the correct floor. They do not want customers meeting other people in the hallway."

On the third floor, Kotani slid a key card into the lock for room 9 and the door clicked open. The African Room resembled the photograph in the lobby, but the zebra-skin rug was frayed and the room smelled like lemon-scented disinfectant.

Hollis went into the bathroom and found a whirlpool tub with a rock façade and fake tropical foliage. He returned to the bedroom, pushed back the leopard-print curtains, and looked down at the streetlight. No fire escape. The door was the only way out.

"Where's the closet?"

Kotani looked confused.

"Most hotel rooms have a closet."

"People do not stay here for long."

Hollis inspected the African carving hanging on the wall and the four-poster bed covered with mosquito netting. Still looking a little drunk, Kotani sat down on a rattan chair and smiled. "Why are you suspicious? No one knows we are here."

"In a few minutes someone is going to show up with a gun for sale. Maybe they'll decide to keep the gun and take all the money."

"There is nothing to worry about. You are the suspicious person, Mr. Wilson. Not Senzo. When you first came to the shop, I thought you were sent by the Tabula."

"I guess you'll just have to trust me."

"But I know who you are. I checked everything with Linden."

Hollis controlled the expression on his face. "And how did you do that?"

"I sent him an e-mail. After he confirmed your identity, I called you on the cell."

"Did you send the e-mail from a cybercafe?"

"I have my own computer at home. No need to worry. I did not use my real name."

"The Tabula could have placed a virus on your hard drive. It's activated when it detects certain words."

"You are much too nervous, Mr. Wilson. Sparrow never talked this way."

"Sparrow is dead. I plan to stay alive."

Both of them were startled when Kotani's cell phone played "Ode to Joy." He switched on the phone and said a few words in Japanese.

"See? Everything is good. Senzo is in the lobby with his friend. They are coming up in the elevator."

"And he's your landlord?"

"Yes. I told you. He offered to sell me the weapon a year ago."

"And so you called him?"

"That was not necessary. He came to my apartment and told me that he was going to paint the kitchen."

"So he just happened to show up at that particular moment?"

"What are you saying?"

"We're getting out of here."

Hollis grabbed Kotani and pulled him to his feet as someone knocked on the door. No way out. He thought about smashing the window, but it was too far to jump.

"Listen to me . . ." Hollis pulled two packets of Japanese currency out of his shoulder bag and stuffed them into Kotani's pockets. "If the Tabula are looking for me, then we've got a problem. But maybe it's okay. Maybe they just want money. Buy the gun and they'll leave."

"I—I understand."

Hollis pulled the ceramic knife from its sheath. As the visitor in the hallway knocked a second time, he dropped to the floor and slid beneath the canopied bed. A cotton mattress cover hung down from the box spring and concealed him. There was a two-inch gap between the hem of the cover and the floor.

Kotani opened the door and two men entered the hotel room. They spoke Japanese, and Hollis didn't know what they were saying. Peering through the gap, he could see one of the men was dressed in a dark blue business suit. The second man wore stained cotton pants and old running shoes. Hollis decided that the second man was Senzo—the landlord who grew up in South America. He had a brisk, friendly voice and his legs rocked slightly as he stood beside the bed.

Senzo did most of the talking while Mr. Business Suit paced back and forth inspecting the room. Kotani's voice was soft and respectful. Hollis tried to breathe quietly as he held the blade of the knife against his chest. *Just pay them the money,* he thought. *Pay the money and tell them to leave.*

After a few minutes of conversation, the man in the business suit began to ask questions. He had a deep, powerful voice and spoke in short sentences. Kotani answered him with a frightened voice.

Silence. And then the man wearing the suit grabbed Kotani and slammed the bookseller against the wall. The man's voice filled the room, demanding an explanation. Kotani fell onto the floor, but his interrogator picked him up and slapped him across the face. Hollis didn't need to understand Japanese to know that Kotani was desperate, begging for mercy. If the bookseller betrayed him, then he would have to attack.

Turning his head slightly, Hollis saw Kotani's scuffed brown shoes. He was standing very close to the left side of the bed. Hollis heard footsteps and a muffled cracking sound. Suddenly, Kotani collapsed onto the floor and blood poured out his mouth. Someone had shot the bookseller in the back of the head.

Hollis glanced to the right beneath the hem of the mattress cover; Senzo was standing only a few feet away. Then he looked left and realized that Kotani's blood had formed a bright red patch beneath his head. The blood trembled when the men walked back and forth. Hollis stopped breathing as the blood trickled toward him.

He crawled to the right, emerged from beneath the bed, and stood up quickly. Senzo was standing a few feet away. Hollis grabbed Senzo's shoulder with his left hand and jabbed upward with the knife, pushing it deep into the man's stomach. As Senzo screamed and fell backward, Hollis jerked the blade away.

A Japanese man with a broad face and slicked-back hair was standing by the rattan chair. He had wrapped a hotel towel around his handgun to muffle the sound. The man raised his weapon, but Hollis was already on him, grabbing the wrist of the gun hand, then twisting it around. Screaming with pain, the man dropped the gun and Hollis drove the knife between his shoulder blades. The ceramic blade hit a vertebra and snapped in two. Hollis let go of the knife, threw an arm around the man's neck, and shoved a knee into his back. As Kotani's killer fell forward, Hollis pulled back with one quick jerk and broke his neck.

He stood up and stared at the motionless body. There were mirrors all over the room so that the couples could watch themselves making love. Hollis could see his wild eyes, his chest heaving in and out. In the mirrors, the dead men looked unsubstantial, like piles of clothing dumped on the floor.

The packets of Japanese money and a loaded 9 mm handgun were lying in the middle of the bed. Hollis stuffed everything into his shoulder bag, and then returned to the man wearing the suit and pushed him onto his back. He ripped open the dead man's shirt and saw that his chest and stomach were covered with a dragon tattoo. Yakuza. A Tabula mercenary.

Akihido Kotani lay next to the bed. Looking down at the dead man, Hollis realized that the Itako had given the correct prophecy; the bookseller's bravery had caused his death. He left the hotel room and sprinted down the hall to the fire exit. Two surveillance cameras were mounted on the wall. Within a few hours, both the Tabula and the Tokyo police would be looking for a murderer, a black man, a *gaijin*, an outsider with no place to hide.

14

When Gabriel had first crossed the barriers, the experience had been terrifying. After a series of journeys, he had learned how to guide the movement of his Light. Though his physical body had nothing to do with this knowledge, the process reminded him of skydiving or bodysurfing—activities where a shift of weight or a slight movement of the arms could propel you in a different direction. Crossing over, his consciousness sensed the right direction and was able to guide his Light to the First Realm. The arrival itself was always unexpected. After passing through the barriers, you were suddenly *there*. It was like lying down in one bed and waking up in another.

* * *

HE OPENED HIS eyes, scrambled to his feet, and saw that he was standing in a long, narrow room with a shattered window at one end. Out on the street, a gas flare blossomed like a bright orange flower from a crack in the pavement. He was in a store that had once sold refrigerators, washing machines, and stoves. These appliances weren't the modern devices with stainless-steel façades that were displayed in New York or London; instead, the washing machines had wringers fixed over an open tub, and the refrigerators were white metal boxes with cooling coils mounted on the top. The old-fashioned technology made each appliance look like a squat little idol-once worshipped, now abandoned in the ruins.

Gabriel turned again and found a shifting patch of darkness on the wall behind an overturned stove. Although this shadow could be seen only by a Traveler, it was a passageway that could be used by Maya, a route back to a specific access point—the hidden chapel at St. Catherine's Monastery. He pushed some of the abandoned machines across the room to mark the way out and walked over to the broken window. The appliance store was on a boulevard lined with other looted shops. A half-burned sofa and a pile of concrete rubble were on the sidewalk in front of him. The trees that had once shaded the area were now blackened trunks and leafless branches that reached toward the light of the flare.

Once again, he wondered if his father had explored this dark city. Gabriel's Pathfinder, Sophia Briggs, had said that only a few Travelers crossed over to the different realms. Many thought that the power to leave their bodies was a hallucination. Others were so terrified by the four barriers that they refused to go any farther.

During Gabriel's previous visit to the First Realm, the commissioner of patrols had mentioned the "visitors" who came from outside the island. Perhaps one of these people had been Matthew Corrigan. When Gabriel thought about his father, he recalled moments when Matthew was driving the pickup truck or working in the garden. Nothing was frightening or dangerous on their farm, but sometimes an expression of great sadness would appear on his father's face. Perhaps he had been thinking about the anger and hate that imprisoned the inhabitants of this dark world.

Gabriel slipped out the entrance and headed down the street. He moved with an alert and cautious rhythm—like an animal that knew it was being hunted. The last place he had seen Maya was at the abandoned school that was used as a headquarters for the patrols. Although it was dangerous to return there, he decided that it would be the center point of an invisible circle. He would start searching at the edges of the city and then spiral inward to the streets around the school.

Hell was a permanent reality, trapped in an endless cycle of destruction, creation, and destruction again. When the last survivor perished, the city would somehow return to that first morning when the sky was blue and hope was possible. The pain of Hell was all the more powerful because of what had been lost.

He had no idea if Maya was alive, but it didn't look as if the cycle of destruction was over. Light oozed through the thick cloud layer that covered the sky. The air smelled like burning tires and bits of ash covered the street. Everywhere he looked, he could see words and numbers scrawled on the walls and sidewalks. X CROSS THE SKY. GREEN 55. HERE IS THE PLACE. REMEMBER. Some of these words delineated certain territories or fiefdoms that existed in the past—like the gang signs in his world. But most of the graffiti was put up by people who believed they would be reborn in a new cycle. Before they died, they left clues and coded directions to hiding places and caches of weapons.

He paused at the corner of a building and peered down a side street. It was dangerous to be here. Eventually, he would be seen by the wolves. He considered different strategies and then decided to leave messages to Maya all over the city. After searching through a burnt-out grocery store, he returned to the street with two pieces of charcoal. Feeling like a teenager in a deserted subway station, he scrawled a Harlequin lute on a brick wall with the words: WHERE U?

The next street over had been turned into a dumping area for broken chairs, two faceless grandfather clocks, and a pile of smashed crockery. Someone had dismantled a carousel and left the wooden horses leaning against a brick wall as if these brightly painted creations were chasing one another down the block. Gabriel touched one of the horses and felt the smooth surface of the black saddle and the flowing mane. He decided to leave another message, but when he raised the piece of charcoal, he noticed faded words written with red paint. Each letter had dribbled at the edges as if they were bleeding. ARE YOU THE TRAVELER? asked the writer. HAVE YOU RETURNED? Below the words was a red arrow, pointing down the street.

Had Maya painted the message? That was possible, but Maya probably would have included the lute or interlocking diamond shapes—Harlequin signs. Gabriel stood beside the carousel horse for several minutes as he considered the possibilities. Then he headed down the street in the direction of the arrow. Two blocks away, he found a second message that led him onward to additional signs. The words were always written in red paint, but the size of the letters varied. Sometimes the message was splattered high up on a building like a billboard. But usually there was only a red arrow, painted on the hood of a smashed delivery truck or on a door still hanging from one hinge.

As he drew closer to the center of the city, footsteps appeared in the soot that covered the pavement. On one block he found a dead man lying on his back. The corpse had been there for some time and was dried out like a mummy. With shriveled lips and yellowed teeth, he appeared to be grinning at the destruction around him.

The red arrows were smaller now, as if the messenger had sensed the growing danger and decided to hide. Gabriel found no further clues on the next corner, so he doubled back and discovered an arrow pointing to the building across the street. The massive structure looked like a bombed-out church with a tower on each corner. Its entrance was a semicircular archway; similar arches shaped each window. Someone had cut words into a marble plaque over the door: MUSEUM OF ART AND ANTIQUITIES.

Wary of a trap, Gabriel stepped into the entrance hall formed by two intersecting arches. The museum once had a ticket booth, a cloak room, and a turnstile, but everything had been destroyed. Apparently, someone had felt particular hatred for the turnstile, and had taken the time to heat up the brass bars in a bonfire and twist them into pincers that reached toward the ceiling.

He had heard about the city's museum and library when he was a prisoner, but he had never been allowed to see the ruins. Turning to the right, he stepped into an exhibit hall filled with smashed glass cases. One still had a brass plaque that read: CEREMONIAL DRINKING CUPS FROM THE SECOND ERA.

There were no flares to light the interior of the museum, but the windows on one side of the room looked out on a courtyard with a fountain at the center. Gabriel stepped through the window frame and approached the fountain. Sea monsters with gaping mouths had once spat water into the fountain pool, but now the green marble was covered with soot and delicate flakes of ash.

"Who are you?" a man asked. "I've never seen you before."

Gabriel turned around, looking for the speaker. There was no one else near the fountain, and the smashed windows that faced the courtyard looked like picture frames displaying sections of the night. *What should I do?* he thought. *Run?* In order to escape to the street, he would have to pass back through the museum to the turnstile.

"Don't waste your time trying to find me." The speaker sounded proud of his invisibility. "I know every part of this building. It's *my* refuge. Not yours. What are you doing here?"

"I've never been in the museum. I wanted to see what was inside."

"There's nothing here but more destruction. So go away."

Gabriel didn't move.

"Go away," the voice repeated.

"Someone painted messages on the walls. I followed them here."

"That has nothing to do with you."

"I'm the Traveler."

"Don't start lying." The voice was harsh, contemptuous. "I know what the Traveler looks like. He came to the island a long time ago and then vanished."

"I'm Gabriel Corrigan."

There was a long pause, and then the voice spoke with a cautious tone. "Is that really your name?"

*　*　*

GABRIEL HAD ONCE seen photographs of an army sniper wearing something called a ghillie suit—a ragged assembly of dark green fabric that changed a person's silhouette and allowed him to blend into the countryside. The dark man stepping through the doorway had created a similar costume for hiding in the corridors of the abandoned museum. Swatches of gray and black fabric were sewn together in a haphazard manner to make a smock and trousers. Rags were wrapped around the man's shoes. A gauzy black veil hung from the brim of a hat and covered his face. Silently, the dark man glided across the courtyard before stopping ten feet away from Gabriel.

"Matthew Corrigan told me that he had two sons named Gabriel and Michael."

"And who are you?"

The ghost hesitated and then raised the veil covering his face. He was a tired-looking older man with thinning hair and very pale skin. Even his brown eyes seemed to have lost most of their color.

"I'm the museum director. When I woke up that first morning, the keys to the museum and some paperwork for a new installation had been left in my apartment. A bill for a new display cabinet was in the folder and my name was at the top of the page." The man closed his eyes as if reciting a sacred incantation. "Mr. T. R. Kelso is my name. At least, that's what the document indicated . . ."

"How did you manage to survive?"

"I hid in the museum during the first wave of fighting and remained here during the different regimes. So far, we've had one
emperor, two kings, and various generals."

"Do you remember when the commissioner of patrols was in
charge?"

"Yes, of course. He's dead now."

"How long ago was that?"

"We don't have clocks and calendars here."

"I know that. But does it feel like a long period of time?"

"It was recent," Kelso said. "The current leader is called the
Judge, but there have never been any laws on the island."

"I'm looking for an outsider, a woman who is a very good
fighter."

"Everyone knows about her," Kelso said. "Sometimes, I leave
the museum, hide in the walls, and listen to the patrols. This
woman frightens the wolves. They tell stories about her."

"Is she still alive?"

Kelso surveyed the entire courtyard as if expecting an attack.
"It's dangerous to stand here. Follow me."

Gabriel followed the ragged figure back into the museum and
through the vandalized display areas. Bits of glass and crockery
covered the tile floor and they crunched and cracked beneath his
shoes. The dark man's movements were completely silent. He
knew where to step and what to avoid. Finally, they reached a
room with a mural that showed men and women in blue overalls
working the levers of enormous machines. Someone had attacked
the picture with an ax or a knife, destroying every face.

They reached a wooden door with a smashed lock in one of
the corners. Kelso opened it cautiously, revealing a staircase and a
dried-out corpse hanging from a noose.

"What happened?"

"You mean the dead man? I found the body on the street and
hung it up here. This is better than a lock or secret entrance. People open the door, see the body, and turn away. You would think
they'd go up the staircase, but that never happens."

Kelso slipped around the corpse, and Gabriel followed. They

climbed up a circular staircase that ended at the top of a tower with a stone balustrade. It was a perfect place to survey the island—the shattered buildings, the overgrown parks, and the dark river. Gas flares rose up from different parts of the city and smoke drifted past the jagged spires of the half-destroyed buildings.

"In the beginning, this really was a museum. The historical exhibits were on the ground floor and works of art were displayed in a first-floor gallery. Whoever designed this place paid a great deal of attention to the details. The relics and antiques have vanished, of course, but I've done a study of the display-case labels. All of them are very specific, mentioning the Twelfth Era or the Third Regime. The island once had a recorded history, a shared story about the past."

"So when was the Third Regime?"

"I don't know. Maybe there's a special book or a government report, but I haven't been able to find it. The people living here can understand what history *is,* but we can't remember the past. History doesn't exist in this world."

"And what kind of art was upstairs?"

"Painful images."

"Torture? Murder?"

Mr. Kelso smiled for the first time. "It was something much worse than that. The museum had paintings of mothers and children, food and flowers, epic landscapes of great beauty. Naturally, the people trapped here hated these images. One of our first dictators said that the gallery confused people and caused discontent. So a squad of men smashed all the sculpture with hammers and burned all the paintings in an enormous bonfire. In this world, the foolish are proud of that fact. They find strength and certainty in their own ignorance."

"It's your world, too."

Kelso raised the arms of his ragged costume and pushed the veil away from his forehead. "It doesn't feel that way to me. The only desire I share with others is the need to escape. Your father disappeared into a passageway and I couldn't follow him.'"

"I'm here to find Maya."

"You mean the demon? That's what the wolves call her. I've

seen her twice, from a distance. She carries a sword and walks down the middle of the street."

"So how can I find her?"

"Why would you want to do that? She'll kill you. Perhaps she once had some goodness in her heart, but goodness can't exist here."

"I don't believe that."

Mr. Kelso laughed. "She kills everyone. No exceptions. I've heard some people say that she's lost her eyes. All you see are little chips of blue stone."

"Can you guide me to her?"

"And what's the benefit to me? Can you get me out of this place?"

"I can't promise that," Gabriel said quietly. "I'm from another world, but you started your life in this place."

"But I'm not like the others here. I swear that's true."

"Everyone has the power to make certain decisions in their life. If you think you're better than the others, then prove it. Maybe your actions will free you when everyone is destroyed and the cycle starts again."

"Do you think that possible? Really?"

"I need to find Maya, Mr. Kelso. If you want to be a good person, you can start by helping me."

Kelso's mouth twitched as if it was painful to be standing there without the veil covering his face. "I heard the wolves talking. They've trapped the demon in what used to be the library. They've probably killed her by now."

"Take me there."

"As you wish." Kelso lowered the veil over his face and started down the stairs. "You remind me of your father, Gabriel."

"What do you mean?"

"He didn't lie to me."

15

Maya had once seen her life as a story with a beginning, middle, and end. That chronological way of thinking had vanished during her time on the island. Although she hid in the rubble and fought in the streets, none of these events were connected to her past. Maya felt as if she were rowing a boat through a swamp where an immense battle had taken place. Sometimes a person's body would float to the surface, and she could see a face, recall a name—and then the boat lurched forward and the face would sink back into the mud and weeds.

The past was fading away, but the present moment was

entirely clear. She was trapped at the top of a pillar—a three-story fragment made of bricks and stone in the middle of the half-destroyed library. Her world was very small: a wooden table, a patch of tile floor, and a storage room where black cardboard boxes were filled with prints and drawings of angels. During the beginning of her captivity, she had searched through all these il-lustrations and discovered that each image was unique. There were smiling, benevolent angels as well as righteous angels smit-ing sinners with whips and swords.

If the wolves had caught Pickering while on patrol, they would have killed him immediately, but the former ladies' tailor used his betrayal of Maya to win some measure of protection. He remained in what was left of the third-floor reading room, sleeping beneath the wooden tables and warming up cans of food on one of the gas lamps. Whenever anyone new appeared in the library, he rushed over to describe the cleverness of his plan and the fact that he still hadn't received his reward. With his encouragement, the wolves stood in the reading room and hurled bricks and chunks of con-crete at the pillar. Maya retreated to the storage area for protec-tion; whenever a projectile hit the metal door, the men cheered like football fans celebrating a goal.

She was resting in the storage room when she heard some-thing heavy slam down on the platform. Peering through a crack in the door, she saw that the wolves had lowered a length of rail-ing between the pillar and the reading room. A bearded man armed with a six-foot pike stepped onto this improvised bridge and moved cautiously toward her. In order to protect his face and upper body, he had punched holes in pieces of blackened sheet metal and tied them together with twine. With each step, this im-provised armor made a clanking sound.

Keeping her sword in its scabbard, Maya left the storage area and sauntered over to the edge of the pillar. The man with the sheet-metal mask shouted threats and jabbed the pike in her direction. He took one step forward, wobbling a bit, as Maya watched his eyes. When he finally entered her attack perimeter, she feinted to the right, ducked down, and grabbed the pike in a twisting motion that made the tall man lose his balance and fall off the bridge. He had a few seconds to scream as he fell sixty feet to the rubble below. The wolves in the reading room stopped cheering, and that gave her a moment of pleasure. She kicked the edge of the railing off the pillar and it made a clattering noise when it hit the ground.

* * *

NO ONE ON the island buried the dead. The bearded man's body was still lying facedown on a pile of half-burned floorboards. This example of her fighting skill seemed to deter attacks for a while, but now a more ambitious plan was being organized. A leader had appeared in the library—an older man wearing a blond lady's wig. His thin, reedy voice could be heard in every part of the library.

Three towers were being built with soot-covered wood re-trieved from the ruins. The men spent a great deal of time cutting off the charred ends of roof beams and straightening bent nails with hammers. The towers were ungainly-looking structures with props and buttresses added on to keep them from collapsing. Slowly, they grew higher until they were about ten feet below her refuge on the pillar. Once each tower had a flat platform at the top, the wolves began building wooden ladders.

Another group of men carried bricks and stones to the reading room and dumped them on the floor. It wasn't difficult to figure out the plan for the assault: the stone throwers would force her back into the storage room while three groups of attackers scram-bled up the ladders. Feeling tired and passive, she sat on the pil-lar with the sword on her lap and watched the preparations.

After the ladders were built and the stones were ready, the wolves carried the railing back up to the third floor and placed sections of wood on the rungs to make a narrow bridge. The men used ropes to lower the edge of the bridge down onto the pillar, but this time Maya didn't kick it away. If they wanted to fight, she was ready.

The man wearing the wig appeared in the reading room,

dressed in a billowy black gown that touched the tops of his boots. Maya wondered if this was some kind of religious costume, but everything became clear when the man took a few steps across the bridge. Wearing the wig and the black gown, he resembled a cartoon version of a British judge.

"Several of my men think that you're a demon," the man said. "But now that I've had a good look at you, I don't see any horns on your head or stubby little wings."

Maya remained silent. The man took a step forward and adjusted his wig. "I'm the Judge, the new ruler of this island. Thank you for killing the commissioner of patrols. That solved a great many problems."

"How can you be a judge?" she asked. "There aren't any laws here."

"Not so! We do have one law. Everyone follows it: *any person or group who has power can kill or enslave those with less power.*" The Judge gazed down at his followers. "Even the most foolish person here understands that law. In fact, they comprehend it better than the clever ones."

"And why are you explaining it to me?"

"Right now, I'm the most powerful person on the island. That means I'm the only person who can save your life."

"Is that why you're building towers and piling up stones?"

"Killing you is the alternative plan. I'd *much* rather have you as an ally. Our enemies in the port area have slaughtered two of my patrols. A small group of traitors shouldn't be a problem for a demon that destroys everyone she meets. You won't have to swear an oath of loyalty—it wouldn't mean anything. Just show the others that you accept my authority. Walk across this bridge and give me your weapon."

"And then you'll betray me."

The Judge chuckled when he heard her comment. "You're not very clever for a demon. Of course I'll betray you—eventually. But you have the chance to organize the others and betray *me*. I accept that possibility."

"And what if I refuse your offer?"

"You'll be killed here in the library. Your death has certain advantages. It shows that I can destroy anything, even a demon."

The Judge took another step forward and extended his hand as if she'd already offered her sword. "Hurry up, now. Don't waste my time. You won't have to trust me, but the two of us can still have an arrangement. One of the most remarkable aspects of this world is that we can work with the people we hate."

"I like where I am right now. Why should I leave?"

"You'll be given food and shelter and other benefits along the way. Let me give you an example."

The Judge wiggled his fingers like a diner in a restaurant requesting his check. Two of his followers left the reading-room area and disappeared down the staircase. They returned a minute later, dragging a prisoner between the tables. It was Pickering.

Someone had gagged the little man's mouth with a strip of white cloth, but he was still trying to talk. Pickering raised his eyebrows and jerked his head back and forth. He didn't look angry, just desperate to explain his point of view.

"This cockroach betrayed you and boasted about it," the Judge said. "I'm sure that angered you, but what could you do about it?"

A rope was tied around one of the tables and looped around Pickering's neck. The Judge didn't see the need to say the prisoner's name or announce his punishment; he simply nodded his head, and the guards tossed Pickering off the edge of the platform. The body struggled for a few seconds, swinging back and forth like a pendulum.

"There you are," the Judge said. "See this as a goodwill gesture. Now come across the bridge and give me your weapon."

Maya looked down at the scrap of flesh and rags that dangled at the end of the rope. The Judge was wrong about one thing; she had become a ghost, not a demon. Her lungs still breathed and her eyes still blinked, but she was hollow inside. The only emotion she could feel was pride. Pride called to her like a faraway voice—difficult to hear, but making its demands. *Never bow to the wicked. Never obey the command of someone who is unworthy.*

Feeling calm and ready for battle, she drew her sword from its scabbard. The Judge saw the change in her eyes. Frightened, he stumbled backward, almost tripping on the hem of his gown. "Attack!" he screamed. "Start the attack! Now!"

The bridge was pulled back to the reading room as bricks and stones rained down on the pillar. A stone struck her shoulder and another grazed the side of her head. Maya crouched down, covered her face, and ran back into the storeroom. A stone struck her left hand as she pulled the door shut.

Kneeling on the tile floor, surrounded by drawings of angels, she listened to the different sounds of each projectile. Stones bounced off the door while bricks and concrete shattered into pieces. Men were shouting, but she couldn't make out the words. She knew they were coming for her in different directions—raising the wooden ladders and propping them up against the pillar.

A proud death. Who had used those words? Her father. And then a memory came to her of a fight in a London Tube station. She was alone, and three men were running toward her. *Where's my father?* she thought. *Why did he abandon me?* A stone hit the storage room door with a boom. Reaching out in the darkness, she felt a handle in the middle of the door. *Go out and face them.*

Maya grabbed the handle and ripped the door off its hinges. With the sword in her right hand and the door held up like a shield, she stepped out of the room and began to inch forward. The wolves on the other side of the gap aimed at the door, but their stones bounced off its metal surface. A chunk of concrete hit the floor, exploding like a bomb, and pieces skittered across the floor.

She shifted to the right and saw the top rungs of a ladder. A big man with braided hair was climbing up to the platform with a homemade sword in his hand. She jumped high as a sword blade flashed beneath her feet. When she came down, she darted forward and stabbed her attacker in the throat.

Turn to the left. Another ladder. Maya took a step and suddenly felt intense pain in her left leg. A man standing on a ladder had jabbed upward with a spear and cut into the muscle a few inches above her knee. Blood spurted from the wound and she found it difficult to remain on her feet. More pikes and spears were thrust in her direction and she had to retreat toward the storage room.

Silence. The stones stopped falling and the faces of her attackers disappeared. Maya peered around the corner of her shield. The men on the other side of the gap stood mute as a burning piece of fabric drifted down from the ceiling. It took her a moment to realize that the library was on fire. When she cocked her head back, she saw smoke leaking out of the walls. The smell reminded her of wet wood burning in the middle of a field.

"Fire!" A voice shouted. Other voices repeated the warning. "Watch out! There's a fire!"

The Judge paced across the checkerboard floor of the reading room. He stopped near the edge of the platform and shouted to his followers. "Take the ladders and pull back! She'll burn to death when the ceiling collapses!"

Maya lowered her shield and let it drop onto the floor. Standing on the edge of the platform, she watched the men carry the ladders through the ruins. They stumbled through a pile of rubble, swore at one another, and vanished out the door. The men she despised, the ones she fought and killed, were actually proof that she existed in this dark world. Without her enemies, she would fade away.

She knelt down and then fell onto her side. Blood flowed from the wound in her leg. She felt as if the Light was leaving her body. Smoke drifted across the empty space like a malevolent spirit and gradually moved downward. Bits of flame appeared on the walls like orange poppies clinging to the side of a mountain. These flames grew larger; they wavered and reached toward her, and she wanted to embrace their bright clarity.

Darkness appeared on the outer edges of her vision. Maya closed her eyes for a few minutes and when she opened them again two figures had appeared in the reading room. A man wearing rags pulled back his veil and revealed a pale, frightened face. He turned and said something as a younger man emerged from the smoke carrying a burning stick of wood. The face looked familiar, but Maya resisted a conclusion. Was it really Gabriel or just a creation of her mind?

The Traveler hurried to the edge of the platform, shouting her name and waving his arms, but the darkness absorbed her again. She was floating on a pond of murky water, sinking beneath the surface. It felt as if she were thrashing her arms and legs to return to the light. When she regained consciousness, Gabriel was kneeling beside her. He scooped her up in his arms and carried her across an improvised bridge. The smoke made her cough, and she saw bursts of flame as the ragged man guided them down a staircase to the street.

"Try to stay awake," Gabriel told her. "We're going to the passageway."

"Passageway—in—the river," she said slowly.

"I found another access point. We can go together."

It felt as if the spear were still jabbing her leg as Gabriel carried her through the ruins of a burnt-out building. The ragged man kept glancing over his shoulder.

"There's a patrol. See them? Near the end of the street."

They started running. Men were chasing them, and she was too weak to fight and protect the Traveler.

"They saw us," said the ragged man. "Go this way, Gabriel. No. *This* way."

"It's too far," Gabriel said. "We're not going to make it."

"I'll stay here and trick them," the ragged man said. "Remember me. That's all I want from you. Remember my name."

And then she was very cold, falling down a long tunnel while Gabriel embraced her. She held him tightly, hearing his heart beat and feeling the warmth of his skin.

"Can you hear me?" Gabriel asked. "We're safe. Back in our world. Open your eyes, Maya. Open your eyes . . ."

16

The night air was cold when Hol-
lis left the love hotel and hiked down the hill to the high-rise office buildings that overlooked the Shibuya train station. The
adrenalin that had surged though his body during the fight had
faded away. He felt as slight and insubstantial as a dead leaf blown
through the streets.

The Chinese-made automatic was tucked into the waistband
near the small of his back. Hollis couldn't ignore its heavy presence—the feel of the barrel and trigger guard touching his skin. It
was dangerous to check into a hotel or return to the airport. Not
knowing what to do, he walked parallel to the Shuto Expressway.

The sodium safety lights made his shadow look black and distinct as it glided across the asphalt.

A few miles north of the train station, he passed a glass-and-steel building filled with retail shops that were closed for the night. A neon sign announced—in Japanese and English—that the Gran Cyber Café was on the second floor.

Internet cafés were all over the world; they were usually large, well-lit rooms where everyone sat close to one another typing on computer keyboards. The Gran Cyber Café had been designed for a very different experience. Hollis entered a windowless room that was kept in constant twilight—like a chapel or a gambling casino—and the customers were hidden in white cubicles. The café smelled like cigarette smoke and the curry dinner that the desk clerk had just heated up in a microwave.

The clerk was a young Japanese woman with studs through her nose, ears, and tongue. Speaking in English, she advised Hollis to buy a "night pack," which would allow him to stay in a cubicle until morning. Hollis walked through the maze of cubicles to number 8-J and went inside. There was a padded leatherette chair, a computer, a television set, a DVD player, and a hand control for computer games.

Hollis stared at the monitor and tried to figure out who could help him. Gabriel and Simon were somewhere in Egypt. His friends and relatives in Los Angeles thought that he was dead or in a third-world prison. When he left the United States he had thrown away his driver's license and credit cards. A bank had seized his house, and Hollis assumed it was sold at a public auction. Although the Vast Machine tracked your movements and monitored your life, it also verified that you were alive.

He returned to the front desk and bought a fruit smoothie, a cup of hot ramen noodles, and a toothbrush. Hollis saw two other customers in the café's library picking through the extensive collection of graphic novels and magazines. Neither of them more than glanced at the foreigner. The Gran Cyber Café was not a place to meet people in physical reality.

Back in the cubicle he removed the gun from his waistband

and placed it in the shoulder bag. Within the gray space of the café, his memory of the three dead men began to lose its power. Hollis decided that the café was part of the Vast Machine, but also a temporary refuge from its control. In the past, people fled from the authorities to the forest or to a church, but even these places were beginning to install surveillance cameras. At the Gran Cyber Café, the customers could lose themselves in various fantasies or pretend to be different people on the Internet. You were truly yourself—and nothing—at the same time. All this revealed the power of the Vast Machine: even your sanctuary was a commercial enterprise.

*   *   *

ALTHOUGH THERE WAS no lock on the cubicle door, Hollis surrendered to his exhaustion and slept. When he opened his eyes, it was ten o'clock in the morning, but the café's artificial environment was unchanged. The main room was still cool and quiet, the customers suspended within its perpetual twilight.

Sharks glided through a turquoise sea created by the computer's screen saver. The cubicle's TV set was still switched on, but the sound could be heard only with a pair of earphones. Hollis watched as a perky young woman presented the news. Snow was falling on the northern coast of Honshū island. There was a car bomb explosion in the Middle East and a coup in an African country. Looking like animatronic figures at an amusement park, the American president and the Japanese prime minister shook hands.

The image on the monitor changed and Hollis saw black-and-white photographs of himself running down the third-floor hallway of the love hotel. The news program cut to shots of ambulances carrying the dead bodies away from the hotel while reporters and TV cameramen stood behind a police barrier. A multiple killing like this was unusual in Japan, and it was getting a great deal of media attention. A blurred close-up of his face appeared on the monitor as a phone number flashed on the screen.

Hollis stood up on the chair and peered over the top of his cubicle. The pierced woman who had welcomed him to the café had vanished, replaced by a young Japanese man with bleached hair. Hollis put on his sunglasses, slipped out the café, and headed for the subway. He felt as if all the surveillance cameras in the city were photographing his passage down the sidewalk.

Kotani had mentioned that one of his former students, a man named Hoshi Hirano, might be dancing in Yoyogi-kōen, the enormous public park in East Tokyo. Hollis got off the subway at Harajuku Station and took the pedestrian bridge across the tracks. It was getting colder, and flakes of snow began to drift down from the gray sky. Near the entrance to the park, he encountered some of the zokus—the tribes that filled the park every Sunday afternoon.

There was a group of teenage girls dressed in black with white face paint and a line of fake blood dribbling from one corner of their lips. The snowflakes swirled around them, clinging to their teased hair. This zoku gathered near the end of the bridge, ignoring the girls who wore satin skirts with petticoats, white kneesocks, and pink hair bows.

Hollis entered the park looking for a rock-and-roll group. Every few hundred yards, he encountered a new tribe gathering at a prearranged meeting place. There was a zoku of young men on skateboards and another group riding trick bicycles. One zoku was comprised of teenagers who had smudged soot on their mouths and eyes as if they were wandering zombies.

Loud music came from the southern edge of the park. A black van with huge speakers mounted on the top was playing military marching music, guarded by a group of nationalists wearing dark green paramilitary uniforms. These fierce young men stood at parade rest with their hands held behind their backs. They watched as their leader—an older man with a shaved head—screamed insults and shook his fist at eight men dancing in unison to "Rock Around the Clock."

The dancers were dressed like the 1950s Elvis—the rockabilly

Elvis, the Elvis of rebellion and dream. Each of the dancers wore motorcycle boots, tight black jeans, and motorcycle jackets with silver studs and chains. But the most elaborate part of their costume was their hair; it was greased and brushed up high from their foreheads into an elaborate pompadour. The leader of the group was only five feet tall, but the boots and the hair and the padded shoulders of his jacket made him appear larger.

The nationalist sound van played a military chorus, and the Elvises countered that with a recording of "Blue Suede Shoes." No distraction from the outside world appeared to disturb their 1950s version of cool. Finally, the nationalists gave up and drove away in their black van. Triumphant, the Elvises danced to "Shake, Rattle and Roll," and then they were finished for the day. Hollis approached the oldest dancer and asked if he knew a man named Hoshi. Speaking in Japanese, the man pointed to their leader—the little man with the padded jacket who had just stuffed his CDs into an athletic bag.

Hollis hurried after the man. "Excuse me, sir. Are you Hoshi Hirano?"

The little man stopped walking and flipped back his hair. "I used to be called that, but I changed my named to Billy Hirano. It's got more style. Don't you think?"

"I'm a friend of Akihido Kotani."

"Yes. My sensei." Billy shook his head sadly. "Do you know he was killed last night at a love hotel in Shibuya? I saw it on the television news . . ."

As his voice trailed off, Billy's face showed surprise—but no fear. Taking out a small pink comb, he touched up the ducktail near the back of his neck. "The police say he was killed by black *gaijin*. Someone like you."

Hollis removed his sunglasses so Billy could see his face. "I swear to you that I didn't kill your teacher. Did he ever tell you about his friend Sparrow? I'm just like that, only I'm from the United States."

"You're a Harlequin? Is that so? So where's your sword, man?"

Hollis unzipped his jacket and quickly showed the handgun held in his waistband. "It's difficult to carry a sword in public. I have a more modern weapon."

"You're either a Harlequin or you're crazy. That's twenty years of hard time if the police find you carrying that." Billy rocked back and forth on the heels of his motorcycle boots. "So what's your name?"

"Hollis."

"And what are you doing in Japan? There aren't any Travelers here. The Tabula killed them all."

"I need to go up to northern Japan and find an Itako."

"An Itako? You mean one of those crazy women who talks to the dead?"

"Can you help me, Billy? I need a translator. I'll pay for everything. All expenses."

"Going north will take two or three days." Billy considered the idea for a few seconds as a greasy lock of hair fell over his eyes. "I guess I could handle it . . ." He took out his comb and repaired his hairdo. "Talking to the dead could be very cool."

"The police are looking for me."

"I understand. You're way too foreign, too—"

"Black?"

"You got it, man. That just adds to the problem."

While Hollis waited in the park, Billy walked across the street to a drugstore and returned with a cane and some supplies in a paper bag. "Put this on," he said, and handed Hollis a surgical mask. "Japanese people wear these masks when they're sick so they won't spread germs. Okay, now put on your sunglasses." He nodded. "Good."

"What about the cane?"

"Slip a pebble in your right shoe and start limping." Billy reached into the bag and pulled out a small oxygen bottle in a nylon sling. "I'm going to be your nurse—which means I'll carry this around and help you walk."

"You think this is going to work?"

"It's bad luck to stare at sick people in Japan. If you look like you're going to die, they'll turn away."

They went straight to Shinjuku station and bought tickets for the next bullet train north to Hachinohe. Billy knew exactly where to line up and what to say to the clerk. As he led Hollis through the sprawling station, Billy explained that he designed the packaging for the Japanese DVDs of Hollywood movies.

"Have you ever been to the States?" Hollis asked.

"Not really," Billy said. "But I'm cool with that." He seemed to prefer his idealized vision of America over the real thing.

They boarded the train a minute before it left the station and found their reserved seats. When people walked down the aisle, they seemed surprised to find a sick black man sitting next to a Japanese Elvis.

"Can you change your hair?" Hollis asked.

"What are you talking about?"

"I look sick, but everyone is staring at *you*."

"This hair is maximum cool," Billy said and took out a mirror to check his pompadour.

"Maybe it was—in 1955."

"I've been attacked on the street because of this hair. My brother won't talk to me because of this hair. This hair has coolness because I say so."

After a whispered argument, Billy finally agreed to replace his leather jacket with a nylon shell. He slipped on earphones and bobbed his head up and down as Hollis watched the train escape from the city. The big apartment buildings disappeared and they passed strips of farmland bordered by ordered rows of pine trees. In Tokyo, the crows were always solitary, but in the countryside the birds gathered together. Crows perched on the power lines and on top of the enormous green cages used as driving ranges by Japanese golfers. Crows clustered in the stumble of frozen rice fields; the bullet train roared past them and they rose up in the sky like points of darkness.

It was night when they reached Hachinohe—a transit town

sprawled between two hills. The only things that appeared to hold the community together were the telephone lines and power cables that ran from one side of the street to another. Snow began to fall when they left the station. Snowflakes piled up on the slanted roofs and balconies of the flimsy-looking three-story buildings. Snow clung to Billy's hair as they checked into a traditional Japanese inn. The inn's owner had just installed new tatami mats; when Hollis lay down on the floor he smelled the yellowish-green reeds. It reminded him of cut grass and summer and those moments when he had been happy. He prayed to Vicki and was able to sleep.

* * *

THE NEXT MORNING Billy left the inn, making two furrows through the slush with his motorcycle boots. He returned after breakfast and told Hollis that the man who shoveled snow at the train station knew all about the Itako. A few years ago, she had moved north to Mutsu, a sea town on the peninsula that jutted out into the Tsugaru Strait.

"And how far away is that?"

"Ninety minutes on the local train."

"Is she still there?"

"Nobody knows, man. He said the Itako lives in the 'dead place.'" Billy rolled his eyes. "So I guess we know what to look for."

An hour later, Hollis found himself riding in a two-car train that was about as large as a crosstown bus in New York City. Steel wheels clicked and clattered as they passed though bare volcanic mountains. Fog. White snow on black rocks. And then the train entered a tunnel that plunged them into darkness. When they emerged, the ocean was about fifty feet away. The train cars shook slightly—like pack animals glad to be finished with such a bleak journey—and they rolled into a train station built next to Mutsu's harbor.

It was cold and windy on the station platform. Rubbing his hands together, Billy hurried off to find a taxi driver. He returned five minutes later with a shy young man who was trying to grow a beard.

"He says he's a part-time driver."

"That means he's going to get lost."

Billy laughed. "We're always getting lost in Japan, but this driver knows how to find the dead place. It's where this company built a pesticide factory. After they killed every tree in the area, they transferred the business to China."

The three of them squeezed into a mud-splattered Toyota and drove away past a row of fast-food outlets. At the edge of the town, a *pachinko* parlor with a huge neon tower stood out against the overcast sky. The young driver turned onto a gravel road, and they entered the dead area around the abandoned pesticide plant. Although the ground was covered with snow, Hollis could see that all the trees had died. A few brown spruces remained standing, as if too weary to fall.

There were a dozen homes in the area, and they stopped at each one so that Billy could ask about the Itako. "Japan is like this weird party where everybody has to be polite," he explained. "People will lie and make up directions so they won't lose face."

For more than an hour, they wandered through a maze of country roads. Coming down a low hill, the Toyota skidded across a patch of ice and slammed into a snowbank. Everyone got out of the car, and Billy started yelling at the driver.

A prefabricated home with aluminum siding was about thirty feet away. Hollis watched as an old woman wearing a black parka and red rubber boots came out of the house and hiked down a gravel driveway. The woman walked in a slow, solid way through the slush as if it would take a bolt of lightning to knock her over. Her face was strong and her eyes focused as she examined the three intruders who had blundered into her world.

When she reached the car, she put her hands on her hips and began asking questions. Billy tried to answer with some rock-and-roll swagger, but his confidence quickly melted away. When the old woman had finished her interrogation, she turned away and climbed back up the driveway to her house. Billy stood in the middle of the road staring at the toes of his motorcycle boots.

"What's the problem with the old lady?" Hollis asked. "Are we on her property?"

"That's the Itako. She says she's been waiting for you."

"Yeah. Sure."

"Maybe it's a story or maybe it's true. All I know is that we got to follow her into the house."

"And then what happens?"

"It's just like you want. She talks to the dead."

* * *

THE TWO MEN entered the foyer of the house and took off their jackets and shoes. The Itako had disappeared, but a door was open to the living room, where an old man sat on a western-style couch and watched a karaoke show on television. He turned his head slightly—showing no surprise or curiosity—and pointed to the left.

Billy led them down a hallway. He slid back a door of thick paper and entered a room with lace curtains covering the window. There were a few floor pillows on the tatami mat, but the only real furniture in the room was a low wooden table that had been turned into an altar. The table was covered with cat statues. A few of the smaller cats were carved from wood or jade, but most were ceramic souvenirs with painted-on whiskers. All the cats stared at a bowl containing three shriveled-up oranges and a martini glass filled with polished stones.

Hollis sat down on one of the floor cushions and tried to figure out what to do. He had traveled thousands of miles to find this place. Three men had been killed, the Tabula were looking for him, and here he was sitting in a house with a crazy old lady who collected ceramic cats.

The Itako came back into the room wearing a short white cotton jacket with Japanese symbols printed on it. She extended her hand, said something in Japanese, and Billy Hirano gave her five thousand yen. The Itako counted the money like a peasant who had just sold a pig, and slipped the currency beneath one of the cats. Then she bustled around the room lighting candles and incense.

When the candles were burning, the old woman knelt and opened up a polished wooden box. She took out an elaborate necklace and carefully draped it around her neck. The necklace was a dark rawhide strand that held old coins with holes in the middle, yellowed bear claws, and a few twisted pieces of wood. She stared at Hollis for a few seconds and spoke in Japanese.

Billy translated. "She wants to know what you're looking for."

"This is ridiculous. I can't believe Sparrow actually talked to this woman. Let's get the hell out of here."

"Don't make her angry, Hollis. An Itako is very powerful."

"As far as I can see, she's just an old lady with a lot of souvenir kitty cats."

"Do what she says," Billy pleaded. "Tell her what you want."

Hollis turned to the Itako and spoke in English. "A friend of mine has died. I want to talk to her."

Billy translated the request. The Itako nodded calmly, as if someone had just asked her for directions back to the train station. She reached into the box, took out a long strand of stone prayer beads, and held a fistful of the beads in both hands. Closing her eyes, she rubbed the beads together as she began to chant a Buddhist sutra.

It felt as if the cats on the altar were staring at him with mischievous smiles on their little white faces. The Itako looked old and tired, and a few times she seemed to lose her way through the long recital of prayers. Suddenly, she stopped chanting and her chin slumped down to her breast. Seconds later, her head snapped back up and her entire body became rigid. A convulsive force passed through her body and the prayer beads fell onto the mat. The Itako sucked air into her lungs and, when she exhaled, a sound emerged from her slack mouth.

At first, it was nothing but nonsense syllables, and then a mix of Japanese and English words. It felt as if someone were moving a tuner, scanning through different radio stations. More words. A garbled phrase here and there.

"Hollis."

It was her voice. Vicki's voice. But he couldn't believe that was possible.

"Hollis?"

"I—I missed you so much, Vicki. And maybe I'm just hearing your voice in my mind. This can't be real."

A long silence. The Itako's body shivered and her eyes rolled upward.

"The first time we made love was in the loft in Chinatown. Maya and Gabriel had gone somewhere and we were finally alone. You placed the mattress on the floor. Afterward, we lay together for a long time. It was so cold in the room that steam came off our bodies and melted into the air."

Hollis felt as if he had cracked open and was falling apart. "Where are you?" he asked.

"Gone. But here."

"I'm so lost, Vicki. So goddamn lost. I don't know where I'm going."

"You're on the right path, but you still can't see it. If you remember who you are, you'll know what to do."

"I can't forgive the people who killed you."

"Know this, my love . . . Believe this, my love . . . the Light survives."

The Itako breathed out one last time, and collapsed onto the floor as if the life force had been ripped from her body.

17

Michael Corrigan accepted a flute of champagne from a young woman with a silver tray and began to wander through the crowd that had assembled in the college cloisters. The Brethren's annual meeting drew delegates from all over the world, and everyone wanted to talk to the young American who had just become the new executive director. Before he could cross the room, Michael encountered Mr. Choi, the delegate from Singapore, who wanted him to meet Mr. Iyer from India.

None of these people could be considered his friend—or even an ally. Michael knew he was in dangerous territory. A year earlier, he was a prisoner of the Brethren, lying on a surgical table with wires in his brain. Now he was running the Evergreen Foundation, and many of the delegates seemed surprised by this sudden transformation.

Mr. Westley and the other half gods had told him what to do when he returned to the ordinary world. But Michael wasn't about to reveal their plans. Instead of describing the wet crawlers and the executions on the visionary screen, he informed the Brethren that he had explored a rock-filled, uninhabited landscape and that he had heard gentle voices, like angels, whispering in his ear. He had asked these angels for technological knowledge, and they had transmitted the design for a memory chip that could store an enormous amount of data.

He made sure that Dr. Dawson sent the executive board an enthusiastic description of this new technology. Many governments and corporations had been overwhelmed by the personal information obtained by the Vast Machine. Now they would have the memory to store every detail about billions of people. Every recordable activity in a person's life could be saved, evaluated, and linked almost instantly.

While Michael's description of the Fifth Realm was like a blurry photograph, his request for power was clear and explicit. If the Brethren wanted to receive more information, then Mrs. Brewster had to resign so that Michael could take control of the research effort. Of course, he would continue to be guided by the Brethren's collective wisdom, but the change of leadership would make the Foundation a more responsive and efficient organization.

Mrs. Brewster spent a week trying to organize opposition to his plan, but the corporate leaders serving on the board were tempted by the power implicit in the new technology. Within twelve hours of his victory, the Evergreen Foundation issued a press release that transformed Michael into a successful real estate investor and international philanthropist.

This conference in London was the next step in his plan. The Brethren's annual meeting was usually held on Dark Island or at

Wellspring Manor in southern England, but Michael wanted to stay away from the two locations where Mrs. Brewster still controlled the security team. Remembering that it was the two hundredth anniversary of Jeremy Bentham's invention of the Panopticon, Michael came up with a new proposal. If the meeting was moved to London, they could hold the welcoming party in the South Cloisters at University College where the philosopher's body was kept in a glass case. The Brethren's executive board was so enthusiastic about this idea that even Mrs. Brewster was forced to smile graciously and make the vote unanimous.

After the Foundation made a generous donation to the college's maintenance fund, the board of governors allowed them to use the cloisters for the evening. Michael volunteered to make the opening remarks to the guests, and he contacted the more powerful members of the board to get their suggestions. "I think we need to make a strong statement," he said, and everyone agreed with him.

* * *

MICHAEL FINISHED HIS glass of champagne as another group of delegates prattled on about their fears and desires. Finally, he shook hands and turned away. In a few minutes he would begin his speech, and he wanted to get some inspiration from the dead man at the end of the hallway. Nodding to members of the board, he threaded his way through the crowd until Mrs. Brewster stopped him. Although he had taken her public role as the head of the Evergreen Foundation, she was still in charge of the Brethren. For this event, she was wearing a royal blue dress and pearls, but her face was a tired mask.

"It's clear that I haven't been informed of all the *arrangements*." Mrs. Brewster's voice had the clipped, precise tone of an educated Englishwoman who had just found something rotten on her lawn.

"Is there a problem?"

"It's the *chairs*." She gestured to the rows of chairs set up at one end of the long hallway. "Are they really necessary for a short welcoming speech?"

"The speech might be a bit longer than we discussed. I believe that this organization is at a crucial point in its history. We need a new strategy for the future."

"And what is that strategy going to be?"

"I'm sure that you'll support it," Michael said, and left her alone in the middle of the room.

He checked the speech in his suit-coat pocket as he made his way to the south end of the hallway. The glass-and-wood cabinet that contained Jeremy Bentham's body had been surrounded by delegates at the beginning of the party, but now the dead philosopher stared out into empty space.

Bentham had believed that the remains of famous men should never be cremated or hidden in tombs. Instead, their bodies should be turned into something he called "Auto-Icons" that would inspire future generations. Dressed in his own clothes, Bentham's skeleton sat on a chair with a cane resting on his leg. A broad-brimmed hat partially covered the wax model of his face.

Michael felt no sense of awe looking at this effigy. But he was impressed with the fact that—even in death—Bentham demanded acknowledgment. Recently, the University College had fired the security guard protecting the glass case and had replaced him with a CCTV camera mounted on the wall. The creator of the Panopticon was now on the grid.

"Excuse me . . ."

Michael pivoted and saw that Nathan Boone was watching him. The head of security for the Evergreen Foundation was as solemn as a funeral director, in a dark blue business suit.

"Do you have a question, Mr. Boone?"

"The schedule says that you're giving the opening remarks. In the past, the staff has been allowed to circulate with drinks and refreshment for the duration of the party. But your e-mail indicated that you'd like the staff removed from the area."

"Yes, this is a speech only for the Brethren. No outsiders."

Boone raised a communications device and spoke softly. "The executive director's speech starts in a few minutes. Please clear the staff and guard the door."

Two of Boone's security men stepped from the periphery of the crowd and whispered something to the waitresses. Still holding their silver trays, they headed for the exit. But Boone didn't walk away. He stared at the Traveler intently as if Michael's necktie could give him clues about what might happen.

"Is there anything else, Mr. Boone?"

"The London staff informed me that you've organized a new team of employees."

"That's correct. It's called the Special Projects Group."

"And you're using my men."

Michael concentrated on Boone's face. The head of security was trying to control his emotions, but his eyes and the corners of his mouth betrayed him. Like Mrs. Brewster, he was being eased out of power, and he appeared to understand the implications.

"Yes. I accessed the database and hired a few of the men you used for previous operations. I wanted to get things moving along and you were busy with your other responsibilities."

"Can you explain to me what these 'special projects' might be?"

"I *do* have a plan, Nathan, but I'm not prepared to give the full details at this time. After this speech, I'm going to ask for full authorization from the executive board. It's clear that the Brethren have been focused on local or regional goals. It's time we committed ourselves to a more aggressive worldwide strategy."

Boone's fingers trembled as if he wanted to choke Michael. "We've been fairly aggressive in the past."

"You've been an outstanding employee, Nathan. We all appreciate your loyalty and hard work. You've shown us the right path. I'm just taking us a few steps farther."

"When can you give me more information?"

"You'll be the first to know." Michael reached out and slapped the older man's shoulder. "With your help, I'm sure we're going to be successful."

He left Boone in front of Bentham's body and strolled to the end of the hallway. The delegates were sitting on folding chairs or standing near the interior windows that looked out at the cloister garden. Michael stepped behind the podium, took the speech from his coat pocket, and gazed out at the crowd.

Studying the faces of the delegates, he realized that they could be placed in three categories. Some of them were openly suspicious, while others were curious about their new leader. The small group that sat around Mrs. Brewster was hostile, glaring in his direction and then whispering to one another.

The last waitress disappeared out the doorway, followed by the two security men. Nathan Boone stood behind the seated guests and nodded to Michael. Everything was ready. *Speak.*

18

"Everyone in this room seems to know about my background and my special gift. The late Kennard Nash, a man of great insight and wisdom, was the first member of the Brethren who realized that a person like me could be an asset to your cause. I will always be grateful for his faith in me. He was supported by a number of people here—in particular, Mrs. Brewster. Her dedication and hard work continue to be an inspiration to all of us."

A few of the delegates applauded Mrs. Brewster. She nodded and raised her right hand as if to say: *Please, it's not necessary*. Then she looked back at Michael with a look of barely disguised rage.

"At first, General Nash had questions about my loyalty, and I had my own doubts about this organization. But I have gone through a complete transformation. These days, I stand in awe of the Brethren and your vision of a stable, orderly society. What we decide here in the next few days will determine the future of this troubled world. Although the Panopticon was never built during Jeremy Bentham's lifetime, our generation has the opportunity to turn his dream into reality.

"I recently crossed over to another world and then traveled back to you with the first of many technological miracles that will finally allow us to achieve our goals. But what is even more important is this: I came in contact with minds of great wisdom who showed me that the so-called virtue of freedom is actually dangerous illusion and that firm, but fair, social control is the salvation of mankind.

"The Brethren are right and have always been right throughout history. After I learned this great truth, I had only one objective: to return and help you in any way possible. But before we start down this road together we need to understand our present situation and where we're going in the future. In some ways, we've never been stronger. Almost every electronic transaction and act of communication can be detected and linked to a particular individual. This information can be placed in centralized databases and stored forever. We can create a 'shadow' image of each person and monitor their daily behavior.

"Yes, there are a few crazies typing away on the Internet, but the major media is now controlled by a small group of people. These opinion shapers are our friends, and once we give them good stories—with villains and heroes, threats and solutions— we can drown out the scattered voices shouting in the streets.

"Opinion polls have shown that law-abiding citizens don't mind being watched by the authorities. All they want is a decent job and a chance to have some fun: a comfortable, orderly existence. Forget about the radicals and the fringe groups. There's no question that the public is on *our* side. Indeed, this is the moment when we Brethren can stop and ask ourselves: How will the new system benefit our own lives?"

Michael paused so that he could examine the crowd sitting in front of him. Most of the Brethren looked surprised by his question, but a few of them nodded slightly as if to say, *Yes. That's right. What's in it for me?*

"The Panopticon will create a stable society where it's easier to manipulate behavior and stifle dissent. But what are we going to gain from the new system? History has shown us that a severe dictatorship creates a resentful and rebellious underclass. A better goal is combining control—with prosperity. The problem with Bentham's Panopticon is that his prisoners don't work. His old-fashioned prison completely ignores the economy.

"It's time for a *New* Panopticon. Imagine a vast office—an enormous room—filled with billions of cubicles. In my system, there's one electronic cubicle for every citizen in the industrial world. And within each cubicle, what are our citizens doing? Making products or providing services. They are productive citizens who fill out their time cards and don't complain.

"Once we realize that our true goal is a cooperative workforce, a great many issues become clear. It doesn't make a difference if we're talking about doctors, accountants, students, short-order cooks, or steel workers. They're all going to be in their invisible cubicles, watched by our surveillance cameras and controlled by our social-parameter programs.

"Do we care how our workers decorate their cubicles? Are we concerned if they spend their free time watching television or digging in their garden? Of course not. It makes no difference what church they attend as long as their faith doesn't transform their lives. They can vote and slap bumper stickers on their cars if their political candidate doesn't really change anything. When an economic crisis occurs, we'll have the government print money and make superficial modifications, but the basic structure will remain the same.

"The New Panopticon allows us to control the behavior of

people both as workers and as consumers. Our citizen in the cubicle is essentially powerless, but he is still able to express himself at the shopping mall. Freedom of choice becomes the freedom to buy, and our new system gives us powerful tools to manipulate consumer behavior. When our citizen walks through the streets, billboards will recognize his face. Eventually, a centralized computer base will know all our citizen's previous purchases and will make sure he's never offered a product that will challenge his view of the world. It will be like listening to a radio station always tuned to music that sounds pleasantly familiar.

"So this is what I'm proposing—not a prison of sullen, unproductive prisoners, but an interconnected structure that creates obedient workers and trained consumers. This worldwide system will guarantee more money and comfort for yourself and your family. We'll get the stability of the old Panopticon—with a happy face."

Most of the Brethren were smiling and nodding. Mrs. Brewster turned her head back and forth as she watched her influence melt away.

"My plan can become a reality if we don't waste our resources on limited strategies. Instead of waiting for people to join the system, we need to create a worldwide sequence of threats and emergencies that impels citizens to voluntarily give up their freedom. And why would they do this? That's easy to answer. Because we've turned them into children scared of the dark. They will be desperate for our help, terrified of a life outside their cubicle filled with predators and danger.

"We can achieve this goal in a few years if we're ruthless enough to consider every option. We need strength, not diplomacy. We need leadership, not committees. We need to stand up and say: 'No more half measures. No compromises. We're going to do everything necessary to create a better world.'

"I stand before you as a faithful servant: ready to obey *your* orders and create *your* vision. This isn't a dream that might come true. What I have described this evening is an inevitable reality . . . if you're ready for this next step. All it needs is your approval and support. Thank you."

Michael bowed his head slightly, folded up the speech, and slipped it into his pocket. The room was completely quiet, but he avoided looking at the audience.

One person began clapping—slow, insistent—and others joined in. The sound grew louder as it echoed off the walls of the cloisters. When he glanced up from the podium, he saw that Mrs. Brewster was staring at him. Her hands were clenched and her mouth was a tight red line.

She's the first to die, Michael decided. *I need to start a list.*

19

Wearing a paper hospital gown, Maya sat on the edge of an examination table at a walk-in medical clinic in East London. A collection of dog-eared magazines was stuffed into a wall rack near the sink, but she had no desire to read about "The Secrets Men Won't Tell You" or "The One-Week Bikini Diet."

When Maya and the others had returned to London, she had still felt a burning pain from the leg wound she had received in the First Realm. The clinic staff had cleaned the wound, checked the stitches she had received from a Cairo doctor, and given her prescriptions for antibiotics and pain pills. For the last twelve days she had been recovering at Tyburn Convent. The Benedictine nuns had served her bland food while they whispered variations of the word *rest*. Well, she had rested enough, and nothing had changed. The wound was still bleeding, and images from Hell still floated through her dreams.

It was about two o'clock in the afternoon and the sounds of the busy clinic filtered through the walls. Doors were pulled open and slammed shut. Someone pushed a squeaky cart down the hallway while two nurses gossiped about a man named Ronnie.

Maya ignored this background noise and concentrated on the screaming child in the next room. It seemed obvious that someone was deliberately hurting the child. Maya's clothes and sword carrier were hanging from a hook on the door; her knives were in her shoulder bag. She should get dressed, walk into the next room, and kill the torturers.

One part of her mind knew she was thinking like a crazy person. *This is a clinic. The doctors are here to help people.* But a dark compulsion made her slip off the table and take a step toward the weapons. As she reached out to touch the sword carrier, the screaming stopped, and Maya heard the child's mother talking about a dish of ice cream.

She heard footsteps in the hallway. The door popped open and Dr. Amita Kamani entered the room. The young physician had trimmed her hair since Maya's last visit to the clinic, and she was wearing a pink T-shirt beneath her white lab coat that read: CHILDREN ARE OUR FUTURE.

"Good afternoon, Ms. Strand. So how's the cut doing? All healed up?"

"See for yourself."

Dr. Kamani pulled on some latex gloves, sat down on a stool near the table, and began to unwrap the bandage around Maya's leg. One of the nuns at Tyburn Convent had put on a fresh bandage about two hours ago, but it was already sodden with blood. When Dr. Kamani peeled the gauze off, she could see that the stitches still held, but scar tissue had not appeared.

"This is not a normal healing response. You should have come in earlier." Dr. Kamani dropped the bandages into a trash bin. She opened a cabinet, took out disinfectant and surgical cotton, and began to clean the wound. "Does it hurt?"

"Yes."

"Can you describe the pain?"

"A burning sensation."

Dr. Kamani handed Maya a disposable thermometer, then checked her pulse and blood pressure. "Did you take the antibiotics I prescribed for you?"

It bothered Maya that the doctor was treating her like a child. "Of course I took the medicine," she said. "I'm not a bloody fool."

"I'm just trying to help you, Ms. Strand." Dr. Kamani glanced at the thermometer. "Your temperature and pulse rate are in the normal range."

"Stitch me up again and give me some more pills."

"There's nothing wrong with the stitches. I'll give you a prescription for a stronger antibiotic, but that might not help. As I recall, you said you were in a car accident during a holiday in Egypt."

"That's correct."

Dr. Kamani took out some clean gauze and surgical tape. She sprayed a yellow liquid on the wound and began to put on a new bandage. "When you were in Egypt, were you in contact with a sick animal or any kind of toxic chemical?"

"No."

"Did you use any illegal drugs?"

Maya wanted to shout out an explanation, but she stayed silent. *A citizen can never understand you.* Her father had told her that hundreds of times, and it was especially true at this moment. What could she say to a person wearing a white lab coat? *I traveled to a city surrounded by a dark river. The wolves tried to kill me, but I stabbed and cut and beat them down.*

"Just fix me up and make the wound heal," Maya said. "I'll pay you double what I did last time—in cash."

Dr. Kamani pulled off the gloves and began to write on her

clipboard. "All right, I won't ask any more questions. But we are going to run some medical tests before you leave the clinic today."

"Will the test results be placed in a computer connected to the Internet?"

"Of course."

"I won't allow that."

Dr. Kamani looked surprised, but her voice stayed calm and reasonable. "If you wish, I'll make a note to the staff. They'll leave the test results in my message tray and I'll keep them out of the database. If I do that—if I break the rules—you have to promise you'll come back here."

"I promise."

Dr. Kamani started to open the door, then paused and closed it again. "Although you told me you were in a car accident, I don't believe that's accurate. Your wound indicates you were stabbed with a knife, and your behavior follows the pattern of someone with extended exposure to significant trauma. Perhaps you were raped or physically abused. I strongly recommend some kind of psychotherapy combined with medical supervision."

"We don't do that."

"And who is *we*?"

"My family."

The doctor's face showed pity and concern. Maya knew that her father would have been insulted by Kamani's reaction; it implied weakness, and Harlequins were never weak. Mother Blessing would have stood up and slapped her.

"You're in pain, Ms. Strand . . ."

"What's the next step?" Maya snapped.

Dr. Kamani opened the door and stepped into the hallway. "Stay here in the examination room. A nurse will take blood and urine samples."

* * *

AFTER THE TESTS, she left the clinic and took a shortcut past Spitalfields Market to the Liverpool Street Tube station. These days, East London was filled with high-rise buildings and trendy restaurants, but for hundreds of years the neighborhood had been a dark, crowded slum—the home of new immigrants and outsiders. This was where her father had met his first Traveler, a Jewish mystic named David Rodinsky who lived in the attic of a synagogue on Princelet Street. Maya had been introduced to Rodinsky when she was a little girl; he was a strange, stooped little man who knew over twenty languages. A few years later this *tzadik* had vanished from a locked room and was never seen again. "We guard the Travelers, but we don't always understand them," Thorn told her. "The only thing you need to understand is our obligation."

Perhaps the relationship was clear for her father, but in her own life, the obligation had become compromised by different emotions. She was supposed to be cold and rational with no real attachments to another person. Most of the time, she could play that role, but there were moments when she wanted to be back on the plane from Cairo to London. During the long flight, Gabriel had wrapped her up in a blanket and embraced her as if she were a sick child. They had spoken about the First Realm in a cautious manner, trying to step back from the pain of what had happened there.

* * *

MAYA FOUND LINDEN sitting outside the falafel shop in Camden Market, guarding the staircase that led to the upstairs room. A carrying bag for a tennis racket was propped up against the wall, but Linden didn't resemble a man of leisure. His broad shoulders and broken nose made him look like a retired football player—someone once known for his rough play and penalties.

"What did the doctor say?"

"The wound is healing, but it's taking some time. Where's Gabriel?"

"The Traveler is upstairs, meeting with a group of Free Runners. They are figuring out a safe way to establish a communications network."

"That's very ambitious."

"It is clear that he has a plan, but he has not explained it to anyone yet. He wants to hold a meeting of the Resistance in a few weeks."

Maya grabbed a chair and sat down beside the Frenchman. When she shifted her leg suddenly, she felt a jab of pain. *Don't show any weakness*, she told herself. *No one can use an injured fighter*.

"You've been guarding Gabriel for a long time. I'm healthy now and can accept the obligation."

"I would like that very much," Linden said. "I need to solve some problems back in Paris. Apparently, a water pipe is leaking in my flat. I cannot have a stranger fixing it."

"I could take charge for a few days."

"As you recall, there was a problem with your *objectivité*. As Mother Blessing told you, Harlequins cannot have an emotional connection with the people they are guarding."

"I was sick during the trip back to London. I'm better now. I haven't even spoken to Gabriel for the last six days."

"Yes. I noticed that. You have finally started to act in the correct way." Linden looked over at the canal and made his decision. He picked up the tennis-racket carrier and handed it to her. "Here is your weapon. A steel frame holds a sawed-off shotgun with a six-round ammunition drum. Insert your firing hand in the opening."

Maya found an opening on one side of the bag. When she slipped her right hand inside, she felt the shotgun's trigger guard.

"The safety is on. Do you feel it?"

She clicked the safety button on and off. "Got it."

"*C'est bien*. I will leave tonight for Paris and will be back on Tuesday. If there is a problem, you know how to contact me." For the first time in their long relationship, Linden made a point of shaking her hand. "Welcome back, Maya. It is good to know that you are healthy again."

* * *

AFTER LINDEN LEFT the shop, Maya stood guard for ten minutes or so. When she was sure the Frenchman was gone, she picked up the concealed shotgun and went upstairs. There was no immediate threat in the area, but she felt tense and sensitive to any sound.

The meeting was just ending in the little room and the Free Runners were on their feet, lining up to say good-bye to the Traveler. Gabriel touched each person's shoulder or shook their hand while looking directly into their eyes. Maya saw that the young men and women were pleased by the Traveler's attention. Gabriel smiled when he saw Maya in the doorway, but he didn't say anything until Jugger and his friends had left the room.

"Where's Linden?"

"I'm in charge. He's going to Paris for a few days."

"Good. He once told me that he misses hearing French in the streets."

Gabriel took a disposable cell phone out of his pocket and called Winston Abosa. While he talked, Maya tried to dissect her emotions. She still loved him. That would never change. But if she wanted to protect him, she could never show her feelings. She focused on her wound, putting all her weight on the bad leg to increase the pain. When the burning sensation returned, she raised her eyes and stared at the Traveler with a coldness that was close to hostility.

"Are you okay?" he asked.

"I'm getting better."

"Good. We need to sit down and talk about what happened in the First Realm."

"I don't want to do that."

"The experience was difficult for both of us."

"Sometimes we have bad dreams, but we shouldn't waste the day thinking about them."

"What happened wasn't a dream, Maya. The realms are a powerful experience because they're real."

"It's time to deal with the problem in front of us. Why did you call Winston?"

"He's picking us up in the van and driving us over to Bloomsbury. We need a safe way to communicate within our group. Sebastian has been in contact with a computer expert called the Nighthawk."

"What's his real name?"

"No one knows. It took several weeks of negotiations before he agreed to meet us. Sebastian thought that the Nighthawk was in Eastern Europe, but it turns out he lives here in London."

"Has Sebastian ever met him?"

Gabriel shook his head. "All I have is a room number at a graduate student dormitory near Coram's Fields."

"Maybe it's a trap."

"That's why you're coming along."

* * *

ON THE WAY over to Bloomsbury, Maya learned a few facts about the Nighthawk. He had been active on the Internet for over ten years, and had first become famous for breaking into the White House computer system. Even Maya knew about the Nighthawk's most famous exploit. Two years ago, the "Kitty Cat Virus" appeared on April Fools' Day. For three minutes, the virus took control of millions of computers and forced them to display a music video of dancing kittens.

Winston dropped them off on the south corner of Russell Square near the British Museum. Maya was familiar with the area, and she led Gabriel across the square, passing through the plaza that surrounded a central fountain. The Hotel Russell was directly in front of them, its copper-roofed turrets and red-brick

chimneys rising over the tops of the beech trees. Passing an outdoor café, they reached the north corner of the square and crossed
the street. Students with backpacks and book satchels formed
chattering groups outside the hotel and the Russell Square Tube
station. Maya touched the outline of the hidden shotgun as they
continued down Bernard Street toward Coram's Fields.

The fields had once been the site of a foundling hospital
where mothers left their babies in a large basket near the front
gate. There had always been a coin or a locket tied to the children's wrists or braided into their hair—a final gesture of hope
that mother and child would find each other again. The hospital
had been torn down in the 1920s, and now a massive playground
stood on the bones of those children who had died there.

When they reached Brunswick Square, Maya looked down the
street and saw the small white buildings used by the petting zoo and
the children's nursery. There was only one entrance to the Fields,
and a black spike fence guarded the area like a row of spears. Peering through the gaps in the fence, Maya saw three little girls blowing soap bubbles and then chasing them around a playground.

"This is Coram's Fields," she told Gabriel. "My mother used to
bring me here."

"You want to stop for a while? We have plenty of time."

"There's a rule here. Adults are only allowed through the gate
if accompanied by a child. If you leave the Fields—and grow up—
you can't get back inside."

Continuing down Guilford Street, Maya and Gabriel reached
Mecklenburgh Square. The Nighthawk supposedly lived in the
graduate student dormitory on the north side of the square. They
passed through a glass door to a lobby that looked as if it hadn't
changed in fifty years. Foreign students sat around a scratched
coffee table covered with newspapers while a clerk sorted through
the mail and placed letters into numbered cubbies.

A sign said they were supposed to announce themselves at the
desk, but no one stopped them. Gabriel grinned at her and pretended to be a student. "So how did you do on the German Lit
exam?"

"Just keep moving," she whispered, and they wandered down a hallway past a laundry room and a communal kitchen. Maya smelled popcorn and heard a Beethoven symphony blasting through the walls. Room 108 was at the end of the hallway, and the brass door bracket held a smudged card with the name ERIC VINSKY written on it.

If this was a trap, then Tabula mercs would be waiting inside. Maya lowered the tennis bag so that the sawed-off shotgun was pointing forward. She motioned for Gabriel to step back and tried the doorknob. It was unlocked. She centered herself, preparing for battle, then pushed open the door and stepped into the room.

The ceiling light was switched off and the curtains were taped shut. Light came from the bathroom and from three computer monitors glowing with different images: a conversation in a chat room, luminous lines of programming code, and a silent, dancing ballerina. Instead of someone with a gun, they found a man sitting in an electric-powered wheelchair. His hand left the computer keyboard, touched a control lever in the chair's armrest, and it swiveled around toward the open door.

They were looking at a young man with a severe muscular disease. He had a slack face and drooping eyelids, and his long tangled hair touched his shoulders. His entire body was a contorted S-curve—the legs going one way, the stomach and chest going another way, while the head struggled to stay in one position.

"Do I know you?" he asked. Every word was an effort.

Gabriel was right behind her and he closed the door to the hallway. "Are you the Nighthawk?" he asked.

"Nighthawks?" The young man tried to smile, but it was more like a grimace. "You mean the birds? They're members of the nightjar family in the subfamily . . . let me think . . . Chordeilinae."

"Our friend Sebastian told us to come here and talk to someone called the Nighthawk."

"I see. You're from the so-called Resistance. Well, I'm not impressed."

"We need to set up a safe way to communicate through the

Internet. Without that, it's impossible to create a worldwide move-ment."

"Can you help us?" Maya asked.

The young man shifted the chair back and forth as if he was fidgeting. "Sebastian gave you the right information. You have the privilege of meeting the legendary Nighthawk, the Demon of the Internet."

"Right now, our enemies can read our coded messages," Gabriel explained. "They've got a working version of a quantum computer."

The Nighthawk lowered his head slightly. He dropped the sar-castic tone and appeared to be considering the information. "A quantum computer? Really? If that's true, then traditional code is not going to work. Ordinary computers have to test code messages sequentially in a brute-force attack. But a quantum computer can test all alternatives at the same time."

"In other words, they can break any code we throw at them." Maya turned to Gabriel. "This trip was a waste of time."

"It *could* be a waste of time, if you speak rudely to the Nighthawk." Pushing down on the armrests, Vinsky struggled to sit up straight. "I anticipated this particular development in the Internet war, and I've already come up with a solution."

"You just told us that this new machine can test all answers," Gabriel said.

"That's true. A quantum computer can defeat all codes—except for those that use quantum theory. When you look at a quantum particle, it alters its state. My code operates the same way. If anyone tries to read your message, both sender and re-ceiver will know instantly."

"So will you help us?" Gabriel asked.

"How much will you pay me?"

"Nothing."

"I see." The Nighthawk frowned. "Then we have nothing to talk about."

"Perhaps you want something other than money," Gabriel said.

"And what could that possibly be?"

"I think you'd like to extend your influence all over the world and annoy those in power."

"Perhaps. You might be right about that. Annoying other people is the only way I know I'm alive. That's the troll morality. And I'm the King of the Trolls."

"So you'll help us?"

"Would you buy me a new modem?"

"We'll buy you three bloody modems," Maya said. "Just deliver what you promise."

"Oh, I'll deliver. I can promise you that."

"There's another problem you might be able to solve," Gabriel said. "I want to communicate with everyone in the world who owns a computer. The message can't be blocked or filtered. It will simply appear."

"Understand something. This is an act that is vastly more ambitious than putting up a video of dancing kittens. The authorities won't be amused. They'll be very angry. If the message is traced back to me, I could end up in prison." The Nighthawk gestured at his room. "My cell would be as small as this hole, but there would be one terrible punishment—they would take away my computer."

"I need your help, Eric. It's important."

"I realize that the Resistance is against surveillance and control, and I agree with that philosophy. But you want me to risk my freedom. So what is the Resistance *for*? What's your plan?"

"I can only describe the ideal. I realize that it's hard to achieve ideals, but they do determine the direction of our journey."

"Go on . . ."

"This is a mass movement with a simple goal. We want people to acknowledge the fact that each individual life has value and meaning."

"Even *my* life, trapped in this chair?"

"Of course."

"And what gives you the right to say that?"

Maya glanced at Gabriel and shook her head slightly as if to say, *Don't tell him anything*. But Gabriel deliberately ignored her.

"I'm a Traveler. Do you know what—"

"Of course I know. But all the Travelers are dead."

Maya touched the tennis carrier that concealed the shotgun. "This one isn't dead. And we're going to keep it that way."

"Really? So what tricks can you do, Mr. Traveler? Can you glow in the dark? Do you fly? *Can you heal me?*" The Nighthawk's voice was both sarcastic and plaintive. "I have DMD—Duchenne muscular dystrophy. Even with the drugs, I'm going to die in five or six years."

"I can't heal you, Eric. I don't have that power."

"Then you're completely useless, aren't you?"

The Nighthawk lowered his head and Maya wondered if he was going to cry. Gabriel's voice was soft, comforting.

"We wander through our lives and then we die. But for all of us there is one moment, one crucial point, where we have to make a decision between what's right and what's wrong, between different visions of who we might be. This might be that moment for you, Eric. I don't know. It's your choice."

The Nighthawk stayed silent for almost a minute and then he turned back to his computer. "It would have to be a worm, not a virus. A virus attaches itself to an existing program. What you want is a self-replicating code that would sit around in a computer—unnoticed—until it was activated."

"What happens next?" Maya asked.

Pushing his control stick, the Nighthawk spun around in a circle like a madman looking for a vision. Suddenly, he stopped and laughed with pleasure. "It does something quite extraordinary. Something that would be useful to a Traveler . . ."

* * *

TWENTY MINUTES LATER, they left the dormitory and headed back to Russell Square. By now, it was after five in the afternoon, and the streets were filled with people leaving work. There was a crowd outside the Russell Square Tube station, and Maya found it difficult to assess the possible threat from each stranger passing them on the sidewalk. She felt as if they had fallen into a river that

swept them past a news kiosk to the north side of the Russell Hotel. Looking upward, Maya saw cherubs had been carved into the
hotel's stone façade. Their faces were blackened with soot and pit-
ted with age, and they looked angry as they stared down at the citizens and drones.

Maya pulled out her cell phone and called Winston. "We're
done with the meeting. Pick us up on the west side of the square."

The tension she felt when they were pushing through the
crowd only seemed to increase when they crossed the street to the
square. There was a pair of old-fashioned red telephone boxes on
the corner. A man wearing a leather jacket stood inside one of the
boxes, staring at them through a grid of red lines while he held the
phone. Were the Tabula getting ready to attack? Thorn had always
taught her that the most vulnerable moment was after an event,
when people were relaxed and thinking about the trip home.

As they strolled across the square, Maya noticed that the man
in the leather jacket left the telephone box. He appeared to follow
them and became one point of a triangle that included a homeless
man on a park bench and a park worker sweeping up trash near
the fountain.

One small voice in her brain was whispering, *Don't worry,
there's nothing wrong.* But London was transformed into the dark
city of the First Realm. Hatred, fear, and pain ruled this place.
She was surrounded by enemies who wanted to kill her. Maya
lowered the bag, slipped her hand inside, and clicked off the shotgun's safety. A round was in the firing chamber. *Aim and squeeze
the trigger*, she thought. *Do it now.*

20

"Give me the shotgun," Gabriel said. When Maya hesitated, he turned and looked directly at her so she could feel power in his eyes. "It's all right . . ." He reached out slowly—as if he were dismantling a bomb—and took the weapon out of her hands.

"They're going to kill us," she whispered.

"Who are you talking about?"

"See the man sitting on the bench and the two people over by the fountain? Tabula mercenaries."

"You're wrong, Maya. There's nothing to worry about."

Gabriel continued across the square, and Maya followed him.

He had no idea if anyone had noticed the incident. Perhaps they looked like lovers having an argument. They reached the curb together, but Winston wasn't there. Maya's head was whipping back and forth as if they were surrounded by enemies. Finally the white van came around the corner and Gabriel waved frantically.

"They're going to follow us," Maya said.

The van pulled up to the curb and Gabriel yanked open the side door. "That's not going to happen. Those people in the park are just ordinary citizens."

They climbed into the back of the van. Maya looked dazed and unhappy, as if she'd just been awakened from a bad dream. When they reached Camden Market, Winston parked on the street. The drum shop owner knew that something had gone wrong, but he had become cautious after a few months of dealing with Linden and Mother Blessing. He waited for a few minutes, and then spoke softly while watching his two passengers in the rearview mirror.

"Perhaps we could go back to the shop and have a nice cup of tea?"

"Just leave us here, Winston. Maya and I are going to talk."

Winston got out of the van, and Gabriel and Maya sat together, listening to the traffic noise. When he tried to take her hand, she pushed it away.

"Are you going to tell Linden what happened?"

"Why would I do that?"

"I'm not a very good bodyguard if I go completely Tonto in the middle of Russell Square."

"It's not easy to come back from the First Realm and act like nothing happened. It's probably best if you just stay in the secret room and guard me. That won't be difficult. I've decided to cross over again."

"Now you're the crazy one," she said. "Everything will fall apart if you leave."

"I have to go, Maya. I need to find my father. He's the only person who can help me figure out what to do."

"He might not have an answer."

"I'm not even sure if I can find him. But that doesn't make any difference. Almost every important choice in our lives is really just an expression of hope."

"You need to know that . . ." A strange look passed across Maya's face and then she stopped talking.

"What?"

"Nothing," she answered with her cold Harlequin voice.

Gabriel took her hand and squeezed it tightly, then he got out of the van. Aware of every surveillance camera in the area, he followed a complicated route that avoided their scrutiny. A minute later, he was entering the catacombs. And a short time after that, he was lying on the bed inside the secret room.

* * *

ONCE HE HAD passed through the four barriers of air, water, earth, and fire, some essence of his Self was conscious of movement and direction. He knew the way back to the First Realm, and he deliberately moved away from this coldness. Like a miner trapped underground, he followed a narrow passageway toward warmth and sunlight.

* * *

WHEN GABRIEL OPENED his eyes, he saw that he was lying on a beach of pebbles and coarse sand. Waves collapsed on the shore in a constant rhythm, and he could smell clumps of dead seaweed rotting at the edge of the shoreline.

Is someone here? Are people watching me? He stood up, brushed the sand off his jeans, and surveyed this new world. He was a few yards away from a shallow river that emptied into the sea. The sand and stone were dark red, like rusty iron, and the surrounding vegetation seemed to have absorbed some of this color. The seaweed and the big ferns near the river were reddish green, and the scrubby bushes growing near the tide line had bright scarlet berries that shivered with each gust of wind. It was like his world, but with subtle differences. Perhaps all life had started at the same point, and then some small occurrence—the fall of a leaf, the death of a butterfly—had pushed creation into a different direction.

The wavering shadow that marked the passageway back to the Fourth Realm was only a short distance away. Near that point, at the border between sand and shore, someone had built a cairn of rocks with chunks of red sandstone. A narrow pathway led away from the cairn and through the surrounding marshland. Far in the distance, the land rose up to a line of green hills.

A screeching sound startled him, and he stepped away from the cairn. Overhead, a flock of birds with large pointed wings and long necks were circling over the turbulent patch of water where the river current encountered the sea.

And then a revelation came to him. Although these birds were hundreds of yards away, he could enter into their consciousness. This wasn't some allegory where lions appeared and talked to human beings about theology. The birds saw the world from their animal perspective. They were aware of the angle of their own wings, the dark shapes moving beneath the waves, the sun and wind, the sense of rising higher while constant hunger made them look for food.

Turning away from the sea, he allowed his mind to enter into the ivy growing by the river. Unlike the birds, the ivy offered a simple, resonant message—as if someone were playing a single key on a cathedral organ. He was aware of the plant's slowness and strength, the stubborn tenacity of its growth, its reaching search for water and light.

This new awareness felt like a moment out of time. It could have taken only a few seconds or several years. It was the presence of the cairn that pulled him out of the dream. This natural world, without roads or cities, was probably the Third Realm of the animals, but it looked like a Traveler had appeared on this beach and built this particular monument. If he turned toward the mountains, he could see another cairn in the distance that marked a route through a coastal marsh.

Gabriel started up the pathway, his shoes sinking in the muddy ground. A few miles from the beach, the river opened up to a lagoon where two large birds—like reddish-brown swans—floated on the still water. The birds raised their heads, and he sensed their curiosity as he forced his way through a clump of reeds.

Eventually, he left the coastal area and began to pick his way across a rocky patch of ground. There was no path to follow, and he kept glancing over his shoulder to keep the cairn in view. He placed a pebble on top of each new stack of rocks to mark his progress.

Something was watching him. He could feel it. When he spun around, he saw a small animal—like a chipmunk—peering out from a crack in the rocks. When Gabriel laughed out loud, the animal squeaked a protest and disappeared into his hole.

As he gained elevation, a line of boulders appeared that resembled the broken pieces of an ancient wall. Gabriel's shoes crunched on gravel as he found a gap between two stones and scrambled up the slope to the edge of a long plateau covered with grass. Mounds dotted the area; it looked as if a giant had fallen into an endless sleep near the base of the hills and now his body had been absorbed by the earth and covered with a green comforter.

The grass brushed against Gabriel's legs as he began to search for the path. In the distance, dark shapes floated through the meadow and then vanished behind one of the mounds. A few minutes later, a herd of horses trotted over the top of the rise.

The horses saw him and stopped, milling around in what looked like a haphazard manner until he realized that the mares and their colts had moved to the center of the herd. The horses had shaggy manes and tails and were smaller than the thoroughbreds of his world. Their clunky hooves were out of proportion to their bodies, and there was a pronounced ridge on their foreheads.

It felt as if his Light was entering into theirs and he sensed thoughts far more complicated than the hunger of the seabirds. These animals had a sense of themselves and one another. They could smell him, see him, and there was a memory of another vertical creature that walked on two legs.

The speed and power of the horses' bodies gave them a certain pleasure, a kind of pagan joy. But something was wrong. His appearance had distracted the herd for a moment; they had ignored a more significant threat. The stallions snorted loudly as they kicked at the earth. *Danger. Look around you.*

Three lion-sized animals emerged from the grass and began to stalk the herd. Gabriel could see that they had large heads and massive jaws. Their fur was golden brown, and they had distinctive red markings on their sides.

As these predators crept forward, Gabriel could feel them evaluating the herd. *Which horse is old or small? Is there any sign of sickness or injury?* For a brief moment they disappeared into a hollow, but the trembling grass marked their passage. When the animals reappeared, they had formed a crude triangle—with the largest predator in front and his companions on each side.

Fear passed through the herd like a wave of frantic energy, and the horses began running. A yearling horse galloped in one direction, stopped and realized it was alone, then tried to join the others. In that instant of confusion, it became the target, and the lead predator dashed forward with long, powerful strides.

When the creature leaped, the red markings emerged from its body, becoming stubby little wings that propelled it through the air and onto the back on its victim. Gabriel felt both the pain of the yearling horse and the exhilaration of its attacker. Down they went, the yearling screaming and kicking as it tried to break free. But the creature dug its claws into flesh, locked its jaws onto the horse's mouth and nose, and held on tightly. Unable to breathe, the yearling made one last attempt to break free, then collapsed and died.

The horses stopped on a mound about a half mile away and looked back at the fallen yearling. If the herd was a single living creature, then one part of the body had been sacrificed to save the rest.

One of the predators saw Gabriel and made a deep chuffing sound. Gabriel's calm objectivity disappeared and he ran toward the next cairn, stumbling through the grass. In this world, at this moment, he was no longer the toolmaker who ruled all living things. It was humbling to realize how vulnerable humans were: a weak little primate with small teeth and useless fingernails.

When he reached the cairn, he gazed back across the meadow and saw the three predators feasting on their victim. A blood-red patch appeared in the middle of the green. And now he thought of the creature's wings—wings of flesh, like a bat. With the addition of an eagle's head, this creature would have looked like the legendary griffin. And what about the horses? The bony ridge on the forehead made them resemble unicorns.

Generations of Travelers had visited this Eden and then returned to the human world. Their stories had become transformed into myths and legends; the unicorn was a medieval symbol of purity, and images of the griffin decorated swords and palaces. But the power of such symbols had concealed the origin of the tales; the myths were a link to these parallel worlds.

* * *

THE PATH REAPPEARED at the edge of the plateau and followed a brook that meandered down from the hills. Huge trees with rough gray bark had thrust their roots into the soil and formed their own kingdom of green. Their branches were so heavy that they bent nearly to the ground, forming a canopy that sheltered the earth from the sunlight. The trees grew fruit that reminded Gabriel of dried figs, and provided nourishment for songbirds and small animals that resembled squirrels.

There was a flowery, sweet smell in the air. Gabriel sat beside the brook to gaze up at the trees. Entering into their slow sense of the world was like stepping into an enormous cathedral with dark spaces and light filtered through the panes of a stained-glass window. The trees were indifferent to time, but were aware of the squirrels scrambling through their branches, scratching the bark, and squeaking in triumph when they found something to eat.

Gabriel knelt to drink and splash water on his face. When he opened his eyes, he noticed something for the first time. A stick about two feet high had been shoved into the dirt. Someone—or something—had marked this point.

He walked in a spiral around the stick and found a second stick about fifty yards away. Someone was leaving signposts to the passageway.

He was cautious now, moving quietly as he tried to stay hidden in the undergrowth. Following the stick markers, he headed up the slope to a line of red cliffs that looked out over the trees. The cliffs had cracked and eroded over time, and there was a pile of debris that looked as if an hourglass had shattered and all the sand had dribbled out onto the ground.

A trail cut through this pile of talus and then zigzagged up the cliff to the mouth of a cave. Something was hiding in the darkness. He could sense the creature's consciousness—feel its cruelty and intelligence. *Run away*, he told himself. But then the creature in the cave felt his presence and stepped outside.

Gabriel looked up the slope at his brother.

21

Michael ducked back into the cave. When he reappeared, he had a talisman sword slung over his shoulder. Both brothers were aware of the distance between them. Even if Michael charged down the pathway, Gabriel would have enough time to get away.

"Well, this is a surprise," Michael said. "I start looking for one Traveler and find the other."

"Is Dad here?"

"No. But someone was living in this cave for a while. They built a fire near the entrance. Maybe they wanted to keep the animals away."

Michael took a few steps forward and Gabriel retreated. "You think I want to kill you?"

"Seems like a good possibility."

"So why aren't you carrying your sword? Did you forget to bring a weapon?"

"I'm not taking that kind of journey."

Michael laughed. "You really haven't changed. You always were a dreamer. When we were in Los Angeles, you spent all your time in a daze—reading books and cruising around on that motorcycle."

"We can't change who we are, Michael. But we can make choices about how we're going to live our lives."

"You're wrong about that. I've changed completely . . ." Once again, Michael took a few steps down the slope. "When we were kids, all I wanted was to fit in and be like everyone else at school. Remember when I took that job at Sloane's hardware store?"

"You wanted to buy blue jeans."

"No, I wanted the *right* kind of jeans and the *right* kind of shoes—all the stuff that everybody else was wearing."

"It didn't make a difference."

"Correct. I bought the clothes, but other kids still thought we were strange. It took me a long time, but I finally learned my lesson: I'm *not* like everyone else. I've been to the Fifth Realm and talked to the half gods. Now I understand that the only reality in all six realms is *power*. And you demonstrate your power whenever you control another person's life."

"Do you really believe that?"

"It's not a belief, Gabe. The half gods have discarded all this idealistic bullshit. They see what's true."

"You shouldn't trust them."

"Oh, I don't." Michael laughed. "The half gods are jealous of me, jealous of all Travelers. They're trapped in their particular reality and they want a way out. So I'm using them to get what I want. They've already sent us the design for a new computer chip that will help create the Panopticon."

"You can build all the computers you want. People aren't going to follow you."

"Of course they will. I just have to give humanity a little push in the right direction. Maybe your new friends don't want to live on the grid, but everyone else wants that feeling of security. As long as you leave up the window dressing—the superficial trappings of freedom—people are more than happy to give up the real thing."

"Some of us know what's going on."

"So what? You can't stop the transformation." Michael took another step forward. "The group with the most power always wins. That seems pretty damn clear to me."

"The kind of victories you're talking about fade away in a few years. The walls crumble and people pull the statues down. Our world is pushed forward by compassion, hope, and creativity. Everything else turns to dust."

"Say whatever you want, Gabe. You're still going to lose."

Gabriel looked up at Michael, feeling the dark energy within his brother. They were connected, but apart—like two particles in a single atom that would explode if they came in contact with each other. Turning away, he headed down the hill. It was only when he reached the trees that he looked over his shoulder and made sure that Michael wasn't following him.

Alone, he passed through the tall grass and returned to the shore.

22

As the hired car left the Inter-
Continental Hotel in Bangkok, Nathan Boone told his driver to
turn up the air conditioner and direct the vent toward the backseat. The hotel concierge had given him a bottle of chilled water,
but Boone took only a few sips. He didn't want to use the bathroom at the prison and would avoid touching anything while he
was there.

The car traveled a few blocks, eased into an intersection, and
jerked to a stop. They were surrounded by pickup trucks, motorcycles, and *tuk-tuks*, the garishly painted auto-rickshaws that carried
people around the city. A traffic officer in a white uniform stood on

a box and waved his hands, but everyone cheerfully ignored him.
Street peddlers threaded between the stalled cars, tapping on the
windows. They were selling coconut slices and lottery tickets, neon-
green condoms, and a rooster in a bamboo cage that squawked and
flapped its wings as if he knew he was about to be plucked.

After much horn-beeping, the car cut around a stalled truck
and glided past a food stand dotted with flies. A prostitute wearing a pink minidress pressed her palms together and made a *wai*
gesture to two Buddhist monks. An old woman reached into a
plastic bucket and pulled out a live squid. The smell of car exhaust and fried food pushed into the car and Boone couldn't escape the noise. When the *tuk-tuks* raced past, it sounded like an
army of lawn mowers roaring in a concrete canyon.

* * *

FOR THE LAST six years Boone had been allowed to hire his own
employees without oversight from the executive board. It was his
job to protect the Brethren and destroy their enemies. Both Kennard Nash and Mrs. Brewster preferred not to know the specific
aspects of Boone's activities.

Everything had changed since Michael's speech to the
Brethren. The Special Projects Group was organizing events in several different countries, but Boone didn't know the details. He had
been sent to Thailand to find an American named Martin Doyle
who was serving time in a prison near Bangkok. Boone had no
problem with that particular responsibility. What bothered him
was the phone call he received from Michael Corrigan.

"The Special Projects Group has given me the file on Mr.
Doyle," Michael said. "He's a difficult individual, but he's suited
for a particular job."

"I understand."

"Hire him. Put him on a plane back to America. And . . ."

There was a hissing noise on the phone and Boone lost contact with London.

"Hello? Mr. Corrigan? I didn't hear you."

"Make an *impression*, Mr. Boone. Make sure he's completely under our control."

"And how am I supposed to do that?"

"It's not my job to figure out every little problem."

*   *   *

IT TOOK AN hour to reach Klong Dan Prison, a large area sur-rounded by guard towers and a brick wall. Boone told the driver to wait in the parking lot and walked into a three-story adminis-trative building with lattice balconies on the upper floors. He mentioned Captain Tansiri's name to a guard and was immedi-ately ushered into a waiting room crowded with women and chil-dren waiting to see the prisoners. The room smelled of sweat and soiled diapers. Babies screamed as old ladies ate from plastic con-tainers filled with shredded papaya and bean sprouts.

When prisoners appeared on a television screen near a door in the waiting room, everyone shouted to one another and rushed in-side. For a few seconds, Boone stood alone in the middle of the room and contemplated a pair of discarded chopsticks.

"Mr. Boone?"

He faced a Thai prison guard wearing a tan uniform that was too large for his skinny body. The guard took a cigarette out of his mouth and grinned, displaying an array of teeth that looked like chunks of yellowed ivory.

"You must be Captain Tansiri."

"Yes, sir. We just received a call from the minister's office. They said you might drop by for a visit."

"I'm here to see Martin Doyle."

Tansiri looked surprised. "Are you from the embassy?"

"I work for the Department of Homeland Security." Boone reached into his left shirt pocket and took out a fake ID card. "We have reason to believe that Mr. Doyle has information about ter-rorist activity."

"I think someone was misinformed. There is nothing political about Mr. Doyle. He is just a very bad person. Don't you know why he's here?"

The Special Projects Group had only sent Doyle's name and location. Boone assumed that the American was being held on a drug charge. "Perhaps you could give me the details."

"We think he kidnapped and killed several children in the Khian Sa district."

Boone was so surprised he couldn't hide his reaction. "He killed children?"

"Well, technically, there was no evidence, but children would disappear when he was near a village. The police watched him for several months and were not successful. Mr. Doyle was far too clever."

"So why is he in prison?"

"They arrested him on a passport charge and the judge gave him the maximum sentence." Captain Tansiri looked satisfied. "This is Thailand. We solve our problems with foreigners."

"That's a good policy, Captain. But it's probably best if I talk to Mr. Doyle and get some information about what happened."

"Of course, sir. Please follow me."

The captain led Boone into a visitor's room divided in half by a barrier of steel bars, wire mesh, and Plexiglas. Two children knelt on the floor and played with a toy dump truck while family members used phone handsets to talk to the prisoners. Tansiri unlocked a door and they entered a much smaller room where five Thai men sat on benches, gossiping and smoking cigarettes. They wore flip-flops, dark brown shorts, and T-shirts. Each man had either a homemade club or a short whip lying on the bench beside him.

"We have too many prisoners and a very small staff. These trustees help us run an efficient operation."

Boone noticed that three of the men had knives concealed beneath their T-shirts. The trustees were the power here. If this place was run like most third-world prisons, then they were far more dangerous than the guards.

The trustees followed them into a corridor lined with prison cells about twelve feet wide and twenty feet deep. Each cell had a squat toilet, a water jug, and a television mounted on a wall bracket. There were no beds.

"This is where the prisoners are locked in at night. Each cell contains about fifty prisoners."

"That's quite a few people, Captain. How do you squeeze them all in?"

"They sleep sideways—one man's head to another man's feet. If you pay a small sum to the trustees, you can sleep on your back."

"And how does Mr. Doyle sleep?"

"He has a mattress and a pillow."

"So how does he pay for that? Does he get money from somewhere?"

"Mr. Doyle has no friends, and we have not heard from his family. He makes a few *baht* doing translations for the other prisoners. Without such work he would have to eat the prison food and bathe in the prison shower room. In a city where people squint, you must squint, too."

Captain Tansiri unlocked the final door and they stepped into a prison yard. Around the perimeter of the yard, people had set up shops, selling medicine, fruit juices, and food cooked on a propane stove. It was about one o'clock in the afternoon, and the sun burned down on the packed dirt and dead grass. A few of the younger men kicked a soccer ball back and forth, but most of the prisoners sat in the shade of the main building, gossiping and playing cards.

As their little group walked across the yard, Boone considered why he had been picked for this particular assignment. Michael Corrigan must have looked at his file and found out what happened many years ago. Perhaps the trip to Thailand was just an elaborate way to test his loyalty.

Martin Doyle sat on a plastic barrel and used a packing crate as a desk. He was writing something on a notepad while one of his translation clients sat on a second barrel. Doyle was a big man with black wavy hair and full lips. At one point of his life, he might have been handsome, but now he had a bloated, fleshy appearance.

Boone stopped in the middle of the yard and motioned to Captain Tansiri. "I'd like a private conversation with Mr. Doyle."

"Of course, sir. I understand. We will remain in the area in case you . . ." The captain tried to think of something polite to say. "In case you require assistance."

As Boone approached the packing case, Doyle finished his translation. He took a few *baht* from the Thai prisoner, and then flicked his hand like a potentate telling a servant to go away.

"Welcome to my office," he said to Boone. "You don't look like a prisoner, so I'm going to assume that you're from the embassy."

Over the years, Boone had learned how to talk to people who might want to kill him. Be polite and slightly formal, but never show weakness. If you think someone has a concealed weapon, then watch his hands. If the man is unarmed, then watch their shoulders. A person who wants to punch or strangle you will usually hunch up his shoulders before an attack.

"I'm sorry to disappoint you, but I have no connection with the American embassy."

"I have sent over twenty letters to the ambassador."

"Perhaps your case isn't a high priority."

Boone sat down on the plastic barrel and placed a fake business card on the packing crate. "I'm Nathan Boone, a field officer for Active Solutions, Ltd. We're a privately held security firm with offices in Moscow, Johannesburg, and Buenos Aires."

Doyle studied the card for a few seconds and snorted loudly. "Sounds like a bunch of mercenaries."

"We hire, train, and supervise former police and military personnel. They're paid to deal with a wide range of security problems."

"Look, I've been all over the world—Africa, Asia, and South America. I've met people like you before and I know what you do. You kill people and get away with it. Don't worry. I'm okay with that."

Something scurried up Doyle's right arm to his shoulder. It was a gray mouse with a long tail. Cautiously, the mouse crept up to the base of Doyle's neck. Its black eyes stared at the prisoner's lips. Meanwhile a second mouse crawled up Doyle's leg to the left pocket of his jeans. The quick movements of the two rodents made it appear as if Doyle was a large and powerful creature with little bits of life clinging to him.

"My pets," Doyle explained. "The men here keep scorpions for fighting, but you can do more things with mice." Doyle plucked the first mouse off his shoulder. Holding it by its tail, he let the animal swing frantically in the air. "You like mice, Mr. Boone?"

"Not especially."

Doyle opened an empty matchbox and dropped the mouse inside. "You're missing out on a lot of fun."

Boone had never been scared of any kind of animal, but the mice made him uncomfortable. There was a demon inside Doyle's head that wanted control over anything that was small and defenseless. Doyle winked at Boone and then plucked the second mouse off his lap. Holding its tail, he raised it up above his head and opened his mouth as if he was going to swallow the creature.

"Think I won't do it? Huh? Pay me a couple hundred *baht* and I will."

Boone shrugged as if he received offers like this all the time. "Not worth it."

"Just kidding . . ." Doyle opened a second matchbox and dropped the mouse inside. "So why does someone from Active Solutions want to talk to me?"

"We want to know if you would be interested in working for our company."

"Sure. But if you haven't noticed, I'm locked up in this shit-hole."

"I think I could arrange for you to be expelled from Thailand and placed on a chartered plane. At the end of the employment period, you will be given a new passport and fifty thousand dollars in cash."

"Great! I'm your man. Where do I sign?"

"You don't have to sign anything, but you do need to be clear about the conditions of your employment in the United States. If hired, you will follow my orders without question and work with other individuals on the team."

"What's the job?"

"It would involve those activities that placed you in this prison."

Doyle laughed. "All this was just a lot of bureaucratic bullshit. I overstayed my visa. No big deal."

"I know why you're here."

"All right, I confess." Doyle chuckled. "I screwed up and bought a fake passport stamp from this guy who promised me that—"

"I know why you're here," Boone repeated. "As do the police in the Khian Sa district."

Doyle jumped up and knocked over the packing crate. The two matchboxes fell onto the ground. "And who the hell are you? An FBI agent? Some kind of cop? I'm not talking to anyone without a lawyer."

"Sit down, Mr. Doyle."

Doyle stood there, breathing hard, and then sat back down on the barrel. The trustees were standing about ten feet away. They looked disappointed that they couldn't use their whips and clubs.

"My company has been asked to run a somewhat unusual operation," Boone said. "I don't know all the facts, but I'm going to assume that it requires someone with your particular *skills*."

"What the hell are you talking about? What skills?"

"My employers want to cause fear—and then panic—in a certain region of the United States. Your activities would help us achieve that goal."

"Forget it. You're just setting me up to be arrested."

"That's a false assumption, Mr. Doyle. It's in our interest to protect you. The fear remains in the population only if you don't get caught."

Doyle stared down at the dirt for a few seconds, his shoulders twitching. When he glanced at Boone, the demon was under control. "I'm not going to do this."

"I hope nothing happens to your work as a translator." Boone stood up as if he was about to leave. "Without the money, you'll have to sleep on a concrete floor with someone's feet in your face."

"Hold it!" Doyle said. "Just—hold it." Doyle's hands opened and closed, again and again.

"I'll do this if you get me out of here."

"Do what, Mr. Doyle? And don't tell me stories about passport violations."

"It'll be just like what happened in the Khian Sa district. I'll make people scared—really scared—when their children disappear."

No, you won't, Boone thought. *You'll try to run away at the first opportunity.* But there were ways around that.

"You're now an employee of Active Solutions. Don't mention this conversation to anyone. We'll be in touch."

Boone headed back across the yard. Over the years, he had hired hundreds of mercenaries for the Brethren. He didn't care what they had done in the past as long as they obeyed orders. Some members of his team had killed the children at New Harmony, but what happened there was as precise and organized as a well-run military operation; his men had their assignments and they completed them without emotion. But Martin Doyle bothered him. The Panopticon was about order and control, and there was nothing controlled about Doyle's actions. He was the living embodiment of the perverse randomness that existed in the world.

Boone was moving so fast that Captain Tansiri had to run to catch up with him. "Is everything all right, sir?"

"No problem. Thank you for your assistance."

"Perhaps you could join me for refreshments in the officers lounge. It's air-conditioned and the prisoners won't be there—aside from the serving staff."

"Sorry. I've got an appointment in Bangkok."

A prisoner in rags was squatting in the middle of the yard. As Boone passed, the prisoner glanced up and it was *her*—her face—here in this fragment of hell. No. Blink your eyes. *No.* And the vision dissolved into a toothless old man, raising his cupped hands as he begged for money.

23

Hollis woke up from a dream and found himself in a cold, dark room. There were no streetlights in the village of Shukunegi, and Billy Hirano's aunt turned off everything electrical before she went to sleep. Back in Los Angeles, Hollis could always hear traffic noise or a police siren. Now the only sound came from the wind whistling through a crack in the shutters.

He slid his hand across the quilt and then reached out to touch the handgun lying near the edge of the tatami mat. The weapon reminded him that he was still a fugitive. Hollis breathed deeply and tried to relax, but at that moment it felt as if sleep was in a far-off land and he didn't know how to travel there. And then the memory of the Itako chanting and clicking her prayer beads returned to him. He could still recall the old woman's dead eyes as Vicki's voice emerged from her body.

* * *

AFTER THE ITAKO finished the ritual, Hollis walked out of the house. For several months, a continual anger had directed his actions and given him a fierce power. Now that anger was gone, and he felt tired and confused. Billy Hirano stared at him as he stood in the middle of the country road. Exhaust drifted from the taxi's tailpipe, but Hollis didn't get back in the car.

"I need to stay out of sight for a while," Hollis said. "Do you know a good hiding place?"

Billy looked like a doctor who had just been asked a complicated medical question. Shoving his hands in his pockets, he paced around for a few seconds, then kicked a stone into the roadside ditch. "It is dangerous to hide in a Japanese city. There are police everywhere, and they would notice you. In a village, people would also have questions. But maybe I could take you to Sado Island."

"Where's that?"

"It's off the west coast of Japan. My aunt lives there in a village called Shukunegi. There are thousands of tourists on the island every summer, but right now it's just the fishermen."

"So what is she going to say when I show up?"

"They have television sets in Shukunegi, but they only get one channel. It's a village of old people. They watch the game shows, but they don't care about the news."

"I'm still going to stick out in that location."

"Of course you will." Billy grinned. "You'll be a new source of entertainment. Watching foreigners make mistakes is a traditional Japanese pastime. But on the islands, people live their own lives. They do not like to talk to the police."

The rest of the day, they took a series of regional train lines over the mountains to western Japan. The fields were covered with long sheets of white plastic as if the soil had to be gradually introduced to sunshine. All the train conductors stared at the black foreigner, but Billy told them that Hollis was an American choreographer who had come to Japan to study traditional dancing.

During the ferry ride over to Sado Island, the boat passed through flurries of snow and rain. At one point, the sun broke through the thick cloud cover and light streamed down on the gray-green ocean like a shaft of divine energy. Hollis doubted if anyone saw it; the other passengers on the boat lay on the floor of a carpeted television room dozing or staring at music videos. He wondered if that was the true secret of history: great changes occurred in the world, but most people spent their lives half asleep.

"What happens when we reach the island?"

"We take a bus to the village and meet my aunt Kimiko."

"What if she doesn't like me?"

"You are my friend, Hollis. That is all I need to say. We are guests for the first few days, and then we have to work."

* * *

THEY ARRIVED AT Shukunegi in the evening. The village was a settlement of about fifty homes squeezed into a coastal canyon. At the mouth of the canyon the fishermen had built a bamboo wall with a pair of gates at the center. The wall made the village look like a fort built to resist barbarian invaders, but the real enemies were the ice storms that roared out of Siberia and hit the western side of the island.

Billy led Hollis through the gates and into the village. The modern two-story houses had electricity and running water, but they were built very close to one another, with dirt passageways between the buildings. A stream ran through Shukunegi; the sound of rushing water mingled with the wind and the faint echo of laughter from a television set in someone's home.

Following the stream up the canyon, they walked past a com-

munity center and a sprawling graveyard filled with statues of the
Buddha and lichen-covered gravestones. Aunt Kimiko's two-story
home was in the middle of the graveyard, toward the end of the
canyon. Like many of the villagers, she had placed a black rock on
each roof tile. The rocks were supposed to keep the wind from ripping up the tiles, but they made the roof look like an odd board
game that was waiting for players.

There were no locks on any of the houses in the village—only
wooden latches. Billy slipped off his muddy shoes and then entered the house without knocking. Hollis remained alone on the
doorstep and listened to a woman's voice coming from within. The
voice was high-pitched and happy, as if Billy's arrival was an unexpected gift. A few minutes later, an elderly Japanese woman—
as small as a child—hurried to the door, bowing and welcoming
her guest.

* * *

BILLY SPENT A few days on the island before returning to Tokyo.
He would talk to the other men who danced to rock-and-roll music in the park and see if there was a safe way for a foreigner to
slip out of Japan. Hollis explored Shukunegi and quickly found a
job that would help the village. A brick retaining wall at the base
of the cliff was beginning to collapse. Using Aunt Kimiko's tools,
he would tear the wall down and build a new one. The fact that a
strong foreigner had agreed to do a difficult job for free made the
villagers very happy.

Aunt Kimiko woke around six in the morning. She would serve
Hollis a breakfast of sticky rice, miso soup, and one dish that was
always a surprise. Once she presented him with an enormous sea
snail and watched him rip the salty brown flesh out of the black
shell. After Hollis finished breakfast, he performed some martial
arts exercises, then carried his tools over to the retaining wall. Usually, two or three old women wearing pink rubber boots would
sit on benches and watch him work. Hollis had never been so
conscious of his own body, the strength of his arms and legs.

Whenever he lifted something heavy, the old women murmured to one another and clapped their hands to show approval.

Working every day calmed him down and brought some order to his life. First he dug a trench, then he began to lay bricks, filling the cavity behind the wall with buckets of gravel he had taken from the beach. Hollis was slow and deliberate with each part of the job, using a length of twine to make sure the foundation was level. As he mixed concrete and slapped it on the bricks, he began to see his past choices with a new sense of clarity.

Vicki had told him that he was on the right path. *"If you remember who you are, you'll know what to do."*

So who am I? Hollis wondered. Back in Los Angeles, he had taught his students never to use violence for negative goals. The true warrior used both mind and heart. The true warrior was calm within, not ruled by anger. He remembered standing on a London rooftop with a sniper rifle and felt ashamed.

More bricks and more mortar. Build the wall higher. Straight and true.

* * *

IT WAS HIS fifteenth day in the village. After working on the wall in the morning, he ate some rice and tempura and wandered through the graveyard that surrounded the houses. Dead flowers. Old coins in a rusty kettle filled with rainwater. A line of chubby stone Buddhas with white cotton caps and little bibs tied around their necks.

He went out the gate, and then walked along the tide line to a black sand beach littered with plastic bottles, automobile tires, and all the other debris of the modern world. Pine trees clung to the rocks like bonsai, and the waves fell softly onto the shore.

Know this, my love . . . Believe this, my love . . . the Light survives. Vicki had traveled a long way to tell him that and now it was the foundation of his faith. If someone truly thought you were a good person, it could change you forever. Perhaps that's why God had created holy men and women. They saw the Light within others, and sometimes that inspired people to live up to an ideal.

Gabriel couldn't have known about the brave bookseller and the yakuza with the gun and the killing in the hotel room, but perhaps he had seen the general direction of Hollis's journey. *Who am I?* Hollis asked himself again. He would always be a warrior, but now he needed to be fighting for something more important than revenge. Staring out at the waves, he felt as if he had cut away all the clutter and confusion that had held back his understanding. *If you remember who you are, you'll know what to do.*

"Hollis!"

He spun around and saw Billy Hirano striding down the beach. Billy must have bought a fresh tube of hair gel in Tokyo—every hair of his Elvis pompadour was in its proper position.

"These old people like you. My aunt says you are a good worker. If you want, you can stay here forever."

"Your aunt is a wonderful person, but I need to move on."

"Yeah. I thought you would say that. I talked to some people. There is a safe way for you to get out of Japan. We take a ferry down to Okinawa and the southwest islands. If you pay enough money, the fishing boats will carry you anywhere you want—Taiwan, the Philippines, even Australia."

"Sounds like a plan."

"These villagers will miss you." Billy smiled. "I will miss you, too. It is very cool to know a Harlequin."

"I wanted to talk about that, Billy. Now that we're friends, I can tell you my Harlequin name . . ."

He was still Hollis for a few more seconds. Gazing out at the horizon, he felt very aware of this choice. He was giving up all attachments, a normal life.

"My Harlequin name is Priest."

"*Priest.* Yes. Very good." Billy looked satisfied. "I never really thought you were called Hollis."

24

Boone arrived with his team half an hour before Martin Doyle was supposed to be released from prison. The motorcycle riders zoomed up and down the road a few times, and then everyone waited beneath a banyan tree growing in a field across from the prison parking lot. Children, small and delicate, climbed the branches of the tree and gazed down at the three Thai men and the three foreigners. One of the little girls wore a garland of flowers around her neck. She plucked off the orange and yellow petals and watched them flutter to the muddy ground.

The motorcycle riders were Thai military policemen who wore

jeans and flashy silk shirts instead of their uniforms. They stood beside their bikes smoking cigarettes and avoiding eye contact with Boone and the two Australian mercenaries.

The older Australian was a chunky little man named Tommy Squires who followed directions and got drunk only when the job was over. Tommy had brought along a friend named Ryan Horsley. Boone was starting to dislike the young man. Horsley was an ex-rugby player who thought he was tough. There was nothing particularly wrong with that idea, but Horsley also thought he was clever—and that was a sad error. Boone always preferred employees who were smart enough to be aware of their own stupidity.

The heat and humidity made everyone feel slow. The policemen bought fruit drinks from a road vendor while Squires and Horsley inspected the lances. One of Boone's contacts had purchased the lances in Singapore, where they were called ECCDs—Electrified Crowd-Control Devices. They were six-foot-long white plastic poles with blunt ends. When the tip came into contact with a human being and was compressed slightly, it delivered a 50,000-volt shock.

In China, the ECCDs were used for breaking up demonstrations in which the crowd locked arms or sat down in the street. The problem with Tasers or pepper spray was that the demonstrators never knew when the officer was going to pull the trigger. If a crowd encountered a line of policemen carrying Plexiglas shields and ECCDs, they could see their punishment heading down the street, getting closer, a little closer. When the tip of the lance was jabbed at their faces, they would usually panic and run.

Boone took out a pair of compact binoculars and scrutinized the prison administration building. A Thai driver named Sunchai had parked his delivery van near the entrance. Boone checked his watch. If everything went according to schedule, Doyle would be released in five or ten minutes.

"You ready?" he asked the Australians. "We'll wait until the van pulls out of the parking lot, then follow about one hundred meters behind. I know it's hot, but make sure you wear the motorcycle

helmets. I don't want Doyle to glance in the rearview mirror and
see three foreigners."

"So when is he going to break and run?" Horsley asked.

"I don't know. With traffic, it's a two-hour drive from here to
the airport."

"But he's definitely going to do it?"

"Very few things in life are definite, Mr. Horsley."

"This whole thing doesn't make sense. When he strolls out of
the building, we should cuff the wanker, pull a sack over his head,
and toss him in the van. Instead we're going to ride around holding these pig stickers."

Squires raised his hands like someone trying to stop a runaway
shopping cart. "Ryan doesn't mean to offend, Mr. Boone. He's just
the curious type."

"What if your neighbor owned a vicious dog?" Boone asked.
"And what if he let his dog wander freely around the neighborhood? Don't you think that would be irresponsible?"

"You bet it would," Horsley said. "I'd take a shovel and kill the
brute."

"We don't want to kill Mr. Doyle. But we want to show him
that negative actions have negative consequences."

"I get the picture," Squire said and turned to his younger
friend. "This is just like what they taught us back in church school.
We want this bastard to feel the wrath of a righteous god."

Boone's handheld computer began to beep, so he walked
around the tree and leaned against the trunk. His staff in London
had sent him an urgent message: *HSC Columba. Images attached.*

Three months earlier, Boone and Michael had left Skellig
Columba with Matthew Corrigan's body. Before the helicopter returned to the mainland, Boone sent one of his men down to the island's dock to install an HSC—a hidden surveillance camera. The
device was battery powered and had a solar chip for recharging. It
would send images only if a motion detector triggered the shutter.

A red flower petal landed on Boone's shoulder. He glanced up
at the branch above him, and two little girls giggled at his reaction.
The tree was filled with children, and more children were squat-

ting on the dirt in front of him. Boone tried to ignore them as he studied the eighteen images attached to the e-mail. In the first few photographs, an old man arrived on the island in a fishing boat and began unloading supply containers. In the sixth photo, a group of nuns was standing on the dock. It must have been windy that day; their cloaks and veils were flapping wildly. The nuns looked like giant black birds about to fly off into the clouds.

In the fourteenth image, a new person appeared in the camera frame: an Asian girl wearing jeans and a quilt jacket. Boone placed a grid over the girl's face and made the image larger. Yes, he knew her. It was the child he had encountered in the classroom building at New Harmony. She had disappeared into the New York subway tunnels with Maya and ended up on the island.

The girl in the quilt jacket was a threat to the Brethren's security. If her story appeared on the Internet it would challenge the carefully prepared explanation of what had happened at New Harmony. According to the Arizona state police, a dangerous cult had destroyed itself, and no one in the media had challenged that theory.

The solution to the problem was clear, but Boone didn't feel like giving the order. This was all Martin Doyle's fault; he was a blister that wouldn't go away. For six years, Boone had tried to establish the Brethren's vision. The electronic Panopticon was supposed to usher in a new kind of society where people like Doyle would be tracked, identified, and destroyed. But now a demon was being set free, and Boone was the man unlocking the prison door.

The handheld computer beeped again as if it were demanding a response. Boone switched on his satellite phone and called Gerry Westcott, the head of operations in London.

"I saw the images from the island."

"Did you recognize the Asian girl?" Westcott asked. "She's also in the surveillance photos taken in the New York subway."

"I don't want a termination," Boone said. "We need an acquisition so that I can question her."

"That might be difficult."

"You have ten or twelve hours to get it organized. If they're going to London, they'll ride the ferry from Dublin to Holyhead."

"I agree. It's too risky to take the plane."

"Give me updates every three hours. Thank you."

As Boone switched off the phone, a flower petal fluttered down and landed on the top of his head. All the children giggled loudly as Boone flicked the petal away.

"Excuse me, sir." Squires stood in front of him. "I think Mr. Doyle is coming out of the prison . . ."

Boone took out his binoculars and circled the trunk of the banyan tree. Captain Tansiri had just escorted Doyle from the administration building, and the big American was climbing into the delivery van.

"That him?" Horsley looked like a boy about to go hunting.

Boone nodded. "Let's get ready."

The three foreigners put on the motorcycle helmets, grabbed the lances, and climbed onto the motorcycles behind the Thai riders. Seconds later, they were following the van as it headed toward the Bangkok airport. Nothing happened for the first few miles. The van moved slowly down a two-lane road past thatch-roofed houses and vegetable gardens. Boone's helmet didn't have any vents, and sweat trickled down his neck.

"This bird's not going to fly," Horsley said into his radio headset. "Maybe he sees us with these pig stickers."

"Stay on the bike," Boone said. "We're following him all the way to the airport."

About twenty miles from the prison, the van entered a large town that appeared to specialize in the manufacture and sale of silk fabric. Crimson dye trickled out of a home workshop and flowed into the gutter. Lengths of silk dried on backyard clotheslines—the fabric so thin and delicate that sunlight made the colors glow. Once again, Boone found himself thinking about the Asian girl standing on the dock with the nuns.

There was a marketplace in the middle of the town filled with wooden booths the size of small closets, carts piled high with manufactured goods, and women squatting behind pyramids of oranges. The van stopped to let an oxcart pass. All of a sudden, Doyle climbed out of the van. He wasn't frightened of the driver or worried about the police. He shouted a threat over his shoulder and sauntered through the crowd.

"Mr. Horsley goes first," Boone said into the headset, and the Australian slapped his rider's shoulder. The motorcycle took off—its back tire spitting off flecks of red mud. Doyle heard the engine above the din of the market. He stopped, twisted his head around, and saw a man with a tinted helmet and a white staff speeding toward him like a knight on the battlefield.

The fugitive began running. He stepped behind a young woman with a basket of peppers balanced on her head, but she saw the bike approaching and flung herself to one side. The lance hit Doyle on his left shoulder blade. It was just a brief shock, but it made the American stagger.

Squires attacked a few seconds later, hitting Doyle in the lower back. This time, Doyle fell to his knees as the bike continued past him. The fugitive looked back and saw that Boone was about a hundred feet away, lowering the lance into a horizontal position. In a few seconds, he was back on his feet and stumbling down a narrow pathway between two stalls.

Boone grabbed his rider's belt and held on with one hand as the bike skidded in the mud. They made the turn and roared through the gap. Doyle was about twenty yards ahead of them—his head down, his arms extended as if he wanted to run on all fours. As the motorcycle got closer he dodged to the left, but Boone's lance hit the big man's leg and the shock flung him forward.

The two Australians reached the site and jumped off their bikes. Boone decided that more pain would teach a stronger lesson, so he let them jab their lances a dozen times. Doyle rolled in the mud like an epileptic having a seizure. "It's the righteous god!" Squires shouted. "Feel that righteous god!"

* * *

A LOCAL POLICEMAN ran up, but the riders showed their military identification and announced that they had just arrested a terrorist. The van arrived a minute later, and plastic restraints were placed on Doyle's wrists, arms, and legs. Finally, he was gagged with a swatch of duct tape and loaded into the van like a slab of meat.

"Tell the riders to take you back to the hotel," Boone told Squires. "Your money will arrive tomorrow morning."

"Yes, sir. Is there any other way we can help you?"

"Tell Mr. Horsley to keep his mouth shut."

Boone got in the back of the van and told the driver to head to the airport. Then he took a syringe out of his shoulder bag and jabbed it into a vial filled with a powerful tranquilizer. Doyle was lying on this back. His eyes rolled wildly when he saw the needle.

"When you wake up in America, you'll have a wound on your right hand and another on the middle of your chest. We're going to insert tracer beads between your skin and muscle. These devices will tell us where you are at all times."

The syringe was full. When Boone leaned forward, Doyle moaned; he was trying to open his mouth and say something.

"If you run again, I'll hunt you down just like we did today. You can't escape, Doyle. It's just not possible. I'm going to watch you until your task is done."

25

Alice Chen decided that she was still the Warrior Princess of Skellig Columba. Through no fault of her own, she had been taken prisoner by the Queen of Darkness and was being transported to the City of Doom.

She held this vision in her mind for about ten minutes, and then the tea cart rattled down the corridor of the train. Alice opened her eyes and found herself sitting in their train compartment while Sister Joan read a leather-bound breviary. Although Sister Joan was dressed in black, she was definitely not the Queen of Darkness. Instead she was a fat nun with spectacles who cooked delicious scones and got all weepy when someone read a news story about a brave dog who saved his family from a house fire.

And Alice knew she wasn't any kind of princess. According to the nuns, she was a disobedient little girl who had been given chance after chance to behave in a decent manner. It was bad enough that Sister Maura found her leaping across the cliffs, but when Alice was marched back to the convent, the butcher knife had fallen out of her belt. That evening she had waited upstairs in the sleeping room while the nuns prayed for Alice's soul and discussed the problem in hushed voices. Finally, it was decided: Alice would be taken to Tyburn Convent in London and put under the supervision of the Benedictine nuns. After inquiries were made, she would be sent to a Catholic girls' school—probably one called St. Ann's in Wales.

"This will be better, dear," Sister Ruth explained. "You need to be around girls your own age."

"Field hockey!" Sister Faustina said with her big, booming voice. "Field hockey and proper games! No more jumping around with knives!"

It was easy for the Tabula to monitor air travel, so Sister Joan and Alice rode local buses across Ireland and caught the ferryboat from Dublin to Holyhead. Now they were on a train to London, and Maya would meet them at the station.

Sister Joan had packed the geometry textbook in Alice's knapsack. If Alice wandered around the train and bothered the conductors, she would have to read the chapter on right angles as punishment. Sitting by the window, she stared at the little Welsh towns and tried to pronounce their names. Penmaenmawr. Abergele and Pensarn. Thick clouds covered the sky, but the Welsh were outside plowing fields and hanging up laundry. Alice saw a farmer shoveling feed into a trough for a mother pig and her babies. The pigs were white with black spots—not like the pink ones she had seen in America.

Crewe was the last stop before London. So far, they had been alone in the compartment, but a crowd of people got on the train, and Alice watched them pass down the outside corridor. As the train lurched forward and left the station, a stout woman in her sixties with dyed-black hair pulled open the sliding door and checked the seat numbers. "Sorry to bother you. But we have a reservation for two seats."

"Do we need to move?" Sister Joan asked politely.

"Heavens, no. You got on earlier—so you get the windows." The stout woman stepped back into the corridor and spoke like she was calling her dog. "Here, Malcolm! No, it's here!"

A pudgy man wearing a tweed suit appeared in the doorway. He was pushing a large black suitcase on wheels. Alice decided to call the two intruders "Mr. and Mrs. Fireplug" because they reminded her of fire hydrants—short and stocky, with flushed red faces.

The woman entered the compartment first, followed by her husband. He puffed and groaned and finally got the big suitcase up in the overhead rack. Then he sat down beside Alice and beamed at Sister Joan.

"You two traveling to London?"

"It's the only stop left," Alice snapped.

"Why, yes. You're right about that. But, of course, there are *connections*." Mr. Fireplug pronounced this last word with a great deal of satisfaction.

"We're going on," explained Mrs. Fireplug. "We'll see my sister in London, and then fly on to the Costa Brava where our daughter has an apartment."

"Sun and fun," said Mr. Fireplug. "But not too much sun or I'll look like a raspberry."

When the conductor came in to take tickets, Alice leaned forward and whispered to Sister Joan, "Let's go to the dining car and get some tea."

The nun rolled her eyes. "We could have done that four stops ago. No tea for you, young lady. We're almost in London."

Alice left the compartment a few minutes later to go to the toilet. She locked the sliding door and tried to imitate Mr.

Fireplug's Welsh accent. "Too much sun and I'll look like a raspberry . . ."

Alice detested anyone who smiled too much or laughed too
loudly. Back on the island, Sister Ruth had taught her a wonderful new word: *gravitas*. Maya had gravitas—a certain dignity and
seriousness that made you want to imitate her.

Back in the compartment, the Fireplugs and Sister Joan were
talking about gardening. Sister Ruth once said that the British
were a godless people, but they got a holy look on their faces when
they talked about beanpoles and trellised vines.

"A good mulch pile is like money in the bank," intoned Mr.
Fireplug. "Spread it everywhere and you don't need fertilizer."

"I add my kitchen waste—eggshells and carrot peels," Mrs.
Fireplug said. "But no meat scraps or the pile attracts rats."

The three adults agreed that the best way to fight slugs was to
drown them in a pie tin filled with stale beer. Alice ignored the
conversation and gazed out the window. As they approached the
outskirts of London, factories and apartment buildings were beginning to appear. It felt like all the empty spaces were disap-
pearing; the buildings were squeezing together and crushing the
little slivers of green.

"I *am* sorry," Mr. Fireplug said. "But we haven't been properly
introduced. I'm Malcolm and this is my wife, Viv."

"Of course, sometimes I call my husband 'Mush'—which is
short for mushroom," Mrs. Fireplug explained. "Malcolm once
tried to grow truffles in the backyard, but it didn't work."

"Wrong trees. Got to have oak trees."

"Pleased to meet you. I'm Sister Joan and this is—"

"Sarah," Alice said. "Sarah Bradley."

"London! London!" a voice shouted, and then the conductor
hurried past the compartment.

"Well, here we are," Mr. Fireplug said. "Here we are indeed . . ."

He glanced at his wife, and Alice suddenly felt strange. Something was wrong about these people. She and Joan should jump
up and run away.

"A pleasure to meet you two," Mrs. Fireplug said.

Sister Joan smiled sweetly. "Yes. Have a lovely time in Spain."

"We might need a porter," Mr. Fireplug announced. "Viv brought everything but the kitchen sink."

He stood up to get the large suitcase, groaning and struggling as he lowered it down. But this time, Alice was close enough to see his face. The bag wasn't really that heavy. He was only pretending.

Desperate, Alice reached out and grabbed Joan's hand. But the nun smiled and gave her a little squeeze. "Yes, dear. I know. It's been a long journey . . ."

Why were adults so foolish? Why couldn't they *see*? Alice watched as Mrs. Fireplug stood up and reached into her purse. She took out a small blue device that looked like a plastic squirt gun. Before anyone could react, she grabbed Sister Joan's shoulder, pressed the device against the nun's neck, and pulled the trigger.

Sister Joan collapsed. Alice tried to get away, but the big suitcase was blocking the door. "No you don't!" Mr. Fireplug said, grabbing her arm. Alice pulled out her stick and jabbed it at his throat. He swore loudly as the stick snapped in two.

"You're a nasty little creature, aren't you?" He glanced at his wife. "Use the pink one, dear. The blue one was for the nun."

Mrs. Fireplug grabbed Alice's hair and held the child against her large bosom. She took a pink plastic gun out of her purse and pressed it against Alice's neck.

Alice felt a sharp pain and then drowsiness. She wanted to fight like Maya, but her legs gave way and she slumped onto the floor. Before the darkness came, she heard Mr. Fireplug talking to his wife.

"I still think you were wrong about the eggshells in the mulch pile, dear. *That's* what attracted the rats."

26

Maya sat in the crowded waiting room of the Brick Lane Medical Clinic and glared at the wall clock. Her appointment had been scheduled for eleven o'clock, but she had been kept waiting for almost forty minutes. Now she would have to hurry across the city to meet the train arriving at Euston Station.

It was annoying to be in an overheated room filled with shrieking babies and old ladies pushing walkers. Like most Harlequins, she had always seen her body as an instrument for doing things. When she was sick or injured, she felt as if a disloyal employee had let her down.

A Bengali woman wearing a pink smock entered the room and checked a list of names. "Ms. Strand?"

"Right here . . ."

"We're ready for you now."

Maya followed the nurse down the central hallway and into an examination room. When five minutes passed and no one appeared, she took out the random number generator hanging from her neck. *Odd means stay. Even means go.*

Before she could press the button, there was a knock on the door, and Amita Kamani hurried in carrying a manila folder. The clinic physician looked flustered; a rebellious strand of black hair had broken free and was touching her forehead.

"Good morning, Ms. Strand. Sorry to keep you waiting. Any improvement in the leg?"

"No change."

Maya had worn a skirt that afternoon so she could avoid the indignity of a hospital gown. Sitting on the edge of the examination table, she reached down and ripped off her bandage. The wound was still swollen and oozing blood, but she refused to show pain. It gave her some small satisfaction that Dr. Kamani looked concerned.

"I see. Yes. That's somewhat disappointing." The physician took some disinfectant and fresh bandages out of the cabinet. She pulled on latex gloves, sat down on a stool near the table, and started to bandage the wound. "Any problems with the medicine?"

"It made me sick to my stomach."

"Did you vomit?"

"A few times."

"Any other problems? Dizziness? Fatigue?"

Maya shook her head. "I need some more antibiotics. That's all."

"You can pick up a refill on the way out. But we need to discuss certain issues." Dr. Kamani applied one final length of medical tape and stood back up. Now that she was no longer sitting below Maya like a shoe-shine boy, she appeared to regain some confidence. "We still don't know what's wrong with your leg, but it's clear that you should adopt a healthier lifestyle. You need to stop traveling and avoid stress."

"That's not possible. I have certain obligations."

"We all have busy lives these days, but sometimes we have to listen to our bodies." Dr. Kamani checked the folder. "What exactly is your profession?"

"That has nothing to do with my leg."

"You need to talk to a specialist."

"I've had enough of this." Maya's sword was hidden in the carrying case lying on the table. She picked up the case and slung the strap over her shoulder. "You're bloody useless."

Dr. Kamani stood a little straighter. Her eyes widened and her nostrils flared as if she were about to smash a tennis ball back across the net. "And you're pregnant, Ms. Strand."

"That's not possible."

"Well, it's true. I ordered a full range of tests, and that was one of them. The pregnancy is probably why you feel sick to your stomach."

Crazy thoughts pushed through her mind. Maya wanted to be surrounded by enemies at that moment so that she could draw the sword and slash her way out of the room.

"When did you last have sexual intercourse, Ms. Strand?"

Maya shook her head.

"Do you know who the father is?"

She felt paralyzed, frozen within that moment of revelation, but her mouth moved and sounds came out. "Yes. But he's gone away."

"Of course there are alternatives if you want to terminate the pregnancy. I usually ask patients to think it over for twenty-four hours before they make an appointment." Dr. Kamani reached into the door rack and pulled out a pamphlet with the words IT's YOUR CHOICE on the cover. "This pamphlet explains the various options. Are there any other questions I can answer?"

"No." Maya checked the time on her cell phone. "Right now, I'm late for an appointment." She slid off the examination table, brushed past Dr. Kamani, and hurried out of the clinic.

Alice Chen and one of the nuns from the island were arriving in London, and Linden had told Maya to meet them. She found an unregistered taxi parked across the street and climbed into the back.

"Euston Station," she told the driver. "I've got to be there in ten minutes."

As the car jerked forward and headed down Brick Lane, the moment in the examination room returned to her with all its power. She was pregnant with a Traveler's child. At that moment, it felt like being in a plane crash—an instant of comprehension followed by confusion and pain. What should she do? Could she tell anyone? She was in turn angry and sad, happy and defiant before the car reached Whitechapel Road.

If this had happened to Mother Blessing, the Irish Harlequin would have demanded an abortion that afternoon. She would have removed this accident growing inside her—destroyed it like a tumor. The Harlequins' power came from the simplicity of their lives, the single-minded ferocity of their obligation. The body was a weapon that had to be maintained.

By now, Maya was late for the train, but she followed the rules she had learned from her father. For Thorn, a place like Euston Station was an "Argus trap"—a high-intensity surveillance area named after the guardian character in Greek myth that had a hundred eyes. Euston was a particularly dangerous location because it was on the northern boundary of the congestion-tax zone, so cameras took continual images of car license plates. University College London and the bones of Jeremy Bentham were only a few hundred yards away from this central point. If the dead philosopher stepped out of his glass case and sauntered down the street, he would have been a prisoner of the electronic Panopticon.

Maya got out of the taxi, walked down Euston Road, and entered Friends House, the Quaker religious center. Standing in the ground-floor reading room, she could make an initial evaluation of the station. The front entrance had over a dozen cameras pointed at the bus area and the war memorial to the "The Glorious Dead."

In an emergency, she would have simply run the gauntlet and hoped that the Tabula mercenaries would be delayed in traffic. But there was usually a safe way in—even Argus had been defeated.

She went back outside and hurried up Barnaby Street on the east side of the station. The trash-covered sidewalk led her past King Arthur's Pub, a betting parlor, and a shop called Transformation that sold clothes to cross-dressers. Two identical male mannequins were in the window, one with a suit and bowler hat and the other with a blond wig and a red silk cocktail dress. THIS COULD BE YOU proclaimed a sign. *Not bloody likely,* Maya thought. An image flashed through her mind of a different display: a pregnant young woman standing next to a fierce-looking twin with a flat belly.

Barnaby Street merged into a traffic ramp, and she followed it up to an enclosed delivery area on the top of the station building. There were only a few cameras in this area—all of them searching for car license plates—and she followed the concrete ramp that led down to the central concourse. The concourse was lined with shops, including two Burger Kings, two W. H. Smith bookstores, and two Marks and Spencers. Perhaps that was a clue to the future—hundreds of stores that were basically the same.

An announcement board told her that the train from the ferry port at Holyhead had just arrived on track six. Maya passed between two shops to tracks seven and eight, and then peered down through a thick glass window that overlooked track six. Passengers from the Holyhead train were hurrying toward the main concourse: an East Asian family with strollers, three teenage girls with braided hair and backpacks, and a middle-aged couple maneuvering a large wheeled suitcase.

It didn't look as if Alice Chen was on the train. When Maya changed her position, she saw a police officer entering the station, followed by two paramedics pushing a stretcher on a gurney. *This way,* the officer gestured. *Track six. Follow me.*

She checked her knives and shifted the sword carrier so that she could draw the weapon easily. Pretending to search for a passenger, she strolled down the platform for track six. The police officer was there, standing on the steps of the fourth train car. As she passed by the windows of the car, she saw that the paramedics and two train conductors were crowded into the third compartment.

Maya reached the end of the platform as the paramedics reappeared with one of the Poor Claires strapped to a stretcher. The nun was unconscious, but alive. So where was Alice Chen? She waited for someone to escort the little girl off the train, but the two conductors and the police officer followed the gurney out to the concourse. It was clear that no one was searching for a lost child.

Maya took out a cell phone registered to a homeless man in Brixton and called Linden. "I'm at the station," she said. "I was supposed to collect the package, but the situation is not as expected."

"Is there a problem?"

"The person in charge of delivery was unconscious and taken away by paramedics."

"And the package?"

"Not on the train."

"What is your current situation?"

"Our business competitors are not in the area."

"Don't put yourself at risk. This is not our obligation."

"I realize that, but—"

"Leave the area immediately and return to the office."

The call ended, but she didn't leave the platform. *This is not our obligation.* Yes, her father would have said the same thing—and a year ago she would have followed his example. But Gabriel had made her aware of another level of responsibility. It felt as if Linden was imitating the Brethren at that moment. He wanted her to be part of the cause and ignore the individual, follow the rules and betray the deeper knowledge within her own heart.

Her cell phone rang again, but she didn't answer it. A stiletto appeared in her left hand as she boarded the train and hurried down the corridor to the fourth car. The third compartment was empty—no sign of a struggle—but she noticed something on the scuffed floor.

Kneeling down, she picked up two fragments of a sea-smooth piece of driftwood. A policeman would have never understood what the fragments meant, but Maya knew instantly. She had made pretend weapons like this when she was growing up—measuring sticks that were supposed to be swords and pencils held beneath her sleeves with rubber bands. When she fitted the pieces together, the driftwood looked like a dagger.

27

Gabriel had always returned to the familiar reality of the Fourth Realm before he gathered the courage to cross over again. But this time he continued his journey. After the confrontation with Michael, he returned to the beach, and then followed the passageway through darkness to light.

Now the Traveler sat on a flat rock and studied this new world. He had crossed over to an arid highlands dotted with low-lying bushes that had black roots growing out of them like spider legs. Immense mountain ranges topped with snow rose up in each direction. It felt as if they contained the universe within their boundaries.

But the most striking aspect of this realm was the sky; it was a turquoise blue that reminded him of old jewelry. The distinctive color could be caused by the high altitude. Gabriel was breathing quickly and felt a burning sensation in his lungs. There was a harshness here—an austere purity that did not permit compromise.

Gabriel decided that he had reached the Sixth Realm of the gods. The few Travelers from antiquity who had visited this place had left vague accounts of tall mountains and a magical city. Perhaps the city no longer existed; nothing was permanent in the universe. According to his Pathfinder, Sophia Briggs, the different realms were much like the human world; they evolved in new directions and changed over time.

He had no idea how long he'd been sitting on the rock, no sense of time other than the sun's changing position. When he first emerged from the passageway, the sun was low on the horizon. It slowly burned its way across the sky. The day appeared to be two or three times longer than the twenty-four hours of his world. Anyone who lived here would have to adjust to a night that would seem to last forever. Each new sunrise would feel like a miracle.

When the sun reached the highest point in the sky, Gabriel shifted his position and saw a distant flash—like a reflection from a mirror. Perhaps someone was trying to contact him. Standing on the rock, he examined the mountain range. Two of the tallest peaks had a V-shaped space between them and there was a glittering point of light at the bottom of this gap.

Before he could go anywhere, he needed to make sure that he could return to the passageway. Rocks were scattered around the landscape. He picked up the smaller ones and began to build a cairn. When this pile was about six feet high, Gabriel studied the surrounding landscape and tried to memorize every detail.

His beating heart was the center of this world—a clock ticking in an empty room. Turning his back on the hills, he walked directly toward the light. It took less than a mile of hiking to realize that flash floods had cut steep-sided ravines and several large canyons into the rocky ground. If he wanted to travel in a straight line, he would have to climb down to the bottom of each ravine and then scramble his way back up again.

It took a great deal of effort to get past the first two ravines, and Gabriel stopped to rest. At this pace, it would be dark before he reached the mountains. When he resumed the journey, he tried a new strategy—following the top ridge of each ravine until the gap disappeared or a rock bridge allowed him to cross over to the other side.

As time passed, the sun descended slowly toward the horizon. Although the glittering point of light disappeared, Gabriel kept his eyes on the gap between the two mountains. When his throat was so dry that he found it difficult to swallow, he reached a long, narrow canyon with a thin line of water at the bottom. Gabriel built another cairn at the top, and then climbed down the rock wall, forcing his hands into cracks while his feet searched for a ledge that would support his weight. Tough little plants that reminded him of evergreen trees appeared as he got closer to the floor of the canyon. He grabbed on to their branches and lowered himself down.

The water was cold and had a sharp taste of iron. Kneeling in the gravel, he drank again and again, and then splashed water on his face. He was in the shadows now, looking at the turquoise sky. It would have been difficult to climb back up, so he followed the canyon, walking against the trickling flow of the creek. Every time Gabriel came around a bend, he expected to find a tributary or a series of ledges that would provide a way out. Instead, the canyon became even deeper, and the sky above him was like a twisting line of ink. The mounds of sand and pebbles on the canyon floor showed that a powerful river had once flowed here.

He lay down on a patch of sand and fell asleep, waking up when a drop of water struck his face. The sky was gray with clouds, and it had started to rain. Drops fell through the canyon opening and then the storm gained power. Drops splattered on the boulders and more water flowed down the rock walls.

There was no shelter, so Gabriel closed his eyes and felt the rain strike his shoulders and trickle down his face. The storm seemed to go on forever, with new surges of intensity until all at once the clouds disappeared from the sky.

Gabriel assumed that most of the rainfall would wash across the rocky soil and drain into the canyon. But nothing had changed. The creek was still about three inches deep, flowing across smooth red stones. He splashed through the water for a few minutes, and then stopped when he felt a sudden gust of wind from higher up in the canyon. Air was being pushed forward by a surge of water coming toward him. There was no way out. The flood would sweep him along and smash his body against the boulders.

He heard a dull roar in the distance. A few seconds later, a two-foot-high wave came around a bend in the canyon and almost knocked him over. Water flowed through his legs as he trudged over to the canyon wall. He looked up, searching for a ledge or foothold. Nothing.

Dead leaves drifted through the air like birds trying to escape a storm. The roar transformed itself into a deep, echoing sound like a train coming out of a tunnel. The water grew higher—up to his waist—as he looked up and saw a dark line on the opposite wall. Planting each foot carefully, he crossed the canyon and touched the rock. A jagged crack, several inches deep, cut across the wall.

Gabriel extended his right arm, forced his fist into the rock, and then followed with his left hand while his feet dangled in the air. An evergreen bush was growing from the side of the cliff about twenty feet up, and he decided to head toward it. Already his arms and shoulders were aching, and blood trickled from his scraped knuckles to his wrists.

The roaring sound had grown louder—so powerful that it seemed to fill the canyon. *Keep moving,* he told himself. *Just keep moving.* But when he glanced right, he saw a massive wall of water flowing toward him. With one convulsive movement, Gabriel reached up and grabbed the evergreen bush. And then the flood was there. His chest, his neck, and now his head were underwater. He heard a moan and a grumbling noise. It felt as if monsters hidden within this dark surge had grabbed his legs and were trying to pull him under.

28

Gabriel waited for that final moment when he would be forced to take water into his lungs. How much longer would he live? His heart beat once, twice—and then the massive wave passed him by and continued down the canyon. Still clinging to the evergreen bush, he opened his eyes and gasped for air.

Once again, the river appeared harmless, a thin line of water flowing over a bed of smooth stones. Gabriel lowered himself down to a patch of gravel and lay there for a long time, gazing up at the turquoise sky. His first thought was to climb out of the canyon and find the passageway home before nightfall. He would return to his own world and its familiar reality.

And then what? Eventually, he would have to leave the secret apartment and speak to the Resistance. Although he opposed the Brethren's philosophy of power and control, he didn't know how to express his vision in a way that would make sense to other people. Perhaps some higher power could help him. He needed to stay here and learn the secrets of this place.

Gabriel stepped into the shallow stream and sloshed his way up the canyon. At each new curve in the rock wall, he would pause and listen for the sound of another flood. Eventually, he reached an area where a section of the rock wall had peeled away and collapsed into the stream. He climbed up the rubble and jumped onto a narrow ledge. His back was pressed against the wall, his knees were bent, and his feet splayed out like a ballet dancer making an awkward plié. The ledge widened as it led him upward, and a few minutes later he was out of the canyon. Once again, he turned toward the mountains and saw towers outlined against the sky. It was a city—a golden city—built in the middle of this desolation.

His body felt slow and cumbersome as he trudged up a steep path that threaded its way around massive boulders. It looked as if the mountains themselves had exploded, and the debris still littered the ground. He would take a hundred steps, stop to catch his breath in the thin air, and then start climbing again. At one point he had to force his way through the narrow gap between two boulders. When he emerged, he saw that his destination was only a few miles away.

The city consisted of three massive structures built on ascending terraces. Each building had a rectangular base, as white as a block of sugar, with thirty-three floors of windows. Golden towers rose from the roof of each base. Some were simple cylindrical shapes, but there were also domes, minarets, and an elaborate pagoda. Gabriel wondered if he was looking at a fort or a school or a massive apartment building where each black-framed window had a view of the plateau. From a distance, the white buildings supporting the towers reminded him of three enormous birthday cakes with fanciful decorations on top.

Neither armed guards nor barking dogs gave a warning as he hurried up a short staircase to the first terrace—an open space of packed gravel. Gabriel stopped halfway across the terrace and gazed up, expecting a face to appear in one of the windows. It was almost painfully bright, and all the shadows had sharp edges. There was nothing welcoming about the golden city; it was more of a monument than a residence. At first, he couldn't find a way in, and then he noticed an entrance at the far-right corner of the building. The door was made of a greenish metal that resembled tarnished copper. An elaborate metal lotus was placed at the center. When Gabriel pushed this ornament, the door swung open. He waited a few seconds, then stepped inside, expecting to find something magical—perhaps a serpent twined around an altar or an angel in white robes.

"I'm here," he said. But no one answered him.

He was standing in an empty room with white walls and bars on the windows. The bars created little boxes of hazy light on the floor. A second door was set in the wall to the left of the entrance. Gabriel pushed it open and found himself in an identical room.

So where were the gods? As he glanced out the window at the courtyard, he heard the door shut behind him. Moving slowly, he passed through a row of empty rooms until he reached the other side of the building. The silence was starting to bother him. He had never been in a space that felt so empty.

A staircase led him upward into an identical room with another doorway. "Hello!" he shouted. "Anyone here?" When no one answered, he lost his temper and marched forward, slamming each door behind him. Floor after floor, he climbed upward, but there were no room numbers to announce how far he had gone. At a certain point, he entered a room and found a white cube supporting a model of a palm tree made out of bits of colored metal.

The next few floors displayed more artificial plants. Gabriel found daisies and oak trees and sea kelp, but there were also plants he had never seen before. Had the gods created these objects? Was he supposed to offer prayers, or was this building simply an enormous museum? A few floors higher, the plants vanished and models of animals appeared. Fish. Birds. Lizards. And then the mammals. There was a room devoted to foxes and another filled with cats. Finally, a spiral staircase led him out of the building, and he stood among the gold towers.

Perhaps the gods were watching him, testing him in some way. Gabriel crossed the terrace and entered the second building. The rooms were exactly the same, but there were models of tools and machinery. He inspected one room full of hammers and another that displayed lamps. There was a room dedicated to different kinds of steam engines next to one filled with antique radios. Gabriel was getting tired, but there was no quick way out. He climbed staircase after staircase until he reached the second terrace.

From the outside, the third and final building resembled the previous two structures. But when he pulled open the entrance door, he found five staircases that led off in different directions. Gabriel took the middle staircase and immediately got lost in a succession of intersecting hallways. There were no models of the natural or mechanical world in this structure—only a great many mirrors. He saw his bewildered face in convex mirrors, pocket-sized mirrors, and tarnished mirrors held in antique frames.

The sun was directly above the mountains when he finally emerged from this maze and stepped out onto the third terrace. Wandering through the towers, he found shards of broken mirrors and then a spot between two towers where someone had used mirrors to build something that resembled a solar oven. *Would gods make something like this?* Gabriel assumed they could just wave their hands and objects would appear.

Cautiously, he passed between the towers to an open section of the terrace. Fifty yards away from him, a man was sitting cross-legged on a bench. Like a stone idol, the figure waited for Gabriel to approach him. He looked smaller than Gabriel had remembered and his hair was much longer—almost touching his shoulders.

"Father?"

Matthew Corrigan stood up and smiled. "Hello, Gabriel. I've been waiting for you."

"That could have been a long wait. I almost died a few hours ago."

"Hope grows from faith. I always believed that you and Michael would find your way here."

His father's certainty, his calmness, was infuriating. "Is that why you disappeared?" Gabriel asked. "So you could live in this empty place?"

"After those men burned down our house, I hid among the trees near the top of the hill. When the three of you came out of the cellar, I made the decision to leave. I knew you would be safer without me around."

"Mom was never the same after the fire. It destroyed her life."

"When I married your mother, I didn't know that I was a Traveler. All that came later. The Tabula found out and put me on their death list."

"So where did you go after the fire? Were you hiding out in this world while we wandered around like a bunch of homeless people?"

"I was teaching others. I tried to show them a different way."

"Yeah, I know all about that. Remember the New Harmony group in Arizona? The Tabula executed everyone living there. They destroyed the entire community—the men, women, and children you 'inspired' to change their lives."

Matthew bent slightly forward as if taking the pain and sadness into his body. "What a terrible crime. I'll pray for all of them."

"Prayers can't change what happened. Those people are dead because of your ideas. And you want to know something else? Michael became a Traveler, but he went over to the other side. Now he's running the Evergreen Foundation."

Matthew stood up, walked to the edge of terrace, and gazed out at the mountains. "Your brother was always angry. He wanted to be just like everyone else, but that wasn't possible."

"Michael is going to turn the world into an enormous prison. And I'm the only one who can stop him. Was that part of your plan? Did you know we'd be on opposite sides?"

"I can't predict the future, Gabriel."

"People are risking their lives because I'm a Traveler and they think I have an answer. Well, I *don't* have an answer. I wake up at night and wonder if I'm just going to create another New Harmony for the Tabula to destroy."

"Hatred and anger are like two men standing in the street and shouting for revenge. Sometimes, it's difficult to hear the softer voices."

"I know all about hatred and anger. I've been to the dark city. In fact, I've met the crazy museum director who is still waiting for your return. But that's your style, isn't it? You never stay long, not even for your own family. Just one short visit and then you're hiding in some distant world."

"The realms aren't distant, Gabriel. They're parallel to our lives. A student sits in a classroom. An old woman cuts a slice of bread. They think they're light-years from a different reality, but those new worlds are right *there* if they could only reach through the barriers."

"Most people don't want to cross over. They're more concerned with the problems they're facing in their lives. The Vast Machine is becoming more powerful, more pervasive. A few individuals realize they're about to lose their freedom, and they're joining the Resistance. If I make a mistake or say the wrong thing, they're going to get hurt."

"That's possible. We can't control the future."

"What about the gods? This is the golden city. Aren't they supposed to appear and tell us what to do?"

"When I first came here, I searched for them. I explored the mountains and the canyons. I tapped my knuckles on these towers, searching for passageways and secret rooms. There's nothing hidden here, Gabriel. The Light that created the universe endures forever, but the gods have vanished."

"What happened?"

"They left no message, no explanation. I've come up with my own theory. Their disappearance is an opportunity."

"So no one's here?"

"If the gods have left the stage, then it's just the two of us." Matthew stepped toward his son. "So who are you, Gabriel? And what kind of world do you want to live in? I'm not going to tell you what to believe. All I can do is guide you forward, and make sure you don't turn away from your own vision."

29

Lying on the bed in Hollis Wilson's rented room in Camden Town, Maya nibbled on tea biscuits and stared up at the crack in the ceiling. Like a mechanic checking a race car, she stretched her body and evaluated its current strengths and weaknesses.

She had grown up seeing ads of pregnant women advertising everything from vitamins to bank loans. Once she had spent a rainy afternoon at the National Gallery contemplating Renaissance paintings of the pregnant Virgin Mary. Now she realized that both the painters and the magazine photographers had it all wrong; she certainly didn't feel like standing around with her hands on her belly and a mysterious smile on her face. Her fatigue had disappeared and her leg wound had finally started to heal. She felt strong, aggressive, ready for battle.

Her cell rang and she picked it up off the floor. "Good morning," Simon Lumbroso said. "Remember the package we lost at Euston Station?"

"Is there any new information?"

"Apparently our young friends have tracked it down. They want to hold a sales conference at their business office. Is twelve noon a good time for you?"

"I'll be there," Maya said, and switched off the phone.

The "young friends" Simon had mentioned were Jugger and the other Free Runners. The "business office" was their apartment in Chiswick and Alice Chen was the "lost package." Maya wondered if Alice was still alive. Killing a child in a public place would have drawn attention from both the London police and the media; it was a better idea to take Alice off the train. The Tabula could question her—and execute her—in a secret location.

As Maya got dressed and ate a bowl of cold cereal, she wondered how to present the problem to Linden. Her thoughts weren't focused that morning, and her mind wandered in painful directions. The fact that the Tabula had captured the little girl reminded Maya of her own captivity in the First Realm. She could see the gas flares wavering back and forth, the wolves with their clubs and spears, and Pickering's body swinging from a rope. *Can the baby feel all that?* she wondered. *Are all these memories trapped within my body?*

Linden didn't care about anything unless it directly involved the Traveler. She knew what the Harlequin would say when she mentioned Alice Chen: the child was dead—or not important. It was logical to forget about this person and move on.

But Gabriel had shown her a different way to look at reality. What was supposed to be logical was not always what was fair, right, or inevitable. Fighting the Tabula was not particularly logical, and yet people all over the world were joining the Resistance.

And what about this child growing within her? Was there anything logical about bringing a new life into this chaotic world? She shouldn't keep it, wouldn't keep it, absolutely can't keep it. But *yes*, she thought. *Yes. I'm going to do it anyway.*

With the sword case hanging from her shoulder, she strolled over to the drum shop in Camden Market. Her first objective was to get Linden's permission. That wasn't going to be easy.

The French Harlequin was sitting in the kitchen of the secret apartment when she came through the door. The room smelled of spilled wine and the sugary odor of the French Harlequin's hand-made cigarettes.

"How is the Traveler?"

"No change."

"I'll check on the body."

Maya walked to the room where Gabriel's body lay on a narrow bed. She closed the door so that Linden wouldn't surprise her and then touched Gabriel's face with the palm of her hand. "I'm pregnant," she whispered. "What do you think of that?"

The Light had left his body, and Maya knew Gabriel couldn't hear her. She leaned forward, kissed his forehead, and then returned to the kitchen. "Still alive," she told Linden. Her voice was calm and matter-of-fact, as if they were talking about an article in the newspaper.

Linden got up from the table and turned on the gas burner. "Coffee?"

"Yes." Maya took the sword carrier off her shoulder and hung it on the back of her chair. "I got a call from Simon this morning. The Free Runners know where the Tabula took Alice Chen."

"I'm sure that she's already dead."

"We don't know that."

"It's the logical conclusion."

"I think we need to consider every possibility."

Linden opened up a tin and began scooping out teaspoons of ground coffee. "If she's dead, there's nothing to be done. If she's alive, we're not going to waste our resources finding her."

"When I was growing up, my father lectured me about the tensions between Travelers and Harlequins. They don't like us. Not really."

"I do not give a damn what they think," Linden said. "Soldiers go to war even though they may disagree with certain political parties within their country. We Harlequins defend a difficult group of people. But we have accepted that obligation."

"If we do nothing to help Alice and she dies, Gabriel will walk away from our protection. You know him, Linden. You know that's true. If we don't save the child, we lose the Traveler."

The kettle started whistling and Linden poured boiling water into a French press. He waited a minute, then pushed the plunger down. "You might be right."

"I'll handle the problem," Maya said, and tried not to smile.

Linden gave her a cup filled with coffee so thick that it reminded her of chocolate cake frosting. Maya resisted the temptation to add sugar and took a sip of the black sludge.

"Too strong?" Linden asked.

"Just right."

* * *

SHE LEFT CAMDEN Market, waved down a taxi, and told the driver to take her to suburban Chiswick. During the journey, she counted every surveillance camera the taxi passed on the street. Some of them simply recorded images, but others used sophisticated face-scanning programs. A few of the citizens noticed there were more cameras—*Yes, they just put up that new one in the square*—but the walls of the new prison were invisible. In Britain, the plan to centralize all databases was called Transformational Government, an innocuous phrase that implied that this sort of change was both positive and necessary. These changes were being made for "Your Protection," for "Efficiency and Modernisation." They were Styrofoam words—light and unsubstantial, packing materials to blunt the sharp edges.

When the taxi reached Chiswick, she got out near a school,

and then walked three blocks to a street lined with tidy row houses. There was a faded Harlequin lute chalked on the pavement in front of the second house from the corner. The Free Runners had been living in the ground-floor apartment for the last few months.

Simon Lumbroso had already arrived and was sitting gingerly on a saggy couch in the living room. He seemed out of place amid the cast-off furniture and the trash cans overflowing with crushed beer cans and fast-food cartons.

The only neat and organized area was a long worktable with three monitors attached to a homemade computer. One monitor showed cars driving past the entrance to Wellspring Manor—the country estate owned by the Brethren. Another showed the entrance to the Evergreen Foundation office building near Ludgate Circus. The third was the main page of a secret Web site set up by the Polish Free Runners; their Internet team had accessed the security cameras near other properties owned by the Foundation. Six small boxes on the monitor displayed street scenes in four different countries.

Roland, the quiet young man from Yorkshire, sat at the table answering e-mail while Jugger bustled about the room. His appearance hadn't changed since joining the Resistance; his T-shirt was too small and revealed a patch of his flabby stomach.

"Tea?" he asked everyone. "How about a nice cup of tea?"

"Not right now." Maya sat down on the couch. "Tell me what you've learned about Alice Chen."

"Yesterday afternoon, I talked to the nun who was traveling with Alice," Simon said. "Apparently, a man and a woman got on the train at Crewe and entered the compartment. They injected the nun with a powerful sedative right before they arrived in London. The man wore a tweed suit and had a Welsh accent. They were carrying a large rolling suitcase."

Jugger scratched his stomach. "After Simon gave us that description, we searched through the images taken by one of the City of London traffic cameras near the Evergreen Foundation office. Go ahead, Roland. Show Maya what we found."

Black-and-white images appeared on the screen along with a time stamp at the bottom right-hand corner. The city-owned camera took a photograph every five seconds, but most of the images showed only the street and the entrance to the Foundation building. As Roland searched through the images, Maya noticed that several of the foundation employees had been tagged with nicknames and other information. SUSIE SECRETARY ARRIVES AT 8:20HRS. FRIENDS WITH MR. BALD HEAD.

"This is the feed two days ago when the little girl was kidnapped," Roland said. "I remember these people because of their suitcase."

The image on the monitor showed that a London taxi had stopped in front of the entrance. A middle-aged woman wearing a rain hat stood on the curb watching a man lift a black suitcase out of the trunk.

"I recognize them," Maya said. "When I arrived at the station, they had just left the train with the other passengers."

In the next five images, the couple maneuvered the rolling suitcase onto the sidewalk and pushed it into the building.

"Return to the third image," Maya said. "No—the one after that."

The monitor showed the man using two hands to pull the suitcase onto the curb.

"See that? It's heavy because Alice is inside. That's how they got her out of the train."

"We're fairly sure that she's still in the building," Jugger said. "None of the subsequent images show either a child or a large container being removed from the area."

"Where's Nathan Boone?" Maya asked.

"We hacked into the computer of the woman who handles travel arrangements for the Evergreen Foundation," Roland said. "Boone traveled to Thailand on a commercial flight six days ago."

"Boone wants to question the child," Maya said. "They'll keep her alive until he returns to London."

"So what are you going to do?" Jugger asked. "Ever since the attack in Berlin, the Tabula have increased their security. Even at night there are at least four armed guards in the Foundation building."

"Alice Chen is the only surviving witness to what happened at New Harmony," Maya said. "But there is a larger issue. When Gabriel met the Nighthawk, he said that the Resistance is more than just destroying the Vast Machine. We need to believe that each individual life has value and meaning."

Jugger nodded. "Sure. I think that's right."

"Alice's life has value and meaning, and that means we're going to save her. I'll need your help to break into the Foundation building."

"Sounds like you're talking about Harlequin business," Jugger said. "We don't go around fighting people."

"I saved your life, Jugger. I pulled you and Roland and your friend Sebastian out of a burning house."

"Yes, and we—we appreciate that," he stammered.

"You have an obligation."

"We're grateful, Maya. Everybody's grateful. All I'm saying is that we're not like you and Linden. I'll go on the Internet and organize people, paint slogans on walls—things like that. But I'm not going to be part of an attack on a Foundation building. That could bloody well get us killed."

The anger she had felt all morning surged through her body and she jumped up from the couch. The heels of her boots clicked across the floor as she approached Jugger and pointed her finger at his face.

"I just said something. But I guess you didn't hear me."

"I'm—I'm listening."

"Good. Because when a Harlequin says, 'You have an obligation,' that does not mean that there's a choice. I'm not *wishing* for your help. I'm not *hoping* for some benevolent impulse. I'm expecting your help *now*."

"Right. No problem. Glad to be helpful." Jugger was sweating. "But it's going to be difficult to get into the building with a weapon. After you pass through the door, there's an L-shaped hallway that leads to the security desk. I'm sure they do a backscatter scan of all their visitors."

"If we can't go in the front door, then we'll have to break in from the top, the bottom, or the sides."

"The walls are too thick," Simon said. "And we would have to gain access to a nearby building."

"What about a hot air balloon?" Jugger seemed desperate to offer a solution. "You could float across the Thames and land on the roof."

"Underground?" Maya asked Simon.

"Possibly. This is an old city—like Rome."

"Hold it! Wait! I know what you need!" Jugger said. "You need an *incredible* disguise."

"A few months ago, this old lady was at the Hope Pub," Roland said with a solemn voice.

Jugger looked annoyed. "We don't want to hear about some old lady. We're trying to solve a problem here."

"She was handing out pamphlets—about freeing the rivers."

"What rivers are you talking about?" Simon asked gently.

"The lost rivers. The ones that flow under the streets."

"So where are they?" Maya asked. "Any underneath Ludgate Circus?"

Roland shrugged. "Can't tell you that. And I won't say something that's not true."

"We called her Crazy Nora," Jugger said. "She had maps . . ."

* * *

A QUICK INTERNET search gave them an address in Finchley, and a few hours later Maya and Simon were walking past the cricket grounds on Waterfall Road. There appeared to be a great many parks and playing fields in Finchley. Jamaican nannies with phone headsets pushed baby carriages while schoolboys kicked a ball. But the largest space in the neighborhood was taken up by the weeping angels and mausoleums of the Great Northern

Cemetery. Maya had a vision of thousands of dead Victorians traveling on a ghost train to this final resting place.

Simon turned the corner onto Brookdale Street and stopped under a flowering cherry tree. "Are you all right?" he asked.

"Just a little tired. That's all."

"You were harsh with Jugger and Roland. Usually, it is better to be kind with your friends—*gentile*. The Free Runners want to be helpful, but they are frightened."

"I don't have the time to be diplomatic."

"Anger can also waste time," Simon said. "You have always been like your father, careful and deliberate. But lately—not so much."

"I'm worried about Alice Chen. She's the same age I was when a lot of bad things happened."

"Would you like to talk about that?"

"No."

"Is there anything else you would like to talk about? I'm sure it troubles you that Gabriel has crossed over . . ."

For a moment, she wanted to break down, embrace her father's old friend, and tell him about the pregnancy. *No tears*, she told herself. *Tears won't save Alice or Gabriel or anyone else in this world*. As Simon watched, she rearranged her sword carrier and stood a little straighter.

"I'm all right. Let's find this woman and see if she has any underground maps."

They continued down the street until they reached number 51—a two-story brick house that had once displayed grand pretensions. Greek columns created a portico leading to the front door and a Doric façade ran around the edge of the roof. Signs had been placed among the weeds and brambles of what had once been a front lawn. FREE THE RIVERS. *INQUIRE WITHIN.*

Maya and Simon walked up a flagstone pathway and knocked on the door. Almost immediately they heard a woman's voice coming from a distant part of the house. "I'm here!" The woman kept shouting as she passed through different rooms. "Here! I'm here!"

Maya glanced at Simon and saw that he was smiling. "Someone dwells within," he said pleasantly.

The door was flung open and they faced a small woman in her seventies. Her long gray hair went off in every direction, and she wore a T-shirt that displayed the slogan BREAK YOUR CHAINS.

"Good afternoon, madam. I am Dr. Pannelli, and this is my friend Judith Strand. We were walking to the park and saw your signs. Ms. Strand is curious about your organization. If you are not busy, perhaps you could tell us a bit more."

"I'm not busy," the woman said with a big smile. "Not busy at all. Come in, Mr. . . . I didn't hear the name."

"Dr. Pannelli. And this is my friend Ms. Strand."

They followed the woman into what had once been the front parlor. All the chairs and tables were covered with stacks of pamphlets, books, and yellowing newspapers. There were plastic pails filled with smooth river stones and glass jars sealed with red wax and marked with cryptic labels.

"Just push away the clutter and find a place to sit." The woman took a stack of books off a wicker chair and dumped them onto a folding cot. "I'm Nora Greenall, the chairwoman and chief recording secretary of Free the Rivers."

"An honor to meet you," Simon said smoothly. "So what exactly does your organization *do*?"

"It's all rather simple, Dr. Pannelli. Free the Rivers describes our vision and our goal. I could have called it 'Free the London Rivers,' but once we're done here, we'll move on to the rest of the world."

"Is the Thames not free?" Simon asked.

"We're talking about all the *other* rivers that used to run through London, like the Westbourne, the Tyburn, and the Walbrook. Now they're covered up with brick and concrete."

"And your organization wants to—"

"Blow up the concrete and let the rivers run free. Imagine a London where pensioners can fish in their neighborhood trout stream. A city where children play and lovers stroll along the banks of a babbling brook."

"A charming vision," Simon said in a soothing voice.

"It's more than charming, Dr. Pannelli. A society that frees its rivers can take the first step toward freeing its minds. Children need to realize that rivers don't follow straight lines."

Maya glanced at Simon—*This is going nowhere*—but he didn't seem to mind.

"I work near Ludgate Circus," he said. "Is there a river in that area?"

"Yes. The River Fleet. It starts in Hampstead, and then runs beneath Camden Town, Smithfield Market, and Ludgate Circus."

"And you're sure it's still there?" Maya asked.

"Of course it's there! You can cover up the rivers, dam them, and fill them with rubbish, but they will always fight back. In time, all the skyscrapers and office buildings will fall down, but the rivers will remain."

"Brava, Ms. Greenall! This sounds like an outstanding organization." Simon reached into his coat pocket and took out his wallet. He hesitated and then—very deliberately—put the wallet away. "You speak with such passion and sincerity that it feels *indelicate* to ask any question."

"Be my guest," Nora said. "Ask away!"

"Do you have any proof of your statement? Do you have photographs or maps of these rivers?"

"Maps? I've got plenty of those." Nora pulled out a cardboard box, and everything fell onto the floor. Quickly, she knelt down and began scooping up pamphlets.

"Do you have a map of the River Fleet? Ms. Strand and I enjoy exploring London. It would be most educational to follow the course of the Fleet through the city."

"The Fleet starts up on Hampstead Heath and empties out of a nasty little drainage pipe beneath Blackfriars Bridge. The rest of the time, it's underground, flowing beneath our madness and confusion."

"I see. But *you* know where it goes."

Nora finished picking up the pamphlets and made a sly smile. "And you would, too—if you become members."

Once again, Simon took out his wallet. "Do we pay dues? Sign a petition? What's the procedure?"

"Five pounds apiece and you get membership cards, although I might have misplaced the cards."

Looking flustered, Nora hurried off into what had once been the dining room and began to rummage through boxes and paper bags.

Maya leaned forward and spoke quietly to Simon. "Do you believe any of this?"

"That the River Fleet is still there? There's no question of that. And ten pounds is a fair price for a good map."

"Here we are!" Looking triumphant, Nora Greenall stood in the doorway and waved her treasure. "Membership cards!"

30

Wearing a yellow hard hat and a reflector vest with the City of London logo, Maya stood across the street from the Evergreen Foundation building on Limeburner Lane. It was about ten o'clock in the evening and no one was out, but she was wary of the surveillance cameras mounted on the wall over the building's entrance.

Roland was halfway down the block searching for a storm drain that emptied rainwater into the Fleet River. According to Nora Greenall's map, the river was directly below them, flowing in the darkness toward the Thames.

At night, the Evergreen building looked like a chessboard—

a grid of lines marking out black or gray squares. Light came from the vertical line of windows marking the emergency staircase and from two curtained windows on the fifth floor. *Maybe Alice is being held there*, Maya thought. *Or maybe some accountant forgot to switch off his desk lamp.*

Roland raised his hand and she hurried down the street to join him. The Free Runner was also wearing a hard hat and reflector vest. He rummaged through a knapsack and pulled out a flashlight attached to thirty feet of nylon fishing line.

"This drain is the closest we can get to the building. But I can't promise you that the outflow pipe leads to the river."

"Do it anyway. It's better than nothing."

Roland switched on a flashlight with a dark red bulb and lowered it through the grate. "When you walk north, you'll see green, white, blue, and red lights. This red flashlight is the most important one. It means you're thirty meters from the target."

He tied the end of the fishing line to the grate, and they hurried down the street to Ludgate Circus. A hundred years ago, this had been a busy square filled with peddlers, but now it was just another sterile intersection with a grid of yellow lines on the pavement. There were plenty of storm drains in the area, and they lowered the blue flashlight through a grate near the lane. Continuing down New Bridge Street, they lowered the white flashlight near the Blackfriars pub and headed for the Thames.

The fourth flashlight was left in a drain near the Unilever building, a large cream-colored structure with an outer façade that made it look like a Greek temple. Maya knew the building was just another statement of power, but the grand gesture in the classical style was very appealing. *And what's the symbol for my generation?* she wondered. *A surveillance camera?*

When they reached Blackfriars Bridge, they took a staircase down to Paul's Walk, the pedestrian pathway that ran alongside the river. Blackfriars Railway Bridge was directly overhead, and Maya heard the click and clatter of a train crossing over to Waterloo Station.

Jugger sat on a bench with a waterproof knapsack that carried her equipment. He finished a conversation on his cell phone and switched it off. "I just talked to Sebastian. He followed the char-woman back to her flat."

"I don't want her working tonight," Maya said.

"No worries. Simon Lumbroso called her and said the building was closed because of a chemical spill. She won't be coming in."

Maya walked over to the parapet wall and gazed out at the city lights reflected on the Thames. In the daytime, the river was sim-ply part of the scenery. Tourists rode to the top of the Millennium Wheel and took snapshots of Westminster. But at night the Thames seemed dark and powerful, passing like a silent force through the flash and bustle of London.

A steel ladder was bolted to the parapet. It allowed mainte-nance workers to climb down to a culvert that dribbled water into the Thames. According to Nora Greenall, this outlet was all that remained of the mighty River Fleet.

Roland and Jugger stood beside her with the gear. During the last few days, they had purchased most of her equipment and helped her organize the plan. Both Free Runners were still wary of her anger and Jugger looked tense whenever weapons ap-peared. After rummaging through his knapsack, Roland pulled out a pair of rubber waders. "Better put these on. You're going to be walking up a river."

A grim-faced jogger ran past them followed by an East Asian couple holding hands. No one seemed surprised that she was pulling on the waders. With their hard hats and vests, Maya and the two Free Runners looked like city employees about to deal with a drainage problem.

Jugger held up the waterproof knapsack and she slipped it over her shoulders. She adjusted the straps, pulling them tight. When everything was ready, she placed the two special shotgun rounds into the outer pocket of the waders.

"I thought the shotgun was already loaded," Jugger said.

"Linden gave me these. They're breaching rounds for blowing out a door lock."

"Bloody hell . . ." Jugger looked impressed.

Roland handed her the bolt cutters, and she clipped them to a ring attached to the waders. "Watch out for sinkholes and don't touch your eyes," Roland said. "Rats live in the tunnels. If bacteria from their waste enter your body, you might get something called Weil's disease. It's difficult to cure."

"That's a pleasant fact. Anything else I need to know?"

Roland looked embarrassed. "I would like to ask one last question."

Because you think I'm going to die, Maya thought. But she nodded to the Yorkshireman. "Go ahead."

"You Harlequins say: 'Damned by the flesh. Saved by the blood.'"

"That's right."

"So whose flesh and whose blood?"

"We're damned because we're human beings. But we're willing to sacrifice ourselves for something more important than our own lives."

Roland nodded. "Good luck, Maya."

"Thank you. You've fulfilled your obligation."

Both Free Runners relaxed and Jugger made a nervous smile. "It was an honor to help you, Maya. I swear that's true. During the last few days, Roland and me have felt like honorary Harlequins."

Mother Blessing would have slapped him across the face for that presumptuous statement, but Maya let it go. If everyone's life had value and meaning, then she had to respect citizens and drones.

"Keep your cells switched on," she said. "I'll call you when I get out of the building."

Maya scrambled over the wall and climbed down the ladder to the grate. Using the bolt cutters, she cut off a rusty padlock, pulled open the hinged grate, and stepped into the culvert. Mother Blessing had always insisted: *Weapons come first. Everything else is second.* Maya's two knives were already strapped to her forearms. Shifting the knapsack, she pulled out her sword and a combat shotgun with a carrying strap. She tied the sword's scabbard to the side of the pack and slung the shotgun strap around her neck. Finally, she pulled out a high-intensity headlamp and touched the switch on the power pack.

Moving the light beam back and forth, Maya studied the culvert. She had expected to find a large concrete pipe, but the Fleet was contained within a brick-lined tunnel about eight feet high with a level floor, curving sides, and an arched ceiling. Although London's citizens took the Tube to work, they rarely thought about what was underground. The River Fleet had flowed through London during riots and wars and the Great Fire of 1666. It had existed in Shakespeare's time and in the Roman era. Perhaps it had drained the melting glaciers from the last Ice Age. All that was past, and now the river was held captive. The lower part of the tunnel was covered with algae, and the rest of the tunnel had a white crust that reminded her of toothpaste left in a sink.

Knee-deep in the cold water, she took her first step forward. Ripples appeared and waves sloshed against the walls. The base of the culvert was covered with silt mixed with gravel. When her boots sunk six inches into the muck, she realized it would take time and effort to reach Ludgate Circus.

Her shadow glided across the walls as she headed up the tunnel. Ten minutes later, she saw the glow of green light coming from a drainpipe that emptied into the tunnel. At least she was moving in the right direction. There was a Y-juncture about twenty yards north of the light. Using a can of spray paint, Maya made a diamond sign on the wall. She went to the left, following the river where the current felt stronger.

She couldn't find the white flashlight near Blackfriars pub, but continued onward. The culvert became smaller—about five feet high—and her hard hat scraped against the rough brick surface. Fiber-optic cables appeared, fastened to the top of the culvert with brackets. The communications companies who wired the city for the Internet had realized that ripping up the streets would cost millions of pounds. Somehow they had persuaded the city authorities to give them free access to the Fleet. Maya wondered if Internet cables followed the routes of the other lost rivers.

Throughout her journey, she had passed through pockets of

sewage. When the culvert turned right, she smelled an even stronger odor. Grease. Cooking oil. She was walking beneath a London restaurant that was draining its waste into the river.

A rat—about eight inches long from nose to tail—scurried across the bricks. As the cooking smell grew stronger, more rats appeared, and she felt sick to her stomach. Some of the rats ran away from the light, but others stayed frozen on the sloping sides of the culvert. Her light made their eyes look like little red beads. The culvert angled left, and when she came around the corner she saw hundreds of rats clinging to the wall. The light caused a panic, and some of the rats leaped into the river, making high-pitched squeaks as they splashed over to the other side.

The river current pushed the rats toward her. The water was high now, almost to her waist, and she could see the rats' sharp noses and thin tails. Maya drew her sword and used the tip of the blade to flick the rats away. The grease smell was almost unbearable. A drop of water fell on her forehead. *Don't touch your mouth or eyes*, she told herself. *A child is inside you, growing within this body.*

After twenty yards of culvert, the rats began to disappear. A few stragglers scurried away when she sloshed up the tunnel. She found the blue light near a Y-juncture, but there was no indication about which way to go. She took the right fork and was relieved to see the red marker.

How far to the Evergreen building? Was it thirty meters? Forty? She continued up the culvert until she found two fiber-optic cables that ran into the culvert from a maintenance pipe in the ceiling. The pipe was about three feet wide and sealed with a hinged steel plate. When Maya tapped the plate with her knuckles, she heard a hollow sound.

Water swirled around her and white foam clung to the waders. Trying not to slip and fall, she loaded one of the breaching rounds into the shotgun. Then she held the weapon close to the plate and fired. The noise echoed down the tunnel. It was so loud that she almost fell backward. A six-inch hole had appeared in the plate, and she used the bolt cutters to hack through the steel.

Sweat covered her face, and she tried not to panic when it touched her lips. After transferring her weapons to the knapsack, she tied the bag to a nylon cord and looped the other end around her shoulders. Grabbing one of the cables, she began to climb hand over hand, the knapsack swinging beneath her. The cord dug into her skin and the dead weight tried to pull her down, but she kept climbing until she reached a closet-sized switching room. The breaching round had been very loud—the noise might have been picked up with a sensor. Perhaps the guards had been notified and now they were there, waiting for her.

Maya took a deep breath and kicked open the door.

31

Maya found herself in a basement with old desks and chairs stacked against the wall. Using the light from her headlamp, she crossed the room and inspected the main electrical panel. Taped to its cover was an inspection certificate that gave the building address: 41 Limeburner Lane. Her fatigue disappeared and she smiled. Nora Greenall was right: the lost rivers could take you anywhere in London.

She zipped open the knapsack, removed her gear, and tossed the bag and the waders into the closet. The Free Runners had supplied her with a pink smock bearing a company logo, cleaning supplies, and a plastic bucket. Pulling on the smock, she considered an immediate assault on the four guards, then rejected the idea and placed the sword and shotgun in a nylon bag.

Her mind shifted into the Harlequin way of thinking as she left the basement and climbed up a short flight of stairs. Two doors were on the landing, one marked MAINTENANCE and another fastened with a padlock. She cut off the lock, slipped it into the front pocket of her jeans, and stepped into the building's emergency stairwell. *Seize the summit*, Sparrow wrote in his book of meditations. *It is easier to fight your way down the mountain than to fight your way up.*

When she reached the fifth floor, she opened the door and stepped into a lobby in front of the elevators. A burly security guard sat behind a desk reading a men's magazine. He looked startled by her sudden appearance.

"Evening," Maya said, using a strong East London accent. "Where do I start cleaning?"

The guard hid the magazine beneath a newspaper. "And who the hell are you?"

"The regular girl was sick. I'm Lila." She gestured to her pink smock. "From the Merry Maids."

"This is a restricted floor. You don't clean here."

It was important to get closer to him, inside the range of her knife. Smiling, she approached the desk. "Sorry! I talked to the guard at the entrance and he told me to go up the stairs." She stopped near the side of the desk. "If I made a mistake, *please* don't tell my supervisor. I've only had this job for three days. Don't want to get sacked . . ."

The guard checked out her breasts and grinned. "Relax. A girl as pretty as you can make all kinds of mistakes."

One step closer, she thought. *Use the stiletto, not the throwing knife. Best target is the lower neck, between the shoulder blades.*

"I'm calling down to the main desk," the guard said. "I just want to see what's going on."

Maya came around the desk and stood behind him. "Thank you. I can see you're a real gentleman."

As the guard picked up the phone, Maya remembered the

padlock she had cut off in the stairwell. She reached into her jeans, slipped the lock into the palm of her hand, then hit the guard on the side of the head. He lurched forward—dazed, but still conscious—so she hit him a second time in the middle of the forehead. The guard was propelled backward onto the floor. Maya reached down and touched his carotid artery. Still alive.

She took a roll of duct tape out of the nylon bag, gagged the young man, and taped his ankles and wrists. Then she picked up her supplies and hurried down the hallway. There were three locked doors, and all of them used wall-mounted sensors instead of keys. Her lock picks and bolt cutters were useless.

Maya returned to the desk and crouched beside the guard. She wasn't surprised to find a small scar on the back of his right hand; in order to get the job he had agreed to carry a Protective Link chip beneath his skin. She grabbed the guard by his feet and dragged him down the hallway. When they reached the first door, she pulled up the guard's hand and passed it in front of the sensor. Nothing. Perhaps he wasn't authorized to enter that room. A cut on the guard's head smeared a line of blood across the carpet as she dragged him over to the second door. Once again, she raised his hand. This time the door clicked open.

She entered a residence suite that was probably used by the members of the Brethren who visited London. The living room was filled with modern furniture, and framed photographs of nature scenes were on the wall.

The living room was connected to a kitchen and a small dining room. A hallway on the left led to a bedroom. Maya drew her knife, moved cautiously to the open doorway, and peered inside. A night table. Dresser. Bed. And there was Alice Chen with her black braids lying like two strands of rope on a pillow.

"I'm here," Maya whispered. "I've come for you . . ."

Alice opened her eyes and sat up in bed. "Don't come in the room, Maya! An alarm will go off!"

Maya stood a short distance from the doorway and saw that

cameras had been mounted in each corner of the room. The four cameras clicked and whirred, following every movement of the child's body.

"Take off your nightgown and put on your street clothes," Maya said. "I'll count to three and then you'll run out of the room. We'll be halfway down the stairs before they respond to the alarm."

"No. I can't do that. The machine is watching me." Alice pushed back the quilt, revealing a thick plastic shackle fastened around her ankle. "They call this a Freedom Bracelet. If I leave the room, I get a big shock."

"Okay. I understand. Get dressed and I'll figure out a plan."

The cameras panned back and forth as Alice jumped out of bed and hurried over to the dresser. Returning to the living room, Maya took out her sword and the combat shotgun. *How do we get out of here?* she wondered. *And what would happen if we just ran out of the apartment? We can't return to the underground river—the water level is too high for a child.*

Rummaging through the kitchen, she found a coffee mug in the cupboard and filled it with water. Then she boiled the water in a microwave oven and used a dish towel to carry the hot cup down the hallway.

Alice had pulled on jeans and a sweatshirt. She was sitting on the edge of the bed, tying her shoes. "What are we going to do, Maya?"

"Stay there. Don't move. We need to find out what kinds of cameras are watching you. Machines can be very clever and very foolish at the same time."

Maya tossed the cup into the room and it rolled across the carpet. Instantly, the surveillance cameras detected the object, panning back and forth and making little whirring sounds as if they were talking to one another.

"See how the cameras follow the cup?" Maya said. "They're infrared devices, focusing on your body heat. The computer program attached to the cameras is making sure that one warm object—about your size—is in the room at all times."

"Then you better leave me here. Boone said the guards will hurt anyone who enters the building."

"You met Nathan Boone?"

Alice shook her head. "A man named Clarence brings my food. Once he handed me a cell phone and said that Boone wanted to talk to me. Boone no longer controls the guards in this building. He said he'll try to help me when he comes back to London."

"He's lying." Maya watched as the four cameras turned away from the cup and focused on Alice. "Are there extra clothes in the closet?"

"Clarence bought some stuff at a department store."

"Go to the closet. Put a few sweaters on the same hanger, then place it in the shower and turn on the water as hot as you can."

"Okay."

"When the clothes are soaked with water, come out of the bathroom holding them close to your body."

"I understand. Then the cameras will focus on the warm clothes and not on me."

"I hope so . . ."

Alice hung two sweaters and a wool skirt on a hanger and hurried into the bathroom. Maya heard water surge through the pipes as the shower started running. A few minutes later, Alice came back out holding the wet clothes.

"Now what?"

Maya held up the bolt cutters. "Place the hanger on that gooseneck lamp over there, then immediately come through the doorway. Are you ready?"

"I'm okay. Let's try it." Alice hung the clothes on the lamp and was out the door in three steps. Moving quickly, Maya cut the Freedom Bracelet off with the bolt cutters and tossed the shackle back into the room. The cameras had been agitated—whirring back and forth—but now all four of them were focused on the wet clothes.

Alice stared at the shackle lying on the carpet a few feet away from her. "Would that really hurt me?"

"Yes."

"Very much?"

"Don't think about it anymore."

Alice embraced Maya, holding her tightly. "I thought you might come. I made a lot of special wishes." She let go and stepped away. "I'm sorry, Maya. I know you don't like to be touched."

"Just this once." Maya extended her arms, and the girl hugged her again. "We need to be careful, Alice. It might be difficult to get out of this building."

"All the security guards have guns. I've seen them."

"Yes, I know. So when I touch your shoulder like this"—Maya squeezed Alice's shoulder—"then I want you to close your eyes."

"Why?"

"Because that's what my father did when I was a little girl and he didn't want me to see bad things."

"I'm getting older."

"I know you are. But just do this for me. We're going to leave this room, go down the staircase, and—"

Maya heard a faint *plop* and spun around. Heavy with water, the clothes had just slipped off the plastic hanger. The cameras were moving again, and little red lights flashed on their holding brackets.

"Does the computer know what happened?"

"Yes. We've got to get out of here."

Clutching the shotgun, Maya ran out of the suite with Alice. They stepped around the unconscious guard and ran into the stairwell. Her mind was calm and detached as she tried to assess the danger around them. Three armed guards were still in the building and there was only one way out.

Maya took two steps at a time, grabbing the railing and turning quickly at each landing. She reached the ground floor first and got ready to fire the shotgun as Alice caught up with her.

"Are you going to shoot someone?"

"Only if I have to. Stay here until I come and get you."

Maya tried the door to the lobby. It was locked. The shotgun was already loaded with regular shells, but she loaded the second breaching round and pumped it into the firing chamber. *Get ready*, she told herself. The breaching round blew a hole in the door, and she kicked it open.

The entrance guard drew his handgun, dived behind his desk, and fired two wild shots in her direction. Maya fired her shotgun directly at the desk and pellets hit its metal panel. With the folding stock pressed against her shoulder, she stepped forward, firing again and again. The pellets hit a glass security barrier, and it disintegrated into shards.

When she reached the desk, she lowered the weapon. All she could see was the guard's hand emerging from behind the desk. A line of blood trickled across the floor. Maya hurried back to the stairway door and yanked it open.

"Let's go!" she shouted. As they both left the building, Maya reloaded the shotgun, folded its stock, and wrapped the Merry Maids smock around the weapon. "*Walk*. Don't run," she told Alice. "All we have to do is get down to the river. The Free Runners are waiting for us there."

They entered Ludgate Circus and waited for the stoplight before they crossed the intersection. It was close to midnight; only a few cars were on New Bridge Street. Maya felt as if she had just emerged from a collapsing house, but no one had noticed.

"Maya! Behind us!"

Two men wearing white shirts and black neckties ran around the corner. Maya pulled Alice down Pilgrim Street, a narrow lane lined with office buildings. For a few seconds she thought they were going to be trapped in a dead end, but a staircase led them up to Ludgate Hill.

St. Paul's Cathedral was directly in front of them. Spotlights on the building made its white dome and two towers look as if they were floating above the city. Maya tried to wave down a taxi, but the driver didn't stop. A group of drunken teenagers were on the opposite sidewalk, clapping and laughing as one of the girls tried to dance.

"They're getting closer, Maya!"

"I see them."

Maya and Alice crossed over to St. Paul's and followed the cobblestone walkway that ran along the left side of the cathedral. A young busker was scooping up the tips from his guitar case and he bowed gracefully. "What's the rush, ladies? I'll play you a song!"

At the end of the lane she looked left and saw a sign for the Tube station at Panyer Alley. Now they were running as fast as possible, not caring if anyone saw them dash down the alley to the station entrance. They hurried down the stairway, passed through the turnstile, and jumped on the escalator.

Maya took sunglasses out of her jacket and the dark lenses dulled the glare from the fluorescent bulbs on the ceiling. The escalator glided downward with a faint grinding sound. Posters for a West End musical showed a woman leaping over a man's head.

When they reached the transit area, Maya saw that a second escalator led to the eastbound trains. She glanced upward. The two Tabula mercenaries had just reached the top of the escalator, and one of them was pulling out a handgun. A NIGHT OF STARS! one of the theater posters read. YOU'LL NEVER STOP LAUGHING!

Maya handed the cell phone to Alice. "Go to the platform and take the next westbound train. Get off at Bank, change onto the Northern Line to Camden Town. Ask for the African drum shop and avoid the cameras."

"What about you?"

"We can't keep running."

"But they both have—"

"Do what I say!"

Alice headed down the short corridor that led to the Tube platform. Maya followed her for a few yards and dodged behind a pillar. The two mercenaries would reach this point in about five seconds.

The shotgun was ready. Her thoughts were clear and precise. Years ago, her father had abandoned her in a Tube station like this so that she could learn to fight alone. He had wanted her to be strong and courageous, but instead she had felt betrayed. That memory stayed with her like a wrathful spirit. But now, at this moment of danger, close to death, it had finally lost its power.

"They're taking the train!" a man shouted.

She pumped a round into the shotgun's firing chamber, stepped into the corridor, and saw the two mercenaries. When she fired, the sound was immense, echoing off the walls of the tunnel. The shotgun pellets knocked the first man off his feet. Turning slightly, she fired again at short range. The second man's chest seemed to explode from within and blood sprayed across the tiles.

Maya wiped off the shotgun with the pink smock and dropped it onto the floor. Leaving the two dead men behind her, she walked slowly onto the platform. Alice was there with her eyes closed and her hands clenched into fists.

When Maya stroked the child's hair, Alice opened her eyes. "You fired the shotgun."

"That's right."

"What happened?"

There was a slight movement of air, as if the earth itself were breathing out, and then a train rolled into the station. Maya turned her back to the platform camera and took Alice's hand. "We're safe," she said. "But we have to keep moving."

32

Gabriel sat with his father on a balcony near the top of one of the towers. That morning they had wandered up the slope and picked some green berries from one of the hillside plants. Matthew boiled water in the solar oven and used the berries to brew tea. The tea had a sharp citric taste, but it seemed to go well with the cold mountain air and bright sunlight.

After days of conversation, the relationship between father and son had reached a certain equilibrium. They were both aware of each other in subtle ways, and complicated emotions could be expressed with a smile or a quick movement of the eyes. Gabriel's

father reminded him of the figures created by Alberto Giacometti. The Italian sculptor used wire and clay to make a horse
or a dog or a human being, then slowly cut away every unneces-
sary detail until only the elemental form remained. Matthew
Corrigan had gone through a similar transformation. His face was
thin and bony, and his clothes hung loosely on his body. Like
Giacometti's statutes, he was spare and unencumbered. He had
lost the vanity and pride that others wore like armor in the Fourth
Realm.

Matthew picked up a pot that was carved from a dark green
stone and poured some tea into his cup. "You look very serious this
afternoon."

"I'm trying to figure out why these parallel worlds exist. Are
there only these six realms?"

"Of course not. Our set of six realms is only a reflection of our
human world."

"What if there was another form of life in the Alpha Centauri
system?"

"I would assume that those beings would have their own set
of realms. The parallel worlds are infinite."

"So what about the gods and the half gods? Did they create
everything?"

"They don't have that power. The creator goes by many names,
but Aristotle called it the 'Unmoved Mover'—that being that is
eternal and indivisible. The half gods in the Fifth Realm are something else. I see them as 'bad angels,' and the 'good angels' were
living here."

"So why did these good angels build the golden city?" Gabriel
asked. "Someone designed these buildings in a particular way."

"Tell me what you felt when you walked through the first
building."

"At first I thought it was a trap, and then I realized it was
empty."

"Yes. It's like an immense museum without guards—or
visitors."

"I looked around a little bit, but there didn't appear to be any shortcuts or hidden staircases. So I walked through every room until I reached the second terrace."

"And then you entered the next building . . ."

"It was the same thing. There was only one way to go."

"Did you examine the various wall paintings and the displays?"

"I looked at a few of them. But after a while I just wanted to get to the next level."

"That was also my reaction," Matthew said. "But then you entered the third building."

"The staircases and corridors went off in every direction. There were dead ends and windowless rooms. I got lost a couple of times."

"It was frustrating."

"Definitely."

"And frightening?"

"Sometimes."

"Did your frustration and fear make you wish you were back in the first two buildings?"

"Not really. Maybe I was lost, but at least it wasn't boring."

Matthew held his stone cup with two hands and stared at the surface of the tea. The soft drone of the wind blowing around the towers reminded Gabriel of the lowest note on a wooden flute.

"During my stay here, I've tried to understand this world using the theories I learned when I was studying physics. I think that the buildings are a lesson for anyone who finds their way to this world. The first two buildings show us a universe where our destiny is predetermined. There's no freedom of choice; there's only one direction for humanity. The entire structure has been set up by some all-powerful architect, and we are children forced to trudge through the rooms in the same direction."

"And the third building?"

"It's a model of the chaotic nature of reality. You can take this staircase or another, get lost, and wander back the way you came."

"You sound like Maya talking about her random number generator."

"Quantum physics shows us that you can't predict the position of subatomic particles. An electron or a photon of light is never in a particular place. It's in a sort of super-position of all possible places at the same time. It's only when something is observed that all these possibilities collapse into one actuality. What this means is that all options are possible and there are an infinite amount of pathways. We don't live in a deterministic universe."

"Okay. Fine. The universe is random and chaotic. But knowing that isn't going to change anything."

"I disagree, Gabriel. Religions and governments that follow a determinist model have caused the deaths of hundreds of millions of people. The strangest aspect of this rigid view of history is that the founders of every major religion believed in free will and made choices throughout their lives. Moses decided to lead his people out of Egypt, Mohammed decided to preach in Mecca, and Buddha sat down beneath a Bodhi tree. For me, one of the most significant aspects of the Passion story is that Jesus made a *choice* to enter Jerusalem and be crucified. The deterministic view is added on by followers *after* the founder's death. When people decide that a certain way of faith is destined and inevitable, hatred and intolerance follow. Instead of saying, 'The Light is within you, choose the Light,' the message becomes 'Agree with our version of history or we'll kill you.'"

Gabriel frowned and shook his head. "That's what the Tabula believe."

"Their views are shared by many governments and political parties. The two failed ideologies of the twentieth century—Communism and Fascism—both advocated a deterministic model of history. Communism was supposedly a 'scientific' theory that predicted the inevitable collapse of the capitalistic system. And Adolf Hitler believed that the so-called master race was destined to take over the world."

"Maybe they failed, but we're still fighting with each other."

"People don't believe they have power. Because they're scared, they want magic spells and secret passwords. It takes some bravery to accept the implications of free will and negative consequences. But we can't solve our problems with surveillance cameras and tracking programs."

"A member of the Tabula would say that the world is a dangerous place. We need safeguards to protect us."

"I'm not going to deny that there's pride and anger and greed in the Fourth Realm. We can find those negative qualities in our own hearts and see them in others every day. But the Panopticon is a system that automatically assumes that *everyone* is guilty. It can never conquer fear. It actually makes people even more suspicious and frightened because it ignores the inherent connections between us."

"Are you talking about our spiritual connections?"

"I'm always wary of calling anything spiritual, Gabriel. It's such a fuzzy, vague word. What I'm saying is that we really *are* connected to each other, and that the Panopticon tries to ignore this particular reality."

Gabriel laughed. "I don't think you can prove that with physics."

"Perhaps we can. When I was in graduate school, we studied something called the EPR Paradox. In the 1930s, Einstein and two other physicists had come up with a thought experiment that attempted to show the illogical nature of quantum theory. Physicists knew that electrons and other subatomic particles revolve like two kinds of tops with their axis pointing either up or down. Often one of these particles pairs up with its opposite so that their up-and-down movements cancel each other out and become zero."

"So what's the paradox?"

"The three physicists described an experiment where an atom was blown apart and two paired particles flew away from each other at close to the speed of light. If one particle was spinning down, then quantum theory predicted that its lost twin had to spin up. Einstein wrote that it was 'spooky' to believe that something that happened at one point of the universe influenced another point light-years away."

"Of course. That's impossible."

"It might sound impossible, but a number of experiments have shown that Einstein was wrong. French scientists measured paired photons several kilometers apart and discovered that the particles were still linked together, joined by their wave function, acting in response to each other. The entire universe is a strange sort of spiderweb connected by gossamer strands of energy.

"These theories both describe and explain what we see in reality. The walls of the Panopticon cannot last: freedom is the essence of our lives—not surveillance and control."

Gabriel nodded. "You could be right. But I haven't met any gods here who actually know the truth."

"Maybe their departure was a gift to mankind. The human race is clever enough to make its own choices. The ultimate power that created the realms will always exist, but perhaps our good angels are telling us: *'You're not children anymore. Stop making excuses and accept responsibility for the fate of your own world.'*"

Gabriel stayed silent for a while and finished drinking the tea. He thought about Maya and all the problems waiting for him back in the Fourth Realm.

"I've come up with a plan to stop the Tabula," he said. "But I don't know if it's going to work. Only a few hundred people are committed to the Resistance. According to Michael, we've already lost."

"And do you believe that?"

"I have one opportunity to get past the censors and speak directly to a great many people. I wanted to find you because I didn't know what to say. I think you should come back and make the speech yourself."

"You said that the Tabula have my body locked up in a room."

"I'll talk to Maya and we'll find a way to get you out."

Matthew turned away from his son and gazed at the mountains. "I know that I'm sitting here with you and we're talking and drinking this tea, but I don't feel completely human anymore. I've been away too long and I'm not attached to our world. If I spoke to people, they would sense that my heart has lost its connection to their hopes and desires."

"But what about your physical body?"

Matthew shook his head. "I'm not really connected with that either."

"What are you telling me, Father? Are you going to die?"

"That may happen fairly soon. But this is just one stopping point of our eternal journey. Every human being has the power to send their Light forward to another world, but they only discover that when they pass on."

Gabriel reached out and touched his father's arm. "I don't want to lose you."

"Don't worry. I'm still here for a while. The gods have vanished, but this place is a suitable residence for a questioning mind."

"I'm the one who has to leave," Gabriel said. "I've got to return to our world."

"I understand. You love someone in the Fourth Realm, and you're worried about all those people who are losing their freedom."

"So what do I tell them?" Gabriel asked. "How can I convince them to step away from the Vast Machine?"

"Unlike me, you're still connected to their lives. Instead of 'telling' them what to believe, try to answer the questions that are in your own heart."

"I'm not one of the gods. I don't have all the answers."

"That's a good start." Matthew smiled broadly. At that moment, he resembled the father who had made kites for his two sons, then watched these fragile creations rise up above the trees. "Look outward, Gabriel. This city is beautiful at sunset. The golden towers don't have their own energy, but they do reflect the light . . ."

33

If a physicist living in Los Angeles had dropped by Mar Vista Park that afternoon, he might have seen a classic example of something called "Brownian motion." The children in the park moved in erratic patterns like tiny bits of pollen suspended in fluid, bouncing off one another and floating away in opposite directions. Someone gazing down from the heavens might have decided that these particles of life behaved like the electrons in a quantum game of chance.

* * *

SITTING ON THE benches near the children's play area, the adults saw cause and effect instead of chaos. Shawn was thirsty and kept running back to his mother for a sip of apple juice. May Ling was playing with two mean girls—Jessica and Chloe—and sometimes they accepted her and sometimes they ran away. The positions of the adults also followed a certain order. A group of elderly Chinese men and women sat on the east side of the play area, proudly watching their grandchildren; Mexican nannies with expensive strollers stood on the opposite side, chatting on cell phones or gossiping in Spanish.

Ana Cabral was separate from both groups. She was Brazilian, not Mexican, and she was watching her own children—eight-year-old Roberto and his four-year-old brother, Cesar. Ana was a small woman with a large handbag who worked mornings at a plumbing parts store. Although she didn't own a closet full of clothes, her tennis shoes were new, and her blue headband matched the color of her blouse.

At this moment, little Cesar was playing with his dump truck in the sand, and Ana's only worry was that an older child might pull the toy from his hands. Roberto was more of a problem. He was an active boy who had come out of her womb with his hands clenched into fists. Because of the dirty air, he suffered from asthma, and Ana had to carry an inhaler in her handbag in case of emergencies.

Roberto needed to run around with other boys, but Ana felt better when her sons were inside the house with all the doors locked. In the last few weeks, twelve California children had disappeared from playgrounds and schoolyards. The police in San Francisco said they had arrested a suspect, but two days ago a little girl named Daley McDonald had disappeared from the backyard of her home in San Diego.

Don't think bad thoughts, Ana told herself. *Victor is right. You worry too much.* She glanced into her bag, made sure the inhaler was there, then leaned back on the bench and tried to enjoy the day. A little blond girl wearing pink overalls was watching Cesar play with the truck while Roberto lay belly down in one of the swings and pretended he was flying. Ana heard the sound of traffic behind her and the voices of the nannies. Back in Brazil she would have known each woman and the history of her family. That was the most difficult thing about Los Angeles—not the gangs and learning English, but the fact that she was surrounded by strangers.

Mar Vista Park was dotted with picnic areas and Scotch pine trees. The hazy Los Angeles sunlight gave the landscape a slightly flat, colorless appearance, like the drawing of a park in a faded illustration. If Ana looked left, she could see a large soccer field with artificial grass. On her right was a fenced-in concrete oval that was used for roller hockey. The play area was at the center. Four plastic and metal structures built to look like beach shacks were surrounded with sand. If you left the sand and walked across a strip of dead grass, you came to a red brick building that was used for basketball games and Boy Scout meetings.

Beyond that was a side street where someone had parked an ice cream truck.

*　*　*

WEARING A RADIO headset, Martin Doyle sat in a windowless compartment between the ice cream machines and the truck cab. He leaned forward and stared at a monitor as a little girl wearing a pink sundress approached the truck and ordered a vanilla ice cream cone with chocolate sprinkles.

A Tabula mercenary named Ramirez was in charge of selling the soft-serve ice cream. He took the child's money, handed her the cone, and watched her walk away. "What are you doing?" he asked Doyle.

"I'm not quite ready to start the target search. Give me a few more minutes."

Doyle continued watching the monitor. He had a scar on the back of his right hand where the Tabula had inserted a radio chip. An even more powerful chip had been injected into his chest—

between his chest muscles and his sternum. *I'm a slave*, he thought. *Boone's little robot*. These days, the team was traveling all over California. If he kept alert, there might be an opportunity to escape.

The high-tech equipment gave him access to private homes and public playgrounds, but he was never allowed to savor the experience. When the team wasn't working, Doyle lay in bed and ran through his memories; it felt as if he were touching each image, holding it up to the light like a cherished photograph. There was Darrell Thompson, the little boy alone in a backyard decorated for a birthday party. Everyone else had gone inside for cake, but Darrell was still jumping on the Moon Bouncer. Doyle remembered Amanda Sanchez, the girl who cried, and Katie Simms, a blond charmer with a Band-Aid on her scraped knee.

The images he cherished most were the quiet moments when the children first encountered him. Doyle enjoyed the look of surprise on their faces and their frightened smiles. They always stared at his face, really *looked* at him in a very intense way. Did they know him? Was he going to be their new friend?

Doyle swiveled in his chair, reached up to a shelf, and took down a clear plastic box that held a dragonfly clinging to a twig. He shook the box gently and the insect moved its wings. The dragonfly had been turned into something called a HIMEMS: an acronym for *Hybrid Insect: Micro-Electro-Mechanical-System*. Ramirez and the other mercenaries simply called them "robobugs."

For many years, the CIA and various European spy agencies had used insect-sized spy drones designed to resemble dragonflies. These high-tech surveillance tools could hover over an antiwar rally and take photographs of the demonstrators. According to Boone, the mechanical dragonflies had several vulnerabilities. They couldn't hover for more than ten minutes and were blown sideways by strong crosswinds. But the biggest problem was that the drones were obviously little machines. When one of them fell onto the Champs-Élysées during a Paris protest against global warming, the marchers had irrefutable evidence of government spying.

A HIMEMS looked exactly like an ordinary insect. When the dragonfly was in a nymph stage, a silicon chip and a tiny video lens were inserted into the larva. As the dragonfly grew larger, its nervous system became attached to the chip, and its movements could be controlled by a computer.

Carrying the plastic box with him, Doyle pushed open a sliding door and stepped around the driver's seat. He opened a second door and strolled over to the picnic table near the park's soccer field. Making sure no one was watching, he opened the box, took out the twig, and carefully placed the HIMEMS in the middle of the table. The hybrid dragonfly was a blue-eyed darner with a long body, strong, transparent wings, and bright blue spots on its abdomen.

The dragonfly had been captive in the box for several weeks and seemed relieved to be outside. Doyle felt that he understood the dragonfly's reaction; he had also been a prisoner, and it was a pleasure to be back out in the world. Slowly, the insect moved its two pairs of wings, feeling the wind and the afternoon sunlight. Doyle tapped his finger on the table, and the startled insect flew away.

Doyle returned to the ice cream truck, stepped into the compartment, and activated the HIMEMS program on the computer. The first image on the monitor showed something dark, with a rough texture, and Doyle guessed that the dragonfly was resting on a tree branch. He attached a joystick to the computer and gently pushed the lever forward. The dragonfly responded like a toy airplane, taking off and heading east. Doyle could see the parking lot and the tops of some trees.

In San Diego and San Francisco, he had learned how to control the hybrids. You couldn't direct precise movements, but you could send the dragonfly in a general direction and then make it stop and hover. Using a HIMEMS meant that he didn't need to draw attention to himself as he watched the children. Doyle had escaped his fleshy, fumbling body. At that moment, he was a dark angel, floating above the children, watching three boys wander away from the play area.

* * *

THE CHINESE GRANDPARENTS were leaving, and Ana checked her watch. It was almost five o'clock. She would let the boys play for a few more minutes, and then she had to get home and start making dinner. Cesar was still playing with the blond girl, but Roberto and two other boys his age had gone over to the park building. They stood near the doorway—probably watching some older boys play basketball.

Something passed through the air near the edge of her vision. When she looked up, she saw an insect right above the swings. What did they call that in the United States? A dragonfly. In Brazil, sometimes they called it a *tira-olhos,* which meant "eye thief."

As the dragonfly darted away, Cesar approached her carrying the dump truck. "Broke," he said in English, and held up the toy.

"No. It's all right. I can fix it."

Ana turned the truck over and began to scrape sand away from the dumping mechanism. When she looked up again, Roberto and one of the boys had disappeared, but the third boy still lingered in the doorway.

The second boy came out of the park building, but Roberto wasn't with him. A minute or so passed until the fear switch clicked in Ana's brain. She stood up and asked the blond nanny to watch Cesar for a minute, please. She strolled past the swings to the dead grass. The two little boys who had been standing near the doorway were coming toward her, but when she asked, "Where's Roberto? Where's my son?" they shrugged as if they didn't know his name.

She reached the open doorway of the park building and peered inside. The basketball room had a polished wooden floor and two baskets—a hollow room with echoes bouncing off the bare walls. Two half-court games were being played: one involved two teams of El Salvadorans, and the other game was between a group of teenage boys with bushy hair and slogans on their T-shirts.

"Have you seen my son?" she said in Spanish to an older El Salvadoran man. "He's a little boy wearing a blue jacket."

"Sorry. I didn't see anyone," the man answered. But his skinny friend stopped dribbling the basketball and approached her.

"He went out that door a few minutes ago. There's a water fountain out there."

Ana hurried down the centerline of the basketball court as the games continued on either side of her. When she walked out of the doorway on the north side of the building she found a small parking lot and the street. Ana took a few steps forward and looked in every direction, but she couldn't see her son.

"Roberto," she said quietly, almost like a prayer, and then a feeling of panic overwhelmed her and she began to scream.

34

The first step in the sequence of events leading to Mrs. Brewster's death was announced by a soft beep and a text message on Michael's handheld computer. Mrs. Brewster was staying at Wellspring Manor and a security guard there was watching her movements.

Michael was four thousand miles away from southern England, sitting in one of the resident suites at the research center outside of New York City. Wearing a terry cloth bathrobe, he finished his coffee and read the message: *Mrs. B. to Portreath airport this evening.*

A spy program had been placed in all of Mrs. Brewster's

computers—Michael had been reading her e-mail for the last three weeks. From the moment he had taken control of the Evergreen Foundation, she had criticized his decisions and organized a small opposition group. In the Fifth Realm, Mrs. Brewster would have been torn apart on a public stage. But Michael didn't want to cause dissent within the Brethren. Mrs. Brewster would die discreetly, without a visible executioner.

Michael saw himself as an author creating different stories in countries around the world. Mrs. Brewster's little story was about to end, but he had invented far more elaborate narratives. First there would be a criminal action or a terrorist attack, then a period of growing tension and instability. Finally, there would be a solution—offered by the Evergreen Foundation or one of their surrogates. The introduction of the Panopticon would give each story a happy ending.

In California, fourteen children were missing. In Japan, envelopes of anthrax had been sent to the emperor and other members of the royal family. In France, a mysterious terrorist group had set off bombs in three major art museums. While these threats dominated the news cycle, three new stories would be introduced—in Australia, Germany, and Great Britain. The message of all these stories was simple and clear: there was no safe place in any country.

* * *

MICHAEL TOOK A shower, and then sent a reply to the guard at Wellspring Manor. *Tell me when she leaves.* When he was dressed, he strolled across the quadrangle to the Kennard Nash Computer Center. Michael had full security clearance for every room in the building; sensors detected the Protective Link chip implanted beneath his skin and doors opened as if he owned the world.

He entered the lobby and Dr. Dawson hurried out to greet him. "It's wonderful to see you, Mr. Corrigan. I was told that you might be leaving today."

"That's right. I'm flying to California to give a speech."

Dawson led Michael into the control room, where Dr. Assad

was studying graphs on a monitor. She pushed a lock of black hair beneath her head covering and smiled shyly. "Good afternoon, Mr. Corrigan."

"I was told that our friends in the Fifth Realm had sent us some more data."

Dr. Assad swiveled her chair around. "It's a design for a radically new computer. The system is quite unlike anything in this world."

"In the beginning, computers were simply computational," Dawson explained. "Now they're learning how to think like human beings. This would be the third evolution—a machine that would seem to be omniscient."

"How is that possible?"

"In school we were taught that it's impossible to calculate any phenomenon that involves a large number of factors. If a butterfly flaps its wings in the Amazon rain forest, then this slight disturbance in the atmosphere could conceivably trigger a long series of events that eventually becomes a hurricane. But this new machine has the power to simultaneously process an immense variety of factors. In some ways, it would have total knowledge."

"So what's the difference between this computer and God?"

The two scientists glanced at each other. It was clear that they had discussed the idea. "God created us," Dawson said softly. "This is just a machine."

"Can you build one?"

"We're assembling a design team," Dr. Assad said. "Meanwhile there have been some new messages." She motioned to a workstation, and Michael sat down in front of a monitor. "As you can see, they want you to return to their world."

"Unfortunately, I'm busy right now," Michael said. "That's not going to happen."

His handheld computer beeped, and he read the text message: *Mrs. B. in her car. Going to airport.* When Michael was in England, he had taken a car from Wellspring to Portreath airport. It took about an hour to get there. Quickly, he erased the message and called his driver.

"Get my luggage from the visitor suite, then contact the charter company at the airport. Tell them that I'm on my way."

He was annoyed to see that Dawson was still hovering around the workstation. The scientist was like a child who desperately wanted to be invited to the party.

"They sent another message this morning, Mr. Corrigan. It's there on the second page: *Remember the story.* What story are they talking about?"

"I described our current civilization to our new friends. It was clear to them that complicated ideas are no longer valued by our media or the general population. Take a look around you. Is anyone reading political manifestos these days? How many people would sit still to listen to a lengthy, sensible speech about our current problems? This world is moving fast, and our consciousness has mirrored that reality."

"But what's the story we're supposed to remember?"

"As ideas lose their power, stories and visual images become more and more important. Leaders offer competing stories, and this is what passes for political debate. Our friends are reminding me to create a powerful story. Let the tension build for a while and then tell a new story that offers a solution."

. Ten minutes later, he was sitting in the back of a limousine being driven to the airport. Cherry trees were flowering in the suburban countryside and their pink blossoms trembled as the car raced down the two-lane road.

Remember the story. Well, he could do that. The news articles he was getting from California showed that everyone was frightened. Parents were keeping their children home from school, and the police kept arresting the wrong suspects. With one decisive move, he had created a crisis that motivated people to enter an invisible prison. Once everyone was inside, a Traveler would watch them and guide their lives.

Michael saw his face reflected in the tinted glass and turned away. Who was he these days? The question kept drifting through his thoughts. The only way he could define himself was by thinking of others. He wasn't his father—and he certainly wasn't Gabriel.

Both of them worried about small things, what a particular person did or said. But most individuals weren't important in the grand narrative of history. For gods and great men, the world was a blank page to be filled with their own vision.

The limousine entered the airport through a side gate and stopped at a building where charter pilots filed their flight plans. A six-passenger jet was waiting on a side runway while the maintenance crew inspected its landing gear.

"Tell the pilot to get everything ready," Michael said. "I need about five minutes to finish some business."

"Very good, Mr. Corrigan." The driver took Michael's luggage from the trunk and carried it over to the plane.

Michael switched on his notebook computer and used a satellite phone to reach the Internet. Ten days ago, he had told his staff in Britain to register all the Evergreen Foundation vehicles with a British company called Safe Ride. Now Mrs. Brewster's Jaguar sedan was connected to the company's computers. The Safe Ride staff could give travel directions to Mrs. Brewster, unlock the car doors if she misplaced her keys, and track her vehicle if it was stolen.

It took only a few seconds to find the Safe Ride Web site and enter a code that allowed him to access the tracking system. Typing in the Jaguar's registration number brought up a satellite photograph of the Cornwall coast. And suddenly, there it was: Mrs. Brewster and her driver were a little red dot traveling on the B3301 rural highway.

Typing quickly, Michael put the local British time in one corner of the screen—it was 7:38 in the evening. Mrs. Brewster was rushing to the Portreath airport to meet the head of Argentina's top antiterrorism unit. The Young World Leaders program connected her to police and military staff in dozens of countries. When these powerful men flew into the local airport, Mrs. Brewster was waiting for them, all charm and smiles.

Michael pushed his cursor across the monitor screen. He followed the route to the airport, noting where the narrow coastal road came close to the sea cliffs. The images provided by the GPS

satellite were amazing. He could see bridges and beaches, towns
and farmhouses. A request for more information created another
box on the screen; now he knew the exact speed of the car and the
fact that an authorized key was in the ignition. Mrs. Brewster had
spent most of her life trying to establish the Panopticon. *We're almost there*, Michael thought. *And you're the one being watched.*

The red dot passed through the town of Gwithian and reached
the coast road. Michael quickly scrolled back and forth across the
screen, and then made his choice. He accessed a second Web site
set up by Nathan Boone's technical staff that allowed him to control radio-chip devices. A day earlier, his contact at Wellspring had
opened the Jaguar's hood and placed an explosive squib on the
car's power-steering fluid container and a second squib on the
car's brake line. Both squibs were small—about the size of an
American penny—and would leave no trace once they exploded.

Figuring a ten- to fifteen-second lag time, he set off both explosives. Michael wondered what it was like inside the car. Too
bad there wasn't a spy cam. The driver would suddenly realize that
the steering wheel no longer responded to his touch. Perhaps his
foot would slam onto the pedal, but nothing would happen.
Would there be time to scream as the car smashed through the
guardrail and glided downward into the sea?

On his computer screen, the little red dot veered off the road,
traveled across a thin patch of cliff, and then disappeared. Michael
turned off the notebook computer, closed it with a snap, and got
out of the car. The pilot and his driver were waiting for him like an
honor guard as he strolled across the tarmac to the plane.

35

Three seagulls sat on the edge of a railing and contemplated the half-eaten breakfast on a serving tray. Michael waved his hand at them—*go away*—but the birds weren't intimidated. Finally he took a piece of muffin and threw it at the ocean. The birds squawked, glided downward, and immediately began squabbling with one another.

He was sitting on the balcony of a three-room hotel suite in West Los Angeles. If he turned slightly to the right, he looked out at beach, ocean, and blue horizon. Young men played volleyball, flinging themselves across the sand, while a girl wearing a bathing suit and roller skates practiced her figure eights on the pedestrian path. Michael sat above it all in a padded chair with a thermos of coffee. The volleyball players and the girl on roller skates had no idea what was about to happen. In three or four weeks, almost every child in California would be part of the Panopticon.

Michael switched on his computer and checked his messages from the different teams working for the Special Projects Group. The anthrax scare in Japan had caused a wave of hostility toward immigrant workers and other foreigners. In France, a new law was being proposed that required a biometric ID card for anyone who wished to enter a government building, a school, or a museum.

New threats were being introduced in three other countries. In Australia, a toxic chemical had been placed in a shipment of oranges that was being sent to regional grocery stores. Two Catholic priests had been assassinated in southern Germany and an unknown Turkish group had claimed credit. In Great Britain, a car bomb was about to go off after an FA Cup match in Manchester.

The half gods had taught him that fear was much easier to sell than tolerance and respect for freedom. Most people were brave only when they saw others taking a stand, and that wasn't going to happen this time. Fear had a strong constituency—those government leaders who realized that the changes would increase their own power.

The door to the suite clicked open and he heard a woman's voice. "Mr. Corrigan! It's Donna!"

"I'm out here."

Donna Gleason pulled the sliding glass door open and stepped onto the balcony. Although she had spent the last ten years in sunny Los Angeles, the public relations consultant was famous for wearing only black. She had very short hair and looked like a nun with a clipboard.

"I just talked to the president of the Los Angeles Press Club. Normally, they fill half the auditorium for these lunchtime presentations, but this event has broken all the rules."

"That sounds promising."

Donna sat down at the table and poured herself a cup of coffee. She talked very quickly, as if everything had to be delivered in thirty-second sound bites. "Three television stations are sending camera crews and there will be reporters from Internet sites, radio stations, and the print media. Everyone was asking me about the title of your speech: 'Save Our Children.' I've told them that you'll start talking at lunch and will be famous by suppertime."

Michael carefully examined Donna's face and saw no signs of deceit or insincerity. In the last few months, he had learned a great deal about the media experts who shaped and packaged images. The good ones had a special talent; if you paid them enough, they became true believers. He wondered what would happen if he pulled out a rifle and announced that he needed to shoot the dangerous skaters and bicyclists on the beach path. Donna might have a difficult transition period, but eventually she would convince herself—yes, it really was a good idea.

"When do we leave?"

"Let me check on that." She turned to the open doorway and screamed, "Gerald! Preston!"

Donna's two assistants reminded him of Scottish terriers, one white and one black. Clutching cell phones, the young men appeared in the doorway.

"Time of departure?"

"We should leave in ten minutes," Gerald said. "They eat a box lunch at twelve thirty and the speech is scheduled for one o'clock."

"Anything else we need to know?"

"Mr. Boone has arrived with one of his men," Preston said. "He wanted to know if you require a security presence."

"Yes. Have them wait in the hallway."

Donna leaned forward. She had three styles of speaking: shrill, flirtatious, and confidential. This was definitely her confidential tone of voice. "I'm sure your speech will be brilliant, Mr. Corrigan. But these days it's all about the visuals. Gerald and Preston installed the video monitors and put up the photographs, but we need something more. It would be great if you could hug one of the mothers . . ."

* * *

THE LOS ANGELES Press Club held its events at a shabby auditorium on Hollywood Boulevard. Every seat appeared to be taken, and the members of the Press Club gossiped with one another while nibbling on potato chips and cheese sandwiches. A dais had been set up onstage, and the club's officers sat behind a long table looking self-conscious. Earlier that day, Gerald and Preston had hung up large photographs of the fourteen missing children. Their cheerful faces didn't bother Michael. Children died every day, but these deaths were going to have a larger significance.

Donna guided Michael onto the dais and introduced him to the president of the Press Club. The meeting began a few minutes later. Donna had written the president's speech, and it included a glowing description of Michael's career path—all of it fictitious. A month earlier, the Evergreen staff had created his past, giving him a series of impressive jobs with nonprofit organizations that were controlled by the Brethren. It was doubtful that anyone would check the facts. But, if they did, false information had been placed on various Web sites.

There was light applause, and the president sat down. As the lost children smiled behind him, Michael took a sip of water and stood behind the podium. He gazed out at hundreds of faces—some curious, some bored. Nathan Boone stood in a side aisle with a sullen look on his face. Michael decided that Boone's story would come to an end during the next few weeks.

"I want to thank the Press Club events committee for inviting me here today. As we drove down Hollywood Boulevard on our way to the auditorium, I asked my friend Donna Gleason what kind of reception I might receive at this event. Donna told me you could be a tough audience and that I'd better say something significant."

A few reporters nodded and most of them seemed to relax a

little. Michael decided that the photographs of the missing children had made the audience uncomfortable.

"There's nothing wrong with being a tough audience. That just means that you're intelligent, informed, and critical. We need all those qualities if we are going to save our children.

"Before I present my proposal, I'm going to anticipate a question that some of you might be thinking: 'How can an outsider, a person who isn't a policeman or a government official, solve the crisis that has touched every family in California?' That's a reasonable thing to ask, and it doesn't require a long answer. I think it helps that I'm *not* part of the system. I can approach this problem from a different perspective and offer a way out.

"The Evergreen Foundation has been around for more than fifty years. We're an international philanthropic organization with offices in London and New York City. Our goals are both idealistic and ambitious. We are dedicated to the health, safety, and stability of human society. Over the years, we've funded the research of thousands of scientists doing medical and genetic research in over thirty countries. Recently, we've gotten involved in the development of technology that fights crime and terrorism. Evergreen has no political agenda or government affiliation. We simply want to make things better—creating a world that's healthy, prosperous, and free from fear.

"And fear is what I see here in California." Michael gestured to the photographs behind him. "Fourteen children have disappeared in the last few weeks, vanished without a trace. Perhaps there are even more cases that have not been officially confirmed.

"Somewhere, a monster stalks through our cities and small towns. This person is a sadistic creature whose only goal is to abduct and destroy our children—the precious little girls and boys who need our protection. Faced with this threat, how have the authorities responded? The parents know the answer. You journalists know the answer. But no one seems to have the courage to say it out loud. The politicians and the so-called experts have done *nothing*."

He paused for a moment and studied the audience. Most of

the reporters nodded slightly as if they had reached the same conclusion.

"I predict that certain out-of-touch leaders, the faces we've seen
blabbering on television, will attack me for telling the truth. They'll
say that an increased number of policemen are on the streets, that
an increased number of cars have been stopped, and that an increased number of suspects have been questioned. But go ahead,
be my guest, ask them: Have these useless activities stopped the
monster that hunts our children?" Michael turned slightly and read
the names at the bottom of the photographs. "Have they saved
Roberto Cabral and Darlene Walker? Will they protect the boys and
girls in danger *right now* while parents mourn the missing?

"These days, mothers and fathers live in fear. They keep their
children home from school. But the fear spreads, like a virus, in-
fecting everyone. Go to the parks of this city. Children no longer
kick a ball or play on the swings. Our communities have lost the
laughter and joy of our little ones.

"But I didn't come to Los Angeles just to criticize the lack of
action by the authorities. I came here to offer a solution. Our idea
is simple, effective, and almost immediate. What's more, the Evergreen Foundation is prepared to fund all start-up costs.

"The Save Our Children initiative is based on proven technology that is already being used in our research facilities. I'm proposing that a Guardian Angel radio transmitter chip with a GPS
locator be placed beneath the skin of every child under the age of
thirteen.

"How does it work? The tiny chips transmit a signal to the local cell phone networks that will be forwarded to a parent's computer or portable communications device. Within seconds, a
mother can know her child's exact location and, if there's a problem, she can instantly contact the police.

"Perhaps this sounds like something from the future, but I can
show you how it works right now." Michael held up his right hand.
"I'm carrying a Guardian Angel chip on the back of my hand.
Donna, would you please connect the Guardian Angel program to
the video monitors."

Donna typed a command into her handheld computer and a satellite image of Michael's hotel appeared on two video monitors. "You're looking at capture images of my movements during the last thirty minutes. You can see me leaving the hotel, traveling on the freeway, and entering this auditorium.

"Now, a parent might say: 'Great idea! But I can't spend all day watching a computer screen!' Well, the Evergreen Foundation has an answer for that as well. It will take us only a few days to connect the chips to a computer that will do the monitoring for you. All the parent has to do is establish what we call a safety parameter—such as the child's school, sports field, and backyard. If the child is taken out of those areas, then the computer will know immediately. The electronic Guardian Angel will contact both the parents and the police.

"These chips work, and the tracking system is amazing. Within a week, every child in California could be safe. Of course, the use of the chips will be optional, but every responsible, loving parent is going to embrace this idea. I can see a day when attendance at a public school will require proof of inoculations and a Guardian Angel chip.

"To summarize: the system works, it's free, and we can start protecting our children within a week. Maybe I should just sit down and eat my lunch while my staff passes out information sheets. But I can't remain silent. I need to tell you what's in my heart.

"The world has become a very dangerous place, but we now have the technology to protect ourselves and others. Who could object to these simple changes? What could possibly be their motivation?

"It's clear that child molesters will be against these changes, along with thieves, rapists, and murderers. Terrorists and the new generation of anarchists demand the perverse 'freedom' to destroy our way of life.

"And who stands with this malevolent crowd? As usual, we have the cocktail-party intellectuals and left-wing college professors who have no clue about the darkness that has descended on our world. But we also have certain right-wing Bill of Rights crazies with old-fashioned ideas of personal freedom.

"The average law-abiding citizen has nothing to fear from these changes. I'm not talking about some Hollywood star with private bodyguards, but the hardworking men and women who want to earn a paycheck, then drive home and watch TV while their kids play in the backyard. Who speaks for these people? Who cares for them? We do. We're stepping forward.

"Fourteen children have disappeared in the last few weeks. *Fourteen children.* Must there be more? Must posters of lost boys and girls be taped on every lamppost in this country? Will you stand up, stand together, and help us save them!"

There was a flurry of activity on a side aisle and Donna appeared with her arm around a small Latina woman. She pulled the woman up onto the dais, guided her over to Michael, and whispered in his ear. "Ana Cabral. You said her son's name."

The mother was weeping as Michael embraced her. *Yes*, he thought. *A good visual*. And flashguns filled the room with light.

36

Around nine o'clock in the evening, Winston drove Maya and Alice across the river to the South Bank and dropped them off in Bonnington Square. Maya had assumed that the meeting was near the Vine House, the illegal squat once used by the Free Runners, but they circled the square twice and couldn't find Edgerton Lane.

The Vine House chimney was still standing, but the rest of the building was a pile of collapsed brick and charred floorboards. Maya paused beside the safety barrier and remembered the night she had dragged Jugger and his friends out the backdoor. A hundred yards away, near the edge of the square, she had killed two Tabula mercenaries with a handgun attached to a homemade silencer. It was a Harlequin rule to never look back or express regret, but sometimes she felt as if the past were following her like a hungry ghost.

"Where's Edgerton Lane?" Alice asked. "Let's call Linden and get directions."

"Linden wanted a blackout on cell phone use two hours before the meeting."

"Don't worry. I'll find it."

Alice ran around the square checking the street signs, then darted into a fish-and-chips shop. She came out with a triumphant smile on her face. "We go three blocks south and turn right."

They left the square and headed down a cobblestone street. Maya glanced up at the windows of the surrounding row houses and saw an older man watching television while his white-haired wife poured tea.

"Why does Gabriel want you to come to the meeting?" Maya asked.

"I thought he told you."

"He spoke to you for almost an hour, Alice. Since he came back, I've only talked to him for a few minutes."

Thirty-six Edgerton Lane turned out to be a vegetarian restaurant called the Other Way. A bulletin board outside was a virtual compendium of the different social and political movements in the last few years. Stop the War and Save the Whales. Raw food and hot yoga. Birth centers and new-age hospices.

She had seen notices like this since she was Alice's age. But this time, there was a significant addition. On the lower-right-hand corner of the board, someone had placed a sticker that showed a surveillance camera with a bar slashed through it. HAD ENOUGH? asked the sticker. FIGHT THE VAST MACHINE.

Maya expected to find a few Free Runners at the restaurant, but the shabby room was filled with strangers. She heard several different languages being spoken as people sipped drinks and waited for the meeting to start. Every table was taken, but Simon Lumbroso had saved them two chairs.

"*Buona sera*. It's a pleasure to see you both. I was worried that you didn't receive the message."

"We got lost," Alice said.

"I didn't think that happened to Harlequins."

"Winston dropped us off on the square," Maya explained. "But we couldn't find the street."

"So I asked the fish-and-chips man."

"Ahhh, I see. You weren't *really* lost." Simon winked at Alice. "As Sparrow suggested, you were cultivating randomness."

While Simon chatted with Alice, Maya studied the crowd that had assembled to hear the Traveler. Everyone in the room could be placed in one of two categories. Jugger and his friends were there along with various off-the-grid tribes that were their natural allies. Regardless of their different political philosophies, the members of this group dressed pretty much the same—jeans, boots, and old jackets. They were an odd mixture of low and high technology: some refused to use credit cards and grew food in rooftop gardens, but their cell phones and computers were cutting-edge.

There was a second group at the restaurant—faces she didn't recognize. Unlike the Free Runners, these new members of the Resistance were citizens who looked as if they paid rent, raised children, and held down regular jobs. They seemed uncomfortable to be sitting in cast-off chairs next to a group of shabby-looking twenty-year-olds.

The owner of the restaurant was a little man with a white beard who resembled a ceramic garden gnome. As both cook and waiter, he scurried back and forth, serving herbal tea and juice smoothies. Maya wondered if any strangers had crashed the meeting, but the gnome was checking names. When he approached their table, he spoke in a low voice.

"This is the monthly meeting of the South London Compost Society. Are you members?"

"We are charter members," Simon said grandly. "I am Mr. Lumbroso, and these two ladies are my friends."

When the gnome had spoken to everyone, he locked the door and hurried back to the kitchen. A minute later, Linden marched into the dining room. Pure Harlequin, Maya thought. The big Frenchman was calm, but alert. Although he didn't show a weapon, there was something about him—some lack of boundaries—that was intimidating.

"*C'est bien,*" he said and Gabriel came in behind him. The Traveler appeared tired and fragile, as if his empty body had spent too many days alone in the secret room. Maya wanted to stand up, draw her sword, and take him away from these people. Maybe they needed him, but they didn't understand the danger.

The Traveler circled the restaurant, personally greeting everyone who had come to the meeting. He stared at each face with a power that allowed him to see split-second changes in a person's expression. Maya doubted if anyone else in the room was aware of this ability, but they knew that Gabriel saw them clearly and accepted their fears and hesitations.

Simon leaned across the table. "Did you see the change?" he whispered. "When the Traveler is here, this becomes a *movement.*"

Maya nodded as she watched the transformation. Even Eric Vinsky, the computer expert who called himself the Nighthawk, tried to sit up in his wheelchair when Gabriel approached him. Finally, the Traveler arrived at their table, touching Alice's shoulder and nodding to Simon.

"Is everything all right?"

"We got lost," Alice said.

"That's not always a bad thing, Alice. Getting lost means you're trying a different path."

He turned away from them and that was it. No words for her. Not even a smile. *I'm carrying your child,* Maya wanted to say. Just thinking it made her nervous. She pressed her lips together so the words wouldn't burst out of her mouth.

Gabriel stood in the middle of the restaurant. When he raised his hands slightly, everyone stopped talking. "This is the first meeting of the worldwide Resistance. I want to thank all of you for coming. According to Jugger, our Japanese friends are stuck in the Frankfurt airport, but we do have delegates from the United States, Canada, Australia, and Poland.

"You are the core, the foundation of our group. I want all of you to get to know one another after I explain the next step in our evolution. The people in this room have different backgrounds and speak different languages. Some of you have unconventional political views, while others see yourselves as liberals or conservatives. This issue unites all of us. It transcends conventional political labels. The real division in our society is between those who are aware and those who choose to remain blind.

"Every person in this room has had a moment when we've looked at the world and have realized that a permanent system of surveillance is being created by the new technology. This system is able to track your movements and monitor your actions. In a few years, it will be able to control your behavior and destroy the privacy of thought that is essential for any democracy. We call this system the Vast Machine, and we are attempting to destroy its power.

"Surveillance technology is the most visible sign of a fundamental change in human society. We are approaching a time when each of us could become another bar-coded object in a world of objects. Distracted by fear and the stress of our contemporary lives, we could only pretend to make free choices. I say 'pretend' because the direction of our lives would be manipulated from birth.

"The people in this room have taken the first step. You've seen what's going on and realized that our freedom is about to be lost forever. The obvious question is: How can we stop this from happening?

"The Tabula and their allies have the power to crush any conventional sort of protest group. They're like Goliath standing on the battlefield with an enormous sword and shield. The only way to defeat them is to act like a modern David. We need to surprise our enemy with quick, decisive action. We need to conceal our organizing efforts until the last possible moment so that our movement will not be compromised or crushed.

"Most of you have heard about the Nighthawk—the person who created our encryption code. He's also developed and released a program called the Revelation Worm, which will allow me to speak to people all over the world. Eric, could you give us some more information . . ."

The Nighthawk moved his wheelchair a few feet from the table. Although his body was still crippled, he seemed happy that he had finally left his dormitory room. "Revelation was released six days ago. I estimate that it's currently hiding in eight to ten million computers, and millions more are being added every day. Remember, this worm can only be activated once, and then security patches will be developed to block it. Think carefully before you pull this particular trigger."

Gabriel nodded, and the Nighthawk rejoined his friends. "The moment I make this speech, the Resistance has to appear and assert itself throughout the world. Some of you feel comfortable about taking part in public demonstrations. Consider yourself the 'Voice of the Street.' Other people here know how to influence the media and members of the government. You're the 'Voice of the Forum,' and should focus on the activities of the Evergreen Foundation.

"Both groups are necessary for our success. You need to start organizing as soon as possible. Send a brief description of what you plan to do to Linden. He's in charge of strategy and will make sure that the different groups don't duplicate activity."

A few people nodded and spoke quietly to their friends. Maya stared at Linden, but the Frenchman avoided her eyes. Harlequins weren't supposed to get involved, but it was clear that Gabriel had pulled him into the Resistance.

"Most of you have heard about the anthrax scare in Japan and the museum bombings in France. These attacks come from unknown groups with vague objectives, but I don't believe that these are terrorist actions. In both countries, legislation was immediately proposed by politicians with past involvement in the Evergreen Foundation's Young World Leaders Program. The new laws would end anonymous activity on the Internet and require mandatory biometric ID cards. There's also been similar activity in the United States. Simon Lumbroso has been monitoring the American media, and he's going to explain the situation."

Simon stood up beside the table and checked a slip of paper with some notes. "Fourteen children have disappeared in California. As the new head of the Evergreen Foundation, Gabriel's brother, Michael, appeared in Los Angeles and made a speech that received a great deal of publicity. Michael used this crisis to set up something called the Guardian Angel system. RFID chips are being placed under the skin of all children under the age of thirteen. They are the first generation of people that can be scanned and tracked like merchandise in a department store."

Gabriel nodded as Simon sat back down. "What's going on in California seems to have created conflict within the Tabula, and this might give our side a unique opportunity. One of their leaders, an Englishwoman named Mrs. Brewster, died a few days ago in a mysterious car accident. In addition, Alice Chen is going to tell us about her conversation with the Foundation's head of security, Nathan Boone. As some of you know, she was taken off a train and held captive at the Evergreen building here in London. During that time, she received a phone call from Boone. Alice, please tell us what he said."

Alice stood up. "Mr. Boone asked if I was okay and if I liked the food and if I was comfortable. He said he wasn't in control of the guards at the building, but that I would be safe because he needed to ask me some questions."

"Go on . . ."

"He said, 'I once had a little girl in my life and I always wanted her to be safe.'"

"What happened after that?"

"He hung up."

"Thank you, Alice. You can sit down. After I talked to Alice, I asked Simon to do some research on Nathan Boone."

"That wasn't difficult," Simon said. "It's all public information."

"Boone has been one of the Tabula's most effective weapons. They might not realize it yet, but he's now become their biggest vulnerability. We know that Boone is currently in Los Angeles. He can be seen in the video footage of my brother's speech. I plan to travel to Los Angeles with Maya as my bodyguard. If we can figure out a safe way to do it, I'll find Boone and talk to him."

* * *

MAYA'S FACE SHOWED no emotion. Boone had killed her father, and now the Traveler wanted to sit down and chat with him. But there was no need for her to express her anger. Almost everyone in the room objected to Gabriel's proposal. They didn't trust Boone and felt it was dangerous for the Traveler to be separated from his friends in London.

Gabriel listened to their arguments, but he refused to change his mind. Throughout the discussion, Maya concentrated on her bandaged leg and tried to appear indifferent. Once, she glanced across the room at Linden, and the Frenchman nodded to show his approval of her behavior. Let the citizens and drones argue about what to do. The Harlequins were calm and steady. They would honor their obligations.

The meeting finally ended two hours later. The various groups began to leave the restaurant and the bearded gnome bustled about picking up cups and dishes. Gabriel accepted a glass of water and sat down at the table next to Alice Chen.

"Alice, I know you like to be with Maya, but she's going with me to Los Angeles. Linden has agreed to protect you, but it's easier for him to do this in Paris."

Alice glanced at Maya as if to ask: *Is this all right with you?* After Maya nodded, the little girl got up from her chair and approached Linden. "Will you teach me how to fight like Maya?"

Linden looked startled for a second, and then he actually smiled. "That can be arranged."

* * *

MAYA FOLLOWED GABRIEL out of the restaurant and into Winston's van. They were silent on the way back to Camden Town, silent as they followed the familiar route through the marketplace to the drum shop hidden in the catacombs.

Winston unlocked the door to the secret apartment. "Will you be all right, Mr. Corrigan?"

"There's nothing to worry about, Winston. Maya is guarding me. Go home and get some sleep."

"Ahhh, yes." Winston's face brightened. "Sleep would be a delightful activity."

Maya went over to Linden's folding cot and pulled off her leather jacket. She placed the sword carrier on the bed, followed by her two knives and the 9 mm automatic she'd been wearing in an ankle holster. As usual, it made her feel vulnerable to be without her weapons. A small mirror in an ebony wood frame had been attached to the wall and, if she moved back and forth, she could see sections of her face. She hadn't washed her hair in three days. No makeup. And she looked tired. *It doesn't make any difference*, Maya told herself. She could be wearing a designer gown and the Traveler would still see the truth in her eyes.

Gabriel was making a pot of tea when she returned to the kitchen. "Are you hungry?" he asked. "We've got crackers and dry sausage, a pot of marmalade, two apples, and a can of sardines."

"Food is food, Gabriel. Anything's okay with me."

Maya thought about her father as Gabriel rummaged through the cupboard and poured hot water into the teapot. Whenever Thorn came back from a long trip, he would buy food at the market, stand in the kitchen, and cook an elaborate meal for her mother. Sometimes, a throwing knife would still be strapped to his arm, but Thorn talked softly as he chopped up peppers and cooked pasta.

"Here we go." Gabriel placed the teapot and two plates of food in the middle of the table. Then he sat in the opposite chair and poured her a cup of tea.

"Do you really want to find Nathan Boone?" she asked. "He killed Vicki and my father. And now you want to talk to him as if he was an ally."

"It's an opportunity. That's all."

"If we find him, you can have your conversation. But when the talking is over—he's dead. You're too idealistic, Gabriel. You don't know who Boone is."

"I know what he's done in the past. But all of us have the power to transform our lives."

"Is that what you learned in the Sixth Realm?"

Gabriel poured some cream into his tea and watched a bubble drift across the surface. "I reached the golden city, but all the gods had vanished. There was only one person there—my father."

"What happened? What did he say?"

"I asked him to return, but he couldn't do it. He's been away too long and doesn't feel attached to this particular reality. I'm not like my father. Because of you, Maya, I'm still connected to this world."

"Is that good or bad?" Maya forced a smile.

"It's good, of course. Love is the Light within all of us. It can survive even when our physical bodies are lost forever."

What's he telling me? Maya wondered. *Is he going to die?*

Gabriel got up from the table and stood beside her. "We can regret the past, but we can't change what happened. We can anticipate the future, but we can't control it. All we have is this moment—here in this room."

No more words. She stood up, and they held each other. The Traveler embraced her doubts and hesitations; he embraced all of her at that instant. *We're here*, Maya thought. *Here.*

37

Nathan Boone established his command post at the Shangri-La Hotel in West Los Angeles. He was about ten minutes away from where Michael Corrigan was staying—a pretentious place on the beach called the El Dorado. Boone saw no benefit to living in the same hotel as the Traveler. It would only make it easier for Michael to interfere with the current operation.

Boone liked the bland décor of the rooms at the Shangri-La. There were no bright colors—nothing that would agitate the mind. But the best feature of the building was that visitors could enter through the parking structure and avoid the desk clerk.

Boone didn't want someone like Martin Doyle sitting on a couch in the lobby.

At this moment, Doyle was watching television in the suite's living room; he particularly enjoyed the news updates about the lost children. Carlo Ramirez, the Peruvian mercenary working as Doyle's handler, sat beside the little table in Boone's bedroom. He kept fidgeting and avoiding Boone's eyes.

"It was only about five minutes, Mr. Boone. I swear to you—"

"I don't care if it was only five seconds. As I told you several weeks ago, your main responsibility is to watch Doyle." Boone scrawled a few words on a notepad, and Ramirez looked terrified. Perhaps he thought the notepad was some kind of death list.

"He's got scars."

"Excuse me?"

"Doyle has scars, here and here." Ramirez touched his breast bone and the back of his hand. "If he's got two tracer beads inside his body, you can hunt him down at any time."

"Mr. Doyle is like a special kind of weapon that helps us achieve our objectives. But that doesn't mean I want him roaming freely through this city. What are you going to do next time Doyle gets away from you?"

"I'll find him and destroy him, sir."

"Destroy him immediately."

"I understand, Mr. Boone."

"Good. Now send him in here."

Still sweating, Ramirez left the room. Boone sipped ice tea and gazed out the window at the shoreline park on the other side of Ocean Avenue. During the last twenty years, winter storms had eroded the cliffs at the edge of the park. In certain places, sidewalks and flower beds had fallen down the slope to the coast highway. Boone was starting to think that everything around him was falling apart. A few days ago, Mrs. Brewster and her driver had gone off a cliff near the Portreath airport, and the authorities still hadn't pulled the car out of the water.

Martin Doyle swaggered into the room and shut the door.

Since leaving Thailand, he had lost his bloated appearance. Now he resembled an unemployed actor who worked part-time as a trainer at a gym. Doyle made a point of eating special meals that included fat-free cheese, pomegranate juice, and steel-cut oatmeal. He was a walking refutation of the theory that a healthy diet led to a virtuous life.

"It looks like you tied up Ramirez and dunked him in the pool." Doyle chuckled as he sat down. "Good for you, Boone. Guys like that need to be kept in line."

"We were talking about you, Mr. Doyle. I learned that you wandered away from the rest of the team."

"That was no big deal. Just a little mistake. Nothing to worry about." Doyle leaned back in his chair. "So how we doing, Boone? Are people scared enough? Or should I scare them a little bit more?"

"I don't want you to do anything for the next few days."

"Maybe I should go out to the desert."

"No."

"What's out in the desert is the only thing that can hurt us. I created a story for you. A fairy tale about a monster. But the story needs an ending."

"Mr. Ramirez is taking you to a hotel in Culver City. Stay there until you receive instructions."

"Does this new hotel have an exercise room?"

"I think so."

"Good. I'm trying to get back in shape." Doyle stood up, glanced at Boone's open suitcase, and then sauntered back to the door. Suddenly, he turned, and there was a different expression in his eyes—that same mixture of shrewdness and hate that Boone had seen in Thailand.

"Are we doing what we're supposed to do?"

"What do you mean by that?"

"I'm following orders, being a good soldier. I just want to make sure that all of us are moving in the right direction."

Instead of showing anger, Boone took off his steel-rimmed

glasses and cleaned them with a tissue. "Do you remember when we hunted you down like a runaway pig? Remember how you lay on the dirt, screaming?"

Doyle's hands clenched as the demon kicked and scratched inside his brain. "Yeah. I remember."

"Good. That's good, Mr. Doyle. Just checking."

* * *

BOONE DIDN'T RELAX until he heard Doyle and Ramirez leave the hotel suite. Then he went out to the living room, got a bottle of vodka from the mini bar, and poured it into his glass of ice tea. Right now he was vulnerable. Doyle sensed that weakness. *What's out in the desert is the only thing that can hurt us. Well, that's not exactly true*, Boone thought. *I'm the only person who is in danger.* Even this hotel room wasn't safe. If the police arrived, they would find a manila envelope that contained black-and-white photographs of the kidnapped children. It was painful to look at their frightened faces, but Boone didn't have the strength to destroy the images.

His fingers touched the little bottles of liquor in the rack again, and then he turned away from this temptation. For the first time in a great many years, he wanted to talk to someone about what was bothering him, but that was impossible. He didn't have any friends; it was a mistake to reveal yourself to another person. Of course there were always a few people who already knew you well.

Boone returned to the bedroom, switched on his computer, and began to answer e-mail. But certain memories pushed through his mind with such power that his fingers were frozen on the keyboard. Maybe he should go see her and confront the weakness that she represented. *If you have an enemy, you should destroy that person, even if it is just another aspect of yourself.*

* * *

ANTHONY CANNERO AND Myron Riles were the other two members of the team working in Los Angeles. Boone called both men and told them he was going to evaluate a site for a meeting. Then he left the hotel in his rental car and turned onto the coast highway. Route 1 marked the transition point between the continental United States and the blue-green expanse of the Pacific Ocean. It was a borderland with surfboard shops and seaside villas. Boone drove a little faster as the morning fog burned away and patches of reflected sunlight appeared on the water.

Santa Barbara was two hours north of Los Angeles. It had once been a sleepy retirement town with strict construction codes that mandated red tile roofs for every downtown building. These days, the community was an odd mixture of wealth and beach style—the sort of place where the women shopping in expensive boutiques wore torn jeans and T-shirts.

North of downtown, the city planners had allowed strip malls and tract developments of flimsy-looking ranch houses with stucco walls. Boone had once lived in one of those houses, but that was a different life, a different reality. He felt as if he were driving slowly into his past.

Ruth's office was in a two-story office building near the freeway. After their separation, she started working for an insurance agency and was now a licensed broker. Boone entered a waiting room where a young woman answered the phone while destroying space monsters on her computer.

"May I help you?"

"Tell Ruth that her husband is here."

"Oh." The receptionist stared at him as she picked up the phone.

Footsteps on the staircase, then Ruth appeared, a practical-looking woman wearing a blue pants suit and black-framed glasses. "This is a surprise," she said cautiously.

"I'm sorry I didn't call first," Boone said. "Can we talk?"

Ruth hesitated and then nodded. "I don't have a lot of time, but let's have some coffee."

Boone followed his wife out the door to a nearby coffee shop where the counter girl had seashells braided into her hair. They took their paper cups and went outside to a patio next to the parking lot.

"So why are you here, Nathan? Do you finally want a divorce?"

"No. Unless you want one. I was in Los Angeles and thought I'd drive up the coast and see you."

"There's only one thing I know about you. One indisputable fact. You don't do anything without a reason."

Should I tell her about Michael Corrigan? Boone thought. He wasn't sure. The problem with talking to other people was that they rarely followed the script that was in your mind. "So how are you, Ruth? What's new in your life?"

"My income went up last year. I got a speeding ticket eight months ago. But, of course, you probably know all that."

Boone didn't object to her statement. After he joined the Brethren, he arranged to receive monthly reports on Ruth's phone calls. The call sheet was cross-referenced with detailed information about whomever she spoke to more than three times in a six-day period. In addition, the Norm-All program constantly evaluated Ruth's credit-card activity and compared her liquor and prescription drug purchases with the regional norm.

"I'm not talking about the *facts* of our life. I just wanted to know how you are."

"I'm fine, Nathan. I have new friends. I've gotten into bird-watching. I'm trying to lead a productive life."

"That's good to hear."

"What happened to us and the other parents was like a plane crash or a car accident. I still keep in touch with some of the people from the support group. Most of us have moved on with our lives, but we were all injured in a profound way. We wake up every morning, go to work, come home, and make dinner—but we'll never be completely healed."

"I wasn't injured," Boone said. "The incident *changed* me. It made me see the world for what it is."

"You have to accept the past and move on."

"I have moved on," Boone said. "I'm going to make sure that that kind of incident will never occur again."

Ruth touched Boone's hand, but let go when he flinched. "I

don't know what you're doing with the Evergreen Foundation, but it's not going to give you what you want."

"And what's that?"

"You know . . ."

"No, I don't!" Boone realized that he was shouting. A young man glanced at them before he entered the coffee shop.

"You want Jennifer back. She was our angel. Our precious little girl."

Boone stood up, took a deep breath, and regained his self-control. "It's been nice seeing you again. Incidentally, my insurance policy still has you down as a beneficiary. Everything is in your name."

Ruth fumbled with her purse, pulled out a wad of tissue, and blew her nose. "I don't want your money."

"Then give it away," Boone said, and marched back to his car.

* * *

WHEN HE WAS in his twenties, he had gone through a six-week army reconnaissance course on an island off the coast of South Carolina. At the end of the training period, you had to catch a wild boar with a snare, stab the squealing animal with your commando knife, and butcher it on the spot. That was just a test, one more way to show that you could deal with any problem. Thirty years later, nothing had changed. He was compelled to take one last step to prove his strength and invulnerability.

Boone punched in the address on his GPS, but it wasn't necessary. The moment he turned off La Cumbre Road, he remembered the way. It was about five o'clock in the afternoon when he arrived at his destination. School had been out for several hours; only a handful of cars were in the parking lot.

Valley Elementary School was over forty years old, but it still looked cheaply made and unsubstantial. Each of the six grades had its own brick building with an asphalt roof. Covered walkways connected the buildings. Everywhere you looked there were planters filled with ivy and spiky orange bird-of-paradise flowers.

Boone strolled past a classroom with drawings of rainbows taped to the windows. Some of the rainbows were scrawled across the construction paper, while others displayed the different colors in distinct bands.

Jennifer drew rainbows and everything else with wild loops and curves. Her cows were red. Her horses were blue. When she drew her father, Boone became an assemblage of lines and circles with crooked eyeglasses and an upturned grin.

The children ate lunch in a central quadrangle surrounded by the class buildings. A lost sweatshirt was on the ground and a thermos bottle with a unicorn had been left, sad and lonely, in the middle of a picnic table. This was where she had sat. This was where she and others had died. There was no plaque or memorial statue to acknowledge what had happened here.

Boone was ready to test his toughness and his bravery, but his body betrayed him. He couldn't move, couldn't breathe. It felt as if his head had exploded and a scream of sadness and pain had finally been released.

38

Maya and Gabriel stood in the auditorium of Playa Vista Elementary School and watched a class of eight-year-olds receive their Guardian Angel.

A medical area had been set up on the auditorium stage. Folding screens blocked a direct view, so Maya went to the front of the room and stood against the wall. First, a nurse injected each child with a local anesthetic in the right forearm. When the children lost sensitivity, a second nurse led them over to a doctor wielding a silver device that resembled a dentist's drill. A spurt of compressed gas injected the RFID chip between the skin and the muscle, and then a bandage was placed on the wound.

Each child received a button that said: I GOT AN ANGEL WATCH-ING ME! A handful of parents sat quietly as a teacher's aide led the students back to their friends. Maya wondered what the mothers had told their children. Some of the eight-year-olds looked fright-ened, and one little boy was crying. All they knew was that they were being forced to walk up some steps and receive a quick jab of pain. The true lesson was implicit in the matter-of-fact behavior of the adults. *We know best. Everyone is doing it. You don't have a choice.*

Maya rejoined Gabriel in the rear of the auditorium. "Seen enough?" she asked.

"Yes. They're well organized. Josetta said the plan for the in-jections was announced three days after Michael made his speech."

Maya nodded. "The Evergreen Foundation was already using the Protective Link tracking device with their employees. The Guardian Angel is just the same chip with a different name."

They left the school auditorium and walked back out to the street. Josetta Fraser, Vicki's mother, was waiting for them in a car decorated with Isaac T. Jones bumper stickers. Josetta was a heavyset woman with a broad face who hadn't smiled since pick-ing them up at the Los Angeles airport. "You see them doing it?" she asked when they got back in the car.

"They're processing a child every two minutes."

"And that's just one elementary school." Josetta turned the car back onto the street. "They're doing it at clinics and at some churches, too."

"But not at your church?" Maya asked.

"Reverend Morganfield preached against it. He said Isaac Jones warned us about the Mark of the Beast. But it's up to the parents, and most of them are going along with the plan. People get angry if they don't see a bandage on your child's arm. It's like: 'What's the matter with you? Aren't you a good mother? Don't you want to stop this killer?'" Josetta sighed loudly. "You could argue with them, but there's no point to that. The Prophet wrote: 'Don't waste time singing songs to the deaf.'"

They were traveling north, passing through an area where massive cinder-block walls had been placed on both sides of the freeway. Maya guessed that the walls were there to block the sound from the traffic, but the design made her feel as if she were trapped in a corridor with surveillance cameras attached to every road sign.

"Where are we going?" she asked.

"I'm taking you to the safest place I know," Josetta said. "There aren't any cameras in the area, and nobody is going to check your ID. You can spend the night there. Tomorrow morning, I'll bring you a car with a clean registration."

"What about a handgun or shotgun?"

"The Prophet wrote that the Righteous should not touch the Machinery of Death and—"

Maya interrupted her. "Gabriel is a Traveler and the Tabula are trying to kill him. A Harlequin died trying to protect your prophet. I thought that some of you believed in 'Debt Not Paid.'"

"The debt *was* paid, and my daughter paid it. Everybody in the church knows about her sacrifice." Josetta's face showed pain and anger as she touched one of the heart-shaped lockets hanging from her neck. "I'm helping you because Mr. Corrigan was kind enough to call me up and tell me that my daughter died."

At the north end of the San Fernando Valley, they turned off the freeway and drove into low foothills dotted with coastal oak trees. The two-lane road followed a serpentine route up a canyon as signs began to appear: RANCHO VISTA—A PLANNED COMMUNITY.

"I'm a loan officer," Josetta explained. "Rancho Vista was going to be a new subdivision, but the builder lost his financing. Now my bank owns the property, and I'm in charge until the lawyers stop yelling at each other."

Josetta pulled up to a gatehouse where a young security guard sat listening to a baseball game on a radio. He recognized her face, raised a gate, and the car turned onto a private road.

"Does the guard know that we're staying here?" Maya asked.

"He doesn't need to know anything. He's off in twenty minutes.

When I drive back down the hill, a church deacon will be on the night shift."

Rancho Vista was supposed to occupy a series of terraces cut into the foothills, but only one building had been finished completely. It was a ranch-style house with a three-car garage and welcome signs posted on the front lawn. Farther up the street were two houses with no lawns, and then the wooden frames of a half-dozen abandoned structures. Past that point, jimsonweed and manzanita bushes had reclaimed the hillside.

"This is the model house," Josetta said as they pulled into the driveway. "The builder set this up so that people could see themselves living up here in the hills."

She got out of the car, opened up the trunk, and removed a large nylon sack and a grocery bag filled with food. Then she led them up the brick walkway and unlocked the front door. Maya thought the model home would be empty, but it was filled with dust-covered furniture. Cocktail glasses and liquor bottles were on a sideboard, and a big bouquet of tulips was in the middle of a coffee table. It took Maya a few seconds to realize that the bottles were empty and the flowers were colored silk and twisted strands of wire.

"There's no electricity," Josetta said. "But they've left the water on."

They followed her into the kitchen. It had a central serving island with a granite countertop and expensive-looking appliances. Wax apples and pears filled a copper bowl; a plastic cake was on a serving plate in the middle of the breakfast table.

Josetta dropped the nylon sack on the floor and set the groceries on the counter. She ignored Maya and directed all her comments to Gabriel. "I bought you some sandwiches for dinner and blueberry muffins for breakfast. A flashlight and two sleeping bags are in the sack. It gets cold up here at night."

"Thank you," Gabriel said. "We really appreciate this."

"When my daughter called me from New York, she always spoke very highly of you, Mr. Corrigan."

"Vicki was a wonderful person," Gabriel said. "She had a pure heart."

Josetta grimaced as if someone had jabbed her with a knife and she began to cry. "I knew she was special even before she was born. That's why I named her Victory Over Sin Fraser. I just wrote a little pamphlet about her with the help of Reverend Morganfield. People want to read about her. Victory is not just my daughter anymore. She's one of the angels."

The Traveler nodded sympathetically. Maya wondered if they were going to have to sit around the breakfast table and watch Josetta cry. But Vicki's mother was stronger than that; she picked up her purse and headed for the door.

"I'll come back around eight in the morning. Be ready to go."

They stood in the living room and watched Josetta drive back down the hill to the gatehouse. "They're turning Vicki into a saint," Maya said.

"It sounds like that might happen."

"But she was just a person, Gabriel. She wasn't a face in a stained-glass window. Remember the night she sang at the karaoke bar? Remember when Hollis taught her how to dance?"

"A saint is just an extraordinary person plus a few hundred years."

They sat at the kitchen table and watched the sun drift down to the foothills like an orange balloon leaking helium. Gabriel decided to take a shower. Maya heard him sputtering beneath the cold water as she switched on her computer and sent a coded message to Linden.

Josetta was right—the bankrupt housing development was a safe place to spend the night—but certain aspects of the model home made her uncomfortable. Someone had placed framed photographs in each room of a married couple and their two children. In one photograph, the family was standing on a dock, and the little boy held up a trout. In another, the little girl wore ballet shoes and a snowflake costume.

Gabriel returned to the kitchen with wet hair. He took the

sandwiches out of the grocery bag and placed them on the kitchen table. "When I was growing up, I fantasized about a house like this. New furniture. A backyard. Parents who gave parties and invited lots of friends."

"I wanted something like this, too. A brick house in Hampstead and a father who didn't travel around the world killing people."

* * *

THE KING-SIZED bed in the master bedroom turned out to be a plywood platform concealed with a comforter. When it got dark, they placed their sleeping bags on the platform. Gabriel lay next to Maya with his arm beneath her head. At that moment she felt as if they were an old married couple who had known each other for a lifetime. She had always thought of love as passion and sacrifice, but it was also like this—a moment of quiet closeness that felt as if it would last forever.

Gabriel smiled. "Is it against the Harlequin 'rules' to say that you're beautiful?"

"I think we've already broken most of the rules."

"Good. Because you *are* beautiful and I'm happy to be here tonight."

He kissed her one last time, lay on his side, and went to sleep. Maya sat up and tried to anticipate what might happen. The next few days were going to be dangerous, but at least her leg wound had almost healed. Although she was sick to her stomach in the morning, she still didn't look pregnant. Gabriel hadn't noticed the vitamin pills and the snacks Maya carried in her shoulder bag. She decided to wake up early and nibble a few crackers before starting the day.

A night wind blew out of the canyons and cut around the edges of the house. Gabriel shifted over to his left side and she gazed down at the Traveler. There was a three-quarter moon outside and a band of moonlight touched his body. Cold light. That's what her father had always called the moon.

Maya heard a muffled noise in the distance—the sound of a

car coming up the street. Barefoot, she walked across the cold tile floor to the living room and peered through a gap in the curtains. A two-door hatchback had parked in front of the house, its headlights pointing up the hill. The shadow driver turned off the engine and got out of the car. He had something in his right hand. When he stepped onto the sidewalk, she saw the stubby silhouette and curved ammunition clip of an assault rifle.

She ran back to the bedroom and shook Gabriel awake. "Hurry up and get dressed. We need to get out of here."

"Why? What's going on?"

"Someone's outside the house."

Still half-asleep, Gabriel pulled on his pants and shirt. "It's probably just Josetta's friend."

"I don't think a church deacon would carry an assault rifle."

A fist thumped on the front door. Gabriel finished tying his shoes as Maya grabbed the flashlight and slung the sword carrier around her neck.

"Hurry up. We'll go out the back."

Gabriel pushed open a sliding glass door and they stepped into the yard. Maya considered running up the street, using the thick underbrush as cover, but immediately rejected the idea. She didn't know the terrain, and an attack could come in any direction. The Harlequin rule was: *choose your enemy's path.*

Something slammed inside the house. The man with the rifle had forced the front door open. He shouted something, but the words were indistinct.

"Stay with me," Maya whispered. "We're going to set up a position in another house."

They ran up the sidewalk and then darted across the street to one of the houses that had never received a driveway and landscaping. Gabriel circled around the back and kicked in the kitchen door. The empty house smelled of roof tar and pine board. There were no light fixtures; bare wires hung down from the ceiling like roots in a cave.

Maya led Gabriel down a short hallway to a bedroom. "Now what?" he asked.

"We wait."

"What if he finds us?"

"Then he's going to get an unpleasant surprise." She handed Gabriel the flashlight and pointed to the opposite wall. "You sit here. The moment he steps into the room, shine the light directly in his eyes."

"And you?"

Maya pulled her sword out of its sheath and moved over to the doorway. "He's carrying an assault rifle. I'm going to respond as fast as I can."

Five minutes went by before the attacker kicked in the front door. Shoes thumped on the bare floor. The doors creaked open as the man searched the house. He swore softly every time he found an empty room.

Footsteps. And then a dark form stood motionless in the hallway. Gabriel switched on the flashlight and Maya raised her sword.

"There you are," said a familiar voice.

"Hollis! This is a surprise!" Gabriel laughed and lowered the flashlight. "How did you find us?"

"I crossed the border from Mexico and contacted Linden. He told me you were here."

Maya stepped through the doorway. "It's good to see you, Hollis. We could really use your help."

"I've got a shotgun in the car and two safe cell phones. But we have to talk about one thing straight up. I've changed my name, Maya. Linden has accepted that change. I'm also asking for your permission."

Gabriel looked confused. "What are you talking about? You don't need permission to use a fake name. We're all using cloned passports."

"He's not talking about passports." Maya slid her sword back in its sheath. "What name will you be using?"

"Priest."

"Do you really want this life, Priest?"

"I accept it."

"Do you really want this death?"

"I accept that as well."

She remembered Hollis holding hands with Vicki as they strolled down Catherine Street in New York City. Those two lovers were gone forever.

"Damned by the flesh," she said softly.

"Yes," Priest said. "But saved by the blood."

39

It was rush hour when Boone drove over the Sepulveda Pass and returned to Los Angeles. Thousands of cars were edging forward on the freeway like sluggish blood cells in a clogged artery. Most people sat listening to music or the endless blathering of drive-time talk-show hosts. Boone had monitored a few of these radio shows and was amused by the constant use of the word *freedom*. The new social order had nothing to do with freedom. It was more like a factory he had once visited in Hong Kong where carrot peelers glided by on a conveyer belt: a computer automatically picked out the anomalies while the rest were boxed up to be sold.

For the last eight years, he had dedicated himself to destroying the Brethren's enemies and establishing the Panopticon. Sometimes the work was dangerous or unpleasant, but he had experienced few moments of doubt or introspection. Now it felt as if the sky had cracked open like a crystal globe. Boone tried to concentrate on the tasks before him—*move into the exit lane, watch the car in front*—but his rebellious mind kept raising questions. He was pleased when Carlos Ramirez called him on the cell phone. It was a welcome distraction.

"We got a problem, Mr. Boone. Doyle is sick."

"He seemed all right this morning."

"Yeah, I know. After he talked to you, we drove over to Culver City and checked into the hotel. Everything was okay until after lunch. Then Doyle said his stomach hurt and he went to bed."

"Where is he now?"

"Still in bed, moaning and sweating a lot. Cannero and Riles are here with me. They were thinking that it might be some kind of disease that Doyle picked up in Thailand. You know—malaria or something like that. Should we take him to the hospital?"

"No."

"Then what do we do?"

"Put some ice in plastic bags and place them near his neck or beneath his arms. I'm in the car right now. I'll be there in ten minutes."

Culver City was an incorporated city surrounded by the rest of Los Angeles. During World War II, it had been the location for most of the Hollywood movie studios, but only one of them remained. The Culver Hotel was a triangular brick building in the center of the downtown. It looked like a stodgy grandfather surrounded by a chattering crowd of wine bars and hip restaurants.

Boone passed through the hotel lobby and took an elevator up to the two suites he had reserved on the eighth floor. No one answered when he knocked. Had his team already taken Doyle to the hospital? Why hadn't someone called him?

The rooms had been paid for with a credit card from a shell

corporation registered in the Cayman Islands. Boone returned to the lobby and presented the credit card to the young desk clerk. He received two key cards, returned to the eighth floor, and entered the first suite.

Myron Riles, a former police officer from Texas, lay dead on the floor surrounded by a patch of blood. The second member of the team, Anthony Cannero, was sprawled on the couch with a bullet hole in the center of his forehead. The wall behind him looked as if someone had splattered red ink on the white plaster.

Boone drew his gun, approached the bedroom door, and pushed it open. Carlos Ramirez was lying beside the bed with his head thrown back and a startled look on his face. Somehow Doyle had managed to grab the smaller man and keep him quiet while he broke his neck.

Then what? Boone returned to the suite's living room and noticed that chunks of foam rubber and shreds of linen were scattered across the floor. Doyle had taken Ramirez's gun and thrust it into a bed pillow: the pillow had muffled the shots when he entered the room. And now he noticed the other details: two wallets left on the rug and an empty money belt on the couch. Both mercenaries had been wearing jeans and their pants were dark with blood. Crouching down, Boone examined their wounds. After they were dead, Doyle had shot both men in the groin.

So where had he gone? The desert? That was the logical choice. Boone remembered the expression on Doyle's face during the conversation that morning. *I created a story for you. But the story needs an ending.*

The suite seemed unusually quiet—a kingdom of the dead. Boone considered calling the police, then rejected the idea. His image had been captured by the hotel surveillance cameras, and he had spoken to two—no, it was three—hotel employees. The police would immediately decide that Boone was the prime suspect. As for Doyle, there was no longer any evidence that he even existed: during the last few weeks, the Evergreen Foundation computer team had systematically removed Doyle's presence from the databanks in a half-dozen countries. The killer had become a modern ghost, a creature that floated through the world like a phantom in a haunted house.

Boone retrieved the three wallets with their fake IDs, placed DO NOT DISTURB signs on both doors, and used the emergency staircase to leave the hotel. Driving north on residential streets, he passed a two-bedroom house that looked like a miniature castle and a cottage with a six-foot high crucifix planted in the front lawn. On Lincoln Boulevard, cars were lining up at a drive-through restaurant with a giant chicken standing on the roof. *Stay calm*, he told himself. *What is the immediate objective?* He needed the packets of money left in his room at the Shangri-La Hotel. Doyle would be a few hours ahead of him, heading east to the Mojave Desert.

He called Lars Reichhardt, the director of the Berlin computer center. "I'm calling from Los Angeles. Do you recognize my voice?"

"Yes, sir."

"Our three contract employees are no longer able to work for us in any capacity. The fourth employee, the one from Thailand, is no longer in contact with a supervisor."

There was a long pause as Reichhardt dealt with the implications of that statement. "I understand, sir."

"Our group has been using credit cards issued to a corporation registered in the Cayman Islands. I want you to cancel these cards immediately and erase any data regarding this company."

"That will take some work, sir. We'll need to enter a bank database."

"Then get on this right away. We have only a few hours until these personnel issues become public knowledge."

He tossed his phone onto the passenger seat and slowed down for a light. There was about $20,000 in his hotel room. After he found Doyle—and killed him—he would try to step off the grid.

Boone hadn't designed the Panopticon, but he knew every room of the invisible prison. If he truly wanted to hide, he could no longer use a registered cell phone or have a conventional e-mail account. He would have to pay cash in all situations and avoid airports and government offices. Cameras tracked him as he entered the hotel parking structure, got out of the car, and hurried down the hallway to his room. Boone entered the suite and stopped. Something was wrong. The door to the kitchen was partially open, as was the door to the bedroom. Had he left them that way?

As he drew his gun, the kitchen door swung open and a black man with dreadlocks stepped out carrying an assault rifle. It took Boone a second to recognize Hollis Wilson.

"Put the gun on the floor, Boone. Go ahead. Nice and slow. Now take two steps back."

"Whatever you say, Hollis."

"Nowadays, I'm called Priest. But you shouldn't worry about that. Put your hands behind your back and lock your fingers together. Good. That's good."

The bedroom door opened and Maya came out carrying a shotgun. Boone remembered when he saw her in Prague striding down the cobblestone streets. Only a year had passed, but she looked much older. And now he was going to die for causing her father's death.

The Harlequin picked up his automatic and thrust it into her waistband. "Did you search him?" she asked Hollis.

"Not yet."

Maya placed the shotgun on the couch and a stiletto appeared in her right hand. She approached him quickly and Boone waited for the shock of the blade sliding between his ribs. Instead, she used the knife like an extension of her hand, pushing open his jacket and finding his holster. The point of the blade glided down his outside leg and jabbed at his ankles, making sure he didn't have a weapon there. When Maya was done, she stepped back and studied his face.

"We thought that you'd be walking in with a few mercenaries. What's the problem, Boone? Is the Evergreen Foundation cutting back on staff?"

"Three of my men are dead," Boone said. "This is an emergency. I need to speak to Gabriel Corrigan. Can you contact him?"

The two Harlequins glanced at each other as Gabriel stepped through the bedroom doorway.

"That can be arranged."

40

As a child, Maya had been taught to plan, but never anticipate. There was an important distinction between these two ways of thinking. When fighting with a kendo sword, she tried to be ready for anything and never assume that her opponent would behave in a certain way.

That might be possible in combat, but it was hard to extend the lesson to the rest of her life. Ever since her father's death, she had wondered what would happen when she finally tracked down Nathan Boone. In these fantasies, Boone was usually weak or wounded. He would admit his various crimes and beg for mercy.

Now the real Nathan Boone was standing in the middle of a hotel suite next to a glass coffee table and a flower arrangement. The head of security for the Evergreen Foundation didn't appear weak or frightened. Ignoring the two Harlequins, he answered Gabriel's questions.

"So you found this man, Doyle, in Thailand, and brought him back to America?"

"That's correct."

"And he murdered fourteen children?"

"No—the children are still alive. I ordered two members of my team to take them out to the Mojave Desert. We leased an abandoned gold mine near the town of Rosamond."

"But you were going to kill them eventually," Priest said.

"I wasn't sure what was going to happen. This is an unusual situation for me."

"You sure as hell weren't going to let them go." Priest glanced at Gabriel as if to say, *let me kill this bastard*, but the Traveler concentrated on Boone's eyes.

"I understand why you couldn't do it," Gabriel said. "You didn't want those children to die like your daughter."

"Who told you about that?"

"The story was in all the newspapers. The estranged husband of your daughter's teacher came to the school and shot his wife. Then he murdered several of the children standing beside her."

Boone was breathing hard. "He hated his wife, but why did he kill the children? My daughter was innocent."

"A year after the incident, you joined the Evergreen Foundation," Gabriel said. "You either found them or they found you."

"I got a call from Kennard Nash, and they flew me to New York. They had my file from the army and they knew about my intelligence background. Nash showed me this model of the Panopticon and explained the system. He said that my daughter would still be alive if everything was controlled and monitored. The General told me what to do and I started working. You need to understand something—*I've always obeyed orders.*" Boone spoke as if this last statement was the catechism of his faith.

"Your daughter was killed," Maya said, "so you hired this man, Martin Doyle, to kill more children?"

"That's why you have to let me go. I think Doyle is driving out to the desert to finish the job."

Gabriel turned to Maya. "Go out to Rosamond with Boone. See if you can save the children."

"Maybe he's lying, Gabriel. We don't even know if Martin Doyle exists."

"We'll go over to the Culver Hotel. If the story checks out, I'll call you on your cell phone. You'll know in the next twenty minutes if Boone is telling the truth." Gabriel turned to Priest. "You're going to help me find my brother and deal with his bodyguards."

Maya went into the bedroom, pulled the blanket off the bed, and wrapped it around her shotgun. For a moment, she thought about calling Gabriel into the room and telling him her secret, but she quickly discarded the idea. She was going on a journey with the man who killed her father.

* * *

BOONE AND MAYA walked out to the hotel parking lot and stood beside the rental car. "I'll drive," he said. "You can sit behind me so you can shoot me whenever you wish. The best moment will be when we reach the entrance to the mining site."

Maya waited until Boone got behind the steering wheel, then slid into the back and placed her shotgun on the seat. She drew Boone's automatic and clicked off the safety. It annoyed her that he was right—the best time to kill him was when the car stopped at the mine. But she could also make up an excuse and tell him to turn off the road when they were close to their destination. She would have to make her decision in an hour or so.

By now, she was used to the Los Angeles landscape—so unlike London or Rome. Its freeways were massive rivers that flowed though parks and neighborhoods. Signs for car washes and smog-testing centers were everywhere. In the Vast Machine, both cars and humans were movable objects that could be tracked.

Her cell phone rang and she heard Priest's voice. "Where are you?"

"On the freeway, heading east."

"The man you're traveling with told us the truth. We just found three dead rats."

"Get out of there and help our friend find his brother. I'll call you when I get more information."

When she switched off the phone, Boone glanced over his shoulder. "What did Hollis Wilson say?"

"There were three bodies in the hotel room."

"Doyle is clever. It's not going to be easy to kill him."

"Keep driving," Maya said. "I'll think up a plan when we get there."

They turned onto State Highway 14, a four-lane road that climbed a range of eroded hills covered with dry vegetation. Every ten miles or so, a commuter town appeared with the same chain restaurants placed between a Starbucks and a McDonald's. Maya studied each new road sign, but her eyes always returned to the man driving the car. *The best moment will be when we reach the entrance to the mining site.*

"You killed my father."

"That is correct. I tried to get his cooperation, but it didn't work. Thorn was a very stubborn man."

"You would have killed him anyway."

"Correct. There was no logical reason to keep him locked up somewhere."

Boone glanced in the rearview mirror and changed lanes. His calm voice, his lack of emotion, reminded her of one particular person—her father.

"I am planning to kill you," she said. "But in some ways you're already dead. You're a cardboard box with nothing inside. You don't care about anyone, and no one cares about you."

"I cared about my daughter." For the first time, Boone's voice was hesitant and filled with pain. "I would have died for her that day, but I lived. I don't know why I lived."

They came over the hills and saw the shops and street lights of the two adjacent communities of Palmdale and Lancaster. This was the farthest extension of the suburban sprawl—a daily commute from downtown Los Angeles to a single-family house with a low mortgage. But the moment they passed through this area, the Mojave Desert surrounded them. The only bright features in this region were illuminated billboards for Indian casinos and plastic surgeons. *CHANGE YOUR LOOKS! CHANGE YOUR LIFE!* shouted one of the signs, and a photograph of a surgeon named Dr. Patmore grinned like a smooth-skinned idol of perfection.

Rosemond was a desert community for the pilots and military personnel who worked at Edwards Air Force Base. The population was so mobile, so impermanent, that they passed a lot where prebuilt houses had been placed on trailers. They turned off the freeway, glided past a shopping center, and took a right turn near the local high school. Joshua trees lined the road and a mountain with three peaks was visible in the distance. The mountain was separate from everything else, so deliberate that it looked as if the earth had rejected something malignant and thrust it upward toward the sky.

Boone turned off the paved road and stopped at a cattle gate with a large sign. PRIVATE PROPERTY! TRESPASSERS WILL BE PROSECUTED.

"This road goes up the mountain to the mining site."

"How far away is it?"

"Three or four miles."

"Switch off the headlights and go slowly."

Boone opened the gate, got back in the car, and drove up a dirt road that led to the mountain. Light came from the stars and moon, but the road was overgrown with weeds; it would be easy to get lost. After the first half mile, Maya rolled down a side window. She could hear cicadas and the crunch of their tires on patches of gravel.

Boone stopped at the entrance to the abandoned gold mine halfway up the mountain. A Cyclone fence topped with strands of razor wire surrounded the mining claim and NO TRESPASSING signs were everywhere. Someone else had arrived earlier; a red sedan was parked in front of gates held together with a lock and chain.

They both got out of the car. Now that Boone had guided her to the gold mine, there was no longer any need for his existence. The shotgun was a noisy weapon. She should draw one of her knives and slit his throat.

"He's here," Boone said. "This is one of the rental cars driven by my employees. Doyle took the car after he killed the men at the hotel."

Maya stepped away from the gate and looked up the slope. Outdoor lights marked a winding pathway to the top of the mountain.

"Who's guarding the children?"

"I left two employees here. They'll be suspicious if Doyle shows up alone."

Boone went to the red sedan, opened the door, and inspected the garbage Doyle had left on the passenger seat. Maya touched the outline of the stiletto hidden beneath her jacket, but she hesitated and left the knife in its sheath.

Let fate decide, she thought, and pulled out the random number calculator hanging from her neck. An even number would cause his death; an odd number would postpone the decision. She pushed the button; "3224" flashed on the screen. The random number indicated death, but it caused a counterreaction that was immediate and certain. *This isn't what I want*, she thought. *This isn't who I am.* She concealed the device before Boone emerged from the car.

"I found some sterile bandages and gauze."

"Do you think one of your men wounded him?"

"I doubt it. Doyle probably bought a knife and cut out the tracer beads inserted beneath his skin."

Maya reached into her waistband and grabbed Boone's automatic. He stood calmly—as if he expected to be executed—but she reversed the weapon and handed it to him. "Don't make any noise as we walk up the hill. We'll become an easy target the moment we step into the light."

Priest had supplied her with a sawed-off shotgun that had a leather carrying strap. It reminded her of the *lupara* that men carried in Sicily. She slung the strap over her shoulder, stepped on the roof of the sedan, and climbed over the gates. Boone followed, and they headed up the hill to the mine. The air was cold and clear and smelled like sage. The only noise came from the mine's power generator; it sounded like a puttering lawn mower that some confused citizen had left in the middle of the desert.

The first building was a clapboard house with a sheet-metal roof. Light glowed through the old newspapers taped to the windows. "What's inside?" Maya asked.

"This is where the two guards sleep and cook their meals."

A wooden plank creaked when they stepped onto the porch. Maya tried to peer through the windows, but the newspapers completely covered the glass. She raised the shotgun and whispered to Boone, "Open the door and step away."

He turned the knob slowly, then pushed open the door. Maya charged inside. The house was one long room filled with a refrigerator, a propane stove, and a kitchen table. A dead man lay on the floor next to an overturned chair. A blotch of dark blood was in the middle of his white T-shirt and there was a second wound below his belt buckle.

"You know him?"

"He's a former Austrian policeman named Voss."

"Where are the children?"

"We put some cots in the building where they refined the ore."

They returned to the darkness and continued up the hill past the stamping machinery used to crush the rocks. After the ore was reduced to gravel, it was sent through filtering screens and metal troughs, then loaded into handcarts and pushed over to the refinery shed.

Lights burned inside the shed, and Maya could hear cheerful music coming from a television. She pressed the shotgun stock against her shoulder, then yanked open the door. Folding cots were in the middle of the room. A television placed on a table played a video of dancing animals. Another dead man lay a few feet away from the television with his mouth and eyes open.

"Only two people worked here?"

Boone nodded. "Maybe Doyle took the kids out to the desert."

"I don't think so. It's dark. He couldn't find them if they ran away. Let's go to the mine."

They left the shed and followed the narrow railway track that once guided the handcarts. Near the top of the mountain, a framework of steel struts had been built over the mine shaft. An electric motor powered a winch that raised and lowered a steel cage. When the mine was active, the handcarts were filled underground, rolled into the cage, and raised to the surface.

"This works like a freight elevator?"

"That's right," Boone said. "If he's got the children down in the mine shaft, they can't run away and we can't save them."

"Why do you say that?"

"Doyle will hear the winch moving when we raise the cage up to the surface. He'll kill the children before we reach them."

Maya left the area near the mine shaft and began to search the site. "Did you ever read Sparrow's book, *The Way of the Sword*?"

Boone nodded.

"There's a chapter about evaluating your opponent. The weakest opponent is the one who expects a victory."

"And you think Martin Doyle is in that category?"

Maya picked up an old towel covered with grease. "He's waiting to hear the elevator, but that's not going to happen."

She ripped the towel in half, slipped the shotgun strap around her neck, and climbed onto the elevator struts. Wrapping the towel around the cable, she swung out into the middle of the shaft.

"I'm going to follow you," Boone said.

"That's not necessary."

"This is my responsibility."

Slide down a few yards. Stop. Slide down a little farther. Stop. A year ago, she had met her father in Prague and stabbed a man in an alleyway. Since then, her life had been shaped by what was hidden from view. Maya felt as if she were descending into a secret world. Somewhere beneath the surface, the innocent were about to be destroyed.

The cable swung to one side, and she almost lost her grip. Looking upward, she saw that Boone was about thirty feet above her, swaying back and forth as he followed her down. Maya tried to move a little faster, pressing her feet against the cable to control her descent.

Finally, she reached the top of the elevator cage and stopped, waiting for Doyle's attack. When nothing happened, she climbed down into the mine's main tunnel. Light came from dust-covered bulbs attached to an orange power cable. The tunnel went off in two directions, but she could hear voices coming from the left. Children were singing a frightened, wavering chorus:

"If you're happy and you know it,
Clap your hands . . ."

With the shotgun close to her chest, she followed the tunnel into the heart of the mountain. Small hands clapping. Voices singing. Then she heard a man's voice echoing off the stone walls. "Louder, everyone! Louder!"

As she came around the bend of the tunnel, she saw the captive children. A man stood in front of them like a choir director who wasn't satisfied with their performance. The children watched him—obedient, terrified—as the big man swung his hand to beat out the time:

"If you're happy and you know it
And you're not afraid to show it—"

"You're not clapping," Maya said. Drawing a handgun, Doyle spun around to face her, and she fired the shotgun. The pellets knocked him backward and he collapsed on the floor of the mine. His body convulsed, and then relaxed. The malevolent power that had propelled him through the world melted away, leaving nothing but a dead body.

Maya was frozen in that moment of destruction until the children started crying. Their tears and frightened faces changed everything. She slung the shotgun on her back so they couldn't see it, then stepped forward and spoke with a soothing voice.

"Don't worry. No one's going to hurt you."

She took a little girl's hand and guided her and others back down the tunnel. "You're safe. The bad man is gone," Maya said. "We're going to take you back to your families."

Boone was waiting for them at the base of the mine shaft. The elevator gate made a shrieking metallic sound as he forced it open. The children scurried into the cage like baby chicks trying to hide from a hawk, but instead of following them inside, Boone shut the gate and turned to Maya. He looked as if they had just lost the battle.

"There was another child."

"What?"

"A girl's body is at the end of the tunnel. She wasn't on the list."

Maya felt sick to her stomach. They had entered the mountain and destroyed this demon—and failed. Without thinking, she touched her belly. All her caution disappeared as she followed Boone down the tunnel to a T-intersection. She was prepared for a dead body, but found only gravel and dust. Suddenly, Boone pulled the automatic from his waistband and faced her. There was no way she could defend herself.

Boone stared at her for what felt like a long time. She could see his sadness and pain.

"Forgive me."

Maya nodded. *Yes. I forgive you.*

Boone raised the gun with one quick motion and shot himself in the head.

41

Priest used Boone's key card to enter the room at the Culver Hotel. Immediately, he saw two dead men, one on the carpet and the other on a couch. The Harlequin slipped a plastic shopping bag over his hand, turned the doorknob, and entered the bedroom. The third mercenary was lying beside the bed with a surprised look on his face.

As he stood beside the dead man, Priest remembered a line of scripture from *The Collected Letters of Isaac T. Jones*: "The foolish man calls forth a demon to harvest his fields and carry his water. But the demon will destroy his master."

"Hell, yes," Priest muttered. It looked as if Boone's particular demon was killing everyone around him. Trying not to step in the blood, he checked the bathroom and the closet, then called Maya on her cell phone.

"We just found three dead rats."

"Get out of there and help our friend find his brother," Maya said. "I'll call you when I get more information."

Priest left the building and returned to the car. When they had searched Boone's hotel room, Maya had found a manila envelope filled with black-and-white photographs of the kidnapped children. Gabriel was sitting in the front seat, examining each photograph.

"Boone was telling the truth. There were three bodies in the room. Now what do we do?"

"This could be the moment that we challenge the Brethren. If the children are still alive, then it substantiates our own story."

"Will you make your speech?"

"Let's wait to hear from Maya. If the news is good, we'll activate the Revelation Worm. I've got a laptop and a Web camera in my pack. We need to go on the Internet at a location where we won't be disturbed."

"We can probably use my martial arts studio. It's still being run by my students."

Priest turned south and drove through his old neighborhood. All the familiar sights seemed to float past the windshield. An elementary school surrounded by a chain-link fence. A doughnut shop with barred windows. A line of palm trees, their trunks defaced with graffiti that marked off the borders of different street gangs.

There were skyscrapers in downtown Los Angeles, but the urban style was distilled into cheaply made two-story buildings with stucco façades. These days Priest felt no connection to a city or a language or a name on a passport. So many things in the world were just glitter tossed on a dance floor.

His old martial arts school was in a mini-mall on Florence Avenue. The liquor store was still there, but the video outlet had been replaced with a shop that sold beauty supplies. His two best students, Marco Martinez and Tommy Wu, hadn't changed the words painted on the front window, but they had placed a sign on the dirt strip near the sidewalk. The sign showed four people—black, white, Latino, and Asian—flying through the air with a variety of capoeira moves. THINK. FEEL. BE REAL, the sign read. DEFEND YOURSELF!

"Do we have to break in?" Gabriel asked.

"There's a key for emergencies. It might still be there."

A clay pot filled with cactus was near the entrance to the school. Priest dug his fingers into the dirt and found a fake rock with a secret compartment. He took out the key, opened the door, and led Gabriel into the reception area.

The glass case with his karate and capoeira trophies was still there, but someone had added a new display. Now his framed photograph was hanging from the wall with a sign that read HOLLIS WILSON. OUR TEACHER. OUR MASTER. OUR GUIDE. Beneath the photograph was a shelf where people had left votive candles, gold medals won at recent competitions, and folded pieces of paper. Priest unwrapped one of these messages and read: *The warrior uses the power of the brain to be deliberate and the power of the heart to be instinctive.* He had told them that. A lifetime ago.

"This is new."

Gabriel laughed. "You always had a big ego. But I didn't think you'd put up an altar to yourself."

"That's what it is. An altar. It's like I'm dead."

"Now you have the opportunity to see your legacy. It's clear that you changed some lives."

They walked past the two dressing areas and entered a long windowless room with a mirror on one wall and a little office at one end. Someone had installed a bookshelf and had cleaned up the messy desk. While Priest set up the Web camera and attached the computer to an Internet cable, Gabriel called Simon Lumbroso.

"I think we're going to offer the world a Revelation. Tell all the groups to get ready."

Gabriel sat down at the desk and switched on the Web camera. The Traveler's face appeared on the monitor, but it was half concealed by shadows. Priest turned on all the lights in the office and adjusted a desk lamp. When everything was ready, Gabriel went online and used the cell phone to contact the Nighthawk in London.

"This is your friend in America. It might be time for the message. I'm on your site right now. Can you see my face? What about the sound?" Gabriel lowered the cell phone and turned to Priest. "We need the microphone in the backpack. He says it's difficult to hear me."

"No problem." Priest plugged in an audio cord and attached a microphone to Gabriel's shirt.

Gabriel switched off the phone and began adjusting the lamp. "Right now, all we can do is wait. Let's see what happens out in the desert."

Priest left the office, found the school's refrigerator, and took out two bottles of water. He gave a bottle to Gabriel, then paced back and forth in the workout room and watched himself in the wall mirror. What would happen when Tommy or Marco opened the school the next morning? Would they notice that someone had been there? He had spent years of his life in this room, teaching people, trying to show them a better way. Now Hollis Wilson had turned into a house god, a minor spirit protecting a new generation of students.

He heard the cell phone ringing and hurried back to the office. Gabriel was smiling as he talked to Maya. "That's wonderful! Okay. I understand. Be careful and come back to the city as soon as you can. I'm sending out the message in five minutes."

Gabriel switched off the phone and began typing on the keyboard. "The children are alive. Maya's calling the local sheriff. She's going to wait on a side road until the police show up at the mine."

"What about Doyle?"

"He's dead, and it sounds like Boone killed himself."

"The Tabula won't be happy."

"Let's give them something else to worry about."

Words flashed on the screen: *Sound good. Image good. Ready for transmission. Nighthawk.* Priest felt alert and ready. For years, the Panopticon had grown larger and more pervasive. Now some of those walls were going to collapse.

Gabriel sat up straight in the office chair. "Give me ten seconds."

Priest raised his hand and counted off the final seconds. Four. Three. Two. One.

And then the Traveler began to speak.

42

"Hello, I'm Gabriel Corrigan.

"I realize that it's a surprise to see my face on your monitor screen. Some of you might be frantically pushing the Delete key or wondering if you should unplug your computer.

"The first thing I need to explain is that your computer hasn't been harmed and none of your data has been lost. My message to you is a onetime event. When I finish speaking, this video will end and will never appear without your permission. You can erase it or play it again by searching on your hard drive for a file called 'Revelation.'

"Right now, I'm in the United States, in California, where

something terrible has happened. Fourteen children have disappeared . . ." Gabriel held up a photograph of one of the kidnapped children. "Including a little boy named Roberto Cabral."

"The people listening to this message have different nationalities and speak different languages. But all of you can understand how the loss of a child evokes powerful emotions. The parents living in California are frightened. They're worried that they can't protect their children.

"Toward the end of this message I'm going to share some news about the lost children, but first I need to explain why all this happened. The disappearances were not some random event caused by a madman. The children were kidnapped because of an elaborate plan created by my brother, Michael Corrigan, who is currently the head of the Evergreen Foundation.

"The Foundation is the public face of a group called the Brethren, a secret organization that has existed for many years. Their members hide in the shadows as they push and guide our leaders toward a system of pervasive social control. Anyone who has noticed the changes taking place all over the world can sense their presence and their power. The men and women who belong to the Brethren have one purpose: they want to control your life.

"Now, some of you might be asking: 'Is the Brethren a left-wing or a right-wing group? What is their political philosophy?'

"These kinds of questions aren't misguided—just irrelevant. Ideology is dying in our new age. Political slogans have become code words for different cultural and economic groups. In most countries, left-wing and right-wing governments share the same goal: to strengthen the technology that watches our lives. This all-pervasive system of electronic surveillance is called the Vast Machine.

"Some of you have already become aware of this new system. One morning, you wake up, look around, and realize that surveillance cameras are everywhere. It feels like you've stepped into a massive electronic prison.

"But the cameras are only a small part of the Vast Machine. Every major government in the world is reading your e-mail messages and listening to your phone calls with scanning programs that react to certain words and phrases. Security agencies and corporations monitor your bank and credit card activity. Your cell phones and your car generate data about your location and activities.

"We can usually see the cameras, but the rest of our prison is invisible. Sophisticated software programs acquire information from your purchases, your work activity, and your medical files to create a shadow image of your life. Separate databases are being combined into a total information system, and this data will be saved forever.

"Many people will gladly trade their personal privacy for small improvements in their lives. 'I've done nothing wrong,' proclaims the honest citizen. 'So why should I be worried?'

"We are being watched, but who is in charge of the watching? Although some of us freely offer up our private lives to the Vast Machine, we have no knowledge of how the information is being used and who is using it. Criminals can duplicate our identities. Corporations can manipulate our spending behavior. Governments can manufacture opinions and crush dissent. We are seen, but they are faceless. We are asked to live in a transparent house, while the forces of power are concealed.

"In order to justify these changes, the Brethren have used the politics of fear. Kings and dictators have always used fear to strengthen and validate their power. Much of history is simply a record of one group of people trying to destroy another group of people who have a different language, faith, or culture.

"But the new technology has made some crucial changes in the politics of fear. Modern media allows frightening images to be broadcast immediately with great emotional impact and power. In addition, there are very few leaders that challenge the public to be brave and take responsibility for their lives. The political credo of our times sounds like an all-powerful parent talking to a child: *Sit down and don't ask questions. We'll take care of everything.*

"Michael Corrigan has created a crisis here in California. He's used the politics of fear to gain support for something called the

Guardian Angel system. In this system, every child under the age of thirteen will have a radio chip implanted beneath their skin. Some of you might think this is an impossible fantasy, but the technology is fairly simple. In China, the authorities are insisting that everyone carry a special ID card. The card can be detected by sensors that allow the Vast Machine to track your movements.

"The infrastructure is already in place for a world where our individual Self becomes just another object like an automobile or a television set. In this system, we become a mobile ID chip, moving through an environment of other chips that link and communicate with each other. Our individual actions are simply more data for the Machine.

"Privacy is the ability to control access to information about one's Self. It's easy to see that this invisible, all-pervasive system will destroy any sort of privacy. We'll lose the power to protect our Self from the scrutiny of unknown groups or individuals.

"And some of you may ask: 'Is there any value to privacy?'

"All new ideas are dependent on some kind of mental privacy—the potential for peace and reflection. The Vast Machine provides information about us and gives the authorities a wide variety of ways to manipulate our thoughts with a subtle power. Everything we hear and see can be shaped to create certain prejudices. Free will—that is, our ability to make real choices about significant issues—becomes an illusion. Gradually, we are surrounded by targeted messages that destroy the opportunity to make our own decisions.

"Freedom of thought isn't the only value attacked by the culture of surveillance. The Vast Machine also gives governments the power to control our actions. At the beginning of this message, I said that ideology is dead. But a new kind of pernicious nationalism has appeared along with the spread of religious fundamentalism. Both groups want to use the new technology to control their citizens.

"And an equal danger exists in democracies. Many elected leaders want to restrict freedom because it appears more efficient or simply because they can. Instead of controlling technology, they serve it. Day by day, the Machine gains power over its creators.

"Some of you have seen the future clearly. For these people, it feels as if we are trapped in a gigantic mall, frightened but hiding our fear, trudging from store to store, carrying objects purchased for some reason—now forgotten. Celebrities appear and disappear on monitor screens while music continues to play.

"When people believe they have no real power, their only choice becomes what to consume. Our society's constant emphasis on buying things has nothing to do with the loss of morality. We feel powerful when we buy something, so we are easily manipulated to buy more.

"I've spoken about freedom throughout this message, but for many of us the word has lost its meaning. The faces on television use the word *freedom* as the justification for war and the expansion of the Vast Machine. The word *freedom* is used to sell airplane tickets and lawn mowers.

"Freedom is the ability to think, act, and express our views. In a free society, our rights are respected as long as they don't harm others. A political system that allows freedom has validity no matter how you view mankind.

"If you believe that humanity is greedy, violent, and intolerant, then free thought challenges bad leaders and corrupt institutions.

"If you have a positive view of humanity, then you can see how freedom allows new ideas and technical innovation. Religious and political dictatorships lumber down the road like an old truck spitting out foul exhaust. The entire country can't turn in a new direction when the scenery begins to change.

"The Vast Machine carries us toward a world where free thought and the expression of those thoughts become difficult—and, sometimes, impossible. And the politics of fear gives our leaders the justification for more control."

Gabriel picked up the photographs. "And sometimes, the threat is exaggerated or even false. Here in California, the Evergreen Foundation made fourteen children disappear. But they are alive—and safe—and their story will validate my message. Of course there are real terrorists, and we should defend ourselves against their attacks. But the anthrax incident in Tokyo, the bombings in Paris, and the poisoned food in Australia are events deliberately created to establish a permanent system of control. Look behind the curtain and ask yourself: Who really benefits from these changes?

"Some of us have had enough of fear and manipulation. In the next few days, we will appear in the chambers of power and in the street. Join us. Stand with us. Who speaks for freedom? It's your choice."

43

Priest switched off the video camera. Gabriel's face disappeared from the monitor, and a few seconds later a message appeared on the screen. *Video statement received and recorded. Quality good. I'll attach the key and send out immediately. My body is captive, but my spirit flies. The Nighthawk.*

The Traveler sighed and pressed his hands against his eyes.

"You okay, Gabe?"

"I don't feel like talking to people. Call Simon Lumbroso and tell him to activate the groups."

"Good idea. Then we should find someplace to hide."

"No. We need to find my brother." Gabriel got up from the desk. "Boone said that he was staying at the El Dorado Hotel."

Priest called Simon as they got back in the car and headed north toward the beaches. The Traveler was quiet and slumped against the door. He stared out the windshield as patches of lights glided across his face.

"What are you going to do when you meet your brother?"

"Michael will see what happened as a setback, but he won't give up. The half gods of the Fifth Realm have changed the way he views reality."

"Do you want me to kill him?"

The Traveler looked surprised. "You really have become a Harlequin."

"He wants to destroy you, Gabriel. It's my obligation to keep you alive."

"I'm the one who needs to deal with Michael. He's my brother. We're connected to each other."

The cell phone rang, and Priest slipped in an ear piece. Simon was calling from Rome. "Tell the Traveler that his message has gone public."

Like a wave gaining size and power, Gabriel's speech began to appear on computers all over the world. Priest knew that it was all because of a complicated package of programming code that could replicate itself and spread to other machines, but he found it easier to see the Revelation Worm as a creature hiding on the bottom of a river. The Traveler's speech needed to be sent only to one computer. Within seconds, the programming key activated the hidden worm. While the speech was being copied multiple times, the worm's Command function took over the computer's video-play capability. Then it was in control, and it insisted that Gabriel's speech appear on the monitor screen. After the speech was broadcast, the individual worm withered and died, but the key continued to spread through the Internet.

Simon called several more times as Gabriel's two-level strategy started to unfold. The middle-class citizens involved in the Resistance were sending out the first of what would be thousands of e-mails to journalists and elected officials. They demanded an investigation into the Evergreen Foundation and challenged the new laws against personal freedom.

These citizens were what Gabriel had called the "Voice of the Forum," but the "Voice of the Street" was also getting organized. It was early morning in Europe. Small groups of Free Runners hurried through streets of a half-dozen cities, putting up posters and spraying graffiti. WHO'S IN CHARGE? LISTEN TO THE TRAVELER! DEFEND YOUR FREEDOM BEFORE IT DISAPPEARS!

Priest turned on the car radio and found a news station. When the announcer came on, it sounded as if he had just run down a hallway to the microphone.

"They're alive! The children are alive! A few minutes ago, the Antelope Valley sheriff's department announced that the fourteen missing children have been found at an abandoned mining operation near Rosemond. Four dead adults were found at the site and law enforcement personnel are attempting to—"

Gabriel leaned forward and switched off the radio.

"Don't you want to hear what happened?"

"It's already in the past."

"What are you talking about? This is going to change everything."

"This is just one battle. The conflict will never end." Gabriel peered through the windshield as if he was searching for a lost friend. "We do have one advantage over the Tabula. Because they worship power, they have a hierarchy and a few centralized locations for their equipment and employees. They may seem strong and efficient, but they're actually more vulnerable than we are."

"We're just a lot of groups."

"That's right. The Resistance is a collection of different groups with different motivations, but the same general goal. We're hard to find, hard to destroy."

"That might be true, Gabe. But all this is happening because you appeared."

"My father has spent years trying to understand why the Travelers exist. Some are killed. Others die in obscurity. Some teach a lesson that survives for a period of time and then fades away. Maybe we're some kind of cosmic anomaly that must keep appearing, again and again, to guide the six realms in a certain direction."

They parked a few blocks from the El Dorado Hotel and got out. Priest had taken a bedsheet from Boone's room, and he wrapped it around the assault rife so that it looked like a wad of dirty laundry. The two men passed through the hotel lobby and took an elevator up to the fourth floor.

"Did Boone tell you the room number?" Priest asked.

"412."

"Let me handle this. I'll get us inside."

As they headed down the hallway, Priest saw a room-service tray on the floor. He concealed the dirty plates beneath their plastic covers, then picked up the tray with his left hand while his right hand clutched the rifle.

"Knock on the door, Gabriel. Then step back."

Priest stood in the hallway with a big smile on his face as a young Asian man wearing a handgun in a shoulder holster answered the door.

"Room service for Mr. Corrigan."

"He didn't order—"

Priest threw the tray and all its contents directly into the mercenary's face. As the man stumbled backward, Priest laid him on the floor with a leg sweep, then clubbed him with the butt of the assault rifle. On the edge of his vision, he saw Gabriel slip into the bedroom. First he secured the area, making sure there were no other bodyguards, then he heard the two brothers arguing.

"No, you won't!" Michael shouted. "That's not going to happen!"

Priest ran across the living room and yanked open the bedroom door. There was an open suitcase on the bed and a smaller bag on the breakfast table. He stepped around the corner of the bed and stopped.

Two bodies lay motionless on the floor—alive, but lifeless, empty of their Light.

44

The four barriers of air, earth, fire, and water stood between the different realms. For some Travelers, the barriers were their only experience in a different reality. They would have a nightmare that they were drowning in a whirlpool or wandering alone across a barren plain. The experience could be so terrifying that Travelers never wanted to return to that place. They would spend the rest of their lives afraid of sleep, clinging to the familiar world that surrounded them.

* * *

WHEN GABRIEL OPENED his eyes, he was falling through blue sky. His brother was far ahead of him, a black speck of anger and desire, as small as a starling flying through a cathedral. Michael shifted his body, reached the passageway, and disappeared. And Gabriel followed him, gliding across the sky toward a shadow.

* * *

DARKNESS. WHEN HE opened his eyes again he was standing on a desert plain. There were no mountains or canyons to be found in this earth barrier—just coarse red dirt, cracked and weathered from an eternal drought. Michael was about a mile away, kneeling on the earth like an athlete who had lost his footing. When he saw Gabriel coming toward him, he jumped up and began running. Both brothers sensed where the passageway was hidden, but Michael appeared cautious and uncertain. Twice, he stopped as if he was going to face his brother, then he changed his mind and started running again. Gabriel widened his stride and tried to shorten the distance between them. But Michael reached the passageway and disappeared.

* * *

GABRIEL PASSED QUICKLY through the dark green waves of the water barrier and suddenly he was standing in an empty town surrounded by a dead forest. This was the fire barrier, and everything around him was burning. If he stayed here long enough, he could watch the endless cycle of destruction and renewal.

A massive wall of smoke rose up from the burning trees. Orange sparks and bits of ash drifted through the air. The two- and three-story buildings were linked by a sidewalk made of pine and the loose boards squeaked and shuddered as he ran toward the town church. Smoke pushed its way through keyholes and letter slots. Gabriel glanced through a window and saw a barber chair on fire, as if a flame creature had sat down for a shave.

When he reached the church, he yanked open the heavy wooden door and stepped inside. The rafters were burning, and embers glowed on the floor. Directly behind the altar, fire flowed up the walls like shimmering lines of water.

Gabriel walked up the central aisle and stopped when he saw the passageway that floated on the surface of a stained-glass window. Had his brother already crossed over? If that was true, then Michael could be in any of the six realms. He could search for hundreds of years and never find him.

The door squeaked on its iron hinges and Michael entered the church. He stopped when he saw Gabriel and smiled slightly. Even in this place, he played the role of the confident older brother.

"Why are you standing there? Take the passageway."

"I'm staying here with you, Michael."

Michael shoved his hands in his pockets and strolled between the pews as if he was a tourist visiting a minor attraction.

"I've experienced the whole cycle in this barrier. Everything burns down, and then it reappears again."

"I know."

"There's no food in this place. No water. We have to cross over and move on."

"That's not going to happen, Michael. You're like a virus that infects everyone who comes near you."

"I'm a Traveler—just like you. Only I see things as they are."

"And that means killing children?"

"If that's necessary . . ."

The altar caught fire, dry wood crackling as it burned. Gabriel looked behind him and saw fire touch the dead roses held in a copper vase. The flowers shriveled slightly and were transformed into tiny points of flame.

When he turned back around, Michael was standing on a bench, trying to climb onto the frame of the stained-glass window. Gabriel sprinted across the room, grabbed his brother, and they fell onto the floor. Kicking and punching, Michael tried to break free while Gabriel held him tightly. They rolled sideways, knocking over the benches, and Michael rammed his elbow into his brother's chest. He jumped up and scrambled back to the window. This time, he stacked up the benches and formed an improvised platform.

"You can stay here!" Michael screamed. "Stay here forever!"

A ceiling beam broke away from the wall. It twisted as it fell, flinging off sparks, then hit Michael's shoulder and knocked him to the floor. He lay stunned for a few seconds as another beam fell and then a third. Michael pushed his palms flat and tried to get up, but the weight held him down.

Gabriel saw the hate and rage in his brother's eyes. He knew that he couldn't save Michael, nor could he leave him to die. Sitting on the floor, Gabriel crossed his legs and waited. He accepted the moment, accepted it so completely that it felt as if all his questions had been answered. *Breathe. Breathe again.* And a luminous field appeared in front of him, infinite, expanding, accepting.

* * *

THE ONLY TWO streets in the town met at a central square with park benches and a stone obelisk inscribed with a circle, a triangle, and a pentagram. Anyone standing by this memorial would have watched the final moments of the conflagration when flames cracked windows and burned their way through doors. Finally, the buildings themselves began to collapse, the burning timbers unable to hold the weight of the upper floors. The church with its wooden pillars and white cupola was the last to go. It seemed to explode from within, creating a point of energy as bright and powerful as a new sun.

45

There was no air-conditioning in their apartment in Rome—just a collection of antique electric fans. A fan occupied a side table in each of the eight rooms, and Alice Chen had decorated them with red and blue ribbons that rippled in the air whenever the blades were spinning.

Because of the September heat, they woke up early in the morning. Priest pushed the living room couches and club chairs against the wall and turned the area into a gym. After drinking two cups of espresso, he did his push-ups and stomach crunches on the white marble floor, then ran through a complicated series of martial arts exercises. When he was done with his own workout, he started Alice's karate lessons.

Now that she was seven months pregnant, Maya found it difficult to jump and kick, so she sat on a yoga mat, stretched her muscles, and offered advice. She and Priest would finish the morning workout sparring with kendo swords. She felt fat and awkward, but her reaction time hadn't changed, and she knew a wide range of fakes and maneuvers. In a ten-minute session, she could usually block Priest's attack and jab him with her bamboo blade.

After a light breakfast, they would leave the apartment and shop for food and supplies on the side streets near the Piazza Navona. In the afternoon, Maya would take a nap while various tutors came to the apartment. Priest was learning Italian, and a college student was teaching Alice history, literature, and mathematics. Linden had returned to Paris. With his help they were beginning to accumulate a collection of fake ID cards and cloned passports that would enable them to travel anywhere in the world.

Simon Lumbroso usually arrived at seven o'clock, bringing a bag of fresh fruit or a carton of gelato. They would cook supper at the apartment or stroll through the quiet evening streets to a restaurant in the old Jewish ghetto. The staff spoiled Alice with special desserts and everyone asked about Maya's *l'arrivo benedetto*—the blessed arrival of her child.

Maya refused to read newspapers or watch television, so Simon was her main source of information on what was happening in the world. Some changes had taken place in the months that followed Gabriel's speech. In the United States, the Guardian Angel program had been canceled and most parents had removed the RFID chips from their children's bodies. A mandatory ID card law had been rejected by several European countries, and the German legislature had made it illegal to monitor store purchases that did not involve dangerous products.

An organization called We Stand Together had started in Britain and quickly spread to a dozen other countries. Initially, the group criticized the activities of the Evergreen Foundation, but now each chapter was involved with local issues involving personal freedom. While this had been going on, the Free Runners had continued to organize informal demonstrations against the Vast Machine. Jugger had come up with a slogan—*No More Fear!*—and these three words were scrawled on walls and bridges all over the world. In Spanish-speaking countries, the slogan had evolved into the words *No Más* next to the cartoon image of a little man looking frightened. Along with the graffiti, there had been local demonstrations like the infamous "Poke in the Eye" night in Glasgow, when the lens of every surveillance camera in the city had been sprayed with black paint.

All these public activities were being reported by the media while other developments took place in the underground culture. People were creating blogs and chat groups that explained how to create a parallel identity. They were publishing pamphlets and setting up Web sites that challenged the politics of fear.

After Simon described all the latest developments, he would take out a large white handkerchief and wipe his brow. "Gabriel's speech made a big splash, like a rock tossed into a pond. In some places, the water is the same again. But the ripples spread out and we don't know how they'll change the world."

* * *

IT RAINED TUESDAY night, and the following day was hot and humid. When Simon arrived in the late afternoon, they decided to stroll over to the park that surrounded the Villa Borghese. It took about ten minutes of walking to reach the Piazza del Popolo, a large cobblestone oval with an obelisk at the center. They cut across the open space and followed the zigzagging stairway that climbed up the Pincio Hill to the gardens. As usual, Alice led the way like a scout guiding them through a forest. Maya and Simon followed. The baby started kicking inside her about halfway up, and Simon stopped several times to point out a distant building.

Priest followed them, carrying his sword in a black tube with a shoulder strap. Maya still had a knife strapped to her left fore-arm, but her own sword was stored in a closet back in the apartment.

Alice reached the top of the hill first and waited for them in the main square that overlooked Rome. If they stood beside the wall, they could see most of the city—from Monte Mario to the Janiculum. The dust and pollution of that summer's day softened the light. The church domes and marble monuments had the yellowish-white color of antique ivory found in a museum.

They strolled down a pathway toward the Giardino del Lago at the center of the park. Huge pine trees and Lombardy poplars sheltered them from the sun until they reached an artificial lake near the center of the garden that Alice called "the Sea." In the summertime, the lake water was green with algae and dotted with lily pads. Families rented aluminum rowboats and spent afternoons bumping into one another and tossing bread crumbs at the swans.

Maya sat down on a park bench and ate two biscotti. Directly across the lake was an Ionic temple dedicated to Aesculapius, the god of health; it felt like good luck to gaze at his statue.

Alice had too much energy to endure such sedentary pleasures. She ran around the park tossing pebbles into the lake and searching for a group of baby ducks hidden among the bamboo and banana trees. Finally, she returned to the bench and approached Simon.

"Let's go to the River. Did you bring a boat?"

"Instead of just one vessel, I've brought a fleet."

Simon reached into his canvas shopping bag and took out a piece of balsa wood with a stick mast and paper sails. In the middle of the gardens, someone had built a brick and concrete canal about the size of a drainage ditch. Alice called this ornamental gesture "the River," because the water in the canal meandered down a low hill, passed beneath tiny bridges, and finally emptied into the Sea. The Italian children liked to send chips of wood or paper boats down this miniature waterway, but Alice had insisted on a "real" toy boat. Three weeks ago, Simon had shown up with a balsa-wood craft. His creations had gradually become more sophisticated.

Alice peered into the bag. "How many did you make?"

"Five. An eighteenth-century warship. A Polynesian outrigger. A rich man's yacht. The ocean liner. And a tugboat. I'll admit that most of them look the same, but you have to use your imagination."

"Who gets the fifth boat?"

"The fifth one is Fate's vessel and *quel dio* sails it wherever he wishes. But you can pick your own, Alice."

"Let's test them first," Alice said. "We'll sail each one to the first bend in the river."

"An excellent idea." Simon bowed to Maya. "We shall perform a quick test of seaworthiness and then return."

The two of them walked off together and Priest sat down next to Maya. "I get the feeling that Alice is going to end up with the fastest boat."

"I think you're right about that. And Simon will be a gentleman and take the slowest."

Maya sipped from a bottle of water and gazed out at the Sea. West of the park, the sun was approaching the horizon, and the light around them began to change. The shallow man-made lake gradually began to look ageless and deep. When a light breeze touched the branches above them, shadows danced upon the ground.

Hollis Wilson might have chatted about where they were going to go for dinner that night, but Priest could sit for hours without saying anything. The rage he had shown after Vicki's death had disappeared, leaving a quiet seriousness that intimidated strangers. He picked the right name, Maya thought, and wondered if her friend would always look sad whenever he saw lovers walking through the park.

"Alice said you got a message from Linden."

"I was planning to tell you. Over the weekend, Linden and two of his mercenaries traveled to England and raided Wellspring Manor. They were going to rescue Matthew Corrigan's body, but all they found was a grave. According to a log book, the Traveler's heart stopped beating about two weeks ago."

Maya gazed out at the swans and tried not to panic. Did this mean that Gabriel had also died? After the incident in Los Angeles, the bodies of both brothers were taken north and concealed in the cellar of a Jonesie church in the Sierra Mountains.

Priest saw the fear in her eyes. He touched her arm and spoke in a soothing voice. "Don't worry. Tommy Wu drove up to northern California last weekend to make sure everything was okay. Both Gabriel and Michael were still breathing. Their hearts beat every two or three minutes. That means they're still alive."

"When I was a little girl, my father used to tell me stories about the sleeping hero," Maya said. "There was always a legendary person who was hidden in a cave—like King Arthur in Britain or Prester John in Africa. They're sleeping, but alive, waiting to emerge once again."

"So we wait?"

"We wait, but encourage the Resistance."

"We're going to have a race!" Alice ran up to the bench and danced around them. "I get the yacht, Maya gets the outrigger, and Priest gets the warship."

"And I have chosen the ocean liner," Simon said solemnly. "Like its owner, it's somewhat awkward in the water."

They left the lake and followed a dirt path that meandered up the hill. The River started at a marble fountain that dribbled into a leaf-clogged pool. They placed the boats in the water and watched as the current pushed them over a thin lip of concrete and into the canal. Although Alice's boat appeared to be the fastest, all five vessels stalled at the first bend in the River. "Don't push them," Simon told Alice. "Let them go their own way."

When Simon wasn't looking, Maya picked up a stick and tossed it into the water. This Harlequin catalyst drifted down to the first bend and struck the warship—which promptly bumped into the other vessels.

That was all that was needed. One by one, the balsa-wood boats slipped around the bend. Excited, Alice darted back and forth, cheering each boat on. Simon followed her, making up the beginning of what would become an epic story about the race. Even Priest was drawn into the competition. He smiled slightly as he jumped across the River.

Maya stood alone and saw everything, the sun touching the western horizon with a blaze of light, her three friends and the dark green canopy of leaves. No angels appeared with clarion trumpets. But she knew at that moment—knew with a subtle, quiet certainty—that she was carrying a new prophet, carrying a Traveler.

And the four little boats and the fifth boat as well continued on their journey, stopping and turning, then racing to the Sea.